O Beautiful

Also by Jung Yun

Shelter

O Beautiful

A NOVEL

Jung Yun

ST. MARTIN'S PRESS
NEW YORK

First published in the United States by St. Martin's Press, an imprint of St. Martin's Publishing Group

O BEAUTIFUL. Copyright © 2021 by Jung Yun. All rights reserved. Printed in the United States of America. For information, address St. Martin's Publishing Group, 120 Broadway, New York, NY 10271.

www.stmartins.com

Library of Congress Cataloging-in-Publication Data

Names: Yun, Jung, author.
Title: O beautiful: a novel / Jung Yun.
Description: First edition. | New York: St. Martin's Press, 2021.
Identifiers: LCCN 2021027557 | ISBN 9781250274328 (hardcover) |
    ISBN 9781250274335 (ebook)
Classification: LCC PS3625.U53 O24 2021 | DDC 813/.6—dc23
LC record available at https://lccn.loc.gov/2021027557

Our books may be purchased in bulk for promotional, educational, or business use. Please contact your local bookseller or the Macmillan Corporate and Premium Sales Department at 1-800-221-7945, extension 5442, or by email at MacmillanSpecialMarkets@macmillan.com.

First Edition: 2021

10 9 8 7 6 5 4 3 2 1

To my parents, who chose a strange and wondrous place to call home

I hope she'll be a fool—that's the best thing a girl can be in this world, a beautiful little fool.

—F. Scott Fitzgerald, *The Great Gatsby*

The agony of my feelings allowed me no respite; no incident occurred from which my rage and misery could not extract its food.

—Mary Shelley, *Frankenstein*

O Beautiful

1

Men talk to her on planes. She doesn't invite it anymore; it's just something that happens. Usually, she travels with things to armor herself against unwanted conversation. Headphones. A sleeping mask. An oversized sweatshirt with a hood. But there was no time to pack today, only a few frantic minutes to throw clean clothes into a bag. She doesn't remember bringing the Restoril—she doesn't even remember having a prescription for Restoril—but thank God, she thinks. Thank God. Elinor shakes a capsule loose and examines the strange combination of colors pinched between her fingers—half calming blue, half urgent red—with the words FOR SLEEP etched on the blue half. Across the side of the bottle are the usual warnings, small icons with lines drawn through them, telling her not to drink, drive, or operate heavy machinery. She taps her empty plastic cup on the tray table, trying to reconstitute a full sip of Bloody Mary from the thin ring on the bottom. The capsule is horse sized, too big to be swallowed dry.

The man in the window seat looks at her. He's been looking at her every few minutes since takeoff.

"Will someone be waiting for you when we land?" he asks. "Or were you planning to rent a car?"

It's the third or fourth time he's tried making conversation. She presses her call button for a flight attendant.

"I don't need a ride, thanks."

"No, I just meant—you know we're only like two hours away, right?"

He motions toward the pill with his chin. "My ex used to take those. They're really strong."

Elinor doesn't know what to do with this information except pretend that she didn't hear it. She scans the nearby rows, wishing there was an empty one she could move to, but the plane is small and full. Someone at the magazine made all her travel arrangements. If it had been up to her, she would have chosen another flight, another carrier. Anything to avoid flying in such a small plane. There are only forty or fifty seats in the cabin. Four per row, two on each side of a narrow aisle, a low ceiling that slopes even lower at the edges, as if the walls are curling in on them. Elinor is tall, a hair shy of five foot ten. She wonders how this man, who's at least a head taller and pressed up against his window, can stand it.

"I don't mean to pry," he says. "I just remember trying to wake her in the mornings. She'd be completely knocked out."

"I'd prefer that right now."

"Oh, sure." He laughs. "But what happens after we land?"

Sleeping pills rarely work for her. She's cycled through enough prescriptions to know. The ones that actually make her fall asleep never keep her in that state for long. But even a restless half hour would be better than fending off a conversation that she doesn't want to have. She flicks the man a tepid smile.

"I won't be able to get out of this row if you're passed out." Now he's smiling back.

"You'll have to climb over me then." She pauses, second-guessing her choice of words, which she worries he'll interpret as playful, maybe even flirtatious. She puts the capsule on her tray table, wondering when the flight attendant will notice her call button so she can order another drink. She can feel the man looking at her again—staring this time, she thinks.

"You have some interesting tattoos. I don't see a lot of Asian women with tattoos usually, not like that, at least."

Elinor has been freezing since takeoff. Because of the cold, because of him, she's been sitting with her arms crossed for most of the flight.

But even this position can't hide the abstract patterns that extend from her shoulders to wrists, the dark black ink alternating with the negative space of her skin.

"I have a couple too." The man pulls up his sleeve, revealing a skull wearing a red beret, with two rifles crossed underneath like pirate bones. The banner above the skull reads 187TH INFANTRY DIVISION, DESERT STORM. Farther up his arm are three women's names, centered and stacked on top of one another in ornate cursive font: AMANDA. ASHLEY. ALYSSA. Ex-wives or daughters, she imagines. She dislikes tattoos that function as biography. She doesn't think people should talk about them—their own or anyone else's. She rubs her arms again, standing the fine hairs on end.

"Are you cold?" He unzips his jacket. "Here . . ."

"It's fine, really. I don't need it."

"But I'm actually getting hot in this."

In his rush to take off the jacket, he pulls his elbow back too far and knocks it against the window. His face stiffens for a moment, and then recovers with a tight smile. When he finally offers her the jacket, she decides it's too cold to refuse. She drapes the soft black fleece over herself like a blanket, grateful for the warmth but not certain how to avoid talking to someone when she's wearing his clothes.

"So . . ." He pumps his elbow back and forth. "Are you from Chicago, or did you just connect in O'Hare?"

"I'm from New York."

"Ah. Fun city. You must be like an artist or a musician," he says, glancing at her tattoos again.

In her late teens and twenties, men usually assumed that she was a model. The polite ones plied her with drinks and conversation before asking the question outright, while others simply cornered her in crowded nightclubs and bars, shouting things like "You! Don't I know you?" They didn't, of course. By industry standards, she had a prettier-than-average face, but not a well-known one. Not the kind that could fetch ten grand a day just for getting out of bed. She had over fifteen years of steady catalog work and the occasional print ad.

Once, she shot a commercial for suntan lotion that never aired but for which she still got paid. Toward the end of her career, her main source of income was a company that made sewing patterns. She appeared on the front of their pattern envelopes, modeling the finished products—matronly, shapeless clothes that resembled colorful sacks. It's been years since Elinor had any work, but she still has difficulty presenting herself as something other than what she was.

"I write," she says, rolling the Restoril back and forth between her fingers. She considers just swallowing the capsule dry, but worries it will lodge in her throat.

"You mean like Stephen King?"

"No. I write nonfiction."

"Oh, so you're a journalist." This seems to impress him even more. "What newspaper do you work for?"

She's not a journalist, not in the way that he probably means it, with a beat to cover and a daily filing deadline. Elinor glances across the aisle at a middle-aged redhead playing a card game on her phone. They make eye contact for a moment and the woman smiles at her as if to say *God, I'm so sorry.*

"I write for magazines, not newspapers . . ." Elinor realizes this makes her sound more successful than she really is. "As a freelancer."

After a moment in which no question is asked, the man says, "I'm in finance."

This strikes her as untrue. He's a salesman of some sort. A salesman flying coach. She can tell by the jacket he loaned her, the black canvas bag at his feet, the notepad wedged into his seat pocket. They all have the same circular logo with a white letter *H* drawn inside. Haines, she thinks. *Businessweek* recently did a feature on their CEO, a smug-looking man who'd allowed himself to be photographed in a Stetson, standing akimbo in a field of pumpjacks and staring dreamily into the horizon.

"So are you headed to North Dakota to write an article about the oil boom? Because I work in the industry, you know, in case you have any questions."

"I actually grew up in the area, so I already—"

"My company manufactures hydraulic drills. We were one of the first to focus on sales and service in the Bakken." He exhales sharply. His breath still smells like the Jack and Cokes he drank earlier. "I've been making this trip to Avery at least once a month since 2006. It was pretty much a ghost town back then, but six years later and I hardly recognize the place. Nothing but roughnecks and field reps everywhere you look now."

It's not clear if he heard her say that she grew up in North Dakota, or whether he even cares. What is clear is that the polite shrugs and disinterested smiles aren't working. Even her curt, unfriendly replies have failed to shut him up. Directness, she suspects, might be her only hope.

"I'm sorry, but these small planes make me nervous, so I was just hoping to get some sleep on this flight."

"You think this is small? You should have seen the vomit comets we used to fly in before everyone and their mother started coming to the Bakken."

"Yes, well . . . I'd really like to sleep for a few hours before we land."

"Oh, sure." He pauses. "But you know that pill's probably going to knock you out for longer, right?"

She leans into the aisle, wondering where the flight attendants have gone.

"Whenever my ex took one of those—" He whistles and swings his forearm down, felling an imaginary tree. "Eventually, she had to switch prescriptions because she'd wake up so groggy, she wouldn't be able to take the kids to school."

"Look . . ." She tells herself to end it finally. Be kind but unambiguous. He's tested her patience long enough. "I appreciate your concern, but I'm not in the mood to talk right now. I hope you understand."

He nods a few times, as if he needs a moment to process. "Okay then. No problem." He picks up the unopened bottle of water from his tray table and places it on hers. It's the miniature kind, shaped like a hand grenade. "Here. You can have this. To take your pill with."

"You don't want it?"

He shakes his head.

"Would you like your jacket back?"

"No. You hang on to it. I wasn't lying when I said it was getting too hot."

She can tell that he's trying to sound casual and obliging, but his cheeks are a bright, mortified shade of red. He rifles through his bag and removes a magazine, tearing the plastic wrapper off with his nails. Just when she thinks their exchange is over, he turns to her again.

"I was only making conversation, you know. I don't pick up random women on planes, if that's what you're thinking."

"I didn't think you were trying to pick—"

"Yeah, well, don't flatter yourself. You're not my type."

His anger seems disproportionate to what she said and how she said it, but Elinor decides not to worry about this now. She cracks the seal on the bottle's cap and swallows the Restoril with some water. The capsule goes down slowly, leaving behind a bitter, unpleasant aftertaste. She finishes off the rest of the bottle and sits back in her seat, burrowing under the heavy fleece. From the corner of her eye, she watches the man flip through his magazine, which appears to be about motorcycles. The way he flicks his wrist, so quickly and forcefully, causes some of the pages to tear.

"Thank you for the water," she says.

"You're welcome."

He turns off her call button and returns to his magazine, still redfaced and tearing pages. Under different circumstances, she might worry that she came off as rude, but he's a stranger, she thinks—someone she'll never see again after they land, no different from the other men on the other trips whose names she can't remember or never really knew. It used to seem adventurous, meeting someone on a flight, deciding if she liked him enough to give him her number or even follow him back to his hotel. If she were a couple of decades younger, she probably would have been more receptive to this one.

She used to revel in attention, good or bad, but forty-two and twenty-two are so different. She's not the same stupid girl she used to be.

Elinor sinks into her seat and feels herself slipping, giving in to the startling efficiency of the pill as a heaviness spreads through her body. She tries to brush a stray hair from her face, but lifting her hand suddenly requires both thought and effort, more effort than her muscles are capable of now. The loss of control frightens her; a beat of panic flutters through her chest. She reminds herself that this is how sleeping pills are supposed to work—the exhausted body giving in before the restless mind. The white noise of the plane thickens, a whir of gears and fans and metal. She blinks back sleep, struggling to keep her eyes open until she can't anymore. Then the dark tide drags her out.

2

A crowd is forming in front of her. People she doesn't know. They rush past without excusing themselves and assemble shoulder to shoulder. She stares at their backs, a high wall of black—black hair, black overcoats, black suits. Elinor can't get around them, but she senses that she has to. They're hiding something. She wants to know what. She moves toward the edge where the crowd is thinnest and wriggles through the wall of bodies, her fear of tight spaces momentarily suspended.

No one in the crowd wants her there. Someone steps on her foot. Someone else brushes roughly against her side. There's a pulling sensation, and then a grabbing, like people are closing in on her, not letting her through. Elinor tries to push forward, resisting the onslaught until she can't anymore. When she turns to leave, the sensation stops for a moment. Then it starts again, crawling slowly up her hip. But this isn't some ragged dream, is it? And it isn't a crowd of strangers with outstretched hands. Is she touching herself, she wonders? Pressure registers against her skin, urgent and firm. It travels down her chest and between her thighs, the same path she sometimes traces at night. She's touching herself. Or someone is touching her. Someone is groping the space between her legs, spreading them open, massaging her there. Is the man—is the man sitting next to her doing this? Groping her beneath the jacket? Is he the warmth she feels on the side of her face, breathing against her skin?

Elinor sits up with a start, clutching her armrests. Her eyes are slow to adjust to the dim cabin. Everything around her looks and feels warped. The woman across the aisle is asleep, her chin tucked tightly against her chest. A few rows ahead, someone's reading light casts a halo over his silver hair. She wants to turn and look at the man sitting next to her, but she's terrified of what she might see, what he might do. Elinor pulls forward on the armrests and launches herself into the aisle, stumbling toward one of the flight attendants in the back of the plane. Her vision is clouded at the edges, as if she's walking through a poorly lit tunnel. She grips every headrest she passes, putting one tentative foot in front of the other. Twice, she stumbles into someone's arm or leg, provoking irritated, half-asleep glances.

The flight attendant in the galley is snapping a trash bag off the end of a roll. Elinor reaches out and catches her by the sleeve.

"Ma'am?" she says, not looking at Elinor's face but her offending hand. "What is it that you need?"

It was so clear to her a few seconds ago. But now the doubt begins to settle in. What should she say? How does she know it was real? What if it was just the pill and the alcohol, making her imagine?

"*Ma'am?* You need to take your hand off me, do you understand?"

Elinor stares at her, trying to focus. The contents of her stomach begin to bubble up toward her throat. "The bathroom," she says hoarsely. "It's where?"

The flight attendant frowns. She doesn't look angry or annoyed so much as confused. "It's behind you. Literally two steps behind you. Is there any . . ."

Before she can hear the end of the question, Elinor locks herself in the bathroom.

"We'll be landing soon," the flight attendant says loudly.

"What's the matter?" a man asks.

"Oh, I have no idea." The flight attendant lowers her voice, still audible through the closed door. "Some woman just went in there looking all crazy."

"Crazy's going around on this flight. The guy in 9C wanted another whiskey. I'm like, '*Sir*, we're about to land and you've already had five.' I swear, we go through more booze on this route . . ."

Elinor stares at her reflection in the mirror. She does look crazy. Wild, almost. Her long black hair is matted from leaning against the headrest. Her forehead and upper lip are beaded with sweat, and a line of dried white spit streaks diagonally across her chin. She tries to wash her face, but the sink basin is too shallow and the water that trickles from the tap is warm. The effect isn't bracing; it doesn't shock her awake. All it does is smear her mascara, which she rubs off with shaking hands and paper towels along with the rest of her makeup. Elinor leans toward the mirror, trying to focus on her pupils, which are severely constricted, no bigger than the tip of a pencil. She tells herself it was just the pill, it was just the pill, it was just the pill.

The plane hits a patch of rough air and pitches sharply off to the side. She puts her hands out to steady herself, unnerved that she can touch both walls. The bright blue chemicals in the toilet, sloshed around by the sudden rocking motion, sting her nostrils with the scent of ammonia, mixed with something that reminds her of dirty diapers. She can't be in this bathroom much longer, not with these walls, this smell. When the plane rocks again, more violently than it did before, she opens the door an inch and looks outside. The cabin lights and fasten seat belt signs are on. Everyone is waking and preparing to land. The captain is making an announcement about turbulence, only half of which she can hear through a thin crackle of static. Elinor walks slowly, watching the back of the man's head as she approaches their row. She takes her seat again, barely hovering over the edge of it, and leaves her seat belt unbuckled. He ignores her, yawning into his fist as if he's tired or bored. He makes no comments about her nap, asks no questions about how she feels, which seems odd to her. She wants to look at him now, to read his face and see what it says. Elinor turns as dots of amber appear outside his window, the beginnings of Avery's sparsely lit grid.

"What—what did you do?" she asks.

"Huh?" His voice has lost all the coaxing charm it had before.

"Did you . . ."

"Please put your seat belt on, ma'am." The flight attendant, the same one from the galley, stops and watches Elinor until she does as she's told.

The descent makes her nauseous again. Every air pocket lifts and lowers them, as if the plane is made of paper. Elinor tries to brace herself on the armrests but grazes the man's elbow and recoils. She shuts her eyes and sits compactly for the rest of the landing, elbows propped on knees, forehead cupped in hands. Somewhere, not far from where she's sitting, a little girl's voice rises with curiosity.

"What's wrong with that lady?"

Elinor doesn't need to look up to know that she's the lady. The girl's mother shushes her as the nose of the plane drops toward the ground and the landing gear extends into place beneath them, the discomfiting sound of metal grinding against metal. Elinor rummages through the seat pocket for an air sickness bag, but finds only a safety card and a sticky candy bar wrapper left behind from a previous flight. She leans forward again, squeezing her eyes shut as the plane hits the tarmac too hard and bounces. Once, twice. It touches down the third time and every mechanized part in the engine roars in deafening unison. The plane continues to speed, much longer and faster than it should, on and on until she thinks there can't possibly be any runway left. As soon as she's convinced of this, as soon as she imagines the plane careening into a barrier wall and bursting into flames, it's over.

Bells ring. Metal buckles release. People shift and gather their things. Elinor sits up, blinking back spots, her teeth sore from the set of her jaw.

"Hope you had a nice nap," the man says.

There's something in his voice now, something both menacing and slightly mocking. It infuriates her. She grabs her bag and pushes into the aisle, cutting ahead of people who mutter under their breath as she moves toward the front of the plane. A flight attendant stands beside the cockpit door with a brittle smile.

"Have a good evening," he says.

Elinor stops in front of him. "I think I might have been . . ." Why can't she just say it? What is she even trying to describe? It felt real to her, but not exactly.

"Did you forget something?"

A man squeezes past, bumping Elinor in the back with his suitcase.

"Ma'am, would you please move out of the aisle? People need to get by." The flight attendant steers Elinor into the galley by the elbows, startling her with his icy hands. "If you forgot something in your seat area, you'll just have to wait here until everyone deplanes."

Elinor is so aware of her breathing, the hummingbird-fast beat of her heart. She can't be in this narrow space while a surge of people comes at her. She can't be here when the man eventually catches up. She steps around the flight attendant and pushes her way onto the jet bridge. Her legs feel stiff and heavy at first, but the more she focuses on distancing herself from the plane, the more she regains control of them. She walks faster and faster, passing people on conveyor belts, eventually speeding through the terminal as if she's late for a connection. The airport is much bigger than she expected. It stretches on and on, all kiosks and newsstands and gleaming new glass and metal. She follows the signs toward baggage claim and the exit, her calves knotted with cramps from pounding against the white marble floors. As she steps onto the escalator, she looks up at a large banner hanging overhead. It welcomes her and her fellow passengers to Avery, North Dakota.

3

There's a warm white light shining on her face. She opens her eyes and finds herself in a car she doesn't recognize, an SUV that still smells factory new. When she turns the key in the ignition, the dashboard lights up with too much information. It's 7:30 in the morning. It's 68 degrees outside. The gas tank is three-quarters full. The radio is set to a country-western station, and a man is singing something about a truck. She turns off the music, trying to collect her thoughts, which feel like pieces of a broken mirror, sharp and shiny and too tempting not to touch. On the passenger seat, she finds a rental agreement, time stamped from 11:19 the night before. "Do you want to upgrade for six dollars a day," she remembers a young woman asking. "Just six dollars more." Slowly, it starts to come back to her. The hard upsell at the Enterprise desk. The sound of her tires swerving off the road. The gas station where she pulled over, unable to keep her eyes open for a minute longer.

She didn't intend to sleep in the car all night, with her doors unlocked, no less. She sits up straight and looks around, her neck stiff, her head pounding and pounding like a drum. She thinks she had three Bloody Marys on the flight. Maybe four, at the most. But the hangover is punishing, as if she drank much more. She suspects the Restoril did this to her. The Restoril mixed with the alcohol. She rummages through her bag until she finds the small plastic bottle in a side pocket. Then she rolls down her window and hurls the bottle out, scraping her knuckles against the door.

"*Fuck!*" she shouts. "Fuck! Fuck!"

The bottle disappears in a patch of weedy grass growing along the side of the road. She stares at the spot where she threw it, embarrassed and enraged. She has so much riding on this trip. This can't be how it starts.

A semi speeds past, leaving a thick cloud of dust settling in its wake. She sucks on her scraped knuckles and looks around, her mouth filling with the mineral taste of blood. The gas station where she pulled over is called the White Wing. It has two ancient-looking pumps that don't have credit card readers and an old wooden sign with a cartoon eagle. CHEAPEST GAS IN TOWN, the eagle declares. Just beyond the gas station is a two-lane road, and beyond the road is a field, green and gold and flat without relief. Pumpjacks scattered around the field bob their heads, rhythmic and slow. She counts six of them altogether, moving in hypnotic, sleep-inducing unison. The motion is soothing. She'd be content to just sit and watch for a while, but the longer her window is open, the more she notices it. A whiff of something that reminds her of petroleum jelly. Not long ago, she read an article about the boom's effect on air quality in the region, quoting residents who said the nonstop drilling made the air smell like Vaseline. During the growing season, it supposedly smelled like Vaseline and manure.

Inside her cavernous bag, her phone begins to vibrate, rattling all the metal zippers and snaps. She digs it out and squints at the cracked screen. The call is from a local number, or local-ish. She recognizes the 701 area code, the same one for the entire state.

"Hello?"

"Well, hello! Good morning. Is this Elinor Hanson?" The voice on the other end is young and buoyant, unnaturally cheerful, especially given the hour.

"Yes. That's me."

"Oh, I'm so glad I finally caught you. This is Hannah from the front desk at the Thrifty Inn in Avery. You had a reservation with us for ten nights starting yesterday, but it says here that you didn't check in yet. We've got a really long waiting list, especially for units with kitchenettes like yours, so I'm just calling to see if you still want the room."

Hannah is talking too loud and too fast, using words that make Elinor feel out of sorts. *Waiting lists*, *kitchenettes*, things she doesn't care about. She removes the phone from her ear and scrolls through her notifications. Three missed calls and two voice mails, all from the same number. She remembers what the irritable old woman who booked her travel arrangements said after finalizing her itinerary: in thirty-five years, she'd never had more trouble finding hotel accommodations for someone. According to Peg, if it hadn't been for a last-minute cancellation, Elinor would have been shit out of luck.

"Yes," she says, rolling up her window. "Yes. I definitely want that room. I'm coming over right now."

As a child, Elinor and her family took a road trip every summer, usually visiting the Badlands in the southwestern part of the state or the better-known Badlands in South Dakota. Sometimes, they ventured farther west to Montana or Wyoming, passing through Avery along the way. The town she remembers was barely a dot on the map back then. Just one main road in and out, and a five- or six-block "downtown" that consisted of a post office and a handful of shops that often appeared closed. To the north and south of this road were houses, and to the north and south of those houses were farms. Her father, a career military officer, was fond of efficiency and routine, even when they were on vacation. He disliked taking unscheduled breaks, but if he had to pull over, he insisted on waiting for a "GFT" town—a town where they could find gas, food, and a toilet—so they could get everything out of the way at once. Back then, Avery didn't even meet these standards. On the handful of occasions when Ed begrudgingly stopped there, it was usually because Elinor or Maren, her older sister, was carsick.

Over twenty years have passed since she last saw Avery, and she understands that things will look different now. But she's still not prepared for how different. A few miles after an exit for Theodore Roosevelt

National Park, traffic begins to slow and she finds herself in a caravan of dust-covered trucks and tankers and semis, all crawling toward the town line. Then the fences appear on both sides of the road where old buildings are being torn down or renovated and nearly every vacant lot is under construction. Signs announce the coming of an Outback Steakhouse, a NAPA Auto Parts store, and a Home Depot. Billboards advertise newly built apartment complexes and housing developments with names that seem chosen at random, without any connection to the landscape at all. The Monarch. The Lyric. The Eldorado. A new Ford dealership stands next to an even newer-looking Walmart, both displaying patriotic GRAND OPENING bunting across their entrances. Even the bright gold streetlights look new, hanging at intersections that probably didn't exist before the boom. The lede of her article almost writes itself. *In Avery, North Dakota, the epicenter of the North American oil boom, one might forget that the rest of the country is still struggling to recover from the worst economic crisis since the Great Depression.*

The Thrifty Inn sits on the main road, sandwiched between a self-service car wash and the fire station. From a distance, it looks like every other budget hotel she's ever stayed at except for the parking lot, which is completely full, littered with signs warning would-be trespassers to keep out. The vehicles in the lot are mostly trucks—passenger, cargo, semi—haphazardly parked in one-and-a-half spaces, sometimes more. Elinor circles the lot twice before pulling onto a scrap of grass, following the lead of two other drivers who simply gave up and parked their huge SUVs on the yellowing lawn.

The lobby has the feel of a train or bus station with people coming and going in every direction. She squeezes through a crowded lounge area where guests—mostly men—are helping themselves to an anemic continental breakfast consisting of coffee, cereal, cups of yogurt, muffins wrapped in clear cellophane, and a basket of waxy-looking fruit. Elinor joins the end of a line at the front desk, surveying her fellow guests, most of whom appear to be middle managers or consultants for oil companies, dressed in button-down shirts and khakis, but no ties. In her hungover state, she makes the mistake of looking at an older man for a few seconds too long. He responds by smiling lewdly at her, his capped teeth gleaming, a glint of something silver. She lowers her head and stares at the dull brown carpet, trying not to roll her eyes at him, even though she wants to. The last time she did that to a stranger for telling her to smile, he followed her for two city blocks, shouting "cunt" at her back.

All around her, men greet each other with backslaps and high fives, making pronouncements like "living the dream" and "another day in paradise"—things she didn't know people really said except on TV. Some of their accents are Southern, ranging from genteel drawls to deep, unintelligible Bayou twang. Others sound vaguely foreign, but she can't identify what countries they're from. The line she joined is moving slowly, so she listens in on nearby conversations: two men trying to one-up each other with stories about how dumb their bosses are; another man arguing with his wife on the phone, telling her it's not his fault that he had to work during their anniversary.

"So what do you want me to do, Paula?" he keeps asking, his voice cracking with a sad kind of desperation. "What the hell am I supposed to do?"

As her line inches forward, Elinor hears Hannah chattering away again, and her head throbs a little harder. She looks up to see a big, bosomy farm girl with rosy pink cheeks, dressed in a too-tight uniform. Her white button-down shirt is about to pop one of its pearl buttons, and her gray blazer puckers at the armpits.

"We'd be happy to send up a cot for fifty dollars a night," Hannah tells a man wearing his mirrored sunglasses on the back of his head.

"You mean fifty dollars total, right?" the man asks. "You're not really charging people fifty bucks a night for some rickety old cot?"

Hannah smiles without apology. "I'm afraid we are, sir. Cots are in very high demand right now. Would you still like one?"

The man doesn't bother to respond before he storms off, sighing with theatrical exasperation. "Everything in this town is such a god-damn scam," he says loudly, which elicits a few chuckles and one "no shit, Sherlock" from passersby.

Hannah must have heard all of this, but her face shows no sign of registering the man's complaint. It just resets to a polite, professional smile as Elinor steps up to the front desk and gives her name.

"Miss Hanson! You made it. I've got your paperwork all ready to go over here." Hannah turns to reach for a file and nearly whips a male coworker in the face with her ponytail. "Now let's get you checked in right away." She types something on her keyboard with pointy laven-der nails. Each click and clack sounds louder than it should, rever-berating through Elinor's temples, scratching behind her eye sockets. "I'm afraid we'll still have to charge you for your first night since you didn't change your reservation before the deadline. But we have you in a nice queen suite on the third floor. I just need to know how many cots you'd like in your room."

"Cots?"

"Yes, you may have heard me tell the gentleman in front of you that they're fifty dollars a night."

The woman who booked her travel said it was shameful, how all the hotels in the area were gouging. Even roadside motels were in-flating their rates by a hundred, sometimes 200 percent, and yet they were still full. Elinor's queen suite at the Thrifty costs $480 a night—a reasonable price in a big city, but unimaginable in western North Dakota prior to the boom. She assumes that most of the rooms here have too many people staying in them, crashing on cots and sofas and floors.

"I don't need any. I'm here alone."

"Oh," Hannah says, drawing out the sound for a beat too long. "Very nice. A suite all to yourself. Alright then, let me just double-check that we have a credit card on file." She narrows her eyes at her computer screen. "It looks like this is being charged to a corporate travel account for the *Standard*?"

"Yes."

"I think I've seen that at the doctor's office. It's a magazine, right?"
She nods.

"Do you work there?"

She nods again, less certain this time.

"Are you like an editor or something?"

"No. Just a writer." The word still feels too big, too pretentious. "I'm writing an article for them."

"Really?" Hannah leans forward, revealing a glimpse of her pale pink bra. She lowers her voice to a whisper. "I'm actually double majoring in English and communication at Avery State. Would you mind me asking how someone can get a job like that?"

Elinor is so tired, so numb with disbelief about where she is and how she got here. She's tempted to tell Hannah the truth: that she dated one of her professors in grad school, that he called less than two weeks ago and asked if she'd like to take over a story he'd been working on for the *Standard*. She remembers it was a Friday because he was on the road, driving to his house in the Catskills, where he usually spent his weekends.

"Can you talk?" he shouted at her over a bad connection, so bad that he had to hang up and call again.

When they reconnected a few minutes later, he explained that he needed to have a hip replacement, something he sounded almost bashful about, sensitive as ever to things that made him feel his age, which was only sixty-three. His doctor had offered him a cancellation date in June, but recuperating from the surgery wouldn't allow him to travel for a while. The article he'd been researching about the oil boom in North Dakota demanded that he travel.

"You grew up near the Bakken, right? That's what I told my editor."

Richard's call was surprising on so many levels. She hadn't spoken to him in over a year, not since she'd graduated from her master's program. And despite his vast network of connections, he'd never helped her find work before, never even thrown so much as a lead her way. A feature article in the *Standard* was something she aspired to—it was something that everyone in her field aspired to—but few ever got the chance. Opportunities like this didn't go to people like her, unagented freelancers working whenever and wherever they could.

"My editor, Lydia—you'll learn a lot from her, by the way, she's always the sharpest person in the room—I think she's a little nervous about how green you are," he said. "But I told her I'd turn over all my research to you. Plus, she liked the idea of assigning the piece to someone who's from the area. You know, someone who has a good sense of the before and after. What do you think, El?"

Absent from their conversation were the niceties that people usually exchange after falling out of touch for a while. *How are you? What have you been working on? Are you seeing anyone these days?* She was relieved about that. Niceties weren't typically his way, not unless he was angling to get her into bed. Their conversation was brief and purposeful; professional, even. He asked if she wanted the assignment. She said that she did.

Standing at the front desk, Elinor struggles with how to boil all of this down for Hannah, who's staring at her expectantly, still waiting for an answer to her question.

"My mentor," she says, trying the word on for size. "He recommended me for the job."

It's a reasonably truthful answer, devoid of any details about her relationship with Richard, which had been complicated, particularly at the end.

"I'd love to have a mentor," Hannah says. "Maybe before you leave here, I'll convince you to be mine."

Elinor manages a tired smile. Richard liked oral sex; he liked it in his office, under a long wooden writing desk that had supposedly belonged to Joseph Pulitzer.

"Maybe," she says, aware that she has absolutely no business mentoring anyone.

4

A large hand waves through the closing elevator doors, forcing them to reopen. It's the man who was arguing with his wife about their anniversary, dragging what appears to be a giant metal toolbox on wheels. He smells like he's been chain-smoking ever since he got off the phone. Elinor glances at her watch. The last time she lit up, it was outside the American terminal at LaGuardia, standing next to several gray-faced smokers on an exiled stretch of sidewalk. That was over fifteen hours ago, possibly a new record for her. She unzips the outer pocket of her bag to see how many cigarettes she has left in her crumpled pack. About ten, minus a few that broke. When she zips the pocket closed, she notices the man looking at her, his thin lips curled upward. She knows the difference between a look and a *look*, and this is one of the latter. Gone is the pained expression on his face, the one that actually made her feel sorry for him earlier. In its place is a strange, almost sleazy grin. So much for your anniversary, she thinks. She's relieved when the elevator dings and spits him out on the second floor, allowing her to ride up the rest of the way by herself.

When the doors open again, she steps out onto the landing and finds a cleaning woman crouched beside an overflowing trash can. Plastic shopping bags filled with garbage, greasy pizza boxes, flattened twenty-four packs of Coors Light, and empty Colt 45 bottles have been piled up next to it. The woman's dark hair hangs in her face as she shoves everything into a bag, the extra-large black kind used by contractors. She's either too distracted or agitated to return the nod of greeting that Elinor offers as she walks past.

"*Cerdos sucios*," the woman mutters under her breath.

Elinor rarely crosses paths with Spanish speakers in her home state, native speakers especially. But *cerdos*, she's almost certain, is Spanish for "pigs." She tries to summon what little remains of her college Spanish classes to translate the rest. *Dirty pigs? Disgusting pigs?* Regardless of the adjective, Elinor agrees with the noun. It looks like a frat house on this floor, not a hotel.

Room 315 is at the far end of the hall. As she inserts her key card into the lock and turns the handle, she braces herself for disappointment, possibly even disgust, at the conditions that await her behind the door. She's relieved to find that the state of the hallways doesn't extend to her suite, which is neat and spacious, with a queen-size bed on one side and a kitchenette and sitting area on the other. Although the olive green and gold upholstery is badly in need of an update, the room is actually larger than her studio in New York. The view is marginally better too. The window overlooks the rear parking lot, and when Elinor cranes her neck at just the right angle, she can see her car, half on the grass and half on the pavement, the angle more diagonal than straight.

"Parked like an asshole," her father would say.

Her skin feels slick and oily, on the verge of breaking out, so she goes to the bathroom and scrubs her face with soap. The vanity light is a soft, pleasing white, so different from the harsh blue fluorescent in the plane, where she washed her face last. The man, the plane. All of it comes rushing at her again. She looks at her reflection in the mirror and tells herself to stop it. There's no use thinking about him now. Even if she called the police, even if the police believed her, what would she say? *I think a man assaulted me, but I'm not sure.* Years ago, she went to the police when she was very sure, but it hardly mattered. She's not about to invite that kind of scrutiny again. She returns to the outer room, looking for something to busy herself with. She hangs up her clothes, sets out her toiletries, makes a mental list of all the things she meant to bring, but didn't. Lotion, lip balm, tampons, socks. None of this keeps her occupied for long, so she fills a Styrofoam cup with water and lights a cigarette. There's a sign on the desk that specifically forbids this in red block letters, but smoking is a distraction too, one of the best.

Two cigarettes later, she checks her email and finds a message from Damon, a friend whose wealthy boyfriend recently kicked him out and cut him off. Damon had some modest success in the nineties doing catalog work for the Gap and Levi's. Now he's broke, couch surfing, and getting by on temp jobs that he's barely qualified to do. He keeps a flip phone around for his staffing agency to contact him, but he pays by the minute and text, so he prefers to email instead. *Would I be in your way if I stayed through the weekend?* he asks. *Last time, I swear.* The question confuses her. The night before she left for Avery, she thought she mentioned being out of town until the end of June, although in retrospect, it's not hard to believe that one or both of them forgot what they talked about. After finishing off a cheese pizza and three bottles of wine, they fell asleep without setting an alarm, resulting in the mad scramble to pack when she jolted awake at noon. *BTW, have you seen my sleeping pills? I'm pretty sure I left them in your bathroom.* So it wasn't even her Restoril, she thinks. He must have placed his bottle on the shelf with her toiletries, which she added to her bag with one clean sweep of her forearm. Elinor types out a quick reply. As penance for taking his pills, she encourages him to stay through the end of the month.

Halfway through her in-box, she sees a name that she hasn't thought about in a while. Kathryn Tasso. Although the two of them took several classes together in grad school, they weren't friends or even friendly, then or now. Kathryn was a former college lacrosse all-star who played on two US national teams. After a brief coaching stint, she retired from the sport in her late twenties to pursue a degree in journalism. Elinor thought it might be worthwhile to get to know her, given the fact that they'd both aged out of their first careers and were trying to launch their second. But Kathryn was aloof and condescending, with an athlete's sense of competition that didn't transfer well to grad school. She treated her classmates like rivals, particularly the women, and the more dismissive she was, the greater her perception of threat. For reasons that Elinor never fully understood, Kathryn seemed deeply threatened by her.

There were other women in their program who were likelier targets for her aggression, women who had graduated from Ivy League universities or already had impressive writing credits to their name. Elinor had delayed college until her midthirties, opting to work and make money while she could still book jobs. By the time she started grad school, she was thirty-nine years old and accustomed to being treated like an oddity in the classroom. Distance, however, was different from outright disdain, and Kathryn often went out of her way to make her feel like she didn't belong. Her gaggle of friends—nervous women who always seemed relieved to be on Kathryn's side rather than in her crosshairs—followed suit, sometimes with contrite, embarrassed looks for taking part in such pettiness. The email neither acknowledges Kathryn's past behavior nor offers any apology for it. *How are you?* it simply begins. *It's been a long time. I was wondering if the two of us could arrange to talk on the phone at some point. Complicated topic, kind of hard to "discuss" by email.*

She assumes that Kathryn heard about the article she's writing. She just doesn't know how. She's not in touch with any of their classmates, in person or online, although the longer she thinks about it, the more obvious it is. Richard was most likely the source. She can easily imagine him boasting to a colleague about helping a former student land a major, potentially career-altering assignment. It wouldn't take long for that kind of news to travel through the alumni grapevine. Kathryn probably wants to ask what it's like to write for the *Standard*, perhaps even ingratiate herself to get a foot in the door. In school, she was always the first to arrive at networking events and alumni mixers, the first to raise her hand during Q and A sessions with famous authors. That was the kind of person she used to be, the kind of person she probably still is. Elinor deletes the email, wondering if Kathryn really expects her to reply and, if so, where she gets the nerve.

In the next room, someone turns on the shower and begins to cough, alternating between hacking and throat clearing for several minutes. She's no stranger to ambient noise—her upstairs neighbor in New York started exercising at all hours of the day and night shortly after her divorce—but the sound transfer is noticeably worse here. She switches on the television, trying to drown out the commotion with a morning talk show.

"One day at a time, sweet Jesus," the man sings, his voice an unexpectedly sweet alto once he's done coughing. "That's all I'm asking from you."

She turns up the TV and continues scrolling through her in-box until she finds what she was looking for, the message in which Richard shared the link to his voluminous research file, giving her access to all his work to date. At his suggestion, Elinor read through the contents before leaving New York, which took the better part of a week. The file, simply titled "Bakken," contains over a hundred articles about the western Dakotas, all written through a different lens—history, business, geology, sociology, public health, popular culture. It also includes census figures, environmental studies, historical photos, news clippings, crime stats, oil industry reports, and the schedule of interviews he'd set up before turning the piece over to her—interviews he strongly encouraged her to follow through with since she had yet to develop any sources of her own. For her benefit, she suspects, Richard also included brief bios of the interviewees—Avery's town manager, the head of a nearby Native American tribe, a woman whose husband sold off their mineral rights, among others.

I contacted everyone and let them know you'd be coming instead, his email says.

The contents of the file confirm something she's always wondered about him. He actually follows his own advice. In grad school, he was forever reminding Elinor and her classmates to cast the net of research wide, to learn as much as possible about a subject before deciding what the story was. Students revered and reviled him for pointing out that what they wanted to write about might not be the thing that deserved to be written about.

Whenever Elinor goes through the file, she can't help but feel conflicted, swinging from one extreme to another. Sometimes she thinks Richard did her a genuine kindness, sharing months' worth of research that he didn't want to go to waste, research that she should be grateful for. But then she finds the instructions and reminders he left for her—brief missives scribbled in the margins of his scanned notes or tacked onto the ends of his lists—and she wonders if the file is his way of exerting control over her, as if she's still his student, someone without a mind of her own. While she appreciates the fact that he recommended her for this assignment, she worries that Richard thinks she's just going to do his bidding here.

I already drafted questions for all the interviews I scheduled, his email continues. *You should feel free to use them.*

By now, she knows him well enough to read between the lines, however casually phrased. When Richard writes "feel free to use them," what he really means is "use them."

5

Her first interview is at town hall at 4 p.m., leaving nearly six hours to kill. Room service is one of her guilty pleasures, but the man who picks up the phone at the front desk chuckles when she asks if they have it. After a long shower, she leaves the hotel in search of a place to eat and regrets her decision to drive almost immediately. In addition to losing her makeshift parking space, the main road—known as Highway 12 outside of town and Main Street within the town limits—is bumper-to-bumper in both directions, making it difficult to turn around or even turn left. She sits in traffic, idling behind a maroon pickup truck with Montana plates and too many bumper stickers: KEEP YOUR HANDS OFF MY GUNS, SPAY AND NEUTER LIBERALS, MCCAIN 2008, ROMNEY 2012. She glances at other plates as she passes and spots vehicles from Texas, Oklahoma, California, Nevada, Florida, Wyoming, and Louisiana. Fifteen minutes later, and she's only seen two cars from North Dakota.

This is the problem, as she understands it—thousands of itinerant oil workers from recession-ravaged parts of the country, descending upon a town of four thousand that was unprepared to take them in. It doesn't require a degree in city planning to figure out why housing is at a premium, why traffic is so bad, why everything is under construction all at once. On the side of a Wells Fargo branch, someone has spray-painted the word *FUBAR* in giant, drippy gold letters, and she pulls the long-lost definition out of a pocket of memory she didn't know she had. *Fucked up beyond all recognition*, which seems about right.

The longer she sits in traffic, the more light-headed she feels. She can't remember the last time she ate and worries it was the pizza she had with Damon two nights ago. Elinor scans the storefronts as she inches past, ready to stop at the first sight of food. Everywhere she looks, long lines have assembled. At the barber shop, the bank, the pharmacy. The lines snake out of doors and clutter up sidewalks. Some even wrap around corners. Unlike the button-down shirt and khaki-clad men staying at her hotel, the men queued up here look like actual roughnecks, either in search of work or between shifts. They're unshaven, unkempt, and tired. White, Black, and brown, all mixed together. A handful of Asians too. She continues along Main, aware at some point that she's never seen more diverse crowds of people anywhere in the state. Before she has a chance to reflect on how surreal this is, a car pulls out of a space in front of a small doughnut shop. She turns sharply into it with a crank of her wheel, even though doughnuts aren't the kind of food she really wants right now. Judging from the relative emptiness of the store compared to its neighbors, no one else wants them either.

The teenage boy working behind the counter at the Donut Hut appears to be very, very stoned. His eyes are bloodshot and heavy lidded; and when the oscillating fan in the corner blows at his back, Elinor catches the unmistakable, skunky smell of weed. She orders the special—two plain doughnuts and a cup of coffee for $1.99—and asks for a receipt so she can get reimbursed, something people apparently never do because the boy's mouth twists with confusion. He lowers his head, frowning at all the keys on the register until he spots the one he wants and presses it with more force than necessary.

Elinor pockets the receipt and takes her order to the small counter where two old men are sitting. The men look like retired farmers—retired, because she doesn't think they'd be in town at this hour if they were still working—and farmers, judging from their worn plaid shirts and dingy, sweat-stained hats, one with a logo for Monsanto, the other for John Deere. She sits down a few stools away from them, her stomach growling with hunger and fluttering with nerves. It's difficult for her to start conversations with strangers. It always makes her feel like she's intruding, the same way she feels when strangers approach her. It's also the complete opposite of how she used to make a living, which a photographer once described as "being quiet and looking pretty."

"Good afternoon," she says, instantly embarrassed by her stiff, formal greeting.

The two men look up from their coffee, startled almost. The one with the thick gray mustache actually turns around to see if she's talking to someone else, even though they're the only three customers in the shop.

"Well, good *morning*," he says.

"Yes, you're right. Morning. I guess I'm a little out of it from flying."

All one of them needs to do is ask where she flew in from, but the old men simply look at each other and then back down at their half-eaten doughnuts. She takes a bite of her own. The texture is dry and dusty, at least a day old.

The bell on the door rings as a mother with two little girls walks in. The boy hops off his stool and waits to take their order, chewing absentmindedly on his black leather necklace. Elinor decides to try one more time.

"Could either of you recommend a place to get lunch around here? Maybe somewhere that won't have a long wait?"

The men look at her blankly, as if she's speaking in tongues. Elinor glances at her arms, wondering if her tattoos are visible through her thin black cardigan. People are sometimes put off by them, elderly people in particular. But the wrinkled sweater she found balled up in the bottom of her bag is finely knit and opaque. The tattoos aren't to blame for the reception she's getting.

"I suppose you're another newcomer," the one with the mustache finally says.

"No. Not exactly." She suspects that being from North Dakota will help her with these men. "I grew up in the area."

"Not in Avery, you sure didn't." The mustached one says this with certainty, as if he's been around long enough to know who belongs and who doesn't. His reaction reminds her why she hates small towns, why she was so glad to leave her own nearly twenty-five years ago.

"Well, I grew up nearby, in Marlow."

The men laugh as if they've never heard anything so funny, doubling over and slapping their thighs.

"Marlow?" the other one whoops. "Who are you kidding? You might as well be talking about Minnesota. Hell, you might as well be talking about the moon!"

Her hometown is only an hour and a half east of Avery, in the central part of the state. The reference to Minnesota—long regarded as North Dakota's more liberal, urbane neighbor—is something she's never heard before, but she finds it annoying. Offensive, even. She had a hard time growing up in North Dakota. It feels like he's telling her she didn't. She drinks her coffee and glances at the boy lurking behind the counter, still waiting for the woman and her little girls to order.

"So let me guess," the mustached one says. "Your father must have been in the military."

She nods, irritated that a stranger can correctly assume this about her based on where she lived. But Marlow is a company town, similar to Redmond, Washington, or Armonk, New York. The company just happens to be the US Air Force instead of Microsoft or IBM. If a person of color lived in Marlow back in the seventies and eighties like she did, chances are, they were stationed there, or someone in their family was.

"And I bet your father probably spent some time in Korea?" Mustache grins. He seems pleased with himself for knowing what kind of Asian she is.

"That's right." Her voice spikes with enthusiasm, overcorrecting for her worsening mood. "He met my mother when he was stationed there."

Her parents, Ed and Nami, spent the early years of their married life on US Air Force bases in South Korea, first at Kunsan in the south, and later at Osan, near Seoul. It was a big deal, Nami once told her, snagging a handsome American serviceman like that. The bases were luxurious compared to the fishing village where she grew up. And the PXs sold things that she and her family had never had access to before—electronics and cosmetics and well-made American clothes. When Nami got pregnant with Maren, Ed arranged for a transfer to Marlow, a Strategic Air Command facility near his hometown. Nami's relatives and neighbors rejoiced. She hadn't been born so pretty for nothing, they said. To them, all of America was "America." They didn't know the difference between North Dakota and New Jersey. They also didn't know that Ed had shipped off to Korea with the intention of bringing back an Asian wife, someone quiet and obliging who would be grateful to have a comfortable home.

Mustache finishes his coffee and wipes his mouth on a balled-up napkin. Then he proceeds to tell her that both sides of his family have been living in the state since the Homestead Act. His father even hauled cement to Marlow when the base was being constructed in the 1950s. It seems like he's playing a strange game of chicken with her, trying to establish that his ancestors were around long before hers were, as if only one of them can remain standing. By now, she's used to this. She's half-white and half-Asian. For as long as she can remember, people have been pushing her out of one circle or another, making her feel less American, less Korean, and now even less North Dakotan than she thinks she is.

"So your father drove trucks?" she asks, picking up on the most benign thread she can. "That's interesting."

"Why's that?"

"I just thought most people around here farmed back then."

He looks at her like she's an idiot. But it's a reasonable assumption, she thinks. The main industry in this part of the state only recently shifted from agriculture to oil.

"My father was a farmer and about ten other jobs that almost broke his back," he says. "That's how he hung on to his farm long enough to pass it on to me."

Mustache is one of those people who talks with the full weight of the chip on his shoulder. The part of her that's curious wants to know what that chip is about, where it came from, if it's possible to ever get past it. She considers asking him about his farm when the two little girls begin whining and banging loudly on the glass doughnut case, prompting their mother to squat down and meet them at eye level. Elinor can't hear what she's saying, but she recognizes the low, threatening growl of an impatient parent. When one of the girls smacks the case defiantly, leaving a greasy little print on the glass, the mother grabs each of their hands and jerks them out of the store.

The conversation drops off again after they leave. Elinor eats one of her doughnuts, forcing the dry crumbs down with swigs of coffee as she steals glances at the second man's fingers. He has a gnarled red nub where his right thumb should be. A farming accident, probably.

"So what brings you to Avery?" The thumbless one grins. "You're not dancing over there at Pandora's, are you?"

Pandora's must be one of the strip clubs she recently read about. "Gentlemen's clubs," they call them here. They've been reproducing like mushrooms on the outskirts of town since the boom started. She tries not to bristle at the suggestion or act on her growing suspicion that these men aren't just old and surly, as she initially assumed. They're intentionally being rude. "I'm writing an article for a magazine called the *Standard*. Have you heard of it?"

The two men look at each other knowingly.

"What?" she asks.

"All those articles do is convince more people to come," the thumbless one says. "We don't need one more person in this town who don't belong here."

She opens her bag and rummages inside. "Would you mind if I quoted you?"

When she places her notebook and pencil on the counter, both men shake their heads. "You just put those away," Mustache snaps. "You don't have our permission to write down anything we said. We were just sitting here, trying to mind our own business before you came along."

She shrugs and slides her notebook back into her bag, trying to appear unrattled. It's not the first time she's been turned down for a quote, but usually, people are more decent about it. "Sorry. I didn't mean to bother you."

Heat floods her cheeks, quickly spreading to her ears and neck. She angles her face away, hoping she doesn't look as red as she feels. The men are like ornery wasps now, disturbed from their nest. When they stand up to leave, the thumbless one mutters to the other about not being able to have a cup of coffee in goddamn peace anymore. He says it just loudly enough for Elinor to hear.

6

The shop is quiet for a while. Elinor picks her second doughnut apart, reducing it to a pile of uneaten crumbs that she pinches between her fingers. The boy behind the register glances at her from time to time. His changing expression—curious at first and then increasingly impatient—suggests that she's wearing out her welcome. He probably wants her to leave so he can light up again. After overworking the doughnut crumbs into a sticky yellow paste, Elinor collects her things and walks toward the door, zigzagging with indecision. Stay or go. Stay or go. Ever since she arrived, she's been thinking about getting high, although she promised herself she wouldn't. Not here, not while she's working on this article. But her conversation with the old men stirred up something inside her. Elinor feels angrier than she has in a long time. She wants to feel something else. Her first meeting is five hours from now. An eternity, as far as she's concerned. Against her better judgment, she stops at the register just as the fan behind the boy blows toward her again. She breathes in deeply, trying to recapture what little remains of the dank, earthy smell.

The boy hops off his stool and waits for her to order. "Another doughnut?" he asks after an awkward pause.

She forces herself to think about the plane, the Restoril, the kinds of things that can happen when she makes bad decisions. But she's not convinced that weed is in the same league as sleeping pills. Weed is just a palliative, after all. Maybe it can even help her forget what happened on the plane for good.

"You need a warm-up, maybe?"

"Yes, thank you." She pushes her half-empty cup toward him for a refill, even though she has no intention of finishing the rest.

"Anything else?"

Although it's not a good opening, it's the only one she has, so she leans forward and smiles. "Would you mind . . . this might sound kind of strange, but would you mind telling me where I can buy some weed around here?"

The boy needs a haircut. His mouse-brown hair hangs in his eyes, which are hooded no more. "W-w-hat?" he asks, his expression owl-like.

"Weed. I was hoping you'd tell me where I could buy some." She can see the denial building up inside him, expanding like a balloon. "I'm new in town," she says reassuringly. "I just flew in last night. Obviously, I couldn't bring any with me on the plane."

He swivels his head around the store, as if there are hidden cameras tucked away in the grimy light fixtures, the grainy black-and-white photos of the original Donut Hut, the framed one-dollar bill that she assumes was the store's first.

"I heard you tell those guys you're writing an article. That makes you what? Some kind of reporter?"

She didn't realize he'd been listening. Having a witness to that exchange just makes her want to light up even more. "This has nothing to do with what I'm writing," she says. "This is just for me."

Richard was the one who reintroduced her to weed. A few unmemorable attempts in high school had left her indifferent to it, but he insisted that even a single drag could make food taste better and lift the clouds hanging over his prose when he was trying to write. She didn't experience the same effects that he did, but she liked how smoking relaxed her, quieting her misgivings about returning to school at her age. Occasionally, she snuck in a hit or two before class to lessen her anxiety about interacting with her younger, seemingly better educated classmates. It helped that Richard only smoked expensive weed, purchased from an organic grower who made weekly deliveries in his Toyota Prius. She has no idea what kind of product a kid working at a doughnut shop might have, but she recognizes that she's the beggar here. She can't also be a snob.

"I'm sorry to come right out and ask you like that. But I swear—I'm not a narc or anything." She pauses, not certain if teenagers even use the word "narc" anymore. "It just hasn't been a good day."

The boy cocks his head at her, frowning. But he's not saying no. The shop feels warm all of a sudden, as if she's standing under a white-hot spotlight. She takes off her cardigan and ties it around her waist, figuring a teenager won't mind her tattoos. With her arms exposed, the boy looks at her like she's a different person. His posture loosens; the tightness in his jaw disappears. His eyes graze her inked skin, hover over her small breasts, and then return to her face. To her relief and alarm, he seems to like what he sees. He walks toward the window and looks outside. Then he locks the front door and turns the hanging sign from OPEN to CLOSED.

"Okay. C'mere," he says, tilting his head toward the back.

"Where?"

"Just c'mere."

Slowly, she follows him through a long galley kitchen that smells like vanilla and yeasty bread. On the wall, there's a whiteboard with schedules for the week and a reminder, written in bright green marker: TYLER, MAKE SURE YOU TURN THE LIGHTS OFF WHEN YOU CLOSE! She wonders if that's the boy's name. Tyler. That's exactly what he looks like. Pimpled complexion, a mouth full of metal, a jelly-stained shirt too big and blousy for his frame.

Tyler unlocks the back door, which opens to an alley filled with junky wood pallets and a dumpster buzzing with flies. He looks cautiously in both directions before removing a small zippered bag from his back pocket. Inside, there's a pipe and some loose weed that resembles dryer lint.

"Come back tomorrow with twenty bucks if you want a dime bag," he says, packing the bowl. "For now, you can have some of mine."

He offers her the pipe and a lighter, which was actually what she was hoping for, more so than the promise of a dime bag later. She accepts them gladly, aware that she's doing a stupid, stupid thing. But the nervous flutter in her stomach hasn't gone away yet. She feels unsettled and agitated; she has ever since she arrived in town. And now she can't stop thinking about the two old men, how they suggested she wasn't really from here, that she had no reason to even be here except to shake her tits in some strip club. She raises the lighter to the bowl and watches the amber flame catch as she inhales, filling her lungs with smoke. It's not high-quality weed; she knows this immediately. It's terrible, in fact. But she takes two long hits anyway before passing the pipe back. Tyler sits down on a plastic milk crate and glances at the empty one beside him. It seems like an invitation, so she sits down, leaning her head against the brick wall as she exhales.

"So where you from?" he asks.

"New York."

"Damn." He touches his tongue with his fingertips, removing a stray bud and flicking it into the alley. "That must be hella exciting."

She tries not to smile at his use of dated slang, which doesn't sound right coming from his mouth. She wonders if he always talks like this, or if he's trying to impress her. "Have you ever visited?"

He shakes his head. "No, but that'd be the place I'd move to if I could."

She remembers thinking the same thing at his age. Every teenager growing up in a small town probably did. On the base in Marlow, her mother used to get her hair cut by a woman who'd lived in New York in her early twenties. Elinor always tagged along to Nami's appointments so she could flip through the woman's fashion magazines and listen to her stories about seeing the Empire State Building light up at night or strolling past the big department store windows during the holidays. Whenever she described her time in New York, neither

Nami nor Elinor could take their eyes off her, as if they were both committing the details to memory for future use.

"I bet it's nice there," Tyler says. "Nicer than this, at least."

It's not, she thinks. It hasn't been nice for a while. The subways are too crowded. It smells in the summer. Anyone who's not a millionaire is getting priced out. She lives as cheaply as she can off her savings, but if she hadn't purchased her apartment in Hell's Kitchen when she was still modeling, she wouldn't even be able to rent in her neighborhood now. She doesn't have the heart to mention any of this to Tyler, whose romantic ideas about New York remind her that she once had some of her own. He should hang on to his for as long as he can.

"So, how old are you?" she asks.

"I'll be seventeen next month."

She wonders how old he thinks she is. Unlike her father's side of the family, pale Norwegian farmers who wrinkled prematurely under the sun, she inherited Nami's good skin. People are often surprised to learn that she's in her early forties, which isn't necessarily a blessing. Twice, she catches Tyler staring at her with too much interest, so she leans away, hoping he understands that she's old enough to be his mother.

"Did those hurt?" he asks, pointing at her tattoos.

She shrugs. "Some. Not all."

The pattern on her arms is similar to a maze, with the lines drawn black and thick. When she turns toward Tyler, waiting for him to pass the pipe, she notices that he's staring at her again. It looks like he's moving an invisible ball through the maze, searching for an exit. She pulls on her sweater, forcing him to stop.

"You know, those guys you were talking to, the Daves"—Tyler takes an extralong hit—"they're real assholes, in case you were wondering." He tips his head back and exhales a thick column of smoke into the air.

"The Daves?"

"They're both named Dave. I can't remember what their last names are. They come in for the special every day, always talking shit about people. Roughnecks, mostly."

"I got the sense they weren't exactly the Welcome Wagon."

Tyler returns the pipe to her. He seems confused by the term.

"I can tell they don't like all the new people in town," she explains.

He looks over his shoulder, making sure they're alone. "It's mostly just the Blacks and the Spanish they got a problem with. You should hear those two when they really get going. It's all 'nigger' this and 'spic' that. I wasn't really sure how they'd take to you at first. I was halfway expecting them to leave when you sat down."

Elinor sits up straight. The rough texture of the brick pokes into her back. She hasn't heard anyone say these words out loud in a long time, except in a movie or on TV. Each instance feels like a blow to the chest, a reaction that must register on her face because Tyler is quick to clarify.

"*I'm* not the one who calls them that. I'm just telling you what the Daves say. I don't think they're used to being around different kinds of people."

There were census summaries in the research file, microscopic ones that she had to magnify again and again in order to read. The population of Avery was nearly all white before the boom, while towns on the neighboring reservation were mostly Native American. Other races barely made up a fraction of a percent, something she remembers from the years she lived nearby, when seeing another Asian face was rare. Then the boom dropped what one writer memorably described as a "diversity bomb" on the western Dakotas. Suddenly, job seekers of every race and ethnicity were arriving in the area. Upon first read, she thought "bomb" was a nice bit of descriptive flourish to account for the scale and suddenness of the changes, but now it occurs to her that bombs destroy things. Bombs are never good.

Elinor is about to take one last hit when she notices the time—11:45, and all she's consumed today is sugar and caffeine, which is making her light-headed. "Thanks for this," she says, returning the pipe as she stands up to leave. "I really appreciate it."

"So you'll come back tomorrow, right?" Tyler is looking up at her, squinting with one eye shut because of the sun's glare. "For the dime bag?"

She doesn't feel stoned yet. She's not sure if she will. She tells him she'll swing by because it seems like he wants her to, and promises to herself aside, maybe she wants to as well.

"You know, my friend can get other stuff. Harder stuff, if you want."

"Harder like what?"

He shrugs. "Meth. Oxy. Smack, if you're into that."

"Are you into that?"

He shrugs again, too young to know what the right answer is.

7

Elinor continues down Main Street, still searching for a place to eat. The farther she drives, the more the businesses begin to thin and spread out. Instead of circling back, she pulls into a Bernie's drive-through with a line of cars nine deep. It's been years, maybe even a decade, since she last had fast food, but she harbors a special fondness for Bernie's, a small Midwestern chain that she assumed had long gone out of business. Whenever she cut class in high school, she'd treat herself to a trip through their drive-through, eating with the windows open so her father wouldn't notice the smell in his car.

By now, she's ravenous—the weed was much stronger than she thought—so she orders a supersize bacon double cheeseburger meal, grateful for her birdlike metabolism. When the food finally arrives, she takes huge bites of the burger, dropping bits of tomato and melted cheese and watery ketchup onto her makeshift plate, which she fashioned out of napkins. She gobbles fries by the dozen, pinching and folding them into her mouth, and sucks so much ice-cold soda through her straw, she almost forgets to breathe. It took twenty minutes to receive her food, and less than five minutes to finish it, scraping the wax paper wrapper clean with her fingers. So many women she worked with used to binge like this. Then they'd slip away to the nearest bathroom and return a short while later, sucking on sugar-free mints. It was one of the few bad habits of the business that Elinor didn't pick up.

From the parking lot of Bernie's, she watches a line gathered in front of a faded brick building on the corner. There's no sign, no address number, nothing that tells her—or them—what kind of business goes on inside. Still, the line stretches halfway down the block, growing faster than it moves. The people waiting are men of all ages, all colors, all physical conditions. She sees more prosthetic limbs than she ever has in one place. Veterans of Iraq or Afghanistan, most likely. The oil companies supposedly love hiring vets. She begins to count how many people are in line and reaches thirty-eight before she sees her first female, a short, middle-aged woman who looks like someone's mother. Behind her are at least a dozen more men.

Elinor wants to know what they're waiting for, what the woman is waiting for, so she examines herself in the rearview mirror, wiping a smear of ketchup from her cheek. Her eyes are a bit droopy, but not the obvious, heavy-lidded kind of droop that she associates with stoners like Tyler.

As soon she gets out of her car, the line registers her presence. The murmur is quiet at first, but quickly, it builds.

"Hey, beautiful."

"Would you look at her."

"Damn, girl."

"*Ni hao ma*."

"What's up, baby?"

She lowers her eyes to the ground, trying not to look up. She hates the way she does this, defaulting to a posture that she associates with shame. How differently she reacts to male attention now.

The first time someone catcalled her, she was a sophomore in high school. The new English teacher had arranged a field trip for his honors students to see a play in Minneapolis. On their way to the theater, they walked past a construction site, and the workers started whistling and making comments at the girls, something most of them had never experienced before. Her female classmates tittered nervously. Some even waved at the men, a motley-looking group dressed in faded denim and orange vests, their skin the color of hide. Elinor had grown faster and taller than most of the boys and all of the girls in her class. At five foot ten, she was more accustomed to being called names than being called pretty, so it took her a while to realize that many of the comments were being directed at her, the "exotic one," the "China doll with the long legs."

Her teacher, Mr. Bender, was a young man still in his twenties. He had a kind face framed by dirty blond curls, and she and several of her classmates had been nursing crushes on him that semester. When he realized what was happening, he rushed toward Elinor and put a protective hand on the small of her back as he led her away. It was electric, all of it. His desire to protect her, the jealous glances from the girls, the bewildered stares from the boys as they tried to figure out what they had missed about her. She walked the rest of the way with Mr. Bender, who advised her to simply ignore men when they did that, as if he knew something similar was likely to happen again. Anyone who observed the bright red flush of Elinor's cheeks when they arrived at the theater probably assumed that she was embarrassed by the incident. But secretly, she was elated. It was the first time she'd ever felt noticed for being pretty instead of being different.

She feels none of that elation now as she crosses the street, trying to pretend that she doesn't notice what's going on around her. But her usual tactics don't work here. The volume, the frequency, the crudeness of the comments being directed at her are greater than anything she's ever experienced before. There are just too many men to ignore, and once the hive begins to buzz, it grows louder and louder.

"What's your name?"

"Smile, baby."

"What's the matter? You deaf?"

"Hey, gorgeous. Gorgeous!"

"Your car broke, honey? Oh, I'll give you a ride."

These are the sentences she can make out, the actual words shouted at her as she passes. But there are noises too. Slick, wet, sloppy, dirty noises. Laughter. The shuffle of feet as men high-five and slap each other on the shoulder, congratulating their friends for getting something into the mix. Elinor's pulse quickens and her skin flushes from cheeks to chest. Everything in her stomach feels like it's about to come back up. She wonders if the weed she smoked is making her paranoid. Then again, if she wasn't stoned, she would have doubled back to her car already and driven away. She reminds herself that she has a job to do in spite of these men, who are everywhere in Avery. She has to be able to walk among them.

Just before she reaches the opposite side of the street, she scans the faces in front of her, trying to decide whom to approach. All she sees are no-good grins and a few menacing stares that wouldn't look out of place in a mug shot. She veers toward the only person she can, the woman.

"Hello," Elinor says.

The woman visibly stiffens. She doesn't turn to face her, but all the men in line do, forming a loose half circle around them.

"I'm writing an article about the oil boom for the *Standard*." Elinor says the name of the publication too loudly, wielding it like a talisman. "Would you mind telling me what you're waiting in line for?"

"Hey, you can interview me," someone yells.

The woman continues staring straight ahead. Up close, she looks like she's in her mid-sixties. She has fine silver hair that hangs in her face, and she's wearing an all-gray outfit. Pants, sneakers, a tight polyester shirt that accentuates the doughiness of her body. Her wire-rim glasses catch the afternoon light, drawing attention to the milky white cataracts forming in her eyes.

"Excuse me. May I ask what you're in line for?" Elinor repeats.

The woman glances at her, but only for a moment. "Halliburton's hiring." Her mouth is drawn so tight, it looks like she just spoke without moving her lips.

"For what kind of job?"

"All kinds."

"And what kind of job are you hoping to get?"

"You want to interview me to be your boyfriend?" someone else shouts.

"Whatever they'll hire me for," the woman says.

In the corner of her eye, Elinor sees the man who offered to be her boyfriend tug at his crotch and take a step toward her. "You want to be my girl, ba—" He stops, quieted by his friend, who's telling him to calm the fuck down.

The entire time she's speaking to the woman, men continue to jockey for her attention, rattling off one terrible line after another and then acting hurt or offended when she pretends not to notice. As a young model, she would have been disappointed to walk into a bar or a club and not generate a reaction like this. Attention was a valuable form of currency. The more she earned, the more she was worth. Now all she wants to do is to blend in, something that's proving impossible here.

"Have you been waiting long?" she asks, trying to keep the conversation going.

"A couple of—"

The woman is interrupted by someone shouting, "Give me a massage!"

Shut the hell up, Elinor wants to shout back. But she knows what will happen if she does. The crowd will turn on her in an instant, replacing their idea of compliments with epithets and accusations. *Stuck-up bitch. Skinny bitch. Chinese bitch.* Things she's heard before that she doesn't want to hear again.

The line advances a few feet and the woman shuffles forward. Elinor shuffles with her. There are so many things she wants to ask. *How old are you? What are you qualified to do for a company like Halliburton? What's it like looking for work in the oil fields at your age?* She tries to figure out how to word these questions with more delicacy, in a way that won't make the woman feel defensive or judged, but it's hard to think clearly with the volume of activity going on around them, which isn't letting up. Elinor feels terrible about this. Before she came along, the woman was just standing in line, wearing her gray clothes like a sort of camouflage. Now they're the center of attention, something she was clearly trying to avoid from the start. Continuing to ask questions will only make the situation worse for both of them.

"Well, good luck," Elinor says casually. "I hope you land something today." She leans toward her and whispers, "I'm sorry I bothered you." Then she returns to her car without waiting for a response, aware that this is the second time she's had to apologize for bothering someone in the past hour, simply by trying to do her job.

Men mock-plead with her to stay and shout comments at her back about the roundness and fineness of her ass. She distinctly hears someone jogging after her, shouting "Hey! Hey!" but the footsteps and jangle of keys soon fall away.

Even after she starts the car, she can still hear men shouting at her over the sound of the engine and the air conditioner blowing hot, stale air on her face. She pulls out of the parking lot without looking at them, relieved that there's less traffic on this side of Main. Only when the line of men disappears from her rearview mirror does she notice the way she's sitting—perfectly erect, both hands squeezing the steering wheel, her knuckles bloodless and white.

8

The town manager's elderly secretary keeps looking at her from across the room. BETTY HILDEBRANDT—the name embossed on her faux-wood desk plaque—clearly means no harm. She's probably just a worrier, the old-fashioned kind who assumes that her boss's lateness will reflect badly on her. Every few minutes, Mrs. Hildebrandt—Elinor has a tendency to think of all older women as "Mrs."—sets down the index cards she's been organizing and glances at her with a pained expression.

"I'm so sorry. He's usually never this late. Are you sure I can't get you something to drink?"

"I'm fine, ma'am. Thank you."

She hasn't called anyone "ma'am" in years, but being so close to home resurrects her father's frequent etiquette lectures. *Be sure to refer to your elders as sir or ma'am or they'll think you're being disrespectful. Make eye contact when you shake hands or people will never trust you. Don't forget to say please and thank you or it'll look like you weren't raised right.* Ed believed that bad manners had consequences, especially among military families that valued order and decorum. Before big events with his colleagues or commanding officers, he always gave Nami the same lectures, as if she were his child instead of his wife.

"And you definitely don't want to reschedule?"

"I don't mind waiting, really."

She understands why Richard set this meeting up. A story about

Avery would be incomplete without speaking to the town manager. But it feels so perfunctory. Elinor assumes that most public officials are guarded. She'll be lucky if she leaves with a decent quote and maybe a new contact or two.

"Well, let me know if there's anything I can do for you," Mrs. Hildebrandt says, picking up her stack of cards again.

Elinor smiles politely and scans the room for what feels like the hundredth time. The furniture in the waiting area is nice, almost conspicuously so. She imagines New Yorkers offering top dollar for the gently used chairs and sofas, attractive examples of mid-century craftsmanship that wouldn't be out of place at a high-end antiques shop. The rest of the decor, however, has a haphazard quality to it. Fake floral arrangements on white pillars; an assortment of trophies and plaques; posters in flimsy, scratched metallic frames. The one on the wall directly in front of her is an enlargement of a vintage photograph with the words AVERY FIREMAN PARADE—JULY 16, 1912 etched directly on the negative. The firemen are marching down the street in suits and ties, their faces dark and sullen.

Years ago, when Elinor was first starting out in New York, she rented a small room in an apartment owned by her modeling agency. Her roommates were a frequently rotating cast of women—girls, actually. Eighteen- and nineteen-year-old girls discovered by the agency's scouts, the same way she was. They decorated their shared spaces like the teenagers they were, with clothing and perfume ads torn out of magazines and covers featuring the supermodels they admired or envied most. In the kitchen, an ethereal Texan who dreamed of walking European runways hung up a black-and-white poster of a street scene in Florence, a photograph that looked like it belonged in the pages of *Life*. To the left of center, there was a tall, elegant brunette with a shawl draped over one shoulder, passing through a gauntlet of Italian men who were all smiling, laughing, staring, and blowing kisses at her. At first, Elinor didn't mind seeing the poster several times a day. It made sense for it to be there. She and her roommates were aspiring models.

They had chosen to be looked at for a living. But the longer she stayed in that apartment, memorizing every detail of the image, the more she understood that something was very wrong.

Her roommates thought she was crazy when she first brought it up. The men weren't bothering the woman, they said. They were simply appreciating her beauty, putting her on a pedestal. "It's cultural!" was their favorite line of protest. But Elinor couldn't be persuaded. She thought the woman looked frightened. Everything about her expression said so. There was the lack of eye contact, the noticeable absence of a smile. There was also the way she held her arms so close to her body, one hand clutching her bag, the other holding up her shawl, as if to keep herself covered. The men in the picture seemed amused by her discomfort. A curly-haired one on a motor scooter was tilting his head at her, his mouth open mid-laugh. Another man in a dapper suit was leaning toward her, his lips puckered for a kiss and both hands shoved deep into his pockets, a detail that always seemed perverse to her.

Several hours have passed since her encounter with the men on the street, but Elinor can't stop thinking about it. If someone had taken a photo of her walking past them, she wonders if it would accurately register her feelings, if there would be any debate about the anger and fear that pulsed through her veins like blood. She keeps seeing the scene unfold as if she's watching from a place outside her own body. When she replays her part, Elinor isn't sure what she could have done differently, other than not get out of the car, which hardly seems fair. She should be able to go wherever she wants without being subjected to that kind of abuse. How far she's come from that awkward teen-age girl in Minneapolis, the one who finally felt seen and appreciated just because men called her pretty. She doesn't want that anymore. At least, that's what she tells herself. She doesn't want to want that anymore. For her, even this is a step.

At 4:40, Alan Denny finally emerges from his office, apologizing for the delay as he smooths out his wispy comb-over with one hand and shakes with the other. He's short and snowman-like, composed mostly of circles. Round head, round belly, round wire-rim glasses that make his eyes look as big as coins. He rattles off explanations for why his conference call ran so long, clearly hating the idea of inconveniencing anyone as much as Mrs. Hildebrandt does. While Elinor didn't necessarily mind the wait, she dislikes the way he leans toward her when he speaks, so close that she can smell the old coffee on his breath.

Mr. Denny ushers her into his office, which is decorated much like the waiting room with the same furniture and trophies and posters. Beside his desk, there's a large window that faces the police station across the street, surrounded by a fleet of newish-looking black-and-white cruisers. She makes a note to mention that all her requests to the police department to schedule a ride-along have gone unanswered. Maybe this is something he can help her with.

"So, the *Standard*'s interested in doing a story about our little town, eh?"

"It's not so little anymore." She takes a recorder out of her bag and asks if she can place it on his desk.

"Be my guest." He moves a tall stack of folders off to the side with his forearm. Mr. Denny, she notices, is a stacker. Everywhere she looks, there's a stack of something, like he's trying to wall himself in behind a fortress of folders and envelopes and boxes.

"So how can I help?" he asks pleasantly, knitting his fingers together and resting them on his stomach. "What would you like to know?"

She's wary of some of the questions on Richard's list, concerned they'll elicit nothing more than generalizations. Sure enough, the first three questions yield exactly that. Text straight out of a stump speech about job creation, economic development, and an unemployment rate that's currently the lowest in the country. If Richard were here, he wouldn't mind. He believed that good interviews required patience, and most interview subjects, particularly inexperienced ones, needed time to feel comfortable with the idea of themselves as interviewees before sharing anything remotely usable. But the longer Mr. Denny goes on, the more Elinor's attention begins to drift. Her eyes keep wandering up to the framed vintage photograph behind his head. This one features three men in aprons standing behind the counter of a mercantile. At some point, Mr. Denny must notice her looking at it because he turns and points at the man closest to the register.

"That's my grandfather from my mother's side of the family. He ran the general store in town for forty-two years."

"Your family goes way back in this area."

"That we do. Seven generations of us, starting with my great-great-great grandfather."

She scans the rest of Richard's questions, irritated with herself for not preparing more of her own. She's used up almost half of her hour with him, asking about things she already knew or never wanted to know.

"So, what else can I help you with?"

Elinor turns the list facedown on her lap, unwilling to continue referring to it. "This may be a little off topic, but something strange happened when I was on Main Street earlier today. I was wondering what you'd make of it."

"Strange in what way?"

She explains how the men surrounded her outside the Halliburton interviews and rattles off some of the things they said and did. Mr. Denny, who has thick gray eyebrows, keeps pushing them together until she can't see the space between them anymore.

"You sure they weren't joking?" he asks hopefully. "A bunch of men like that—maybe they were just goofing around?"

"But if you don't mind me asking, how is that funny? For me, it was actually kind of frightening."

Mr. Denny nods. "You're right, you're right. A lady like yourself should be able to walk down the street without being treated that way." He glances at his tie, a shapeless red knit one that has a spot of something brown on it. He scratches at the spot with his fingernail. "I'm not going to lie to you, miss. Things have been complicated around here since the boom started. A lot of these roughnecks, they're rough around the edges. That's probably how they got their name. They come from all over, from different cultures, different kinds of families. They're not like us Avery boys who know it's bad manners to talk to a woman like that."

This is the angle that Richard eventually landed on for the article—the boom as an economic phenomenon that created a town filled with insiders and outsiders. It was an idea she understood well—the people who truly belonged to a community versus everyone else. But something Mr. Denny just said momentarily distracts her.

"Is it really bad manners, though? Or even a cultural misunderstanding? Or is it just harassment? Misogyny, even?"

He nods again. "I think the boom introduced us to a lot of issues that we've never had to deal with before. I mean, even some of these words . . . People didn't use to go around just saying things like *misogyny*, you know?" He catches himself chuckling and seems to think better of it. "Anyway, as you're probably aware, I started this job back in 2010, a couple months after the incident . . ."

The town council appointed Mr. Denny to replace a longtime manager who retired. Beyond this, Elinor isn't sure what the euphemism refers to. "I'm sorry. Which incident?"

"You know, the Lowell case."

She doesn't know, but it doesn't feel right to say so. She plays along as if she understands what he's talking about, a bad habit she learned from her mother. Elinor often watched Nami pleasantly nod her way through a conversation, only to ask what the teacher meant by this or what the neighbor meant by that once they were alone. Elinor's older sister didn't appreciate having to play the role of interpreter. Often, Maren groaned or rolled her eyes, making no effort to hide how inconvenienced she felt by such questions. But Elinor always did her best to explain if she could. On some level, she knew why their mother acted like this. Nami didn't want anyone to think she was dumb. People often assumed that she was, something Elinor could sense by the way they spoke to her—slowly, loudly, carefully—using simple words that even she, a small child, could understand.

"Remind me..." she trails off, her head swimming with details from all the articles she read before arriving in Avery. She's certain she saw the name "Lowell" somewhere in the file. The first name started with an *L* too. Lana. Lisa. Or maybe it was Leah. "Are you talking about Leah Lowell?"

"Her name was Leanne," he corrects. "Leanne Lowell. I think that case still causes a lot of grief for people around here. I'd be willing to bet that more than half this town—the original residents, I mean, not the transients—more than half of them probably assume a roughneck had something to do with her going missing because things like that never happened before they came. Mrs. Hildebrandt—you met her outside—she was working here back then and she said people kept calling day and night, demanding searches of every man camp in the area. And then of course that case took on ... well, I guess you could say it took on some unfortunate racial overtones. But it really wasn't as bad as the papers made it out to be. It was just a handful of closed-minded folks pointing their fingers at certain kinds of roughnecks, giving them a hard time...." Mr. Denny trails off, watching Elinor scribble notes on her pad.

"My predecessor was stuck between a rock and a hard place, trying to make this a business-friendly environment for the newcomers while keeping the old-timers happy. It's no wonder he decided to take early retirement and go sit on a lake somewhere." He looks around his office, at the stacks surrounding him. A sound that resembles a sigh escapes from his mouth. "Some people may not like all these roughnecks coming to town, but it's complicated. Everybody's livelihoods are tied up with the oil companies now. And remember—ten years ago, we were a dying community. Whenever the high school graduated a new crop of seniors, those kids would head for the hills. They'd end up in Fargo or the Twin Cities or the army, even. None of our young people wanted to stay here until the boom." He pauses. "Well, look who I'm talking to. Mr. Hall said you did the same thing."

It startles her to realize that he knows this detail about her life, that Richard would even bother mentioning it to him. But it happened exactly as he described. Three weeks after Elinor received her high school diploma, she packed her bags and boarded a bus to New York, too young to know any better, too excited to be afraid.

9

Her phone rings while she's trying to open the door to her hotel room. Elinor takes one look at the name flashing across the screen and lets it go to voice mail. Ever since she told her sister that she was coming back to North Dakota for an assignment—a mistake, in retrospect, although it was nice to have good news for a change—Maren has been calling and texting daily, insisting that Elinor visit the farm and spend some time with her family. By now, she's familiar with all of Maren's arguments. *It's been so long since you've been home. You need to get to know my boys. Tom keeps asking when you'll come.* But Elinor and her older sister aren't close. Their interactions consist of cards on Christmas and birthdays—usually belated—and the occasional attempt at a call. If they knew each other better, Maren would realize that she's using the worst possible arguments to persuade her. Elinor returned for an article, not for a homecoming. She feels nervous and awkward around children. And she dislikes her brother-in-law, Tom.

As she enters the room, she notices that it's been tidied up in her absence. The comforter she sat on earlier is no longer hanging unevenly off the bed. And the little red No Smoking sign is positioned directly next to the Styrofoam cup she's been using as an ashtray, as if housekeeping is sending her a message. She opens the window and sets her recorders and laptop on the desk, trying to motivate herself to transcribe while the conversation with Mr. Denny still feels fresh. But transcription has always been one of her least favorite activities.

If she could send her recordings to a service that sped through the work for a dollar a minute, she gladly would, but she doesn't have that kind of budget to burn. Also, Richard transcribed his own interviews and strongly encouraged his students to do the same. He thought the act of listening to something over and over again would help them become more attentive, more familiar with what was being said and how.

She plays back a clip of her interview, surprised by the quality of Mr. Denny's recorded voice. He was kind in real life, but that barely registers once he's no longer sitting in front of her, looking overworked and slightly disheveled. What she notices most is how clearly and evenly he speaks, never searching for the right word or inserting an "um" or an "ah" to buy himself a few seconds to think. He sounds like a politician, someone who's quick on his feet, even when the topics are uncomfortable. She replays the section when he said a woman should be able to walk down the street without feeling harassed, and for a moment, she's glad that he acknowledged that on the record. But the longer she thinks about it, the more irritated she feels. Why are her standards for this man so low? Why was his first instinct to explain away the incident as a joke or bad manners? And why does she sound appreciative when he finally believes her instead of angry that he initially didn't?

"Her name was Leanne," he says. "Leanne Lowell. I think that case still causes a lot of grief for people around here."

She opens Richard's research file and lights a cigarette, figuring she has ten whole days to air out the room. A keyword search for "Leanne Lowell" turns up five results in a new window—news clippings in a huge folder labeled MISCELLANEOUS that she skimmed but didn't have time to study like the others. The first article includes a color photograph of Leanne, a headshot that looks like it was taken at a portrait studio in the mall. She's the all-American kind of pretty that Elinor used to envy as a little girl. Blond, blue-eyed, with a wide, lip-glossed smile that seems like her default expression. It's not hard to understand why her disappearance was such big news in the area. If a woman who looked like this wasn't safe, then who was? Elinor glances at her recorder, aware that she has to start transcribing soon. She has a tendency to let this kind of work pile up and get away from her. She takes another drag and decides to read on until the end of her cigarette.

Avery police looking for missing woman
October 20, 2010

The Avery Police Department is asking for the public's assistance in finding 27-year-old Leanne Jean Lowell.

She was last seen jogging eastbound on Rural Route 1 on October 18 at approximately 8:00 a.m. Lowell has blond hair, is 5 foot 3, and weighs 110 pounds. She was wearing a light blue jacket, black running tights, and a red baseball cap. Anyone with information is asked to call the Police Department at 701-507-5353.

Broken cell phone only clue to
woman's disappearance
October 27, 2010

AVERY, ND (AP)—Police and residents are conducting searches throughout Avery, North Dakota, for a local woman reported missing one week ago.

Leanne Lowell, 27, left her home on Monday morning to train for an upcoming marathon, but never returned. Avery Chief of Police Stan Hauser told KVQR News that a canine unit had recovered her iPhone near her regular running route.

Police believe Lowell may have been abducted or possibly hit by a vehicle, Hauser said. The police chief added there was no evidence that her phone had been left behind after an animal attack, a scenario introduced by local fish and wildlife officials.

Family of missing woman offers reward as
search continues
November 5, 2010

Authorities expanded their search on Friday for 27-year-old Avery resident Leanne Lowell, who went missing in mid-October. The enlarged search area now includes the northwest corner of the North Fork Reservation, where multiple witnesses reported seeing Lowell on the date of her disappearance.

No solid evidence has emerged to indicate that Lowell was kidnapped, authorities said. But FBI agents were called in to assist local law enforcement in the case, and an agency spokeswoman said the possibility of abduction was still under investigation.

Lowell, the manager of the Depot Bar in Avery, left her home for a 15-mile training run at approximately 8:00 a.m. on October 18. Her husband, Shane Foster, reported her missing after she failed to return. On Thursday, Foster announced a $50,000 reward to the person or persons who could provide information leading to her successful recovery.

Human remains discovered on North Fork
Reservation
March 19, 2011

A WinCo Electric Company crew discovered human skeletal remains on Friday afternoon, approximately four miles west of Kittery, authorities said.

Utility workers burying cable on Route 83 discovered the body at about 3:45 p.m. The remains will be transported to Bismarck where forensic analysis will be conducted by the State Medical Examiner's Office.

Flowers and letters have begun to appear along the roadside, fueled by speculation that the remains belong to missing local woman Leanne Lowell, who was last seen on the reservation in October.

Residents in the area will likely experience traffic delays and notice a large police presence until Tuesday. Traffic on Route 83, between Green Trail Road and Elon Road, will be closed throughout the weekend.

Remains found on reservation do not belong to missing runner
April 14, 2011

BISMARCK, ND (AP)—The State Medical Examiner's Office released the results of autopsy and DNA tests conducted on human remains found on the North Fork Reservation last month. The results confirmed that the remains do not belong to missing Avery woman, Leanne Lowell.

Lowell, a 27-year old student and bar manager from Avery, was last seen training for a marathon on the reservation in October of last year. State Police are still investigating her disappearance as a possible abduction. Members of Lowell's immediate family were not available for comment.

According to the medical examiner's report, the unidentified female was approximately 30 years old and died of asphyxiation. Efforts are underway to identify her in cooperation with local authorities.

10

Richard calls at a quarter past ten. Late for him, she thinks, especially with the time difference in New York. He likes to write first thing in the morning. Usually, this means he's in bed by nine.

"You're prepping for Harry Bergum and Amy Mueller tomorrow?" he asks.

It doesn't sound like a question so much as a statement. She can't help but hear other messages embedded in it. A reminder that he's out on a limb for her. A warning not to embarrass him.

"I've been at it for hours," she says, unwilling to admit what she's actually been doing since she returned to her room.

"So . . . you want to ask me anything?"

Elinor has no intention of using his materials again like she did with Mr. Denny. If she's ever going to feel a sense of ownership over this article, she has to diverge from Richard's script and figure out her own. Still, she tries to come up with a question, some small token of the respect or gratitude he seems to be fishing for.

"I didn't understand what you meant here," she says, pulling up a page of his scanned notes on her laptop. "When Mrs. Mueller was talking about her husband, you wrote 'something going on with them' in the margin. Do you know why you thought that?"

Richard is silent for a moment. Then he says to her sharply, "You're not even going to ask me how I am?"

She forgot about his hip replacement. She doesn't remember when the surgery was scheduled, whether it happened already or he's about to go in. How strange this is, she thinks. A whole year without any contact at all, and now he's calling her late at night, irritated that she hasn't asked about him.

"Oh, I'm sorry. How are—"

"Jesus. Never mind."

His voice is hoarse, as if he's coming down with a cold. And he's drinking. She can tell by the sound of ice cubes clinking in a glass, the way he occasionally moves his mouth away from the phone to swallow. She wishes she were drinking with him. It was one of the few hobbies they had in common. In Richard's apartment, a Gramercy Park duplex decorated by his ex-wife, he had a beautiful old bar cart. On the first shelf, there was a double-walled ice bucket and an assortment of tongs and matching spoons with mother-of-pearl handles. Next to them were a half-dozen rocks glasses made of lead crystal, their weight so perfect in her hand. Richard kept a few bottles of good bourbon, vodka, and gin on the bottom shelf for guests. But what he liked most was whiskey. He taught her to like it too, everything from the cheap handle of Jameson to the special-occasion bottles of Yamazaki and Hibiki that his friends sent as gifts. While no one would ever accuse Richard of being miserly, the Japanese whiskeys were apparently so expensive, he kept tabs on their fill levels, discreetly marking their backsides with wax pencil in case one of the many people who entered his home—his assistant, his cleaning woman, the maintenance man, his interns—started to help themselves. It wasn't until after their breakup that Elinor realized she was also one of the people whose consumption he probably wanted to monitor.

She takes a sip of her warm ginger ale, which she's been nursing for hours while sitting at her desk. The taste of it is metallic and syrupy against her tongue.

"So what did I write in my notes again?" he asks.

The television in the next room turns on, followed by two loud thumps in quick succession, like boots being taken off and dropped on the floor. One of her many neighbors has returned. At first, she thought she only had one—the man who kept coughing and singing in the shower. But over the course of the evening, she's heard several others coming and going. How they get any rest over there, she doesn't know. They're constantly slamming doors and listening to the TV at full volume, with no consideration for each other, much less her. She gets up from her desk and moves toward the window to avoid the evening news broadcasting through the walls.

"You said there was something about the Muellers—"

"Oh, right." He takes another drink. "The wife—she just seemed a little off to me. I got the sense it wasn't exactly your typical marriage."

Amy Mueller's husband, Bill, sold the mineral rights to their farm to help pay for his medical bills. Shortly after he passed away, a Dallas-based company named EnerGia notified her that they intended to start drilling two new wells on her property. Mrs. Mueller sued EnerGia to invalidate the agreement, but the court ruled against her on the grounds that Mr. Mueller had never added her name to one of the documents of incorporation for the farm. Forty-plus years they'd worked that land together, and she apparently had no legal right to be consulted. None of this strikes Elinor as particularly unusual though. Her mother owned nothing during all the years she was married to her father. She took nothing when she left.

"What do you mean by 'not your typical marriage'?"

"I don't know. It was just a feeling I got from our phone conversation. You'll have to figure it out for yourself when you meet her."

Richard sounds tired and short-tempered. She thought he'd called to check in on her before the interviews he'd scheduled, but he doesn't seem interested in talking about them at all. She fishes around in her pack and pulls out a cigarette. Her last, unfortunately. She leans out the open window to light it, feeling the warm, humid night against her skin. Beats of music from nearby bars compete against each other. She hears heavy, relentless thumps of bass and imagines sweaty bodies on dimly lit dance floors, their fists pumping in the air.

"You're still smoking, I see. Or should I say 'hear'?"

She moves her mouth away from the phone as she exhales. "I am."

"You're going to regret that one day."

She takes one last drag and drops the cigarette into the cup on the ledge. The water inside is now a filthy, sooty gray. "I know."

"Just wait. When you're sixty and breathing through a tube in your neck, you'll remember I told you so."

He's in one of his moods again. She almost forgot what they were like. Anything related to aging always sent Richard on a rapid downward spiral. Elinor didn't understand why until she looked at his photo albums and clip books. Flipping through the pages, she realized that he'd bloomed late, both physically and professionally. It wasn't until his early forties that his angular face began to look interesting instead of severe. And while men his age started losing their hair, Richard's turned gray and lustrous. At work, he'd been a reliable but seemingly underappreciated business reporter for the *New York Times*, laboring away in relative obscurity for over fifteen years. But then the *Exxon Valdez* struck the shore of Prince William Sound while he was vacationing in Alaska, and he had the good fortune of being one of the first journalists to arrive on the scene. His coverage of the oil spill launched his career as a features writer, which led to a book contract and the lecture circuit, and then three more books and an endowed faculty position. It also led to the end of his marriage and a succession of attractive girlfriends, none of whom appeared in his albums for long. Whenever Elinor studied his photos, she noticed how Richard looked so much happier and more confident as he aged. She assumes he wants to cling to this life, which he's only had twenty-odd years of, compared to forty years of the life he had before he became this version of himself. If this is one of the effects of his blooming late, she wonders what it means that she bloomed so early.

"Hello?" he says, too loudly. "Are you even listening?"

"I am."

"Did you hear me ask how your interview went today?"

"It was fine."

"And you used my questions?"

"Some, yes."

"Some?"

She hears the pique budding in his voice. "Most . . . by the way, do you remember why you kept those articles about Leanne Lowell in your file? She was that Avery woman, the runner, who went missing a few years ago?"

He doesn't say anything for a while. Elinor shakes her empty pack of cigarettes, wishing she had just one more hidden inside.

"That's what a dump file is for," he finally says. "Things you keep in case they're useful later."

"But they never found her, right?" She's not sure why she phrased this in the form of a question, as if she doesn't know. All she's been doing for the past four hours is looking up articles about Leanne Lowell. There were no further sightings, no charges filed, no people held accountable for her disappearance, no evidence of a death. Eventually, the steady stream of news about her case dwindled down to nothing.

"I don't think she turned up anywhere, but I haven't been keeping tabs on it," he says. "Why? What did you find?"

"I was just interested."

"But *why*? What does a missing runner have to do with anything?"

She shakes her empty pack again. She regrets dropping her last cigarette in the water instead of just pinching off the cherry. There were still two or three drags left that she could use right now. She's tempted to tell Richard what she's been reading about—the standing room only public safety forums after Lowell's disappearance; the acts of vandalism at man camps telling oil workers to "go back to where you came from"; the random beatings of Black and brown men, two of whom required long-term hospitalization. Technically, the scape-goating fits into Richard's theory that the boom turned Avery into a community of insiders and outsiders, but something about Leanne Lowell feels like her own private discovery. She doesn't want to be told that she isn't important or have to defend her right to include her in the story, not when she hasn't even decided to yet.

"I was looking through your file for tomorrow and started reading things in the Miscellaneous folder," she says. "That's all."

"What's on the schedule besides Mueller and Bergum?"

"Nothing, really. I just have a check-in with Lydia."

In the background, she hears him set down his drink too hard. The crystal knocks against the surface of the table; the ice cubes in his glass rattle and clink.

"You're talking to Lydia?"

"Yes?" Her voice lifts cautiously, uncertain why his sounds so sharp all of a sudden.

"Why are you talking to my editor?"

She thinks the answer is obvious. She took over the article that Richard was writing. Now Lydia is her editor too. "Her assistant's been emailing me. She said Lydia wanted to set up a call." She pauses. "Is something wrong?"

"No. I just thought—well, I thought you'd both have the courtesy to loop me in since I made the original connection, but I'm in meetings all day tomorrow, so I wouldn't be able to join you anyway."

During the year they were together, Richard was a distinguished professor at the university. He was also a regular contributor to the *Standard* and researching a book on the housing market collapse of 2008. She never knew him to be in meetings all day. She can't imagine his schedule is busier than it used to be when he was writing his book. She assumes he's lying because his feelings are hurt and her impulse is to apologize, to invite him to join them, to offer to reschedule the call. But she's trying to make this story her own now. It will never fully be hers until he backs away from it.

"It's late where you are," she says, looking out the window. "Aren't you tired?"

She waits for him to say something, not certain if he'll let the call with Lydia go, or if this is one of those things he'll clamp onto like a dog, unable to shake it loose from his jaw. She imagines him on the other end of the line, boiling at her unintended slight. The silence continues, growing louder and more awkward with each second. In the parking lot below, two people are smoking in their car. She watches the tips of their cigarettes glow amber and black, amber and black.

"Was I nice to you?" he asks.

"What do you mean?"

"I was nice to you when we were together, right? I never made you do anything that you didn't want to do?"

At first, she assumes that she's not hearing him correctly. It's not like Richard to reflect on the past, which he argues is a useless activity. What's passed is past, he always says.

"Why are you asking?"

"I've been thinking about us lately," he says, pausing to swallow. "I don't know why. I'm just feeling nostalgic, I guess."

11

The bar down the street from her hotel is called Swift's. The signs in the window advertise two-dollar Miller High Lifes and shots of Cuervo, Fireball, and Jägermeister. On the sidewalk, directly below the window, there's an elaborately detailed mural of a football player carrying a ball, with huge bolts of lightning behind his feet as a substitute for the *S*'s in *Swift's*. It's not her kind of bar, she can already tell, but it's close to the Thrifty—just a few doors down the block—and there's a cigarette machine in the corner that she can see through the window. She paces back and forth over the mural, fighting two competing urges—to return to her noisy room so she can finish transcribing, or to buy some cigarettes and have a quick drink. Cars slowly pass through the intersection, their headlights filling her eyes with fluttering dots to match the butterflies in her stomach. She's never felt nervous about walking into a bar by herself. This seems like reason enough to go in.

The first thing she notices about Swift's is that it smells like too many things. Cleaning chemicals, body odor, fryer grease, popcorn, and stale beer. Three steps over the threshold, and Elinor considers turning around and leaving—the smell is that bad. But a handful of people have already noticed her. It would be awkward to leave so soon after she arrived. It's also not busy, which she likes. There are a couple of young guys playing pool in the back, and a couple of older ones watching TV. She buys a pack of cigarettes and slides into a seat at the bar.

The bartender asks what she's drinking. Elinor looks up and tries not to stare, but she can't help herself. He's a huge man in every way. Tall, fat, broad shouldered, beer-bellied. His mustache and beard remind her of a brown bear's fur, so thick and full, with no hint of the pale pink skin underneath. She points at what the old man sitting on her right is having.

"Same as him," she says, ordering a boilermaker. She intended to have only one drink here. Technically, a beer and a shot are two.

The old man seems amused by her order. He gives her a lopsided, red-faced grin that she refuses to return.

"Eight bucks." The bartender slides her drinks toward her from several feet away. "Unless you want to start a tab."

She downs the shot in a single gulp, trying not to grimace at the taste of the cheap well whiskey, which reminds her of lighter fluid. Her expression only seems to amuse her neighbor more. He has a laugh that sounds like a horn on a bike, goose-like and loud, designed to solicit people's attention. She wraps her fingers around her beer, unwilling to give him the satisfaction.

"Anything else?" The bartender seems impatient, as if it's nearing last call, which it's not.

Her stomach rumbles. She didn't bother picking up anything for dinner. Hungry now, she asks for some popcorn.

"Huh?" he says loudly, following up with an even louder, "What's that?"

"Popcorn," she repeats, looking around. "Don't you have a machine in here?"

The man with the boilermaker snorts. "She's saying this place stinks, Mitch! *Ha!*"

"We haven't served popcorn in years." The bartender frowns as he disappears into the back room.

Her neighbor continues laughing. She turns and glares at him, annoyed that the bartender is annoyed with her for something she didn't actually say. *Why would you tell him that?* she wants to ask, but she knows better than to engage with a drunk.

"You don't have to worry about Mitch," the man says. "He's big, so everyone always thinks he's pissed about something, but he's not. I'm Bud, by the way. Like the beer." He grabs his fleshy stomach and gives it a jiggle. "But not as light." He flashes her another grin, a bigger one this time, revealing teeth streaked brown like an old coffee filter.

Mitch returns from the back room with a bag under his arm and a fake bamboo bowl that he places in front of Elinor. He tears open the bag and fills the bowl to the rim with peanuts in the shell.

Bud looks on. "Hey. What about me?"

"What about you?"

"Well, how come she gets peanuts and I don't?"

"That should be obvious. Look at her and look at you." Mitch stows the bag under the bar. "Besides, the last thing I need in here are girls getting shit-faced on empty stomachs."

Bud scowls. "Aw, fuck you, Mitch. Who wants your old sack of nuts anyway?" He gets up from his seat, announcing that he has to take a piss.

Elinor cracks a peanut shell between her thumb and forefinger. It's empty, as if the peanut inside shriveled up and disappeared. Every other one is the same. She doesn't have a second bowl for the shells, so she starts a small pile next to her beer and waits for the bartender to come over now that she's alone. It's a relief when he doesn't. She didn't like the way he referred to her as a "girl" and assumed she couldn't hold her liquor. It's just one boilermaker, after all. She eats a couple of dusty-tasting peanuts while scanning the photos displayed behind the bar, action shots of men playing football. She looks up at the TV, expecting to see more of the same, but it's summer and not the right season for it. Instead, there's a rerun of a fishing tournament on, the 2012 Bassmaster Nationals, taped earlier that month according to the text floating on the screen. She didn't know that such a competition existed, but here it is, right in front of her. Three men in a boat, a leaderboard scrolling across the bottom, slow-motion replays of someone reeling in a giant bigmouth bass. The other man sitting at the bar, the quiet one on her left, has his eyes glued to the TV, riveted.

She watches along with him as she sips her beer. It's warm already, almost undrinkable. She wants another whiskey, but it doesn't seem right to order one when she still has a full beer in her hand. Richard used to criticize her when she drank too much, too quickly. She thinks about his question again—*Was I nice to you?*—not certain what he meant by "nice." When was he ever nice?

A month after they started seeing each other, he invited her to a gala dinner at the New York Public Library, their first big outing as a couple. She thought she looked good that night, but Richard didn't care for the dress she was wearing, a strapless black evening gown that she'd found in the back of her closet, the only one she owned that was suitable for such a formal occasion. He said the fabric looked cheap, like something she'd picked up in Chinatown. And her hair and makeup—they were apparently wrong as well. Her hair was too flat, the makeup too pale. He griped about her appearance during the entire drive, muttering that he'd told people he was seeing a former model and who would believe him now? The two of them were sitting in the back of a cab, and she remembers the way the driver, an elderly Sikh man, kept looking at her in his rearview mirror. He wanted to know if she was alright.

In retrospect, she should have asked him to pull over and just gotten out of the car, but she was struck by an uncomfortable memory. Her father used to tell her mother to change clothes all the time. Ed insisted on long sleeves over short, skirts instead of pants, hemlines below the knee, florals over stripes. Fashion trends and seasons were meaningless to him. He wanted Nami to look feminine and pretty like the other wives on the base, but buttoned up to avoid soliciting the attention of their husbands. Sometimes he'd even lay out the clothes he thought she should wear. If Nami tried to argue, he'd tell her he only had her best interests in mind. He didn't want her to stand out for wearing the wrong thing; he didn't want her to be embarrassed.

In the back of the cab, Elinor fumed as she avoided the driver's watchful eyes. She never imagined herself with someone who felt entitled to comment on her appearance. But before this thought had a chance to fully sink in, they arrived. Suddenly she and Richard were ascending the marble stairs on Fifth Avenue and walking through the library's entrance, flanked by its huge stone lions. And then they were climbing even more stairs and entering the main reading room, surrounded by rose-colored frescoes and old wooden tables and more brass and gold leaf than she'd ever seen in one place. As soon as they joined the party, Richard became a different person. How charming he was. How much larger than life. Men in tuxedos and their bejeweled and perfumed wives crossed the room to say hello to him and introduce themselves to her. She met editors and writers, politicians and philanthropists—people who either made the news or wrote it. She watched as Richard asked about their children, their recent work, their elderly parents. She marveled at how he remembered their birthdays and anniversaries, the colleges that their sons and daughters attended. His public persona exuded such warmth and generosity, so much so that she allowed herself to forget the incident in the car and the pitying looks of the driver. She was grateful just to be in Richard's orbit.

Nice, she thinks, replaying the word over and over again, wondering why he suddenly cares, what he meant when he said he was feeling nostalgic. It couldn't be nostalgia for the two of them as a couple, could it?

Bud emerges from the bathroom, wiping his hands on his jeans. "Time to hit the road," he says to no one in particular. When this fails to elicit a response, he raises his middle fingers at Mitch, shooting them off like guns, complete with sound effects. "*Pew-pew.*" Then he offers a wobbly salute goodbye that barely earns a lift of Mitch's brow.

The man on Elinor's left, the one who's been watching the fishing tournament, chuckles after Bud leaves, banging the door shut behind him. "Jesus Christ. I thought he'd never go home. Another boilermaker over here, Mitch."

Elinor would like another too, but it's hard to justify it, not unless she can get something in exchange for her time. She looks at the man, who's wearing a shirt with a Blackwell Trucking logo. "You know that guy?" she asks quietly.

"We're not friends, if that's what you mean. He's just always hanging around."

"He's kind of a character, isn't he?"

"He's kind of an asshole, that's what he is. I just try to play dead until he leaves." He turns and blinks at her dopily, his eyes baggy from a lack of sleep. "You did a pretty good job of playing dead yourself."

Elinor has had plenty of practice. The irony of her bar crawling days was that she went out seeking attention, collecting it like shiny gold coins, but she didn't care for the conversations that came with it. Now, when men try to approach her, she usually responds with indifference or pretends that she can't hear. If that doesn't work, she'll try feigning drunkenness or claiming that she doesn't speak English, a tactic she's not particularly proud of, but she's learned that "no, thank you" and "not interested" sometimes aren't enough. The man sitting next to her, however, clearly isn't the persistent or aggressive type. He's already staring at the television again.

"I'm writing an article about Avery for a magazine. Would you mind answering some questions for me if I bought your next round?"

"What kind of questions?"

"Just general ones—what it's like to live and work in the oil patch, how the boom has affected you, things like that."

He gives her a careful once-over and then shrugs. "Alright, but you don't have to buy me anything as long as you don't make me drink alone." He waves Mitch over again, ordering a second boilermaker for Elinor. She realizes he was paying a little attention to her after all, but chose to leave her be, which she appreciates.

"So how long have you lived in Avery?" Elinor asks.

"About six months."

She nods, encouraging him to continue.

"Before that, I lived in Oregon for fifty-two years. That's basically my whole life, except the four I spent in the army."

The man, whose name is Steve, doesn't look like he's fifty-six years old. He looks much older, like someone who should be nearing retirement, fishing for bass like the people on TV.

"And what do you do for work around here?"

"I haul sand. Bottoms up."

He raises his glass of whiskey at her and she raises hers at him. They drink and bang their empties on the bar at the same time, the sound loud and hollow and oddly satisfying. It occurs to her that she should stop getting boilermakers because now she's stuck with another pint of beer in addition to the one she's barely made a dent in. She takes a good long drink of the watery pilsner, trying to hurry the end of the glass along.

12

Steve tells her a story that every other man in the Bakken probably knows. In 2008, he lost his job as a warehouse supervisor. That was the first domino to fall. Then the others went down in rapid succession. He got behind on his car payments and credit cards. His adjustable-rate mortgage, which seemed like such a good deal at 1.75 percent, hit the five-year mark and ballooned to 8 percent. He cashed out his IRA, which left him with a tax bill he couldn't repay. Then he borrowed money from relatives and emptied out his daughter's college tuition account. When there was no one left to borrow from and the only people who ever called were creditors, Steve decided he had to do something more drastic than send out job applications that never resulted in a single interview. With four hundred dollars in his pocket, he drove to North Dakota, where he found work in less than a week. Now he makes over $100,000 a year hauling for Blackwell, more than he and his wife used to make combined back in Oregon. The only downside is that he hasn't been able to visit his family, not once since he left.

"I'm the oldest guy on the crew, but the lowest guy on the totem pole," he explains, finishing off his second beer. "Since I was the last one hired, I have to take what my boss gives me. Holidays, third shifts, doubles, it doesn't matter. And I can't complain either because there's at least a hundred guys arriving in town every day who'd jump at a job like this, you know—with housing and time and a half coming out your ears. They're young guys too. They could probably drive all night on a single Red Bull."

"Have you ever considered moving your family here?"

"Here?" He snorts. "What's *here*? I couldn't afford to rent an apartment in Avery, much less buy one of those new tract houses they're slapping together and charging a fortune for. Plus, the camp that Blackwell's got me in doesn't allow women or children, not that I'd ever let my family live in a situation like that, even if they did. So my options are renting an RV and letting my wife and daughter sit in a tin can while I go to work, or just calling home every night."

As far as housing goes, Steve actually ranks among the fortunate. His employer-provided room is at one of the better-run man camps just outside Avery. Elinor has a tour scheduled at a sister facility run by the same company later this week. Unlike many newcomers, Steve isn't living out of his car or trailer in a parking lot somewhere, dodging cops and tow trucks now that there's a town-wide ban on overnight street parking. She's beginning to understand why the housing shortage makes it hard to move to Avery with a wife or a girlfriend, much less kids. She scrawls a possibility in her notebook. *Housing insecurity → gender imbalance?*

"You want to see a picture of my family?" Steve asks. He doesn't wait for a response before opening his wallet to a photo of him, flanked by his wife and daughter at Mount Rushmore.

Elinor leans in for a better look. Somewhere, she knows there's a picture of her family just like this, posing under the four presidents like every other tourist. Her father refused to put it in an album or frame because of the thumb—a big orange blotch on the upper left corner, partially obscuring George Washington's head. Ed lamented it for years, frustrated that the stranger he'd entrusted his camera to had been so careless. Still, it was the rare family photo that captured all of them smiling and looking in the same direction, seemingly happy to be together.

That was the summer they hitched up the trailer and went to South

Dakota, touring the Badlands and the Black Hills for the first time. Fresh from a promotion and pay bump to technical sergeant, Ed sprang for extras that he typically wouldn't. Walking tours through underground caverns glittering with fool's gold. Paddleboat rides in Custer State Park. Tickets to Reptile Gardens, where his favorite trick was hissing in Nami's ear while she examined the snakes and lizards. No matter how many times he snuck up on her, Nami would jump and chase him around the reptile cages, a sight that made Elinor and her sister laugh until they cried. It was a relief to see their parents enjoying each other's company for a change.

At home, Ed often worried out loud about Nami's inability to make friends with the other wives on the base. He had no patience for her protests about the way they treated her, like an afterthought at best, an alien at worst. Ed was an engineer by training, someone who believed that every problem could be fixed. If Nami complained that no one talked to her at a holiday party, he told her to keep working on her English. If she mentioned that the Korean food she brought to a potluck went untouched, he suggested learning more "American" recipes instead. Fitting in required effort, he insisted, as if the fault for Nami's isolation was solely her own. Elinor wasn't sure what she disliked more: the way her parents bickered and argued about the people around them, or the long hours and occasional days after an argument when they barely spoke at all. It was obvious that living in Marlow made them both unhappy—so much so that she often begged her father to hitch up the trailer again and take them somewhere else.

"So . . . are you alright?" Steve asks.

She sets his wallet on the bar, embarrassed that she picked it up in the first place. "Sorry. I was just thinking about all the road trips we used to take when I was a kid."

"You been to Mount Rushmore?"

She nods.

"Where else did you go?"

She's tempted to ask where didn't they go? Ed's parents believed in taking one good family vacation a year, no matter how lean the times.

He made it a priority to carry on the tradition, playing the role of tour guide for his own family every summer. Elinor rattles off the places that first come to mind—Teddy Roosevelt National Park, Yellowstone, Glacier National Park, the Grand Tetons, Devils Tower, Pikes Peak. Steve adds a "yup" after all the sights he's also visited, which is most of them.

"You know, this is the longest my wife and I have ever been apart since we got married. Thirty-eight years we've been together—can you believe that?" He wipes his nose with the back of his hand. "It's hard going from that to being alone all the time, to being lonely." He snaps his wallet shut. "Do me a favor, will you? Don't write that I was getting all sentimental or anything that makes me sound stupid, okay?"

"I wouldn't," she says, although she's touched by the sight of someone who misses his family so much. She needed to meet a man like Steve, a good one.

Earlier that evening, before Richard called, she was thinking about husbands, the kind she often saw on the news. When a woman went missing, when a woman turned up dead, the husband was almost always to blame. She wants to know how the police decided that Leanne Lowell's husband had nothing to do with her disappearance. She wants to know why he never looked sufficiently distraught on TV. There were video clips of him online doing the things that people in his situation usually do: begging for his wife's safe return, announcing a reward for information leading to her recovery, thanking all the volunteers who helped the police search. She watched every video she could find, replaying them multiple times, and not once did Shane Foster seem upset.

When her mother ran off, there were four long days when no one knew what had happened to her. Elinor, who was twelve at the time, still remembers how terrified her father looked during this period, like he was staring into a funnel cloud, waiting for the tornado that would eventually carry their town off into the sky. "My wife is gone. My wife!" he'd shout at anyone who would listen—the police, his relatives, the random coworkers who called to check in. Ed never referred to her by name during these conversations. Even back then, Elinor noticed. Nami was just his wife, the quiet beauty he'd brought back from Korea for the purposes of taking care of his home and family. After he received her letter, telling him she no longer wanted to be married, the terror of those days settled deep into his skin, twisting his expression into a permanent state of rage. This is what bothers her about Leanne's husband. A man in his situation—he should have been wearing it on his face.

"So, how long do you think you'll stay in Avery?" she asks.

The question seems to depress him. "God, I hope not much longer." Steve pauses, scratching at a sticker from an apple or banana that someone stuck to the bar. "Actually, don't put that in there either. My boss doesn't strike me as someone who can read the back of a box of cereal, but just in case, it's probably better to say that I'll stay as long as I've got a good job. . . . Between you and me though, I'm hoping another nine months, maybe a year at the most."

"Even though the money's good here?"

Steve shrugs. "A lot of guys who come to the Bakken, they crapped out everywhere else and this is kind of their last chance at making something of themselves. That guy who was in here before? Bud? He's a good example. I think he's got at least two or three ex-wives and a bunch of near-grown children, but if he was on fire, it doesn't sound like any of them would bother handing him a glass of water. That's how much he screwed up. It's not like that with me though. I've got a family and a home I want to get back to, so the second I have enough money to pay off our debts and put a little extra aside, I'm gone. I'd rather be middle-class in Oregon than rich in this hellhole." He glances at the clock hanging above the top shelf of the bar. It has a green football field for a face and a ball swinging back and forth instead of a pendulum. "Speaking of, I better get going. I've got a double starting in the morning."

It's just after midnight, longer than Elinor intended to be out. She still has Alan Denny's interview to transcribe, and now these notes too, but she doesn't regret the time she spent here. It feels good to finally have an interview of her own under her belt. She flips through her notes, making sure there's nothing she wants to follow up on before he leaves.

"Would you mind giving me your phone number?" She turns to a blank page. "I probably won't need to contact you again, but a fact-checker might."

Steve massages the palm of his hand before taking the pencil. The numbers he scrawls are large and arthritic. He crosses out something that looks like an eight and starts again, making a shaky three. Mitch watches them with interest, the same way he's been watching them for the past hour.

"Can I settle up over here?" Steve waves two twenties at him.

"Oh, no. Let me."

Mitch walks over and takes Steve's money even though Elinor is holding out her card. She doesn't understand why he's been so unpleasant to her all night. Bartenders are usually much friendlier toward her, male ones especially. She frowns at him, not caring if he catches her reflection in the mirror. Perhaps it's the light or the angle he's standing at, but for the first time, Elinor notices Mitch's resemblance to one of the football players on the wall. As he makes change at the register, she glances back and forth between him and the photos, all of which are of him, she realizes. The mural outside the entrance—that was him too.

Steve must notice her noticing because he points at a headshot of a clean-shaven young man in a maroon jersey. "Mitch played for Montana when he was in college. Number thirty-nine, defensive end. The great Mitch Swift. His dad dedicated this whole place to him." His phone starts to vibrate on the bar and a woman's smiling face appears on the screen. He picks up immediately. "Oh, hi, honey. I'm sorry I didn't call you earlier. You'll never guess—I've been talking to a reporter." He slides off his stool and waves goodbye.

She's not certain what to make of Mitch's expression once they're alone. He doesn't seem proud now that she knows what he used to be, like most ex–football players would. He also doesn't seem embarrassed or ashamed to be tending bar in a place that was clearly designed as a shrine to what he used to be, but no longer is. If anything, he just looks worried.

"So, you planning on coming back here again?" he asks.

"Why? Would you actually want me to?"

She meant this as a lighthearted jab—something to counteract this strange, unfriendly man's mood. But Mitch doesn't even crack a smile.

"We don't get a lot of women in here," he says. "It's a sports bar, you know."

She glances around. The guys who were playing pool when she arrived are gone now. Bud and Steve too. He's served a total of five people, including her, during the past hour and a half. "Maybe you'd have more customers if more women came around."

"Yeah, well . . ." He pauses. "I don't need that kind of trouble."

She's bewildered at first, as if he just told a joke that sailed straight over her head. But then she realizes he's serious. Thousands of itinerant men in this town and he thinks she's the one who's going to cause problems for him. She grabs her card from the bar and walks out as her cheeks begin to bloom with the heat of an unpleasant teenage memory. Her father used to call her trouble. Just like your mother, he said. Trouble, whore, slut, bitch.

13

In the morning, there's a voice mail waiting for her. Elinor assumes it's from her sister again, but when she plays it back, all she hears is static—a long, crackling stretch that makes her think the entire message might be nothing more than noise.

"Do you hear that annoying buzz?" An unfamiliar woman's voice cuts in. "Sorry. I'm not sure if you're getting it on your end. Anyway, Alumni Affairs gave me your number, so I thought I'd try calling too, in case you're using a different email address these days. Please get back to me when you can? I'd really appreciate it. Cheers."

It's the "cheers" that helps Elinor identify the caller, more so than her voice or the mention of an alumni office. Kathryn Tasso always signed off her emails and said goodbye this way in grad school, an odd affectation given that she wasn't English and she didn't drink. Elinor turns on the light above her bed and scrolls through her recent calls to see when the message arrived. 5:50 a.m. Even if Kathryn had assumed they were both on East Coast time, she called at 6:50—too early to contact anyone except a family member or very close friend.

Elinor covers her face with a pillow, trying to block out the irritating memory of "if you think about it," a phrase Kathryn often said in class before critiquing someone's work in progress.

If you think about it, that angle's already been done before.

If you think about it, you're framing this from management's perspective, not the union's.

If you think about it, the nurse was the only person who actually made that piece interesting.

It wasn't that Elinor minded her classmates' feedback. She understood that that was what they were supposed to do—help each other see and write their stories better. But she still found it grating, the way Kathryn always commented on her drafts like an authority figure rather than just another student. There was also something about her tone, a cross between astonishment and disappointment, as if she'd been expecting or even hoping that Elinor's work would be terrible.

Being underestimated wasn't a new experience for her. Teachers and professors were often surprised to discover that she wrote well. They made no effort to hide it either, as if they'd already sized her up and decided what she could and couldn't do. The first time Mr. Bender finished reading one of her essays in high school, he set the pages down, looking utterly perplexed. Then he called her sentences "beautiful," a compliment that eventually came to mean more to her than being regarded as beautiful. One required effort and intellect. The other was just an accident of genetics. While she was grateful that her parents' genes had combined in their particular way, allowing her to make a living for all those years, by the time she quit modeling, she was desperate to be good at doing something, rather than simply being something.

Elinor tosses her pillow on the floor. Even if she wanted to go back to sleep, she couldn't. *If you think about it* continues to ring in her ears. It was such a slyly worded insult, suggesting that the writer hadn't *already* thought about what they were doing, that they were somehow incapable of thought. Although Kathryn used this preamble on everyone, Elinor was especially sensitive to it. Her late-in-life college degree, combined with her unfamiliarity with all the books and theories and thinkers that her classmates discussed so freely, formed a delicate Achilles' heel, one that she masked with introversion and weed. More than once, Richard reported overhearing some of her classmates describe her as "cold" or "standoffish," which seemed to amuse him to no end.

Before getting out of bed, she deletes the voice mail and blocks Kathryn's number with a firm press of the button. It feels satisfying at first, to have an assignment that her former classmate is so eager to talk about. But as the morning goes on, she grows more and more agitated at the thought of Kathryn's relentless careerism, her pushy white sense of privilege. Elinor would be too embarrassed to reach out to someone who clearly didn't want to hear from her, who hadn't even attempted to return her previous messages. But Kathryn, being Kathryn, always felt free to knock on every door, certain that the person standing on the other side would be willing to let her in.

By the time Elinor arrives at the Bluebird Diner for her first meeting of the day, she's still irritated about the call and sleep deprived because of her next-door neighbors, who thunked around at all hours of the night. Her mood worsens when she sees her nine o'clock standing in the diner's parking lot with a toothpick hanging out the side of his mouth like a cigarette. He makes no effort to hide the fact that he's scanning her from head to toe, his expression both appreciative and delighted.

"You must be the student that Mr. Hall sent in his place." He shakes her hand, holding it in both of his. "He told me you were pretty, but, my God, aren't you stunning?"

Elinor introduces herself and smiles through a locked jaw, wondering what else he and Richard talked about and why a stranger would repeat something like this. She reminds herself that Harry is in his sixties, possibly even his early seventies. He belongs to a generation of men who still think it's charming to comment on a woman's appearance. She's never sure what to do about people like him, people who seem reasonably well-meaning but whose understanding of the rules is so different from her own.

"I'm his former student," she says, emphasizing the word *former*. "Thanks for meeting me, Mr. Bergum."

"Oh, please. Call me Harry."

According to her file, Harald Olaf Bergum III has a long list of nicknames. In addition to Harry, he's known as the king of Avery, the unofficial mayor, the luckiest son of a bitch alive, and the richest man in town. In a state that's minting millionaires faster than any other in the country, this isn't particularly extraordinary, except that Bergum was the first local to make truly big money in oil—$28 million and counting last year, according to the *Wall Street Journal*. Elinor assumed he'd show up looking the part, with nicely tailored clothes and a foreign sports car, maybe even a pert young assistant in tow. But her image of showy new wealth was all wrong. Harry is dressed in a brown plaid button-up shirt, faded jeans, and old work boots with mismatched laces. He looks like a down-on-his-luck farmer leaning up against his rusty Ford F-350, not a multimillionaire, and certainly not the man responsible for what "modern-day Avery" is, another name that people apparently call him, though not in a complimentary way.

The Bluebird Diner is almost full, but the hostess says she's been keeping Harry's usual table open for him. As soon as he and Elinor sit down, food they didn't order begins to arrive. Mugs of coffee and a platter of pancakes, a side order of bacon, glasses of fruit juice—orange and apple, a small bowl of butter pats wrapped in shiny gold foil. After the tabletop has all but disappeared underneath the food and Elinor's recording equipment, the waitress slides an egg white omelet, a stack of dry toast, and a pale side of fruit salad in front of Harry. From her apron pocket, she hands him a bottle of Tabasco sauce.

"I hope you don't mind, but I took the liberty of calling ahead and ordering for us." He dots his omelet with drops of Tabasco, making a shape that looks like the letter *H*. "The menu's like an encyclopedia here. It takes forever to go through it, so it's just easier this way. You like pancakes, don't you?"

There's nothing she can possibly say in response to this now except yes. She tips the syrup container gently over her stack and a thin amber liquid gushes out, pooling around the edges of the plate. She tries not to look at Harry's omelet, which she would have preferred.

"The Bluebird's famous for its pancakes. I used to get them all the time, but I had a little—what do you call it?—a little cardiac incident a few months ago, so my doctor's got me on this low-fat, low-sugar, low-something else diet that I can't stand." He pauses. "Low salt. That's it. That's the third one."

Elinor takes a bite of her pancake. All she tastes is syrup, the artificial kind that's nothing but sugar and food dye. She checks the red light on her recorder to make sure it's turned on. "So, I noticed there's already quite a few articles written about you." This is something she should have asked Richard when he called—why did he want to talk to someone who'd been profiled in so many other outlets? What more did he hope to get out of him? The questions Richard drafted for the interview weren't particularly probing. Even if they were, she still wouldn't use them.

"Why do you think people are so interested in your story?"

Harry looks over his shoulder, scanning the diner to see who's sitting behind them. Then he turns back to her with a wink. "I've been in the oil business in the Bakken since 1971. I made my money in mineral rights, back when mineral rights were a joke. You know what those are, right?"

"Technically, but it might help to hear you explain them."

"Well"—he beams, clearly enjoying the opportunity to hold forth—"in North Dakota, people can sever the surface rights from the mineral rights on their property, meaning that someone can own the land and the right to use it for farming or grazing or whatever they like, while someone else can own the right to everything below the surface. So back in the seventies, my grandpa died and left me some money, and I got it into my head that I should start buying up people's mineral rights. I was a geology major at Avery State—kind of a disappointment to my parents since they thought I'd study agriculture—but I read a book in one of my classes that said shale deposits were rich in crude oil. Everybody knew Avery was built on a giant slab of shale. The problem was, nobody could figure out how to blast through it to get the oil." He generously butters a piece of toast and then stops, no doubt remembering the rules of his diet. He flips the toast over to the plain side, as if what he can't see won't hurt him. "I said to myself, nobody's figured this out *yet*, 'yet' being the key word there, so I started going to the courthouse after school and figuring out which families still had their mineral rights. Then I knocked on their doors and asked if they wanted to lease them to me. I didn't have to offer much because mineral rights were basically worthless back in the seventies. It's not like it is now, when the people who held out can demand big signing bonuses and higher royalty rates and usually get them." He takes a bite of his toast and chews it thoughtfully, unaware of the crumbs suspended in his snow-white mustache and beard.

"Nobody really understood what I was doing in the beginning. They kept saying, 'You mean I can keep my land and grow whatever I want without having to answer to you or anybody else?' and I'm like 'Yeah, that's exactly right.' They just couldn't get it through their heads that all I wanted was everything under the surface, including the right to poke around. This was long before anyone knew what fracking or horizontal drilling were, so most people just kind of laughed and took my money, figuring there'd never be a way to tap what was stuck in the shale. Now, of course, if Exxon or Kodiak or whoever wants to drill on land that my company holds the rights to, I'm the one they have to pay."

Elinor politely takes notes even though she's familiar with most of this story. She read it in one or more of the profiles about Harry that she found in the file. This is what she was afraid of, that he'd simply re-hash the things he said before, assuming she either wouldn't notice or care. "Let me rephrase the question," she says gently. "You've already talked with a couple of writers about what you did leading up to the boom. Now I'm curious to know *why* you think people find your story so interesting, because they really do, you know."

Harry shoots his lower lip out, nodding as he considers the question. She can tell how much he enjoys thinking about himself in this way. Behind him, a man slides into a seat at the counter and swivels toward their table, trying to listen in. Elinor doesn't particularly care for Harry's oversized ego or his obvious regard for the sound of his own voice. She could tell him that they have a visitor so he doesn't embarrass himself, but she decides against it, curious to see what he says.

"I suppose because it's the American Dream, right? People want to believe they can work hard and get rich and make a nice life for themselves. That's the leap of faith that brought my ancestors to this state in the 1800s. It's the same leap that's still bringing people here from all over the world." He continues to nod, as if he's convincing himself the more he talks. "I've got this Mexican kid working for me. His parents are illegals, but he was born in California. A real hard worker, probably the hardest worker I've ever met, but he just wasn't getting ahead picking fruit, you know? So this crazy kid, he hears about the boom and decides to hop a bus to Avery in the dead of winter." He pauses, chuckling at the thought. "Can you believe that? Nineteen years old, didn't know a soul in North Dakota, didn't even own a proper coat when he got here. Anyway, I thought he had an honest face when I first met him, so I gave him a crappy job and he did it well, so I gave him a less crappy job that paid more money. I've promoted him at least three or four times, I think, and believe it or not, this Mexican kid who's barely old enough to buy beer helped his parents put a down payment on a house somewhere in California. He's also paying for his little sister to go to community college. So . . . to answer your question, I guess Americans just enjoy a good story about people who chip away at a dream and then have something to show for it. Doesn't really matter how big the size of the fortune is."

She might like Harry's story more if he'd stopped calling his employee "the Mexican kid" and used his actual name, just once. The man at the counter who's been eavesdropping clearly doesn't like the story either. He rolls his eyes in such an exaggerated circle, Elinor can't help but stare. Harry, who must notice that he's lost his audience, turns around in his seat and stares with her.

"You got something you want to say to me, Ned?"

The man scowls. "Nice that your little friend is making so much money. You could have hired one of my boys to work for you instead, but no, you didn't think they were good enough, did you?"

"Everybody knows your boys have DUIs, Ned. They can't drive. What good are guys on a drill site who can't drive?" Harry seems to catch himself sounding impatient and exasperated. He turns back to Elinor, smiling weakly. "As you can probably imagine, a boom this big is bound to kick up a fair amount of hard feelings because *some people* are getting rich"—he says the words pointedly—"and some people aren't. But that's not my fault. I made the wells possible. I helped bring good jobs here. The rest is up to the individual."

The man at the counter gets up from his seat. "High and mighty Harry can do no wrong," he says, loud enough to turn heads. "Never mind that he brought the wells and the jobs, but he also brought the oil trash and the crime and everything else that's ruining this town."

14

For several long minutes after Ned leaves the diner, Harry eats in distracted silence, stabbing chunks of melon with his fork. Elinor recognizes the lit match of embarrassment when she sees it. She knows how easily it can turn into something else. Despite the sickly-sweet taste of her pancakes, she finishes off the rest of the stack, sensing that it should be Harry, not her, who speaks first.

"Now do you see what I have to put up with?" he finally asks.

She pushes away her empty plate, still slick with excess syrup. "Does that happen a lot? People getting upset with you personally?"

"You better believe it. Every time I walk outside my door these days, someone wants to pin this whole goddamn mess on me."

The "mess" that Harry's referring to is the town. Since the boom started, every quality of life indicator has taken a hit—crime, pollution, traffic, overcrowding, noise. But Harry, being Harry, has a theory about all of this. People like Ned, they're not pissed off because Avery is supposedly changing for the worse. They're pissed off because they feel left out of the good parts of the change. If they were making money, buying back their farms, riding around in shiny new trucks like everyone else, they might not be so quick to find fault with the boom or the people who are coming here in droves to be a part of it. Harry offers his best quote of the morning when he says it's hard to be happy for others with nothing in your hands.

Once the conversation picks back up again, Elinor asks if Ned had any mineral rights to sell. Harry looks around the diner again and lowers his voice to a whisper. Off-the-record, he explains that Ned's family never had much, least of all property. Instead, what passed down from one generation to the next was a history of drug abuse, alcoholism, violence, and incarceration. A healthy dose of goddamn ignorance too, he adds.

Despite the obvious ill will between them, Harry is surprisingly capable of empathizing with Ned. He imagines out loud what it must be like for him to see strangers prospering in a way that his family probably never will. He suspects it doesn't help that many of these strangers are Black and brown, a sentiment he knows is shared by a handful of longtime residents who apparently complain about a certain "element" taking over the area. When Elinor mentions the random attacks on men of color after Leanne Lowell went missing, Harry shakes his head, offering nothing more than a mumbled "goddamn bigots" directed at his lap. For several minutes, he goes out of his way to convince her that most people in Avery aren't like this; *he's* certainly not like this. He tells her that his company hires "the rainbow" and refers to himself as "color-blind." While he didn't vote for Barack Obama—he's never voted for a Democrat in his entire life—he's not one of those people who wanted to move to Canada right after he was elected either. It makes her uneasy, the way Harry insists that he's open-minded in the same breath that he invokes a stereotype about how hard-working Asians are.

"You and your family probably had to put up with folks like Ned, right?" Harry asks. "Every community has a couple of bad apples."

She shrugs as she flips to a clean page of her notebook. He's not the person she wants to discuss this with.

"The thing that Ned just doesn't get is that no one's entitled to anything in this country. Success isn't a handout; it has to be earned. And you know who understands this best, at least in my opinion? Immigrants like you," he says matter-of-factly. When she explains that she was born in North Dakota, not even two hours away, he adds, "The kids of immigrants too. I bet you had to work really hard to get where you are today. And look at you now, writing for a famous magazine in New York."

Elinor isn't the success that Harry thinks she is. She had a decent run as a working model. But now she's a barely working writer. Before Richard called, she'd been using a website to find freelance assignments, usually pieces of a thousand words or less on random topics— food, wellness, community events. None of them ever paid more than a few hundred dollars, which was starting to become a problem. Ever since she went back to school, she'd been living off the money she earned from modeling, trying to stretch out her savings for as long as possible. But now she has a year, maybe eighteen months at the most, before there's nothing left. The ever-diminishing balance is like a timer ticking down in the background of her days. Although she tries not to think about it, the awareness that she has to make something out of the rest of her life is never too far from the surface. Elinor is forty-two years old and has never held an office job before. Her typing skills are hunt and peck, at best. She's not entirely sure what spreadsheets are for, much less how to use them. In her weakest moments, she imagines her worst-case scenario, which is ending up like her friend, Damon. A faded beauty temping in gray, cubicled offices around the city, fucking up office work that he dislikes too much to learn. The idea has started to keep her up at night.

Her article for the *Standard* has to be great. It has to be better than the best thing she's ever written. But she can't shake the feeling that Richard has pitched her down the wrong path, and a story about the boom creating a schism between insiders and outsiders is just too simplistic for the mess that Avery really is. Something much bigger is happening here. Something potentially more frightening. It's unusual for her to second-guess Richard's professional judgment, which she's always admired. Although she's not proud of this fact, it's still a fact that she stayed in their relationship much longer than she should have because it afforded her certain opportunities to learn. Now she finds herself wanting to scrap his concept in favor of one she can barely explain. She wonders if Lydia would be amenable to letting her pursue a different line of thinking, or at least follow the tenuous threads she's been collecting to see where they lead. After all, Richard's not here. He's not the one sitting with this man who keeps talking and talking at her as if they're simpatico when she knows that they're not.

"My mother—the one who immigrated here—she didn't like living in North Dakota," she says, taking a sip of coffee. "I mean, she tried to at first, but she just couldn't."

Harry startles a bit. "Why's that?"

Elinor smiles, falling back on her instinct to make this man comfortable, even though he's making her uncomfortable, even though she's overwhelmed by the number of stories that come to mind if she wanted to explain. "Oh. You know . . ." She glances at her hands. "It was just very different here. She missed home, I guess."

"You'd be a terrible poker player, miss. Now what were you really going to say?"

Elinor grew up in military housing. On the base in Marlow, families lived in a concrete gray apartment complex where all the living room windows faced a large interior courtyard. Whenever she and Maren followed their mother through the courtyard to go to town or the PX, Elinor felt watched by every nearby set of eyes. The women who frequently gathered around the picnic tables and playground equipment whispered to each other behind cupped hands as Nami passed, while men silently stared at her like a package they wanted to unwrap. At school, their children were much more direct. In outside voices, they asked Elinor and Maren why their father married a mail-order bride, was she a prostitute before they met, what did it feel like to be half-breeds—words and ideas they surely learned at home.

"If you really want to know, people weren't very kind to her here. And she never understood whether it was because she was Korean, or a foreigner, or a woman. Or maybe it was a combination of all those things." She almost laughs at the thought of what she's about to say next. "For a while, my father thought it was because of Vietnam— you know, because the military suffered such big losses over there. But my mother obviously wasn't Vietnamese. At least I thought it was obvious. Anyway, at a certain point, it didn't matter why people were unkind to her. The only thing that mattered was that they were."

Harry nods. "I'm sorry to hear that, miss, but like I said, every community has its bad apples."

Elinor wants to tell him don't. Don't explain it away like that. Nami didn't leave because of a couple of bad apples. She left because she hated her life here. And the people who should have made it better, the people who were supposed to love and comfort and support her—namely her husband and firstborn child—treated her as badly as everyone else. But already, she's told Harry more than she ever wanted him to know about her. She smiles again, trying to lighten the mood.

"I guess you just got me thinking how people always want to have someone to blame when things go wrong. But there's a tendency to oversimplify, don't you think?" She doesn't mention that Nami blamed Ed for bringing her to North Dakota, while Ed blamed her for not being the grateful, docile wife he thought she'd be when they married. Later, he blamed Elinor for what seemed like nothing more than being Nami's daughter, a girl who would eventually become a woman and turn her back on him like she did. "Things are almost never that cut-and-dried," she adds.

"Well, that I agree with." He wipes his mouth on a napkin and signals their waitress for the check, which she deposits on their table. "But simple people tend to look for simple answers, don't they?"

Harry glances at his watch and then swipes the check out from underneath Elinor's palm. She decides not to argue with him about who gets to pay.

"Forgive me, but I've got another meeting I need to run to." He drops thirty dollars in cash on the table and fishes in his pocket for change. He adds fifty-five cents to the total, leaving the waitress a five-dollar tip. Barely 20 percent of the check, which seems cheap for who he is. "Is there anything else you want to ask me before I go?"

She runs through her list of questions, many of which he inadvertently answered without any prompting. She shakes her head. "Not that I can think of for now. But I hope you won't mind if I have to contact you later to follow up."

"Feel free." Harry unwraps a toothpick from a sleeve of blue plastic and inserts it into the side of his mouth. "It's been a long time since a pretty young lady called my number. By the way, who else does Mr. Hall have you talking to while you're out here?"

She lets the first comment pass as she thinks over the second. She's not about to share her full list of interviews with him. But she's curious to know if Harry is friendly with the woman she's seeing next, another lifelong Avery resident about the same age that he is. This was something she always disliked about living on the base. Everyone was connected to each other in some direct or indirect way; everyone knew each other's business. During the last few years of her parents' marriage, when Nami leaned toward displays of kindness like sunlight, it never took long to hear that she'd been spotted talking to so-and-so's husband outside the laundry or accepting a ride downtown from airman so-and-so.

"I'm heading out to see Amy Mueller after this. Any chance you know her?"

He looks slightly stricken at the mention of her name. "Bill's wife, yeah. Sad couple. They got all tangled up in something I don't think they really understood. . . ." He pauses. "You know, I told Mr. Hall on the phone that I didn't want to be part of one of those big-city hit jobs that makes Avery out to be some kind of a terrible place. That's not what you're writing, is it?"

"A hit job? No." She wonders why her mention of Amy Mueller would elicit this. "But to be clear, I'm not writing a tourism piece either."

"Alright. Just be fair. That's all I'm asking."

She's about to ask "fair to whom?" but she thinks she knows the answer already. People from North Dakota are nothing if not loyal. Among friends and neighbors, they might complain about the state of things in their community, but God help the outsider who criticizes the place they call home.

15

The Mueller farm is twelve miles outside Avery, five turns off the main county road. The GPS signal is spotty this far from town—something Amy Mueller warned her about—so Elinor has to rely on the directions she emailed, which are confusingly written. It's hard to tell whether some of the curves in the winding road are actually turns or vice versa. As she looks in her rearview mirror, not certain if she just passed a curve or a turn, she hears the noise for the first time. A thunderous boom, like a wrecking ball smashing against the side of a building, and then the screech of dozens of birds as they streak through the air, their bodies small and black against the darkening sky. She pulls over to the side of the road and waits for the noise again. A few seconds later, there's another boom—louder than the one before—and another. She aims her recorder out the window, hoping it's sensitive enough to capture the percussive crashes, followed by eerie metallic scraping sounds that remind her of broken machinery. When she plays back the recording, all she hears is an indistinct whir.

The source of the noise reveals itself as she drives around a wooded bend in the road. A modest brick farmhouse comes into view. Behind it, there's a blue-and-white-striped drilling rig rising high above the roofline. Although she knows it's an optical illusion—the rig can't possibly be as close to the house as it appears—the fact that she can see it at all is alarming. Farther off in the distance is an identical rig. She guesses this equipment marks the drill pads for what will eventually become Yogi Bear NE-1 and Yogi Bear NE-2, following the recent trend of naming wells after cartoons, movie characters, planets, classic cars, and animals—anything to help people distinguish one well from another.

When Elinor parks and gets out of her car, she hears dogs barking—large, unfriendly dogs in a fenced-off area beside the barn. The screen door of the house bangs open and a heavyset woman lumbers down the front steps, drying her hands on a kitchen towel that she throws over her shoulder. When they were emailing back and forth, she imagined Amy Mueller as a smaller, more delicate woman—a petite strawberry blonde with tiny features, someone who actually looked like an Amy. But Mrs. Mueller is broad shouldered and stout. "Hearty," she imagines some would call her. She looks more like a Margaret or a Helen, with a bad case of rosacea and deeply etched crow's-feet that suggest a lifetime of squinting at the sun.

They meet halfway between the house and the barn, Elinor smiling as much as she can, Mrs. Mueller not smiling at all. She makes no effort to hide the fact that she's giving Elinor the once-over and dislikes what she sees, as if she too expected her to look like someone else.

"So you're Elinor Hanson, huh? You must have married a Viking or something."

Such a familiar line of inquiry, she thinks. Such a familiar joke. "Me? I've never been married."

"You're adopted then?"

She shakes her head, annoyed by the assumption, the audacity of a stranger to say it out loud.

"Hanson though."

"Yes?"

"That means what? Your father was American and your mother was . . . ?"

"American."

Mrs. Mueller's face twists and pulls with confusion. Elinor lets it go on much longer than she should.

"But your parents' people are from where?"

"My father's family is Norwegian and my mother's is Korean." A drop of rain falls on her shoulder. A few more brush the side of her neck. She tells herself to stop playing dumb. Not only is she antagonizing Mrs. Mueller, but they're about to get wet. "I'm sorry," she says, trying to give her a graceful way out. "Is there something wrong? I'm not late, am I?"

She shakes her head, visibly flustered. "No. Not wrong. It's just . . . I don't know. I guess a person hears a name like 'Elinor Hanson' and they figure . . . Well, anyway, you're the student Mr. Hall sent over to replace him, huh?"

The car keys are still in her hand. Elinor tightens her grip, allowing the teeth to poke into her skin. The fact that Richard told everyone he was sending a student in his place is almost as offensive as Mrs. Mueller assuming she was white. It probably never occurred to him that he'd be making her job harder by introducing her like this. He didn't have to think about earning people's trust or establishing legitimacy in the same ways that she did.

"I graduated last year." Elinor wipes the beads of sweat collecting above her lip. The temperature must be in the nineties now and dark, greenish-gray clouds have gathered above them. It looks and feels like tornado weather. She wishes she hadn't put on a black blazer and jeans that morning. The blazer covers her tattoos, but it's made of cheap rayon and polyester, fabric that doesn't breathe.

"Well, alright then," Mrs. Mueller says. "Come on in."

The drops of rain turn into a steady patter as they make their way toward the house. No sooner have they climbed the front steps than the deluge begins. Elinor shuts the heavy wood door behind her, glad to be inside until she realizes it's as hot indoors as it was out. The air also feels wetter than it should, like a greenhouse or a sauna.

"I was about to have a pop. You want some?"

"If it's not any trouble."

Mrs. Mueller points down the hall. "Go on in and take a seat, then."

The living room is unnaturally dim for midday because of the rain and drawn curtains. As Elinor's eyes adjust, she sees stained glass light fixtures and wood-paneled walls; chunky, overstuffed pieces of furniture that probably date back to the seventies. She walks toward the windows and discovers that one of the curtains isn't a curtain at all. It's a vintage American flag. The colors are so old and muddy, the navy blue and red threads are almost indistinguishable from one another. She's never seen a flag used as a window covering before, hanging upside down instead of right side up, no less. The sight of it actually makes her uncomfortable. She's accustomed to flags being treated with more care. On the base in Marlow, uniformed airmen raised and lowered the central flag with gloved hands at the exact same times every morning and night. There was a whole ritual to the folding and unfolding, the hoisting up and the lowering down. If a flag accidentally touched the ground or tore because of wind or debris, it had to be disposed of. Burned, if she remembers correctly.

Mrs. Mueller returns with two plastic cups filled with soda. She places them on the table and snaps open all the curtains, letting in what little light the sky offers.

"I'd normally have a pot of coffee going—"

"But this is exactly what I wanted. Thank you." Elinor takes a small sip, getting a jolt of pure sugar from the off-brand cola.

"You're just being polite. I swear, this stuff will rot your teeth out fast. But there's no way I'm using the water that comes out of the tap these days."

Mrs. Mueller glowers over the edge of her cup as she chews a piece of ice. She seems irritable and tense, but Elinor tells herself she was probably like this long before she arrived.

"Do you mind if I turn this on?" She places her recorder on the coffee table, next to a Lazy Susan filled with too many remote controls.

Mrs. Mueller shrugs. "That's what you're here for."

Elinor sits down on the sofa with her arms pinned against her sides. Underneath her blazer, her white T-shirt feels damp with sweat. She brushes her fingertips against the nap of the worn velour upholstery, which features a busy brown pattern of pheasants and cornucopias. Instead of sitting down beside her, Mrs. Mueller continues to pace, seemingly nervous now that the recorder is on.

"So . . ." Elinor watches her cross the room once, then twice. "You mentioned the water here. Is there something wrong with your well?"

"I'm not about to drink it and find out. You know people all over this area are talking about how their water tastes different after they've been fracked, right? Like one of these companies threw a bucket of kerosene down their well or something. Can you imagine drinking coffee made with water like that?"

At first, it sounds like she's asking her questions, but Mrs. Mueller continues on, clearly not in need of a response. "A friend of mine, she lives a couple towns over, and she can't even take a shower in her own house anymore. She says the water makes her eyes burn, and her hair's starting to fall out. You should go over there and interview her, if you get a chance. Her name's Louise Eddy, E-d-d-y. She's got four EnerGia wells on her property. Four! You'd get a kick out of talking to her, I bet."

Elinor takes notes as quickly as she can, struggling to keep up with Mrs. Mueller's conversational pace. She glances at the recorder again, confirming that the red light is on.

"Would you mind telling me about the noise I heard outside? Does that have anything to do with what's going on here?"

Mrs. Mueller shakes her head. "Welcome to my world. It was quiet for a while—you know, while the case was tied up in court—but as soon as they got their judgment, it was like, *bang.*" She claps her hands together. Specks of dust float through the air, visible as they pass through dim amber slants of light. "Suddenly all the crews came back, big swarms of them, like locusts. It's almost worse now because they're behind schedule, so instead of taking six weeks to install their wells, they're trying to do it in four." She knocks on one of the windows, which offers a rain-soaked view of the road Elinor just drove up. "They're not even halfway done yet, and I don't think I've slept two hours in a row since they got here. How's someone supposed to live with those drills going twenty-four seven?"

"They actually drill overnight?"

"Sometimes. It's never on any set schedule, as far as I can tell. They stop when it rains hard like this, so I might actually get a little bit of peace today. And don't bother asking if I've complained. I've complained so much, I don't even know how to have a decent conversation anymore. Last week, I ran into some folks at the supermarket, and they asked me how I was doing with Bill being gone, and ten minutes later, I was still talking their ears off about how I can't sleep. All this noise, all the time—it feels like I live in Iraq," she says, pronouncing the word *I-rack*. "I just can't take it anymore."

Elinor isn't the kind of person who can function well without sleep. The past two nights in Avery are already starting to take their toll. If she doesn't get some decent rest soon, she'll be babbling like Mrs. Mueller, who seems aware that she keeps going on and on, but unable to do anything about it. Now she understands what Richard meant when he said there was something a little off about her.

"Do you want to talk about the future?" Elinor asks, trying to switch to a lighter subject. "Once the wells are up and running, you'll probably start getting royalties for your share of the oil profits, right? So what do you plan on doing then?"

"Are you serious?" Mrs. Mueller snaps her head back, her mouth stretched into something that looks like a smile at first, but isn't. "You don't know, do you? Oh, you should definitely go talk to Louise Eddy then. The way EnerGia writes their sneaky little Jew agreements, they take a whole chunk out for—what do they call it?—gathering expenses? People are lucky to get a couple thousand dollars a month after all the deductions, which is hardly enough to make up for not being able to farm the land. That's why I took them to court. I started hearing all these nasty things about them, how people couldn't afford to live after they went into business with EnerGia, so I sued to get a new agreement drawn up before they started drilling."

"What . . ." Elinor's mouth feels thick with cotton. She wonders if she's imagining things, if she really just heard what she did.

"My husband, he wasn't a sophisticated man. He saw some of our neighbors getting rich off their wells, so he signed the damn contract before he got a lawyer to look at it. He probably figured it said 15 percent monthly royalties, so that's what we'd get. But Bill didn't realize how all these companies do business a little differently. Some of them are fair, and some of them are just out to screw you." She makes a fist, hitting herself in the meat of her thigh over and over again. "Honestly, I thank God every day that Bill died before he learned what kind of people he was dealing with. I'm sure he thought he was doing a good thing, giving me a little extra income so I wouldn't have to work as hard after he was gone. But if he knew what he'd done—Christ, the guilt would have killed him before the cancer did."

16

Their first hour of conversation is a blur. If not for the limits of her digital recorder, Elinor wouldn't even know how much time actually passed. Mrs. Mueller has a habit of talking until she's emptied her head of everything she wants to say on a particular subject. Most of the time, she's not even answering a direct question, just chasing tangents like a dog that keeps finding and refinding its tail. Elinor takes the occasional note, but it's hard to keep up. It's even harder to listen. She's still stuck in the moment when Mrs. Mueller said "sneaky little Jew agreements" as if it was nothing at all. Like her mother, she struggles with what to do in these situations. The more Nami's English improved, the more she wanted to respond when people said or did things that upset her. But Ed warned her not to ruffle any feathers with his fellow airmen or their wives, as if the people they lived among were soft little birds whose necks would snap if she spoke to them the wrong way. Elinor hates it as much as Nami did—this business of going along to get along, pretending she didn't hear anything out of the ordinary because it's simply easier. But here she is, doing exactly the same thing.

As she swaps one recorder for another, Mrs. Mueller motions toward the window and asks if she'd like to walk around the property now that the rain has stopped. Elinor is still sweating through her clothes, so she stands up before she even answers the question, eager to get out of the house.

Mrs. Mueller points at Elinor's shoes, a pair of black flats with thin soles. "You can't go out there in those."

"Oh, they're old. I don't mind if they get dirty."

"Dirt's not the problem," she says, but she doesn't explain what the actual problem is. She disappears down the hall and returns with an old pair of boots, knee-high galoshes made of rubber, similar to the kind she's changed into. "Here. These are probably going to be a little big on you, but at least you'll be covered up."

She thrusts them at her in a way that makes the offer difficult to refuse, as much as she'd prefer not to wear a stranger's shoes. Elinor slides her bare feet into the clammy rubber, wishing she'd also been offered socks.

The air smells like fertilizer as they walk around the side of the barn, through mud and ankle-deep puddles that swallow their boots, releasing them with loud pops of suction. The dogs she heard when she arrived—only two of them, although they make enough noise for a pack—start to bark as if another storm is headed their way. Mrs. Mueller doesn't pet their heads or coo their names as she passes. They aren't those kinds of dogs. Elinor can still hear them going wild in their pen as she and Mrs. Mueller continue walking toward the first drill pad, which is just past a small slope. When they reach the other side, she spots at least a dozen men dressed in hard hats and neon-green vests, moving around the rig like fireflies.

"This used to be all durum wheat, if you can imagine," Mrs. Mueller says. "For over a hundred and fifty years, we were wheat farmers." It's an unusually economical thought for her to express. When Elinor turns to glance at her, she almost expects to see tears. Instead, Mrs. Mueller just looks furious.

Richard's file included several photos of drill sites, annotated in his careful block script to identify different types of oil field equipment. Elinor has yet to understand the intricacies of how each piece works, but she understands what their presence generally means. If there are rigs, trucks, vans, trailers, pumps, water tanks, and chemical tanks clustered in an area, as there are here, the land is in the process of being fracked or drilled. If there's only a pumpjack, the land has been drilled already and the well is producing oil that feeds into a battery of tanks nearby. And if there are long pipes sticking out of the ground, spewing amber flames into the sky, natural gas is venting out of the earth to prevent dangerous subsurface buildups, a process known as "flaring."

Of all the new information she recently had to take in, this last bit gave her the best sense of how much money is really at stake here. In other parts of the country, the whole point of fracking is to access natural gas, which people often pay a fortune for to heat their homes. But here in the Bakken, it's the crude oil they want. The gas is just a by-product, the waste they burn off into the atmosphere because there's not a pipeline in place to transport it yet. Last month, *Scientific American* published satellite photos of the Bakken at night, the flares so numerous and widespread, it looked like wildfires had broken out across the region.

Elinor narrows her eyes at the equipment in the field, surrounded by a fence that's at least fifteen feet high, topped with a spiral of razor wire. Before leaving New York, she contacted over a dozen energy companies and requested permission to tour one of their drill sites. Most didn't return her calls, and those that did cited safety concerns or too many competing requests from other journalists as a justification for turning her down. When she tried to follow Richard's advice to be more assertive, to use the *Standard's* good name like a battering ram, the doors still didn't open.

"Can we walk over there?" Elinor asks, aware that this might be her best opportunity to see a drilling operation up close.

Mrs. Mueller shrugs. "Let's see how far we get before they try to stop us."

Their boots continue to squish and slap through the muddy grass. When she's not watching her step, Elinor scans the landscape, which turns from farmland into open prairies the farther out she looks. She never minded the stark, almost desolate emptiness of the countryside in

North Dakota. In fact, she thought it was beautiful, how she could see all the way out to the horizon line, uninterrupted by any evidence of people. Now these companies are ruining it, the one thing she actually liked.

"So, have your opinions about fracking or horizontal drilling changed at all over the past year?"

"Changed?" Mrs. Mueller barks. "I didn't have an opinion *to* change. I mean, I knew that kind of stuff was going on around here, but what did I care? I was too busy with the farm to worry about things that had nothing to do with me."

Before her recent crash course, Elinor understood that drilling wasn't good for the environment. But she did so in the same vague, uninformed way that she knew genetically modified foods were unhealthy or methane gas contributed to global warming. At some point, she simply internalized these ideas, accepting them as facts without understanding the evidence. If asked to explain why she believed what she did, she wouldn't be able to, not in any level of detail. But now that she's read hundreds of pages of articles and research studies and environmental reports, nothing about this business seems right. Companies are boring holes miles deep into the ground, turning their drills sideways, and then detonating explosives in the horizontal expanse. She doesn't think human beings were ever meant to do this; it hardly seems sensible or safe. But this is just the prep that happens before the part that really frightens her, when millions of gallons of water and chemicals mixed with sand are pumped through the holes to force the hard shale layer underneath to crack, releasing the oil and natural gas trapped inside. Sometimes, the adulterated water contaminates neighboring wells and reservoirs, or the chemicals leach into the soil. Sometimes, entire fields drown under a viscous, toxic ooze forced to the surface from places deep underground. Despite not being particularly conscientious about the environment, it still seems so wrong to her—all this money, all this manpower to do something so wholly unnatural. Maybe what's trapped in the shale is just meant to stay there.

"Oh, look," Mrs. Mueller says dryly. "Here comes my favorite person."

They're about thirty feet away from the fence when a man starts walking toward them. He's dressed in jeans, a company polo shirt, safety goggles, and a yellow hard hat. He looks like a middle manager of some sort, the kind of guy staying at Elinor's hotel.

"The crew doesn't like it when I come this close. They say it's for safety reasons, but I know it's because they don't want me to see what they're up to."

"Amy," the man shouts, but not unkindly. "We've talked about this. . . . You're not supposed to walk over here. . . ."

"I can walk wherever I want."

"I'm sorry, but that's just not true."

"This is still my property."

"I'm not arguing with you about that, but you signed an agreement."

Mrs. Mueller laughs. "At least once a day!" She turns to Elinor. "At least once a day, one of these bloodsuckers likes to remind me that I signed an agreement, but I didn't sign anything. My husband did, on his deathbed." She waves her hand at the structure looming in the distance. "Will you look at all this? Look at how EnerGia took advantage of a sick old man and now his widow is stuck with a ten-year lease and this goddamn nightmare in her backyard. Does that seem right to you?" She points at Elinor's notebook. "Write that down so people will know. EnerGia took advantage of a sick old man."

Elinor stands stiffly, her pencil frozen above the paper, trying to remember if "bloodsucker" is an anti-Semitic term.

"Who're you?" The man motions toward her with his chin.

"She's a reporter. She's here writing a story about what you're doing to my land."

Elinor hopes that's not what Mrs. Mueller really thinks the piece is about. But before she has a chance to clarify, another boom shakes the ground, like a mild earthquake that might gently rattle dishes and chandeliers.

"Are you perforating?" Elinor asks loudly, a high-pitched buzz now ringing in her ears. She hopes she's using the term correctly. She can't imagine what else is making the ground do this, if not for subterranean explosive charges.

"It's really not safe for you to be so close to the pad right now," he says. "I have to ask you both to leave."

She's not sure what he'll do if they refuse, but Mrs. Mueller doesn't push back.

"Come on," she shouts. "I can barely hear a word anyone's saying out here."

Elinor removes a business card from the pocket of her blazer and offers it to him. *I'm not with this person,* she desperately wants to say. *I'm not responsible for the things that come out of her mouth.* "Any chance you'd be willing to talk to me? We can do it off-the-record if you want."

He puts his hands in the air, as if she's trying to mug him. Then he walks back toward the rig, leaving the card untouched.

When they return to the house, Mrs. Mueller crouches beside a spigot near the back door and turns on the water. With a garden hose, she sprays the mud off her own boots before moving on to Elinor's. The mud washes away into a small drainage ditch filled with dead grass.

"Take a good look at that," Mrs. Mueller says, motioning toward the ground.

In the sunlight, Elinor sees an oily, rainbow-colored film coating the water. She leans over to examine it.

"Now does that look like any mud you've ever seen before?" Mrs. Mueller asks. "And those sons of bitches have the nerve to tell me not to worry about my well."

Elinor nods, not certain where the oily residue is coming from—something they walked through or from the spigot itself.

She's about to stand up when Mrs. Mueller grabs her forearm. "You've got to help me," she says. "I got screwed by that company. Then I got screwed by the judge and my lawyer. It feels like I'm gonna go crazy unless someone actually helps me."

Now come the tears that weren't there before, welling in Mrs. Mueller's bloodshot eyes. Elinor hesitates, unaccustomed to seeing a woman like her cry. She reaches out, about to pat her on the shoulder, when Mrs. Mueller suddenly seems to remember who she is and blinks the tears back. Her face darkens and she releases Elinor's arm, pushing it away roughly.

"Christ. I get so emotional sometimes." She hits herself on the leg again, a tic that must soothe her because she keeps doing it for a while, pursing her lips together until they flatten into a hard, thin line. "Come on. Let's go in and get your shoes."

Elinor follows her into the house, where she changes out of the rubber boots. Mrs. Mueller looks on, nearly expressionless now, as if the outburst outside never happened. As Elinor gets up to say good-bye, she sees a large, framed photograph hanging above the fireplace, which she was sitting with her back to earlier. There are at least twenty adults standing in two rows, and an equal number of children sitting on the ground. Everyone—adults and children alike—is dressed in coordinating shades of red, white, and blue. On the barn behind them, there's a banner that reads MUELLER FAMILY REUNION 2010. Elinor scans the smiling faces, leaning in to search for Mr. and Mrs. Mueller, who are holding hands on the far left.

"That was taken right before Bill got sick."

"Such a big family," she says, thinking of her own, how she and Maren would stand out in a photo like this, surrounded by their tow-headed cousins.

She scans the rest of the row and pauses when she reaches the end. The blond, blue-eyed woman staring back at her is so familiar. She's seen her face before in a slightly different form. When the name finally comes to her, it feels like someone just punched Elinor in the chest, forcing all the air out of her lungs.

"Why is Leanne Lowell in this photo?" she asks.

"What do you mean, 'Why's she in the photo'? That's my nephew's wife."

17

On her third day in New York, Elinor spotted a sign at the flower shop next to her youth hostel: CASHIER WANTED. She had no interest in flowers and no experience in retail, but all the touristy things she'd dreamed of doing—seeing a Broadway show, dancing at the Limelight, taking a carriage ride through Central Park—simply cost too much. With the help of her fellow guests, Elinor decided to apply for the cashier job and put on the nicest outfit she could assemble. A black jumpsuit from the Danish girl down the hall, a pair of white patent heels from her German roommate, and jewelry from the wealthy Italian sisters who seemed conspicuously out of place at the gritty hostel. Whenever Elinor looks back on this day, she wonders if it was fate that sent her next door to ask for the manager, dressed in her borrowed European best. Or perhaps it was fate that caused her to bump into the woman at the register, the modeling scout who was picking up flowers for her daughter's graduation. Whatever that particular force was—fate or luck or coincidence—it feels like it's revisiting her again.

Leanne Lowell was married to Amy Mueller's nephew, a fact that Elinor can't help but interpret as a sign. Suddenly, her curiosity about this woman's life feels validated. Her desire to learn more about her disappearance does too. But the walk around Mrs. Mueller's property added well over an hour to the visit. Then she spent another twenty minutes trying to convince Mrs. Mueller to share her nephew's contact information, a conversation that ultimately went nowhere. Now there's less than an hour before Elinor's first conversation with Lydia, and she has yet to do even the most basic prep.

After a quick rinse in the shower and a change of clothes, she searches the Internet for "Lydia Griswold editor," something she'd planned to do the night before until she decided to go to Swift's. Elinor assumes that Lydia is an accomplished woman—she'd have to be, in order to have the position she does—but the bio that emerges is even more intimidating than she initially expected. Yale undergrad, summa cum laude. Two master's degrees from Columbia—one in journalism, the other in creative writing. Four nonfiction books on American first ladies, all critically acclaimed. Eighteen years at the *Standard*, its first female features editor. Award after award after award. Women like this always make Elinor feel nervous, uncomfortable in her own skin. She knows she can't compete at their level, but the urge to compare is always there.

Whenever she googles her own name, she has to wade through dozens of search results about another Elinor first—thirteen-year-old Elinor Hanson of Colorado Springs, a swimming phenomenon considered to be a top prospect for the next Summer Olympics. Elinor's bylines don't begin to appear until several pages later. There aren't many of them yet, but she always feels a small flutter of pride to see her stories listed on the screen, as well as relief that her digital footprint is based largely on her current work. Despite how many photos she took over seventeen years in the business, there are actually very few images of her available online. The handful of archived catalog photos she's been able to find make her cringe. In the late eighties and early nineties, makeup artists often had no idea what to do with her. Some tried to accentuate her Asian features, while others tried to blur them out until she didn't look Asian at all. The result was a portfolio of photos in which she always appeared to be someone else. Years later, when casting directors began hiring more models with an "exotic" or "ethnic" look, her agent complained that she didn't seem sufficiently grateful for the uptick in demand. *Exotic or ethnic compared to whom?*

Elinor always wanted to ask. Why were the white girls the norm while she was the trend?

Elinor scrolls back to the top of Lydia's search results page and clicks on the images tab, curious to know what she looks like. There are almost too many photos to choose from, taken at glittering fundraisers and book parties. Elinor finds candid shots of Lydia talking with people at receptions while holding a glass of wine in her hand—always red wine, always the left hand. There are staged shots of her posing next to tuxedo- and evening gown–clad guests at various galas, all left-leaning causes like promoting literacy and protecting the environment and raising scholarship funds for inner-city kids. The image she sees most frequently is a professional headshot in which Lydia is sitting at a desk, her face turned to a three-quarters pose, reading a manuscript.

In every photo—candid or staged, casual or formal—Lydia looks the same. Neutral colors, muted makeup, tasteful clothes that flatter but don't distract or draw too much attention. She has porcelain, almost blue-tinted skin, and a long, aquiline nose that the eye simply can't avoid noticing. She isn't particularly attractive, not in the usual ways. But with her silvery white hair and mannish black eyeglass frames, she exudes a quiet, cerebral confidence, a quality that makes her stand out among the sea of Plasticine socialites and trophy wives.

Toward the end of the first page of images, she finds a photo of Lydia and Richard standing next to each other at a Literacy Matters gala earlier that spring. One page later, there's another photo of them at the American Museum of Natural History. Richard always looked his best in a tux; on some level, she thinks he must have known that. It was rare for him to turn down a black-tie invite. This also appears to be true of Lydia, who must have a closetful of evening gowns and cocktail dresses at her disposal. Elinor continues clicking until it finally dawns on her—how frequently the two of them appear at the same events, in the same photos. When she starts zooming in on the images, she notices Richard's hand wrapped around Lydia's waist, positioned low on her hip. It's too intimate a pose for colleagues or even longtime friends. They're a couple, she thinks. They have been for at least eight months, which is how far back their earliest photo together goes. Suddenly the phone conversation she's about to have seems fraught. Does Lydia know that she and Richard used to date, or did he simply refer to her as a former student? And if he's dating this woman, then why did he tell Elinor that he'd been thinking about her when they spoke last night?

Before she has a chance to collect her thoughts, her phone rings. It's a FaceTime request from a number with a New York City area code. She quickly declines it, assuming someone misdialed, but twenty seconds later, another request from the same number appears. She presses the "accept" button hesitantly, not recognizing the young woman with the poppy-colored lipstick whose face now fills her screen.

"Hello?"

"Hi. I'm Ms. Griswold's assistant. Could you hold for her, please?"

"Yes, but wasn't this . . . wasn't this just supposed to be a phone call?" Elinor touches her hair, which is still wet from the shower. The comfortable gray T-shirt she changed into is freckled with holes. She cocks her phone up at an angle so the assistant can't see the largest of them, a fingertip-sized one on the edge of her sleeve. "I didn't think . . ."

"I mentioned it was a video call in my email. She prefers this format. May I put her on with you now?"

The assistant seems convinced of her faultlessness in the matter, so Elinor simply nods. When the screen goes black during the transfer, she quickly searches for the original message on her computer, if only to prove to herself that she didn't make a mistake. But there it is, in the very first line of the first paragraph, seemingly impossible to miss now that she knows what to look for. *Your FaceTime call with Ms. Griswold is scheduled for Wednesday, 6/13, at 3 p.m.* She wonders if Lydia really prefers this format, or if she's just curious to inspect the woman who slept with Richard before she did. Elinor runs her fingers through her hair and pinches her cheeks for some color, mortified that she's underdressed, wearing no makeup, and sitting in terrible light. She wishes she didn't care about such things, but then Lydia appears on the screen, and it's obvious why she should.

"Well, at last," she says, in a voice that sounds like she's smoked all her life. "We finally meet."

Lydia looks as polished as she did in her pictures. A crisp white button-down shirt. A gold choker peeking out from beneath the pressed collar. Shoulder-length hair that must have been blown out by a stylist just that morning. And the way she sits—so elegant and upright.

"Yes. Hello." Elinor straightens up as she tries to smile. She was always good at posing in front of a camera, but her default sitting posture is terrible, with her shoulders tipped low toward the ground.

"How are you settling in?"

"Fine, thanks."

Lydia pauses, as if she expects more. When nothing else follows, she leans back in her chair, an expensive-looking modern one made of black leather and thick tubes of chrome. "I'm sorry it's taken us so long to connect. I can count on my hands the number of times I've assigned a piece to someone without talking to them first, but Richard had so many wonderful things to say about you. It feels like we know each other already."

"Oh?" Elinor's voice cracks at the mention of him. She can't imagine Richard actually doing this and wonders if Lydia is just being polite. "That's nice." If she wasn't on a screen, she'd be tempted to roll her eyes. Even she feels impatient listening to her terse, inane answers, but she's too rattled to think on her feet.

"Well, alright then. Maybe we should just get started." Lydia picks up a black fountain pen that she spins between her forefinger and thumb with a graceful whirl. "Why don't you tell me how it's going, what you've been up to, how your first few interviews have gone."

It's obvious that Lydia just asked several different questions in a row, probably in an effort to elicit something that resembles a conversation. Elinor starts slowly, trying to work through a wall of nerves that almost feels too high to climb. One by one, she runs through her conversations with the town manager, Steve from the bar, Harry

Bergum, and Mrs. Mueller. She thinks she summarizes the takeaways well, but she feels increasingly unnerved by the sight of Lydia's pen, which continues to whirl, faster and faster. When she finishes speaking, Lydia just nods and puts the pen down without making a single note.

"Were you . . . were you able to hear all of that?"

"I could hear you just fine." Lydia's expression has shifted from contemplative to slightly amused. "It sounded a bit like you were giving a book report, though."

Elinor has no idea how to respond to this. The rush of embarrassment she feels transports her back to grad school when Kathryn would lob criticisms at her across the seminar table. Usually, she did so in a tone similar to Lydia's, with a hint of airy condescension that made the words sting even harder.

"I was just telling you what I've learned so far."

"I understand, but you're writing a feature story, not a news article, and all you gave me was information. Why should people care about what's happening there? Also . . ." She pauses, as if to think through what she wants to say next, a sign that something very bad is coming. "Where's your sense of personal investment, or rediscovery? I don't feel like I'm talking to a writer who's *from* North Dakota and returning there after a long absence with new insights. That's the whole reason I agreed to reassign this piece to you in the first place. I mean, who better to write about insiders and outsiders than someone who grew up in the area and was probably a little bit of both at some point?"

Elinor focuses on the bookshelves behind Lydia's head to avoid looking her in the eye. She doesn't know if it's wise to tell her that she thinks Richard's concept is too reductive, smaller than the place that Avery has become. Who is she to question him, after all? To question either of them?

Lydia seems to misinterpret her silence as hesitation, or perhaps even inarticulateness. "Alright, let's try this another way. Why don't you tell me the thing that's struck you most about being back in North Dakota?"

Elinor stares at her lap, going over the events of the past three days, but the answer is already there on the tip of her tongue. "It's the men."

"How so?"

"I've never been in a place where there are so many men. Where I feel completely outnumbered."

"Okay." Lydia nods encouragingly. "That's interesting. The male-to-female ratio must be quite high there with all the oil workers in town, right?"

"It is." In the line outside the Halliburton interviews, she counted well over thirty men before she saw a single woman. "And the way they behave when there are so many of them in one place . . . It's like walking past a construction crew when you're alone, and you just have to brace yourself for whatever they're going to say to you because who's going to stop them . . ." She trails off, thinking about her mother, how men sometimes used to call out to her when Ed wasn't around. If they were friendly, she'd let them approach and make conversation under the guise of practicing her English. Elinor and Maren always tugged on her hands, trying to lead her away until she snapped at them to be patient, be polite. "Anyway, I'm not sure if things like that have ever happened to you, but that's what this place feels like. It's just nonstop."

Lydia, she guesses, is in her late fifties. Possibly her early sixties, at most. Yet her face registers a brief flicker of recognition, as if she too has experienced this before. She writes something down on her notepad finally. "That sounds awful," she says, but for the first time since their conversation started, she actually seems pleased. Intrigued, almost. The sudden shift in her demeanor encourages Elinor to bring up something that she wasn't planning to mention.

"As long as we're talking about what kind of insights I could offer, I was wondering if you'd consider letting me change the focus of the article a little. I don't mean change it entirely or anything, but instead of writing about insiders and outsiders, I thought it might be interesting to examine more specific issues, like gender and race, maybe even class too, and how they're all interconnected here." She sees Lydia's eyebrows and mouth turn downward in the shape of protest. Before she has a chance to respond, Elinor continues. "There was a local woman who went missing a couple of years ago. It's an unsolved case, but it's not hard to imagine a roughneck was involved somehow—that's what the locals think, anyway."

"Oh God," Lydia says morosely. "Please don't tell me you're thinking about writing some sort of dead girl story."

Elinor pauses, unfamiliar with the term. "Dead girl story?"

"You know what I mean. Those stories about missing or murdered women that magazines and news shows can't get enough of lately. They're lurid, I think. Sickening, really." She waves her hand dismissively. "Of course nothing ever changes afterward. The underlying conditions that result in these women turning up dead always stay the same. We just feed the public's appetite for female suffering to sell magazines and bump up our Nielsen ratings."

Elinor doesn't appreciate what she's being accused of. Lydia hasn't listened long enough to even understand what she's trying to do. "But I don't want the story to be *about* the missing woman, specifically. It's just, these kinds of things—they never happened in this area before the boom, and then afterward, there were these attacks on men of color . . . I'm still working it all out in my head, but I think I could use this woman's disappearance . . . mention it, I mean, as a way of framing some of the issues I've been thinking about since I've been here."

"For three days," Lydia says, and then nothing more follows.

"I'm sorry, what?"

"You've been thinking about these issues since you've been there—for three days. But Richard researched this story for nearly three months before he handed it off to you. And I'm guessing—correct me if I'm wrong—that you haven't talked to him about the changes you want to make."

Elinor wonders if she misinterpreted the photos she saw online. If they were really dating, Lydia would know the impossibility of what she's asking.

"Look, I'm not suggesting that you shouldn't add your own spin to what he originally proposed. In fact, I think you'll need to in order to bring some value and connection to the piece. But what you're suggesting right now is a completely different story. It's also kind of a maelstrom of big ideas that would probably be too much for even the most seasoned writer . . ."

She leaves the sentence unfinished, but Elinor knows what she meant to imply.

Lydia smiles at her, conveying both warmth and sympathy at the same time. "Richard opened a door for you. So why in the world are you trying to run through a wall?"

18

Elinor spends the rest of the evening and the next morning transcribing. It's difficult to concentrate; she finds herself starting but never quite finishing anything. Whenever her phone vibrates, she assumes it's Richard. She plays out their entire conversation in her head. He'll call her ungrateful or disrespectful, possibly both. He'll go on and on about how he gave her such an amazing opportunity. He handed the whole thing to her on a plate, *for Christ's sake*, and then what did she do? She embarrassed him behind his back, trying to turn his pitch into something unrecognizable. She'll apologize, as she usually does, and offer an innocent observation about how stories can evolve over time. Then she'll point out that she didn't argue when Lydia told her to do it his way. This is when he'll really lose it. *Who the hell are you to tell me what stories do?* he'll shout. Or *Why did you ever think you had a choice?*

Worse than the anticipation of Richard's anger is the embarrassment that eventually settles in. She imagines Lydia telling him about their conversation, describing Elinor as naive and presumptuous. A familiar feeling of regret sweeps over her, replaying the things she said, followed by all the things she wishes she would have said. When Lydia suggested that Elinor had only been thinking about the story for three days, while Richard had been thinking about it for three months, she should have corrected her immediately. She's been thinking about these issues her entire life, in ways that Richard never had to.

The worst thought of all, the one that makes her blister from the inside out, is how Lydia and Richard will probably share a good laugh at her expense. The words "in over her head" will be repeated in tones both mocking and concerned. Then they'll discuss taking the assignment away, a scenario that Elinor can hardly stand to think about because what else does she have if she doesn't have this?

Freelance work is hard for her to get back in New York. It's not like modeling, when she had an agency pushing her portfolio at photographers and casting directors. So much happens through word of mouth, through friends of friends. Elinor didn't leave grad school with that kind of network. Despite being a capable writer, dedicated to improving her craft, most of Elinor's professors and classmates regarded her with skepticism because of her relationship with Richard, a poorly kept secret that no one ever discussed but everyone seemed to know about. On the rare occasions when a faculty member told her about an assignment that was up for grabs, it was always something fashion or beauty related, which she wanted no part of. She'd had enough of that world and people thinking it was all she could do. Richard had been a difficult person to be with, and dating him had probably cost her things that she can't even estimate the value of now, but she's grateful to him in a way that she isn't toward the others. At least he finally gave her a chance to prove herself capable of more. Who else can she say that about?

Elinor confirms the details of a ride-along with the Avery Police Department—a minor coup given the runaround she encountered while trying to schedule it. She suspects that Alan Denny, who agreed to make some calls on her behalf, helped nudge the process forward. She sends a grateful email telling him so before leaving the hotel.

Her two o'clock meeting is a tour of one of the big man camps located outside town. The farther north she drives, the weaker her cell phone signal gets. Eventually, she has no bars of service left, just strange roaming symbols at the top of her screen that she's never seen before. She wonders if not being able to receive a call when she's expecting a bad one is a form of torture or reprieve. It's unsettling that

Richard hasn't contacted her yet, although it's possible that he's holding off because he knows the wait will make her anxious. Like an actress running her lines, she rehearses all the things she'll have to say in order to calm him down: *I understand what a good opportunity this is. I appreciate and respect the work you've already done. I'm sticking to the plan now; I really am.* When he asks whether she intends to use his questions from now on, she'll tell him yes. Yes. She absolutely will.

Elinor tosses her phone on the passenger seat and stares at the long, dry stretch of road ahead of her. Avery doesn't allow man camps within the town limits, so housing for oil workers is exiled to the no-man's-lands in between towns, just off the main roads. The camps on either side of Highway 19 resemble sprawling fields of crops, with identical buildings spaced out in long, even rows. She can tell how much it costs to stay in them, give or take, based on the size and style of their housing units. She spots a budget version comprised of dozens of modest white trailers, each probably no more than a hundred square feet with a single porthole-shaped window. Across the road is a pricier-looking version with an outdoor recreation area and modern silver trailers big enough for three or four people to share. Elinor's childhood dream was to travel from state to state with her family, seeing the sights and living out of a trailer not unlike the ones she's passing now. She wished this could be her father's job instead of fixing rockets, which was how she understood his work as a missile silo engineer. In her daydreams, however, she imagined her family alone, with no one around to bother them. It was always the people who were the problem. When it was just the four of them, Ed didn't pick at the way Nami dressed or behaved so often. He didn't constantly compare her to other women, other types of wives.

Man camp 18, also known as Simon's Lodge, is supposedly "the gold standard in the Bakken." Richard's contact there said so in an email, which she quickly dismissed. But as she pulls into the visitor's lot, she realizes he wasn't just throwing marketing copy around. Simon's Lodge is at least four times the size of the other camps she passed. Instead of individual trailers, there are dozens of huge, modular buildings that resemble barracks. If she didn't know what she was looking at, she'd assume it was military field housing. Each barrack has a number painted on its side in navy blue, which contrasts sharply against the almond-colored fiberglass. When she gets out of her car, she checks her phone again for a signal, which it still doesn't have.

Her contact, a young man named Brian, is waiting for her outside the main building. He's Black, and the fact that she's surprised by this pinches her with guilt. Only yesterday, Elinor was annoyed with Mrs. Mueller for assuming she was white, the very same offense she just committed. She tells herself that at least she has the sense not to talk about it, although Mrs. Mueller's approach, however problematic, might actually be more honest—to have the thought and then admit that she did.

Brian looks all of twenty-five, with acne-scarred skin that he's liberally doused with aftershave, a grandfatherly scent that reminds her of leather and pine. She can tell that he's former military because of the way he holds his chin up and his chest out as he shakes her hand, referring to her quaintly as "ma'am." As he leads her into the building, he quickly limps to reach the doors before she does so he can hold them open for her. Elinor studies the lower half of his right pant leg, which appears deflated compared to the left. He's young to be wearing a prosthetic. She suspects she knows why he has to.

"Do you mind if I ask . . . did you recently serve overseas?"

"Yes, ma'am. Twenty-first Infantry Division, headquartered out of Baqubah. Were you in the service too?"

"No. My father was though. He was stationed in Marlow. That's where I grew up."

"This place must look pretty familiar to you then."

They pass a laundry room, which has several washers and dryers, none of which are running, and then a room with a closed door that says CHAPEL.

"Our parent company was actually founded by former marines,

so you'll probably see a lot of military influence in the design of this community. Our residents returning from active duty say they feel right at home here."

It's been less than a year since the US withdrawal from Iraq. How strange to leave that landscape and come to this one, she thinks. But many newly discharged servicemen apparently did just that, trading the skills they learned in the military for high-paid work in the Bakken. If Elinor was less tired and more lucid, she might pause to untangle the irony of people trying to make their fortunes in oil after fighting a war that some think was caused by it.

They continue walking down the long, brightly lit hallway, passing an impressive gym outfitted with every possible piece of equipment. Next door is a basketball half-court with the shiniest wood floors she's ever seen. Both spaces are empty. The hallway too. Occasionally, she hears the sound of a car outside or an air conditioner kicking on. But no conversation, no people coming and going.

"Where is everyone?" she asks.

"It's the middle of second shift right now, so most of our residents are either sleeping or on the job. Some might be doing errands in town. In a couple of hours, these halls will be completely full during the changeover."

Her father would have liked Brian. Ever the perfectionist, Ed liked anyone who did his job well. Brian seems to take his very seriously. Elinor dutifully asks the first two questions on Richard's list and he answers in great detail about the construction of the lodge, which has twenty-eight buildings that house 687 men from all over the world. He shows her a model VIP unit, which has a full-size bed, a small desk with a mini fridge wedged under one side, a narrow closet with two shelves, and a flat-screen TV mounted to the wall. Behind an accordion-style door is a private bathroom too small to poke her head into without feeling claustrophobic. Everything in the room is new, but cheaply made of pressboard, nylon, and polyester. It looks like a bad college dorm or a very good prison.

Next to the model unit and the leasing office is a computer room with four workstations. There's a red-faced man sitting at the computer closest to the door, not quite asleep but not fully awake either. He's holding his head up with a fist, staring blankly at his screen.

"Hey, man," Brian says with a wave.

There's something unusually friendly, maybe even a little performative, about his greeting. Elinor wonders if he always interacts like this with the residents, or if he's simply doing it because she's there. The man doesn't seem to recognize him or care when they stop in the doorway. He just continues staring. Elinor notices at about the same time that Brian does. He's watching porn. On his screen, there's a woman splayed out on a filthy-looking bed and two guys shot from chest down going at her from each end. The volume is on mute, but judging from what they're doing to her, Elinor assumes the woman is trying to scream, or wants to.

"Hey, man," Brian repeats, quietly this time. "The signs say you're not supposed to be doing that."

Above each workstation is a laminated sheet of paper, peppered with bright red "No's." Elinor steps off to the side to get a better look.

NO SKYPE WITHOUT HEADPHONES
NO DOWNLOADING PROGRAMS OR FILES
NO WATCHING TV
NO PORNOGRAPHY

"Peter wrote you up for this already," Brian adds.

"And?"

"And I know he told you—the first time was just a warning. We're not in the business of giving second warnings around here."

"You mean Pedro? Half the time I can't even tell if that beaner's speaking English."

Brian pauses. She wonders if she looked similarly pained when Mrs. Mueller said, "sneaky little Jew agreements." Brian probably has battles of his own to fight here. Does he have to fight everyone else's too? He waits a few seconds longer. "*Hey.* We've got a lady present."

The man glances at Elinor. His eyes are completely dead. "So?"

When the man turns back to his screen, Brian says "hey" again, his voice no longer amiable and salesman-like, but sharp and forceful. Suddenly the man jumps to his feet, so quickly that he sends his chair skittering backward on its casters. He stands over Brian in the doorway, looking down his nose at him.

"Hey, what?" he barks. "Hey, what?"

Elinor tugs on Brian's sleeve and says the first thing that comes to mind. "I need to use the restroom. Can you show me where the restroom is?"

The two men continue staring at each other like boxers in the seconds just before a fight. Brian isn't small, but he's small in comparison. He's about to get hurt.

"Please," she says. "I have to go."

Elinor tugs harder, which seems to snap him out of the state he's in. "Okay," he says, blinking at her. "Okay."

Slowly, they walk away, not turning to look at the man or each other. Elinor worries that Brian is about to get jumped from behind. He seems to think so too because he doesn't say a word to her, not until they've gone some distance. When they turn the corner at the end of the long hallway, Brian removes the radio from his belt and asks security to report to the computer room for a resident eviction. After a squawky voice confirms his request, he continues on, following the signage toward the cafeteria. "You didn't really need a restroom, did you, ma'am?"

She shakes her head.

"Then can I interest you in a cup of coffee?" He pushes open a set of double doors. "Or maybe some dessert?"

"No," she says. She means this in more ways than one. No, she's not going to eat dessert and no, she's not going to pretend that everything is fine. "You do understand that I have to ask you about what just happened, right?"

"I could have guessed." He waves hello at a cafeteria worker standing behind the counter as he takes a piece of pie off the serving station.

The long, narrow dining hall is filled with round tables, most of which are empty. Elinor and Brian sit off to the side, far from the two dozen or so men absentmindedly eating while watching one of the TVs hanging from the ceiling. He cuts into his pie, which is blueberry. The filling oozes out onto his plate, a broken dam of purple. He rakes it back and forth with his fork, first in rows, then in circles.

"So, you must have to deal with fights like that all the time with so many men living under one roof."

He chuckles. "Have you ever seen a fight, ma'am? That's not what that was."

She doesn't appreciate the way he answered her question, as if she didn't just witness the same thing he did. "I'm pretty sure you were about to get punched. Would you have considered it a fight then?"

He takes a small bite of pie, which seems like a prop, something he picked up just to keep his hands and mouth busy. "Ma'am, I know what you're probably thinking. But we've got seven hundred men living in this facility. Most of them work really long hours, doing dangerous things, so they're tired and stressed out twenty-four seven." He brushes a crumb from the side of his cheek. "Unfortunately, guys blow their top from time to time, like you just saw. But we've got rules to keep things from getting out of hand. No drinking, no drugs, no women. Absolutely zero violence. And we enforce the hell out of those rules, excuse my language. It'd be chaos if we didn't, so I hope you don't let that one incident give you the wrong impression of this place."

"What—" It feels like she missed something. "What impression would you like me to take away?"

Brian shrugs. "You seem surprised that things got a little heated back there. But given the stress these men are under, I think the bigger surprise is that it doesn't happen more often."

19

She returns to Avery, driving eighty because she can. The only other cars on the road are off in the distance, which is fortunate, given her distracted state. Elinor keeps circling back to a strange thought she had about the man in the computer room. In some ways, it would have been better if they'd caught him with his pants unzipped and his dick in his hand. She might be able to understand a badly timed attempt to masturbate, followed by an embarrassed display of testosterone. But all he was doing was sitting there with his bloodshot eyes and open mouth, too tired to even jerk off. That's the part that disturbs her. That, and the video he was watching, the way the camera zoomed in on the woman's face as mascara-stained tears dripped from her chin. *Fuck you*, she should have said. *Fuck you for watching that as entertainment*.

Elinor has gone home with more men than she can count, some of whom liked to play rough. It embarrasses her that that's what she thought sex was for a while. Although she participated willingly, she never invited that kind of aggression. She didn't particularly enjoy it, but no one talked about consent back then. It wasn't even a choice that she realized she had, not until much later when every other encounter felt like something to regret. Most of them took place when she was young and indiscriminate, and a night out usually ended in a stranger's bed. At first, it felt liberating to cast aside other people's ideas of appropriate female behavior, ideas that never belonged to her. The smoking and drinking, she liked. Still likes. Some of the drugs too. But sex eventually became the least pleasurable thing that she did.

When Elinor was leaving Simon's Lodge, she saw two uniformed security guards escorting the man from the computer room out to the parking lot. All of them were carrying large black garbage bags. The only explanation she could come up with for the bags was that they held the man's belongings. She wonders what will happen to him now, if he'll end up in trouble with the company that rented him the room, or if they'll simply move him elsewhere because his skills or services are too valuable to do without. She tries to recall his face and finds that she's forgotten it already. His features weren't particularly memorable. He was just a guy. White, thirtysomething, average. The thought of this is alarming—how she could cross paths with him again and not even know it. Brian seemed to suggest that evicting him was a good thing. But he was only thinking about his job, his facility. If Simon's Lodge is a microcosm of the Bakken, how many men like this are out there, human powder kegs just waiting to be lit?

She speeds past a construction site where a large truck stop is going up, a lone building that will likely be joined by others as Avery's sprawl continues north. She still can't get over it. This entire stretch used to be a no-man's-land. Soon, it will be nothing but men. What's stranger? she wonders. How different the area is, or how she barely recognizes herself within in it? Everything she hated about this place when she was younger—the tightly knit communities, their isolation from the rest of the world, the boredom and piercing quiet—she suddenly misses because they're gone. However small or stagnant life was, she used to feel safe here. No more though. She's never felt less safe anywhere. She thinks about Ned, the man in the diner who accused Harry Bergum of changing Avery for the worse. She understands his anger now, even if it was somewhat misdirected. She understands what it means to lose a way of life and want it back.

When a sign appears, marking her return over the county line, Elinor checks her phone again. Richard still hasn't called, but there are two new texts from Maren.

I have to drive into Avery today. Any chance we can meet up?

Then fifteen minutes later:

Leaving now. Going to stop by your hotel. Really hope to see you.

She wondered how long her sister's patience would hold out. Maren's invitations to the farm have become increasingly persistent, making it harder and harder to respond. But these latest messages are different. She's no longer suggesting that they should see each other when it's convenient. She's not even asking or insisting. She's just coming to town. A visit from Maren is the last thing Elinor needs right now. If Richard tries to reach her and she doesn't answer, he'll be that much more upset when they finally do connect.

Her phone keeps cycling between no signal and a weak one. When two bars of service appear, she pulls over onto the shoulder of the road and speed dials Maren. The line immediately drops. She tries a few more times, frustrated that the call either won't go through or goes straight to voice mail. She gets out of the car, walking ten feet this way, then twenty feet that way, holding her phone in the air, as if that will boost the signal. Eventually, she decides to give up. What would she even say if she reached her now anyway? *Sorry, it's been years since I saw you last, but please don't come. I'm expecting a call from my ex.* Elinor takes off her jacket, letting the sun warm her skin. The thought of spending time with Maren again makes her anxious. It's too much of a distraction from her work, from the argument with Richard that she knows is coming. On her list of priorities, Maren ranks low, which makes her feel both guilty and sad.

She leans against the hood of her car and tries to light a cigarette, scraping the flint of her lighter roughly against the metal wheel. When the flame finally catches, she looks up and sees something moving in the tall grass, about twenty feet away. It's a doe and two fawns, walking slowly toward the road. She hasn't spotted deer in the wild like this in some time—living and breathing instead of roadkill on a highway or images on a screen. They're as beautiful as she remembered, lithe and long-limbed, with eyes black as coal. She could never understand how people hunted such graceful animals for sport, turning their insides into meat.

She shakes her head and takes a long pull from her cigarette. She doesn't like that memory. She was certain she'd put it behind her, so far behind her that she'd almost gotten rid of it for good. But now it all comes back to her at once. The ramshackle Hanson family hunting cabin near the Canadian line, handed down to eldest sons for generations. Ed's insistence on going there by himself every autumn when the weather turned cold. The blood-purple bags of deer meat he always returned with, some to freeze and others to give away to grateful neighbors.

Elinor saw the cabin only once, shortly after she turned twelve. Ed decided to bring the entire family at the last minute, a strange decision considering his claim that hunting should be a solitary activity. At first, Elinor was overjoyed. She thought it would be fun, like a vacation. But the one-room cabin was frigid and barely inhabitable. And there was nothing to do there. No TV or stereo. They weren't even allowed to wander around outside for fear of being mistaken for prey. Years later, she learned that Ed had dragged them along because of rumors that Nami was becoming too friendly with a local man, someone she'd met while taking driving lessons. According to Maren, he wasn't about to leave his newly licensed wife at home to do God knows what, giving people even more reason to talk about their family. Elinor doesn't remember her parents arguing about this, not specifically. What she remembers is the noise.

She can still hear Ed returning to the cabin from a daylong hunt, shouting at all of them to come out and see. Tied to the roof of his car was a large deer, its lifeless head dangling over half the windshield. Nami took one look and went back inside, but at their father's urging, Elinor and Maren stayed behind. Ed cut the ropes and enlisted their help moving the deer to the ground. Then the three of them used a tarp to drag it to the shed, where he strung up the carcass from a long wooden beam that creaked and bowed under its weight.

"I haven't bagged a ten point in a while," he said proudly, using his index finger to count out each antler tip.

That was the moment when they should have left, when they could still pull themselves away. But suddenly Ed was running a knife down the deer's midline and all the blood began spurting out. It filled two whole buckets before eventually slowing to a trickle, then a drip.

"They shouldn't be here for this," Nami said. She had reappeared in the shed and was standing behind them in the open doorway.

"It's fine," Ed answered, not looking up from his work. "There's honor in killing an animal for food."

"But this will make them dream bad things."

"Oh, stop worrying. They're Hanson girls. They're tough."

She lifted her hand to Elinor and Maren. "Come back to the cabin with me."

Ed laughed. "When we first met, your family was still fishing its dinner out of a river. Now you've got a problem with hunting?"

Nami waited for a few seconds before lowering her hand. Elinor wanted to go with her, but she and Maren had been trained to listen to their father. Nami was trained too, although lately, she'd seemed tired of listening. She turned and walked away, leaving Elinor staring at her older sister.

"It's okay," Maren said quietly. "We have to be tough."

Ed's father hunted. His father's father hunted. Everything he knew about the sport, he said he'd learned from them. Perhaps for this reason, he went about his work with a solemn air of ritual, placing two plastic laundry baskets on a large tarp. One by one, he removed the deer's organs, separating them by their utility. Edible parts went into the blue basket. The heart, the liver, the kidneys. Inedible parts went into the yellow. Ed labored hard and fast, his breath a cloud of steam in the cold shed. He threw without looking at the part or the basket, knowing exactly what belonged where. When he finished removing the head, antlers, and pelt, he carried the yellow basket to the edge of the property, allowing Maren and Elinor to follow close behind. The ground was too frozen to bury the waste, so he flung the contents into a ravine where the crows gathered around, feasting for days.

It wasn't the violence of dressing a deer that frightened Elinor, but the way her parents fought about it, and seemingly everything else, on that trip. At home, their arguments rarely rose above a whisper thanks to the paper-thin walls in their apartment. The possibility that the neighbors might overhear was a threat that hung over them all. At the cabin, the nearest neighbor was several miles away. Ed, who had brought only enough hunting gear for himself, began sending Maren and Elinor out on daily hikes, dressing them in his blaze orange hat and vest. As soon as he pushed them out the door, they could hear their parents shouting about the deer, the cabin, the way their lives were turning out.

Elinor's stomach churns at the thought of the venison Ed made the night before they returned to Marlow. He'd never cooked a meal for them before, not that she could remember. Maybe it was his idea of a peace offering to Nami. Or maybe he knew there was no other way the four of them were going to eat. Whatever the reason, he cooked a large piece of backstrap on the stovetop, preparing it the way his mother did, using only butter, salt, and pepper. Then he sliced the meat into thick pieces that resembled steaks. When he set the platter down on the table, he actually seemed proud to be sharing something that his own family had enjoyed when he was young. His smile didn't last for long though. The medium-rare venison looked red and bloody, an instant reminder of what they'd all witnessed in the shed. When he told them to dig in, no one moved. His mood quickly changed from pride to frustration as he began reciting the list—China, Ethiopia, the Soviet Union, Cambodia—the random atlas of despair where people were starving and yet there they were, in America, turning their noses up at perfectly good food.

Maren was the first to give in, as she always was, washing the meat down with desperate gulps of milk and then offering Ed a timid, traitorous smile. Once her sister folded, Elinor felt she had no choice but to follow. Nami, however, simply crossed her arms over her chest and sat through the rest of dinner, staring silently at the three of them with an expression that wasn't quite sadness but definitely wasn't love.

20

Maren is sitting in the lobby of the Thrifty, typing on her phone. Her face is mostly hidden by her long black hair, which she keeps tucking behind her ear, only to have it fall down again a few seconds later. Whenever she takes a break from typing, she discreetly chews on her nails, something she's done since childhood that no amount of pleading or punishment could make her stop. Elinor wonders if Maren is as nervous as she is. Ever since their father died, they've been trying to rekindle the closeness they felt toward each other as children, but with mixed results. Sometimes, they'll have a few good calls in a row, only to be blindsided by an argument so fierce, they'll both question out loud if distance was the better choice. Elinor knows why they keep trying, despite so many signs that they shouldn't. They were devoted to each other once. When they were little and couldn't point to a single friend at school, it hardly mattered because they already had a best friend in the other.

Now Elinor is hiding behind a column in the lobby of her hotel, second-guessing the seemingly innocuous texts they exchanged when she first arrived in town. Why did she reply when Maren asked where she was staying? How did she not expect something like this to eventually happen? The longer she stands there, ducking awkwardly to avoid the leaves of a nearby plant, the more her annoyance begins to turn outward. She has so much riding on this article. Spending time with her sister is an interruption that she just can't afford. Elinor wishes she could be direct with Maren and simply explain this to her, but she knows there'd be no recovering from that kind of hurt.

She crosses the lobby tentatively, lifting her hand in a half-hearted wave when they finally make eye contact. Maren jumps up and races toward her, pinning Elinor's arms down with a hug. She keeps saying "Oh my God" over and over again, so loudly that a succession of heads turn toward them, craning to see what the commotion is about.

"Hi." Elinor gently presses her elbows out to free her arms, wary of drawing too much attention to themselves.

"I can't believe you're really here." Maren takes a step back. "Oh my God, El. You look so pretty. And those tattoos. Wow . . ."

The last time they saw each other in person, Elinor didn't have any. The difference clearly takes some getting used to because Maren can't stop staring and her smile has turned rigid. Elinor assumes she's on her best behavior, trying not to blurt out what her agent and manager said after she first showed them the work: *Why the hell did you do that to yourself?*

"Your bag." Elinor points at Maren's purse, which is sitting unattended next to her chair, halfway across the room.

Her sister laughs. "We're in Avery, not New York. You don't have to worry about people stealing your stuff around here."

That's not true, she wants to say. But a disagreement of any size, on any topic, is probably a bad way to start the conversation. Instead, she just nods while Maren does that thing that women always do to each other, consuming every last inch of her with her eyes. Elinor is equally guilty of it, although subtler in the execution, she hopes. Her sister still looks good after all these years. A little too tan, maybe, but being a farmer, spending time in the sun would probably be impossible to avoid. Her lacy cream-colored shirt and skinny jeans are tight; it's hard to believe that she's forty-four and has two kids. Elinor wonders if this is her usual outfit for running errands in town or if she dressed up for the occasion. Maren appears to be wearing makeup, a shimmery palette of peach and pearl. She never used to bother with makeup before.

"I'm glad to see you," Elinor says, trying to sound more excited than she feels. "Sorry I didn't reply to your texts. I barely get cell service around here."

"I was worried you might have plans." Maren pauses. "You don't have plans, do you?"

The question reminds her of Harry Bergum, asking if she liked pancakes after he'd already ordered her a plate of them. What could she possibly say now that she's here?

"You actually caught me at a good time. You want to get something to eat?" She looks at her watch, realizing it's that odd in-between hour when it's too late for lunch and too early for dinner. "Or maybe we should just go up to my room for a while?"

"Oh, no. I hardly ever come to town without the boys. Why don't we go have a drink somewhere?"

Maren used to be a teetotaler, so this is an unexpected but wholly welcome surprise. After her tour of the man camp, Elinor would like nothing more. But the only nearby bar she knows of is Swift's, which she has no intention of returning to again. "Just give me a second. I'll go ask the front desk for a recommendation."

"Actually—" Maren checks her phone. "I know of a place. Roswell's. It's a couple blocks from here, off Main."

When they set off down the street together, Maren threads her arm through Elinor's and draws her in close. She smells like coconut shampoo and floral soap and sweet, fruity perfume. Elinor wonders if it's a function of the cheerful scents, or just wishful thinking on her part, but her sister seems so much happier than she used to be. As the oldest daughter, Maren inherited the responsibility of an entire household at fourteen. Cooking, cleaning, shopping—all the things their mother used to do before she left, Ed expected her to take care of. It aged her quickly. Then she married the first boyfriend she ever had when she was barely twenty-one. Too young, in Elinor's opinion. But by then, she'd fled to New York and wasn't around to dissuade her. It seems strange that they're both here now, walking through the streets of Avery, arm in arm like the sisters they haven't been in so long. Their presence doesn't go without notice from men who whistle and stare and occasionally shout come-ons as old as time.

Maren clearly isn't used to this kind of attention. She and Tom live on a soybean farm outside Marlow, where days can probably pass without seeing another soul, other than immediate family. To go from that to this must be unnerving. Elinor tries to ignore everyone else and pulls Maren in closer, encouraged by the lack of resistance.

"Try not to look at people," she says quietly.

"What do you mean?"

"You're looking at people. It's like an invitation for them to look at you." Elinor doesn't think she should have to explain this to her older sister, but either Maren isn't aware of the effect they're having on passersby, or she's actually enjoying it.

"Maybe you don't want anyone looking," she says, still smiling as they continue to turn heads, "but I've been stacking fertilizer bags all day, so I could use a little attention right now."

Maren flicks her hair over her shoulder in a way that Elinor has never seen before, not even when they were teenagers. She can't help but stare, wondering who this woman is. Certainly not the dour, possibly depressed sister she last saw nearly a decade ago. Granted, Maren was pregnant then, with a toddler underfoot, a husband who rarely helped around the house, and a father with a heart condition living in their guest room. But the difference now is still so extreme.

"You dating anyone these days?"

Elinor accidentally lets out a sigh.

"What?" Maren asks. "Is that a bad question?"

"No," she says, wondering why it had to be the first question.

"No, it's not bad? Or no, you're not dating anyone?"

"Both."

"Oh, okay. That's a relief. I thought maybe you and that teacher were back together or something. What was his name again? Roger? Richard?"

Their lives are so separate now, the intersections between them so distinct and discrete. She's startled to hear Maren even guess at

Richard's name. Dating her older, divorced professor isn't a detail she'd usually share with her. But there was a brief period during the relationship's decline, which coincided with the end of grad school, when Elinor began to drink more than usual. Sometimes, she'd wake up and notice hour-long calls on her phone from the night before. Most of them were with Damon. A few were with Maren. She doesn't remember what she confided to whom.

"His name's Richard. He's dating someone else now."

"Well, good riddance to that guy, right?"

She wonders what she said to Maren that would make her talk about him like this, but decides it's better not to ask.

A trio of scruffy teenage boys walk past, ogling them like men. Elinor finds herself abandoning her own advice and staring at the one on the left, whose face is so familiar. When his shy grin widens into a smile and she sees the braces, her heart begins to race.

"You didn't come back yesterday," he says too loudly. His chest is all puffed out. He seems proud to have a reason to talk to her in front of his friends.

The boys stop walking, so Maren stops too, tugging on Elinor's arm to prevent her from speeding away.

"I'm sorry?" Elinor says airily, doing her best to feign ignorance. "Did you say something to us?"

"You didn't come back for your dime bag," Tyler says, clueless. "You still want it?"

She feels like a teenager getting busted for shoplifting nail polish again, waiting for her father to retrieve her from the PX. The seconds begin to crawl as she decides what to do, what excuses to make, how to explain herself.

"I'm sorry," she repeats. "I think you're confusing me for someone else." She pulls on Maren's arm and they continue on their way. Elinor mentally prepares for Tyler to shout something awful at her in an attempt to save face with his friends. But remarkably, he doesn't, which she assumes has something to do with his age. He hasn't been conditioned yet to punish women who cause him embarrassment or shame.

If Maren understands what just happened, she doesn't let on, which is both kind and uncharacteristic of her.

"So you're really not dating anyone?" she asks.

"No. I'm not interested in that."

"Why not, though? There must be so many good-looking men in New York."

"I'm usually pretty busy."

"Oh, right. It's always work with you."

Elinor glances at Maren's sinewy arms, which are tanned and dotted with freckles. As children, Maren used to be the ambitious one, always dreaming out loud about having an important career in Minneapolis or Chicago, maybe even somewhere as far as Denver. Although her goals frequently changed—she alternated between becoming a nurse, an artist, a teacher, or a lawyer—not once did she ever mention becoming a farmer. It's actually the last thing Elinor would have imagined her doing. Because she feels indirectly responsible for the choices Maren backed into, she can never bring herself to ask her sister if she likes her work, if she likes her life.

"You know what these tattoos remind me of?" Maren runs her fingertip over the pattern.

Elinor braces herself. "What?"

"The corn maze." She laughs. "The one dad took us to in Medora? I must have been like eight, so you were six. You remember how—"

"I insisted on going in by myself, but I got lost and started screaming."

"And then I had to run all over the maze looking for you?"

It's one of Elinor's happier childhood memories—her sister barreling through tightly planted rows of corn, creating shortcuts and paths where none previously existed. By the time Maren finally found her, their voices were hoarse from shouting each other's names and Maren looked wild with worry. She had bits of corn silk sticking out of her hair and bright red scratches covering her skin from crashing through the sharp, dry stalks and husks.

"You always wanted to do things on your own terms," Maren says. "Even back then."

Although she's still smiling, her words don't feel like a compliment, just a gentler way of reminding Elinor that she's selfish, which they've argued about in the past.

"And you always wanted to save me," Elinor adds, right before they let go of each other's arms.

21

At Roswell's, she's about to sit down at the half-empty bar when Maren leads her to a booth instead.

"This way, El. I want to be able to see you while we're talking." She slides into the seat across from her. "I haven't seen you in so long."

Elinor doesn't want to get in the habit of interpreting everything Maren says as a slight, so she reminds herself that it has been a long time. Going on nine-and-a-half years. Being in each other's company again should feel like a cause for celebration. But they aren't those kind of sisters anymore. Elinor worries that one of them will trip an invisible wire, setting off another random argument, which is usually what happens on the phone. She tries to choose something easy to talk about. Something reasonably harmless.

"So . . . are you still running these days?"

"Running?" Maren asks curiously. "Not much. Why?"

"Just wondering." She looks away, aware of the sad state of their relationship, how much mental effort is required just to have a minute of conversation.

They order drinks from a passing waitress. A whiskey for Elinor, a rum and Coke for Maren. As soon as the waitress leaves, Maren's initial excitement seems to wear off and the awkwardness of what they're doing finally sets in, as if the weight of their reunion is pushing down on them both. Elinor doesn't know what to do other than scan the room, which has an old-fashioned nautical theme. Fishing nets hang from the wall, and the long, wooden bar looks like something salvaged from a shipwreck, with elaborate carvings of sea creatures and bare-breasted mermaids.

"How did you know about this place?"

"A friend suggested it." Maren squares her place mat against the edge of the table. "Are you hungry? They have food here if you want."

She shakes her head. "What were you doing in Avery today? A supply run or something?"

"Isn't it obvious? I came to spend time with you."

Maren says this good-naturedly, but it startles Elinor nonetheless. "It's almost four hours round trip, though."

"I know, but one of us had to rip this Band-Aid off. And you weren't exactly jumping at the idea of coming out to the farm. I got the sense that if I didn't make the effort, you wouldn't."

She wonders if Maren is trying to pick a fight, or if she's simply stating the obvious. Either way, she's right. Elinor had no intention of visiting Maren or spending time with her family during this trip.

"So how's your article going?"

"Fine. Just trying to get my bearings still."

"You'll have to interview Tom when you come over. He has lots of opinions about fracking."

Her sister simply won't give up. "What about you? You must have opinions too."

Maren shrugs. "Tom's all worried about how it affects the water supply and wildlife and everything, which I get. But if someone offered us a million dollars to put some wells on our land right now, I definitely wouldn't say no."

It's hard to tell if Maren actually thinks companies are paying a million dollars for the rights to drill, or if she's just exaggerating the figure because it's a fantasy for people like her and Tom. Unlike Avery, their town wasn't built on a shale formation. There's no fossilized crude oil under their soybean fields, waiting to be pumped from the earth. No promise of royalty income from any wells that manage to produce. Elinor looked at the distance on a map once. If Tom's family farm had been situated just forty or fifty miles to the west of where it is, they might actually be rich instead of lower middle class.

"You know they don't really pay . . ." She hesitates, trying to figure out how to reword in midsentence. Maren is sensitive about not going to college. Tom is too. They get prickly whenever she says things that make them feel uneducated or ill-informed, so she quickly abandons the thread. "You know they don't give us much paid time for these research trips. Ten days is pretty short."

"Have you written a lot so far?"

"I probably won't start writing until I'm back in New York. It's just interviews for now."

Richard used to read early drafts of her work when they were together. He always took a pen to the text whether she asked him to or not, making note after note in fine blue ink. However critical his feedback was, it still felt like a privilege to go through the dog-eared, marked-up pages afterward, realizing how the introduction of a new paragraph or the movement of an existing one could make such a difference. Even his small edits—a word choice, a deletion—seemed seismic to her. She learned more from reading his marginalia than she did in any class. Studying it made her a better writer, capable of improving her work independently. Elinor wonders if he'll want to see a draft of her piece before she sends the final copy to Lydia. Maybe he'll even want to see multiple drafts, going back and forth over her revisions like they used to. She can't summon the same sense of excitement or gratitude about Richard's involvement anymore. She'd been looking forward to doing this on her own. But even if the byline is hers, even if most of the writing is hers, the story will still be his.

"It's going to be a lot of work. More than I really understood, but it's a good opportunity . . ." She trails off, aware that Maren is texting under the table.

"Sorry, sorry. I just had to deal with something real quick." She sets down her phone as the waitress returns with their drinks.

Elinor assumes that a toast is coming. Something embarrassingly sentimental, but Maren simply picks up her glass and takes a long slug. She decides to do the same.

"So how are your boys?" she asks. It doesn't feel right to call them "my nephews." The oldest, whose name she sometimes confuses with the youngest's, was barely walking the last time she saw him. And the youngest, she's only seen in pictures. Certain childless people, she's noticed, dote on their siblings' kids like their own—something Maren occasionally points out, not making any effort to be subtle. Elinor's former agent was like this, displaying her nieces' pigtailed school photos on her desk and taking time off to attend their Christmas pageants and choir concerts. Elinor admires this kind of closeness, even though she doesn't aspire to it herself.

"The boys are doing good, but Jesus, preteens are hard. They've been driving me crazy lately. You know I caught Nathan smoking a couple weeks ago? And Adam has a girlfriend all of a sudden. Can you believe that? My baby has a girlfriend. Tom says eleven's still too early for a conversation about the birds and the bees, but this girl Adam's been hanging out with . . ." Maren's phone vibrates and she snatches it up with both hands, her face flickering with a strange, almost nervous expression as she types out a reply.

The call from Richard could arrive at any minute. A message might even be waiting for her now. Still, Elinor resists the urge to check her phone. It strikes her as odd, maybe even a little rude, that Maren can't demonstrate the same restraint.

"What were you saying about the girl?"

"Hmm?" She sets the phone down again. "Oh . . . right. Right. He's dating this seventh grader who's really bad news. She's not even thirteen yet, and all the moms I'm friends with call her 'the bicycle.' I mean, I know we probably shouldn't talk like that. She's just a kid after all, but these parents of hers—they let her run completely wild." This also feels like an elbow to the ribs, something to justify the way Maren used to police Elinor's behavior as a teenager, ratting her out to their father at every opportunity. "I'm worried Adam's going to come home one day and tell me she's pregnant. Can you believe I have to think about things like this now? He's *eleven*."

"Wait. Why do you call her the bicycle?"

"You know . . . the sort of girl everyone's taken for a ride."

Elinor blinks at her. She still can't get used to the idea of Maren as a mother, friendly with the kind of mothers who never gave theirs the time of day. This was what Maren always wanted though, to belong to something, to be like everyone else. Elinor can't really blame her, growing up in a place where the kids at school used to accuse them of eating stray dogs and called them "chinks" and "gooks" right to their faces. Whenever their classmates turned their attentions to the Sioux or Mahua girls, they'd both join in gladly, so grateful not to be on the receiving end of the name calling for a change.

She takes another sip of whiskey, noticing that Maren's glass is almost empty already. "And what about Tom? How's he?"

She shrugs. "Tom is Tom."

"Still fixing old cars?"

"When he has time."

"And listening to talk radio?"

"Oh, God. Constantly."

Elinor never knows whether to be upset or disappointed by her sister's choice of husband. However unfair the comparison, she can't help but think of her brother-in-law as an adult version of the shitty little kids they went to school with. Shortly after they eloped, Maren brought him to New York for a long weekend so that he and Elinor could finally meet. At first, she was so embarrassed to be seen walking alongside him, dressed in his pearl-snap shirts and stiff blue Wrangler jeans, gee-whizzing at the architecture as if he'd never seen a tall building before. Although Elinor had been living in New York for over a year by that point, her impostor syndrome still ran deep. She thought she could sense people looking at her because they were looking at him, and she hated what his proximity implied. Occasionally, she found herself wishing that Maren and Tom hadn't spent their hard-earned money to pay her a visit, which made her feel like a terrible sister, a terrible person. But then she'd hear Tom's booming voice, warning Maren not to buy the counterfeit purses from the Africans. Not "the men" or "the street vendors," but "the Africans," he kept calling them, which made her wish they'd both just pack up and go home.

Maren finishes her drink and signals to the waitress for another. It's been less than ten minutes since they sat down.

"Are you okay?" Elinor tries not to sound concerned.

She checks her phone again. "I'm fine. Why do you ask?"

"I don't know," she says, and she really doesn't. In person, Maren is so different from what she remembers, different from what she expected. The drinking and texting and constant distraction seem unlike her, although it occurs to Elinor that she has no idea what kind of woman her sister is now.

22

The jukebox has been playing Jimmy Buffett's greatest hits for the past half hour. Then the dollar bills that someone fed into the machine finally run out and the selections abruptly change. An old AC/DC song that was popular in the eighties starts, the intro a series of long, echoing chords on an electric guitar. Maren sits up straight at the sound of the familiar notes, slapping the table with both palms as the drums join in.

"You remember this one?" she asks excitedly. She finishes off her third drink and shouts "turn it up" at no one in particular.

Elinor sinks into her seat, mortified. She glances around the room, certain that people are staring at them. But shouting at the jukebox is apparently something that people do at Roswell's. It doesn't earn them any extraordinary notice.

Maren's second and third drinks went down as quickly as the first. In between, she told more disjointed stories about her kids, one of which involved an ATV they totaled, and another about living in a house with three males and only one bathroom. Elinor gently pushes a red plastic basket of fries across the table. She wasn't particularly hungry or even in the mood for fries when she ordered them. She just wanted Maren to eat something solid.

"You should help me with these before they get cold," she suggests.

Maren shakes her head and looks over Elinor's shoulder at the door. Roswell's has gotten busier since they first arrived. Every bar seat and table is now taken. The mostly male crowd is a mix of old and young, roughneck and local. A good place to find new sources, if she weren't here with her sister. Maren, whose face is becoming increasingly flushed, surveys the room with the kind of wide-eyed interest better suited to a big city or a natural phenomenon.

"I think that guy likes you," she says, motioning toward the other side of the room. "He keeps staring."

Elinor turns to see who she's talking about and immediately wishes she hadn't. There's a man with a long, scraggly ponytail and Elvis-like sideburns leering at their table. He raises his beer at Elinor and winks.

"Oh, great," she says under her breath. "Some old creep is into me."

"Jesus." Maren almost laughs. "Judge much?"

"What?"

"You don't know he's a creep. He could be a perfectly nice guy if you gave him a chance."

Elinor drinks to avoid saying something she might regret. This is dangerous, familiar territory for them. Maren occasionally accuses her of acting like she's better than other people—namely her and Tom. There's no convincing her that being judgmental and having good judgment aren't the same thing.

"All I'm saying is that you don't have to be such a snob. Someone thinks you're pretty, El. What's so wrong with that?"

His attention isn't a compliment, but Elinor doesn't know how to explain this, not without descending into a narrow valley that would be difficult to climb out of. In the past, she used to enjoy being noticed by men, typically attractive men of means. But why did that feel better than what's happening now? Why was it different when the man looking at her had nice eyes or was wearing a $3,000 suit? Was it actually different at all?

"Maybe we should cancel the next round and get going. You can lie down in my room for a while before you have to drive back."

"I'm not drunk," Maren snaps. "I'm just trying to have a good time."

There's a strange role reversal at work here. Elinor remembers saying something eerily similar to Maren when they were teenagers. She also remembers feeling deeply resentful that she had to say it—there were only two years separating them, after all. Their father, however, was convinced that Elinor would go astray without proper oversight. At his urging, Maren became responsible for keeping her in line, which she interpreted to mean telling her what to do, what to wear, and how to behave. In high school, when she should have been getting drunk at parties, Maren was rummaging through Elinor's belongings and interrogating her when she came home from school, trying to find evidence of her bad behavior. Her sister's vigilance, combined with their father's, was oppressive. And Elinor saw it for what it was—an overcorrection for Nami's absence. She didn't appreciate their efforts to protect her from herself any more than Maren appreciates them now.

The waitress brings over another round of drinks—Maren's fourth, Elinor's second—and tells them that table service is ending. They'll have to go up to the bar from now on. Maren clearly isn't listening. She's almost leaning out of her seat, craning her neck so she can see the door.

"Why do you keep doing that?" Elinor asks.

"Doing what?"

"*That.* Right there. Are you expecting someone?"

Maren leans across the table, lowering her voice. "Okay, listen. There's this guy . . . his name's Gary. He's going to join us for a drink, but I don't want you making a big deal about it."

"Who's Gary?"

"A friend." Maren hesitates, clearly wanting to say more.

"Is he the person you've been texting with?" She realizes this isn't the first time that she's heard the word *friend* since they sat down. "Wait. Is this the same friend who told you about this place?"

Suddenly, Maren grabs both of Elinor's hands, squeezing them tightly in hers. "I think . . . this is going to sound crazy, El, but I think he might be the guy I've been waiting for."

"What does that mean? 'The guy you've been waiting for'? What about Tom?" Elinor pulls her hands away. It feels odd asking about her brother-in-law, a recent Tea Party convert who she can barely stand to talk to. Still, twenty-three years of marriage is a long time. "Maren, are you having an affair?" She stops, aware that the moony smile on her sister's face, the one she assumed was just drunkenness, is getting bigger and bigger. She turns to see a dark-haired, barrel-chested man elbowing his way through the crowd toward their booth.

"Hi, there," he says to Maren.

The two of them attempt to greet each other, first with a chaste kiss on the cheek and then a straight-armed hug that almost turns into a real one. It looks like they discussed how they should behave toward each other in front of Elinor, but they've having a hard time remembering.

"Gary, this is my little sister."

He holds a large hand out in front of her. Elinor shakes it, feeling quarter-sized calluses pressing into her palm.

"You want to sit?" Maren moves over, patting the space beside her. Gary slides in, their bodies now touching from shoulder to leg.

"Nice to finally meet you," Gary says. "Your sister was real excited about you being in town."

Real excited about you being in town. Gary doesn't have an accent, but there's something different about his choice of words, the way he puts them all together.

"You're not from around here, are you?" she asks.

"No, I'm originally from Tulsa."

"But he was an army brat," Maren adds. "He's lived all over the world, just like Dad did when he was young. Tell her, Gary. Tell her some of the places you've lived."

As Gary rattles off a list of bases, Elinor watches her sister abandon all pretense of platonic friendship and snake her arm through his, the same way she did during their walk from the hotel. It's clearly the early stage of whatever this is, when neither of them can stop touching the other. They giggle and squeeze and smile and stroke as question after question racks up in Elinor's head. Who is this guy? How long has this been going on? Does he know that she's married? That she has kids? How much damage have they already done?

"So . . ." Elinor pauses, trying to decide what she can get away with asking. "How did the two of you meet?"

Gary strokes the stubble on his chin and laughs, revealing perfectly straight yellow teeth. "In Walmart, actually. It was my first week in Avery, and I had to grab a couple of things to make my RV a little more inhabitable. I was just walking around the store when I saw your sister here." He looks at Maren and takes her hand. "She was so gorgeous, I followed her around the aisles for nearly an hour, trying to work up the nerve to say something to her."

The two of them seem to think this is funny, but Elinor isn't amused. This man just described stalking her sister in a Walmart. She takes a hard look at Gary, whom she already dislikes. He's too tan, too muscular, too much of a peacock. His biceps bulge out of the sleeves of his T-shirt, a black one that he probably chose because it's tight. He's also wearing a black leather cuff studded with silver around his left wrist. When he turns away, she notices that the skin around his eyes is lighter than the rest of his face, like he's been wearing goggles. And there's a one-inch strip of skin directly below his hairline that's also lighter, right where a helmet might cut off. He's a biker, she thinks. Her sister is having an affair with a meathead biker. As soon as the thought crosses her mind, she realizes this is exactly the behavior that Maren pointed out earlier. And yet she's still not sorry. Her judgment has probably saved her from more bad situations than she can count.

"Maren said you used to be a model in New York. That must have been pretty exciting."

She wishes her sister wouldn't tell strangers this, but of course Gary and Maren aren't strangers. "Mostly I just did catalog work."

"You mean those big phone books they used to send in the mail?"

She nods. "And then some Internet stuff, when the catalogs went away."

His eyes sweep the length of her arms. "I never saw women with ink like that in any Sears catalog."

"These came after," she says, turning at the sound of a bell clanging behind her.

Their attentions shift to a trio of guys standing at the bar. They're all shouting "Chug! Chug!" at a young roughneck who's wearing a lime green T-shirt that says IT'S MY BIRTHDAY. It must be his twenty-first because he barely looks legal with his cherub cheeks and constellation of pimples mapped across his face. He appears to be spilling more beer than he's actually swallowing, but the crowd doesn't seem to mind. When he brings his empty mug down on the bar like a gavel, everyone erupts. Gary laughs and gives him a hand.

"Kids," he says.

Yes, they're kids, Elinor thinks. And the three of us are adults with adult responsibilities.

When the applause dies down, Gary makes a big show of looking at Maren, then Elinor, then Maren again. "You know, I don't think I would have been able to tell who's older or younger if you hadn't said something. You're like twenty-five-year-old twins."

"El's always been prettier," Maren says.

"Bullshit. You're the prettiest woman in town."

He gives her a kiss on the neck and gooses her lower back, which causes Maren to jump. Elinor shoots the rest of her second drink, setting the empty glass on the table harder than she means to. Gary points at it with the gun of his thumb and forefinger. Then he scans the crowd for a server. "Let me get you another."

"You have to order from the bar," she says, hoping to get rid of him for a while. "That's what the waitress told us."

He knocks on the table with his giant knuckles. "No problem. I'll be right back. Don't you two go anywhere."

This strikes her as a particularly dumb thing to say. As he gets up to leave, she notices the back pockets of his jeans, which have eagles wildly embroidered on them with shiny gold thread. The sight of his idiotic party jeans makes her irrationally angry. Her sister has lived a sheltered life. She doesn't understand what's so painfully obvious to Elinor. Gary isn't a guy worth waiting for. He's just a roughneck on the make.

Maren catches her rolling her eyes. "You're not even trying."

"But you have a husband. You have *kids*."

"You don't need to remind me," she snaps. "I know what I have."

"Then why are you doing this?"

"Because he makes me happy, okay? As my sister, you should be happy for me—"

"But—"

"No. No buts, El. I really like Gary. He likes me, and he's fun. You know how long it's been since I've had even a little bit of fun? Am I not allowed to have that in my life?"

Elinor picks up her empty glass and rolls it back and forth, warming it between her hands. By virtue of being the oldest, by virtue of being the one who stayed, Maren had to be the responsible one. She never got the chance to be young and stupid and make foolish mistakes. The part of Elinor that still feels guilty about this wants Maren to be happy, to have her share of fun like everyone else, but the thought of what she's doing to her children is intolerable. What if she leaves them like they were left? For most of her life, Elinor has carried around two equally plausible stories about their mother. One is that Nami ran off because she met someone, a man she loved. The other is that she ran off because of Ed, a man she didn't. Elinor always assumed that if Nami met someone, he was a good and deserving person who promised her a better life than the one she had. But what if he was just some guy? What if she left them for just another goddamn Gary?

"Was I your excuse to get out of the house today?" she asks.

Maren looks at her over the rim of her glass. "I wanted to see you."

"But you also wanted to see him, right? That's why you're dressed like that, why you decided to put makeup on before you left. You arranged to meet him here after we had some time to ourselves, didn't you?"

If Maren is planning to respond to this, she doesn't get the chance. Gary returns to the table, shaking his head. "The line's three deep just to get a drink and there's only one bartender working. How about we take off and meet up with my friends downtown?"

Elinor begins to collect her things, grateful for the excuse to part ways. "Thanks, but I have an interview to prep for tomorrow. I should probably head back to my hotel now."

"No, not yet," Maren pleads. "Come with us. We've barely spent two hours together." She turns to Gary for help.

Of all the irritating things to happen tonight, it's the turn that frustrates her the most. What does Maren expect Gary to do? Why should this stranger be the one to convince her? They used to be everything to each other once, and now Elinor just feels like an excuse to get out of the house.

"You can take a night off to spend time with your sister, can't you? You're not here for long. Plus the Depot's the big place to be in town. You shouldn't leave without having at least one drink there."

She's about to ask him to repeat the name of the bar, but she knows that she heard him correctly. She just doesn't believe it. The Depot is where Leanne Lowell used to work.

"Alright," she says. "One drink then." She glances at Maren, who's beaming now, unaware that this change of heart has nothing to do with Gary. It doesn't even have anything to do with her.

23

They arrive at the Depot to find Gary's friends, Aaron and Fat Mike, waiting in line outside the squat brick building. Fat Mike's sister, Dani, is standing behind them, looking pissed off and put out. The line apparently hasn't moved since they joined it twenty minutes earlier, and all of them are getting impatient. Elinor knows what to do, but she isn't sure that she wants to do it, not until Aaron starts rattling off a list of nearby bars where they wouldn't have to wait. She didn't tag along to spend time just anywhere, or even to keep an eye on her sister. She came to see the Depot.

"Stay here," she tells them, grabbing Maren by the hand and leading her toward the front of the line.

"What are you doing? We can't just cut like this."

"Yes, we can."

The only people in line are men, who react exactly the way she expects them to when they walk past. The bouncer turns to see what all the commotion is about. As Elinor and Maren approach, he examines them from top to bottom, then unhooks the rope and waves them in with a gallant sweep of his arm.

"Wait," Maren says. "What about our friends?"

"How many friends?" he asks.

"Three guys and another girl, so three and three." Elinor points at the rest of their group, hovering near the end of the line.

The bouncer scans the crowd until he spots Gary, Fat Mike, Aaron, and Dani. All of them have one foot in line and another foot on the sidewalk, leaning out to watch what happens. "The one in red's a girl?" he asks, smiling.

Dani and her brother share the same floppy ginger curls and wide, heavyset build. She's big, but obviously a woman.

"It's three and three. If you don't want to let us in, we can go somewhere else."

The bouncer looks at Elinor for a moment. It's not quite a glare. But it's definitely not friendly. "Be nice," he tells her. "Like your friend here."

Maren has barely said a word, which she understands is the point. Elinor feels a current of anger travel through her body, white-hot as it reaches some nerve that she didn't know she had. She wishes she was taller and bigger and stronger. She wishes she were a man so she could get up in his face, the same way the guy in the computer room did to Brian. If she were a man though, there wouldn't be any need to. Men don't tell other men to be nice. This is something they reserve only for women. Elinor wonders if Leanne hired this bouncer, if he treated her like his boss or he treated her like this. As soon as she remembers what she came here for, the heat begins to subside. She wants and needs to go in.

"What makes you think I'm not nice?" she asks.

Her response seems to amuse him, so he waves Gary and the others over. The guys in line break out into jeers when they realize they're being passed by. Gary looks elated as he walks toward the roped-off area, clearly relishing his minor VIP moment, which makes Elinor think even less of him than she did before.

"That was amazing," he says to Maren, giving her a kiss full on the mouth.

"It wasn't my idea, it was my sister's. How did you know that would work?"

Because it always worked in New York, although Elinor thought she'd put those days long behind her. She worries that Maren thinks they just did a good thing. *We're nothing but bait*, she wants to explain.

Instead, she pretends not to hear the question as she walks into the dark bar, holding her hands out in front of her to feel for walls and corners. She takes baby steps behind Fat Mike, waiting for her eyes to adjust to the low light.

"I fucking knew it," he shouts over the music. "It's not even that busy. They just keep that line going so people think there's something worth seeing in here."

Elinor blinks the place into focus. She suspects he might be right. The Depot is barely half-full, awash in the smell of beer, sweat, and aftershave. It's actually more of a club than a bar. Dueling purple strobes circle the ceiling as a live band plays a Metallica cover, long hair and heads flailing despite the small, scattered audience. A pair of women stand in the middle of the empty dance floor, drinks in hand as they shout and laugh at each other. Like Maren, they look like they made an effort to dress up for a night on the town. The skinny one in the black camisole and jeans teeters perilously in stiletto heels, while her friend sways back and forth in a miniskirt and fringed crop top. Surrounding them like the outer rings of a bull's-eye are dozens of men drinking beer, all of whom keep sneaking glances at the pair and mumbling to each other like seventh-grade boys at their first school dance.

"Let's grab that big table over there," Gary says, leading Maren away.

Elinor ends up sitting next to Dani, whose mood improves considerably once she has a drink in her hand. When she learns that Elinor is writing an article about Avery, she becomes even chattier, eager to share how much she knows about the town. It's impressive actually, the volume of history she has stored up in her head. The year the high school was built. The number of farms foreclosed on in the eighties. Dani is a lifer, born to a family of lifers, which makes her a good person to know.

"So what do you think of the Depot?" she shouts. "Isn't it great?"

"I like it. It's different," she says, aware that Dani wants to hear something positive. "I've only been out twice since I got here, and the first place was terrible."

"What was it called?"

"Swift's. It's a sports bar near my hotel."

"Oh, I know it. I drive by there all the time. You meet the owner, the big guy? Kind of looks like a grizzly bear?"

Elinor nods, trying not to let her expression sour at the mention of Mitch. Locals know other locals. She already described his bar as terrible. She's not about to say what she thinks of him only to find out they're cousins. "Is he a friend of yours?"

"My brother used to play football with him in high school. State champions, ninety-four. Go, Steers." She makes a set of horns with her index finger and pinky. "Mitch got a full ride to college after that season. Probably could have gone pro if they hadn't kicked him out."

"Kicked him out for what?"

Dani lifts and lowers her eyebrows. "Eh. Some nastiness involving a girl. You know. Frat party thing. I think her dad, or maybe her uncle, was some big-time lawyer in Billings who got Mitch expelled, so he ended up back here."

Frat party thing. It's strange, how quickly Elinor can fill in the blanks just based on those three words. Although she doesn't remember the specifics of her conversation with Mitch anymore, she remembers the general sentiment. He didn't need any drunk girls hanging around, causing trouble. At least she knows she wasn't imagining his unfriendliness now.

"This club used to be an appliance store," Dani continues. "It went out of business when I was in junior high and sat empty for like fifteen years. Now it's the biggest meat market in town."

"Did you know the woman who used to manage this place? The one who went missing a few years ago?"

She shakes her head. "Read about her in the papers. But knew her, no."

Elinor glances across the table at Maren, who's listening to Gary, Aaron, and Fat Mike complain about a coworker they all know and clearly don't like. Their conversation, which she can't hear well from her end, is liberally sprinkled with words like "cocksucker" and "faggot." Elinor watches her sister for a reaction. A frown, a raised eyebrow, a subtle crossing or uncrossing of the legs—something to indicate that she's bothered by this language and understands that it's wrong. But Maren just sits there, sipping her rum and Coke through a straw, looking as happy as Elinor has ever seen her. Occasionally, Gary leans over her and shouts at his friends, resting his hand on Maren's leg like she's an extension of the table. Now Elinor is the one who's drinking too fast. Her double whiskey, which she'd intended to be her last for the night, is already down to one slender finger.

"Has your brother known Gary long?" she asks.

"They started hanging out a couple months ago. I guess they're on the same crew now."

"You think he's a good guy?"

Dani shakes a piece of ice out of her glass and chews on it. "He's got a real dickish sense of humor—sorry—but so do most guys, I guess."

It's unusual to hear a complete stranger offer her opinion so freely. Elinor is accustomed to people constantly talking around things here, speaking in careful euphemisms or whispering unflattering opinions, but only among themselves. She returns her attentions to the dance floor, which has the quality of a fishbowl. Lots of watching, but very little interaction. A group of men near their table grumble about the cost of Miller Lites at $6 a pop. They seem tired and agitated, and Elinor thinks she understands why. It's a meat market, with hardly any meat. Aside from the two women on the dance floor, she can only make out eight others in the entire club, plus the two working behind the bar. Most of the female customers are with their boyfriends, signified by a proprietary arm draped around a shoulder or waist. She tries to imagine Leanne here. Pretty, blond, petite. Bait.

"I would have expected more guys to be hitting on them," Elinor says, motioning toward the two women dancing.

"It's probably because they're out in the open like that," Dani says through a mouthful of ice. "Takes balls to risk getting turned down with a bunch of people watching. Plus, it's early still, so everyone's probably just holding out to see who else walks through the door. Those two aren't even cute, not that it really matters with the Avery scale."

"What's that?"

"The Avery scale? I guess it's kind of like beer goggles." She frowns, seemingly dissatisfied with her explanation. "Actually, that's not right." Dani scans the dance floor, pausing until she lands on something that she wants Elinor to see. "Okay, watch. Over there. The blond guy getting ready to make a move."

There are at least ten blond guys near the dance floor. It takes a moment to figure out that she means the tall one with wavy, sun-streaked hair, the one who resembles a surfer.

"He's pretty good-looking, right?" Dani asks. "Probably a seven?"

He's tan, muscular, and tattooed. Elinor might say an eight, but she agrees that he's at least a seven.

"And that girl he's about to sidle up to . . . she's like, what? A four?"

It's harder to assign the woman a number than the man. It seems cruel. Elinor takes a drink to avoid having to answer.

"Maybe she's a three," Dani second-guesses. "So keep watching."

The blond ambles toward the women, occasionally looking back at his friends with a playful grin. He zeroes in on the one in the miniskirt and starts dancing behind her, moving way too close, too fast. The woman snaps her head back to see who's rubbing up against her. He gives her a big smile and a shrug of his shoulders as if to say *Can't blame me for trying.* She shouts something at him that Elinor can't hear, but the shape of the word, at least from a distance, looks like "asshole." Then she shouts something at her friend with an exaggerated roll of her eyes as the blond returns to his buddies, earning howls of laughter and a few good-natured thumps on the back.

"See what just happened there?" Dani asks. "A three acting like a ten, and a seven getting shot down like he's a three. That's what I mean by the Avery scale. Everything's all out of whack here."

Elinor no longer wants anything to do with systems that class and categorize people by their appearance. That was all her life used to be.

Every week, she went to go-sees and stood in front of casting directors, allowing them to examine her and order her around. *Walk for us. Pull your hair back. Look over here at the light.* Sometimes, they'd make small talk while they flipped through her portfolio. Most of the time, they'd just study her face or breasts or legs, silent with displeasure until they dismissed her and called the next girl in. The prospect of landing work always used to excite Elinor. The more go-sees her agent sent her on, the better. She can't remember when the thrill of being looked at turned into something she couldn't bear. She only knows that it did.

"It doesn't bother you?" she asks. "Turning women into numbers like that?"

"Hey, it's not like I invented the system. And I've been on the losing end of it my entire life. I'd be a two anywhere other than Avery."

Her instinct is to protest, but Dani just shakes her head. "Relax. I'm not fishing for compliments or anything. I know why you grabbed your sister instead of me when you went to talk to the bouncer. That's kind of the point. I may be a two where you're from, but here, I'm a ten. That girl and her friend with the beak? Both tens. We can have our pick of men in this town because there's so few of us to go around. And you and your sister." Dani laughs. "Don't get me started. You're like thirties here. You can see why Gary keeps pawing at her like that. He wants everyone to know that she's taken and they should all just move the fuck on."

Elinor doesn't want to look over at Maren. She's seen enough. She finishes off the rest of her drink, wishing she had another before she even sets the glass down.

"Hey, how about you and me try to score a free round up at the bar? I don't have a chance of getting laid if I just sit here all night." Dani motions toward Aaron and her brother. "We look like we're here with our boyfriends."

Dani's frankness continues to surprise and maybe even charm her a little. She's not sure if she's ever met someone so forthright, so comfortable with who she is and how things are. Elinor wants to talk to the bartenders and ask if either of them knew Leanne, so she follows Dani to the bar. Two men immediately offer them their seats, which they accept. When Elinor sits down and glances at the long mirror hanging behind the rows of liquor bottles, she sees the men in reflection, their faces shiny with sweat. The smell of chemicals steams off their bodies—gasoline and oil and something almost sulfurous. They hover close by as if they hope to start a conversation in exchange for being chivalrous. Neither she nor Dani pay them any mind.

Within minutes, the black-haired bartender slides another double whiskey and vodka soda their way, explaining that the guys on the end bought their round.

Dani turns to see who she's talking about. "Eights," she mutters under her breath. "Hell, yes."

The men in the Depot are starting to look alike to Elinor. They all have the same farmer's tans that cut off midbicep. They all need haircuts and a good night's sleep. They all reek of loneliness and horniness and desperation, a desire to be the guy who gets the girl.

"Which one do you want?" Dani asks.

Elinor doesn't look over before responding: "Neither."

"You sure?"

"Positive."

"Okay, then. Suit yourself."

She edges away from the bar with her drink. Elinor watches as the crowd of men splits open, forming an aisle that Dani glides across like a queen.

24

The attempts to strike up conversation multiply once she's alone. Men of all profiles—young and old; handsome and grizzled; drunk and sober; Black, white, and brown—take their best shot at her, using every imaginable line. If she wanted to, she could get blackout drunk with all the offers to buy her next round. One man asks for Elinor's hand in marriage, hissing his proposal wetly into her ear. Another man smiles a dazzling gold mouthful of caps at her and says—loud enough to turn heads—that he'll make her scream when she comes. Feigning deafness and disinterest works on most men, but not this one. The dark-haired bartender points an angry finger at him and threatens to get the bouncer involved if he keeps it up.

"Christ. Relax." He peels a fifty off a roll of bills and flicks it at her like a playing card. As he turns to leave, he stumbles into a man who's been waiting to order and tells him not to bother talking to the Chinese girl at the bar. "Bitch doesn't speak English," he shouts.

The bartender picks up the fifty from the floor and examines it under the light. Then she turns toward Elinor, her kohl-lined eyes tired and red. "His money's real, at least." Without asking or offering, she pours her another whiskey. "You deserve that. The dogs are really out tonight."

Elinor stares at the full drink next to her now empty one. She no longer remembers which number she's on. She wishes the bartender would stay in one place for a while so they can talk, but there are too many customers to serve and the other woman covering the far end of the bar isn't being much help. She seems more interested in flirting than taking orders.

"What are you drinking?" the man standing behind her asks.

"I'm all set, thanks."

"Actually, I wasn't offering to buy you a drink. I just wanted to know what you're drinking."

"Oh, sorry . . . It's just whiskey."

The man waits a beat. "I'm guessing you don't drink beer?"

She shakes her head.

"You're probably one of those girls who doesn't like beer because it really packs on the pounds, right?"

Elinor glances at him over her shoulder. He grins at her innocently.

"So how old are you?" he asks, still grinning.

"Why do you want to know?" She regrets following up with a question. She realizes this is exactly what he wanted her to do.

"Because you seem older than some of the other girls in here. Don't get me wrong—I'm not saying you look bad." He brushes something she can't see off her shoulder, nicking the side of her neck as he does it. "Just, you know, older."

"Excuse you—" She jerks her head back, annoyed now. The stupid questions were one thing; the touching, another. She also recognizes the game he's playing, a technique made famous on a television show—some sad reality series designed to help awkward men approach women. The bartender must recognize it too because suddenly she's shouting at him.

"Get the hell out of here with that bullshit."

The man looks around as if he doesn't know who she's talking to.

"Yes, *you*, dickbag. Move on."

He shrugs and walks away with a wink.

"That's twice now you've saved me," Elinor says.

"That fucking guy. You know he was negging you on purpose, right?"

Elinor nods. For a brief period in her thirties, she remembers men coming up to her in bars, gently insulting her because the show said women would be more responsive, more inclined to welcome a man's advances if they were trying to gain his approval. She's embarrassed by the number of times she fell for it before finally catching on.

"That piece of shit thinks making girls insecure is the big secret to getting laid," the bartender says, still visibly annoyed. "I don't know if it ever works for him, but it pisses me off whenever I see him try."

"Has he ever tried it on you?"

"Yeah, right. He wouldn't dare." She laughs as she slaps a pack of Camel Lights against her palm and removes the plastic wrapper. "Sam!" she shouts at the other bartender, waving her cigarettes in the air. "Time for you to get to work, girl."

Elinor doesn't understand what kind of armor the bartender has that she doesn't. They're both about the same age. They're both attractive, tattooed, and dressed somewhat forbiddingly in black. What made that man think one would be susceptible to his tricks, but not the other? She watches the bartender slip out through the side door. Elinor considers following her, but wonders if she should tell someone first. She looks around and spots Dani at the other end of the bar, holding court with three guys who occasionally erupt with laughter. Maren, meanwhile, is off in her own world, making out with Gary right at the table. The way they're going at it reminds her of high school kids, groping each other in public because they have nowhere else to go, or because their hormones have simply taken over, replacing whatever good sense they started out with. She decides no one will miss her if she steps out for a smoke, so she stands up and shoots the rest of her whiskey, unwilling to leave her drink unattended. A swell of nausea rises up from the back of her throat and lingers dangerously. She remains very still, fingertips pressed against the edge of the bar until the sensation slowly passes.

By the time Elinor wades through the crowd and goes outside, the bartender is talking on her phone, several feet away from the door. There's no approaching her now, but it's a relief to breathe in the cool night air, free from the smell of beer and bodies. The exit opens onto a narrow one-way filled with small storefronts, perpendicular to Main. The sidewalks are teeming with people who look ready for a night out. Cars slowly cruise past, windows down, music blaring, a mix of country and metal and classic rock. From the safety of their vehicles, men whistle and shout at the handful of women on the street. They shout at men too, calling them "motherfucker" and "asshole" for reasons that Elinor can't understand. Occasionally, a police cruiser passes, the officer inside keeping a watchful eye. It's not even after midnight, and yet the crowd's energy seems ready to combust.

Elinor leans against the side of the building. She feels protected by the dark, which makes it easier to brush off strangers' beery hellos and attempts to smoke alongside her. Her thoughts cycle through Maren, Gary, Nami, Ed, Richard, Lydia, Dani, and Leanne. But all the alcohol in her system has the semipleasant effect of not allowing her to focus on any one person for too long. She finishes an entire cigarette before she even remembers to check for a voice mail or text from Richard, neither of which she has. Strange how only a few hours ago, hearing from him was the thing that worried her most.

"So, you've finally had enough of that shitshow?" the bartender asks, slipping her phone into her pocket as she walks over.

"I just needed some air."

The bartender introduces herself as Michelle. She lights a cigarette from the still-lit butt she's been smoking and leans against the building beside her.

"Is it always like that in there?" Elinor asks.

"Always."

Michelle has sleeves of tattoos on both arms. The rings of a tree on the left, the entire tree on the right, the branches twisting and gnarling around her bicep and forearm. It's good, detailed work that required a lot of hours in somebody's chair. Michelle is examining her arms appreciatively in return. Neither of them comments on the other's tattoos.

"I haven't seen you around before. How'd you find us?"

"A friend of my sister's convinced me to come." She hesitates to call Gary that, but it's better than the alternatives. "He said the Depot's the big place to be in Avery."

Michelle snorts. "God. That might be the saddest thing I've heard all night." She exhales a huge white plume of smoke over her head. The cigarette she just lit is nearly half-gone already. Only one of her inhalations seems to equal a regular person's three. At this rate, she'll be back behind the bar before Elinor even gets around to the question she came out here to ask.

"Did you, by any chance, work with Leanne Lowell when she managed this place?"

If the question seems odd or abrupt, Michelle doesn't register it. "She'd been missing a couple of weeks when I moved here. Kind of a weird time to be arriving with all the volunteers out looking for her."

"And the other woman working tonight?"

"Sam? She's even newer than I am."

They both take another drag of their cigarettes. Elinor takes two in quick succession, her desire to continue the conversation doing battle with the sick, swampy feeling in her stomach. She regrets coming to the Depot and having so little to show for it. She regrets how much she drank just to get to this point. Her temples are pulsing and everything is starting to look blurry to her, like she's watching the passing traffic through badly smudged glasses.

"Why did you want to know if I worked with her?" Michelle asks.

"I'm a writer." Now that she's drunk, it feels less awkward saying so. "I just think it's an interesting story, that's all."

"You in town for a while?"

Elinor mentally counts backward, startled by how much time has already passed. "Six more days."

A tall, skinny white guy runs past them at full speed. They watch him turn the corner, followed by a half-dozen others.

"You want some advice on how to deal with all these idiots who keep coming on to you?"

It's not the lead she was hoping for, but under the circumstances, Elinor is curious to hear what a woman who works in a bar has to say. "Sure."

Michelle puts out her cigarette under the heel of her boot. "Get yourself a ring. Not a real one or anything. Just a shiny fake, like the kind you can buy at Goodwill for a dollar. Guys are way less likely to hit on you if they think you're married." She pauses. "Well, not all guys, obviously, but more than you might expect. At least half of them are probably married themselves. And if you don't want to go to all that trouble, just pick someone across the room, someone who looks a little juiced up and crazy, like he'd be ready to throw down over nothing. Then when these jerks come up to you, you can point him out and say you're waiting for your boyfriend. Word'll get around. Trust me."

This is sad advice, using imaginary husbands and boyfriends to scare off real men who won't take no for an answer. But she understands that Michelle shared it in the spirit of being helpful. Elinor manages a nod of thanks as she glances at her hand.

"You're not wearing a ring though."

"Most of the regulars around here know I'm only into girls. Like I said, word gets around." She turns at the sound of a glass or bottle breaking nearby. "Actually, my ex—the one I moved here with—she used to work with Shane Lester before he skipped town. Kind of a strange guy, she said. Really quiet."

Elinor feels like she's on a boat, bobbing gently in the water. It's soothing, until she realizes that the motion is coming from her. She's nodding her head over and over again, a sign that she's far beyond her limits. Still, something tells her to keep it together, to pull herself back into the conversation before she misses the thread.

"Who's Shane Lester?"

"Leanne Lowell's husband." Michelle glances at her, startling slightly. "Hey, are you alright? Your eyes—"

The skinny guy runs past them in the opposite direction. The shirt he was wearing only a minute ago is in tatters, the torn hem fluttering like sails.

"You mean Shane Fost—"

Before she can finish, the guy stumbles over something and falls face-first into the street. By the time he gets to his feet, the men who were giving chase catch up and form a loose circle around him. Another bottle breaks and the skinny one starts throwing punches, his long arms spinning like propellers. It's useless. He's no match for any of them. It takes only a few seconds before someone lands a hard right to his chin and he's on the ground again. The men quickly close in, kicking him as he curls up into a ball. Passersby cut a wide berth around the huddle, ignoring the pleas for help coming from the center. Others stand back and watch from a safe distance. Elinor can't help but watch too.

"Come on. Let's get you inside." Michelle pushes her toward the door.

"Shouldn't we do something!"

"About that fight?"

"There's so many of them."

"Men fight," Michelle says, pushing her again.

25

Elinor rereads her note, which she wrote more illegibly than usual. ONE OF THE I-STATES. (INDIANA?) She inserts the words "Shane Foster moved to" at the start of the sentence in the event she can't remember what Michelle told her in the morning. Then she tucks her notebook back into her bag, fumbling with the zipper as she pulls it closed. It's not a particularly good lead, but it's better than the nothing she thought she had.

When they first returned to the bar, Michelle gave her a glass of lukewarm water and told her to drink it slowly. She even watched Elinor take her first few sips before moving on to other customers. The glass is empty now; the water sloshing around in her stomach along with some fries and not much else. Elinor inhales and exhales, inhales and exhales, trying to steady her heart, which is beating too fast. Everything she drank earlier this evening is hitting her all at once. She's grateful for the empty stool that Michelle deposited her on at the dark end of the bar. It's a good place to not be bothered while the room continues to spin and blur and pulse. From her seat, she can see Maren and Gary, who are still making out at their table. It doesn't seem like Maren even noticed that she was gone. Dani is making out with someone too. One of the roughnecks she was entertaining earlier. And Fat Mike and Aaron have moved to the dance floor, hovering along the periphery along with everyone else.

Michelle returns briefly to refill her empty glass. "Slow," she warns, before heading back to the register. "I'm not kidding. Drink it slow."

Just as Dani predicted, more women arrive at the Depot. As soon as they get their drinks, they take to the dance floor in small groups, shouting at each other over the music. The cover band is gone now, replaced by the sounds of autotuned dance hits blasting through the speakers overhead. Despite all the shouting, the women appear less interested in conversation than in simply being seen. There's an element of performance in the way they toss their hair back and laugh dramatically at things that can't possibly be that funny, all the while scanning the room to look at who's looking at them.

Elinor reminds herself that it's not a moral failing to enjoy being the center of attention. She used to behave like many of the women here tonight, casting about with the same flirty glances while wearing the same tight dresses and high, high heels. But when she imagines her younger self walking into a place like this, inviting everyone to take her in, she's flooded with panic at the thought of who else that affected, who it could have hurt. Maybe it's the whiskey clouding her brain, but being in Avery confuses her about how to be in the world. She thinks women should be able to do what they want, look how they want, be as sexual as they want. But is it really that simple? Doesn't Maren's behavior, and Dani's too, have an effect on how men treat other women? Isn't the relentlessness of the attention she receives here partly a by-product of what they're doing now? Of what Elinor herself did all those years ago?

The longer she thinks, the more the questions multiply, generating answers and explanations and exceptions and excuses until her head feels ready to split in two. Then something in her stomach begins to churn, threatening to come up. Elinor pushes her stool away from the bar, knocking it over with a metallic clang that pierces through the music. She catches a concerned glance from Michelle as she walks toward the back of the club, where she assumes the bathroom is. She prays that she's right, prays that it's free. Halfway there, and she hears someone calling her name. She turns, hoping to find Maren or even Dani, but sees only a group of newly arrived young women standing around a high-top table, scoping out the crowd. One of the women is staring directly at Elinor. It takes a moment to realize that it's Hannah—big, bosomy Hannah from the hotel—and she's smiling at her.

"Hiiiiiii," Hannah shouts, waving her plastic cup and spilling some of the slushy contents on the floor. She teeters toward her like an over-sized baby, all wobbly ankles and outstretched hands.

Hannah surprises Elinor with a hug, enveloping her in her soft, slightly damp flesh, which is heavily perfumed with something beachy smelling. When Hannah steps back, Elinor realizes why it was hard to recognize her at first. Gone is her conservative uniform from the Thrifty, the button-up shirt and tweedy blazer. Instead, she's dressed in an aqua top that shows off her considerable chest and white skinny jeans encrusted with crystals. Hannah is as loud and cheerful when she's drunk as she is when she's sober.

"You guyyyyyys, this is Elinor. She's a writer from New York. She's staying at the hotel."

Elinor feels flecks of spittle hitting her cheek every time she slurs out an *s*.

Hannah's friends look over with indifference. A few mumble "hey" but none of them bothers to introduce herself, not even when Hannah grabs Elinor by the arm and pulls her toward their table. Typically, she'd resist this, but it feels so good to have a place to lean.

"So what's going on?" Hannah asks. Her breath smells like cigarettes and strawberries. "I didn't expect to see you here tonight."

"I just thought I'd see how oil workers spend their free time."

It's a silly, perhaps even stupid impulse, but Elinor doesn't want Hannah to know how drunk she is, even though it's obvious that she's drunk too. No one has ever admired her writing career before. Most of her former business acquaintances were bewildered by her shift to journalism and weren't shy about saying so. Even Damon seemed du-bious for a while. The idea of someone like Elinor going to college, try-ing to reinvent herself as a writer but not even writing about fashion or makeup—the things she was supposedly an expert in—just didn't make sense to people. Their skepticism didn't particularly make her want to explain it.

"Is this where you and your friends usually hang out?" she asks, enunciating as carefully as she can.

Hannah tries to take a sip of her drink, but the straw keeps moving, hitting her in the face. Eventually, she pushes it off to the side and takes a big gulp. "We go to lots of places, don't we?" She lets out a loud whoop that no one returns. "We'll pretty much go anywhere that has a good ladies' night." She looks to her friends for confirmation, but they remain as unenthused as Hannah seems excitable.

"Are you liking it at the hotel? Is everything okay there?"

This isn't the time or place to bring up her noisy next-door neighbors. Elinor suspects there's nothing she could do about them anyway. "It's nice. Thanks for asking."

Two of Hannah's friends are staring at her from across the table. One of them says, "I don't know. Half-Japanese, maybe?"

Despite her impaired state, Elinor understands what they're doing. Trying to figure out what she is. Good luck, she thinks. For eighteen years, she lived in North Dakota, surrounded by white people who didn't think she was white. Then she moved to New York, where the Asians she met didn't accept her as Asian, disconnected as she was from that part of her identity. Apparently, she was just enough of both to qualify as neither. Still, Hannah's friends seem to agree on one thing: she's pretty, *too* pretty, which Elinor can hear them grumbling about behind their drinks. The longer she stands there, the harder and less welcoming their expressions become. It's obvious that they want her to move on, to not complicate the mathematics of their four-person hunting party. The feeling is mutual.

"Well, it was nice running into you again. Have a—"

"Oh, wait. Wait," Hannah shouts, waving at someone across the room. "My boyfriend just got here. I'd love for you to meet him."

A guy in a baseball cap saunters over to the table, trailed by three friends. The boyfriend is a full head shorter than Hannah, unshaven, and not as attractive as he seems to think he is. He's wearing his cap backward and his pants a few inches lower than his boxer shorts, which actually makes him look even shorter.

"Come here, Corey. I want to introduce you to Elinor. This is the lady I was telling you about, the writer from New York."

They nod hello at each other, their reserve a sharp contrast to Hannah's enthusiasm. Corey is wearing a large, ridiculous gold pendant that looks like the letter *C* at first glance. On closer inspection, it's actually the sign for cents.

"We're good to go," he mumbles to Hannah.

"Aren't you the best boyfriend in the world?" She plants a kiss on his stubbly cheek.

Corey is a scumbag. Of this, Elinor is certain. There's something about the way he has his arm draped over Hannah's shoulder, his fingertips grazing her breast in public, in front of everyone. And yet he's staring at Elinor, at the other girls at the table, sizing them all up to see if he has a shot with any of them. His friends are doing the same thing, whispering to each other, comparing notes and taking dibs.

"You dance?" one of Corey's friends asks.

Elinor shakes her head, unable to form the word *no* anymore, tired of constantly having to repeat it.

"I do," one of the whispering girls offers.

The friend examines her for a moment, and then extends his hand with a smile. One by one, the others pair off, leaving only Hannah, Corey, and Elinor at the table. He slides a small glassine envelope toward Hannah, who tucks it into her bra.

"You party?" Corey asks, discreetly flashing another envelope at Elinor.

"No, not anymore. Not like that."

Hannah finishes her drink, siphoning off the dregs through her straw. "We don't either usually. Just on special occasions."

"Oh? What's the occasion?"

"It's my first night out since the baby."

Elinor tries not to frown. "You have a baby?"

"Yup. She's four weeks old today. Her name's Corrine, like my great-aunt, but we call her Corey, like her daddy here."

Elinor can't help but glance at Hannah's chest. She assumed the tight shirts bursting at the seams were a fashion choice. Now she wonders if they're something else. "You're not . . ." she pauses, trying to ask the question delicately, but there's no good way to say it. "You're not doing whatever was in that little packet and breastfeeding, are you?"

Corey, whose attentions have drifted off to the dance floor, suddenly turns and glares at Elinor under hooded green eyes. But even his severe expression is eclipsed by Hannah's.

"I'm not dumb," she barks.

"I'm not suggesting—"

"You think I don't know how to take care of my baby?"

"I didn't—"

"We feed her formula, bitch."

Elinor hears herself saying "I" over and over again, trying to get a word in while Hannah hurls insults at her. She's snobby and stuck-up. She thinks anyone who's not from a big city is stupid. She looks down her nose at people who have to do real work for a living. When Hannah calls her a judgmental bitch, it all starts to feel too familiar, like she's having an argument with her sister instead of a stranger.

Hannah continues shouting as Elinor backs away from the table. Eventually, the only thing she can hear over the music is Corey, who chimes in with a "yeah, bitch" of his own. She turns and keeps walking in the same direction she was headed before, resisting the urge to run. At the back of the club, Elinor stumbles into the vacant ladies' room, chaining the door shut behind her. The windowless space smells like a laundry basket, thick with artificial perfume, which makes her feel sick to her stomach again. She braces her forearms on the ancient avocado-green sink, unwilling to put her face near the rust-ringed, piss-splattered toilet. At first, the nausea seems like another false alarm, just drunken dry heaves that will come and go after a few violent waves. But then her throat clenches, she tastes the rising bile, and she vomits a hot spray of liquid into the sink. She repeats this again and again, the force of the expulsions so strong, her back cracks each time she throws up.

When the waves finally pass, she spits into the basin, wiping away the tears that leaked out of her eyes as she clenched them tight. In the mirror, she sees wet strands of hair clinging to her cheeks and chin. The whites of her eyes are an unnatural, watery pink.

Never again, she tells herself, and this time she might actually mean it. *If I make it through this night in one piece, I will never do this again.*

She rests her aching head on her forearms, which are still braced against the sink. It's possible that she briefly falls asleep in this position, awakened by the sound of someone shaking the doorknob. Elinor lifts her eyes but not her head, noticing a small hole below the liquid soap, about the size of a dime—probably the first attempt to anchor the dispenser into the wall. In this awkward position, leaning low over the sink, she can look through the hole and see what's on the other side. Shadows. Movement. Something the color of skin. She squints, and the image slowly begins to sharpen. A woman's exposed breasts, flapping rhythmically back and forth. A man thrusting at her from behind. She leans in closer, blinking back tears as the image comes into focus. It's Dani, bent over the sink in the adjacent bathroom. Behind her, a roughneck is fucking her like a goddamn animal.

26

Morning, and a phone is ringing somewhere. It's been ringing on and off for a while. Elinor opens her eyes and finds herself sprawled out on her bed at the Thrifty, still dressed in the same clothes from the night before. The comforter is bunched up under her back, and all the pillows are on the floor. She reaches over, swatting at nearby objects—an alarm clock, a plastic cup of water, a small bottle of pills that sounds like a rattle when it rolls off the nightstand. Finally, she feels a familiar shape in her hand.

"Hello?" she answers. Her voice is raspy, her throat full of phlegm.

"We're here, waiting," a woman says. "Are we still meeting today?"

She sits upright, her head so heavy with pain, gravity immediately wills it back onto the bed. There's a sharpness in the woman's voice, an irritable spike as she hits each syllable of the word *waiting*. Elinor senses that she's done something wrong, or not done something that she was supposed to. She looks at the ice bucket on the floor, strategically positioned at arm's length in case she felt the urge to throw up in the middle of the night. She peers inside, relieved to find it empty.

"I'm sorry," she says, still not certain to whom she's speaking. "I'm having . . . car problems. Would it be possible to reschedule?"

The voice on the other end of the line is silent. Elinor slides out of bed and rifles through the notes on her desk. Her eyes are slow to make sense of all the letters and words. What time is it now? Who was she supposed to meet today?

"You know, you really should have called me," the woman says. "We've been sitting here for twenty-five minutes wondering if you just decided not to show up."

She finds her schedule in the stack of papers and follows her fingertip down to today's date. Randy Hudson, North Fork Reservation Tribal Offices, 9:30 a.m. Assistant: Shawnalee.

"Yes, I know. I'm so sorry . . . Shawnalee." She assumes this is the name of the person to whom she's speaking. She hears nothing to correct this notion. "My battery's dead. I was trying to get a jump for the longest time. Someone's working on it now. . . ." The excuses keep piling up, one after another. She must not be sober yet, otherwise she'd never be able to lie like this. "Is there any chance I could reschedule?"

"He'll be out of town for two weeks starting tomorrow."

In two weeks, Elinor will be long gone. She can't risk missing an interview that Richard set up for her, no matter how bad she feels. "Well, is there anything else available today?"

The woman is silent again. Finally, she sighs. "He could meet you at eleven. Can you make it here by then?"

"Yes," Elinor almost shouts, not certain if she actually can.

There's no time for a shower. The only nonessential activity she allows herself is a quick check of her phone. Aside from Shawnalee, she hasn't received any other calls this morning. No texts or emails either. Not from Richard. Not even from Maren.

In the bathroom, she slaps cold water on her face and brushes her teeth. Then she attempts to put on makeup, but her hands are shaking and everything she applies is either too thick or too thin. The skin under her eyes looks raccoon-like. The rest of her face has a green, almost ghoulish tint to it that makeup can't hide. She leans toward the mirror and exhales, fogging up the glass. Her breath is still completely saturated with the smell of alcohol. How did she let this happen? How did she even get back to her hotel last night? The thought of Gary helping her, possibly even carrying her, into bed while Maren set out aspirin and water and a bucket to throw up in—she doesn't know if she'll ever recover from the shame. Elinor brushes her teeth again and scours her tongue raw with the brush, but it hardly helps. The amount of alcohol she had last night feels like it's changed her at the cellular level. The only thing she can do is alternate between gum and mints during the hour-long drive to the reservation.

The North Fork covers over a million acres of land. Along the main highway, most of it is flat and scrubby; and when towns do appear, they come and go quickly. A couple of buildings here, a couple of buildings there, sometimes a sign letting people know where they are. She's thankful that the road is relatively smooth. When she was younger, she remembers rutted, unpaved roads crisscrossing the reservation that churned gravel through the wheel wells. She couldn't stomach a loud or bumpy ride in her state. She can barely tolerate the sun shining in her eyes as she drives east toward Kittery, the administrative center of the Mahua Nation. The town was named after the man who negotiated a treaty with the tribe on the US government's behalf. Apparently, Louis Kittery was willing to establish a reservation here because he thought it was throwaway land that could never be farmed, something she read in the file but never learned in school. What's the bigger irony? she wonders. The fact that the largest town on the reservation is still named after someone who actively despised Native Americans, who wished them to die a slow, painful death of starvation? Or the fact that the shale, which was what made the land so difficult to farm, contains the richest concentrations of oil in the entire state?

The main tribal office is located in Kittery's town center, housed in a temporary trailer with a beige horizontal stripe hugging it like a ribbon. A few lots over, a complex of half a dozen new buildings is going up, the exterior walls all covered in bright white Tyvek. While one setup looks too modest, the other looks unusually extravagant. The architect's rendering on the construction sign features a mid-rise office building surrounded by single-story structures, all clad in matching gold brick—nicer than anything Elinor has ever seen on the reservation before. She wonders what would have happened if Richard hadn't set this meeting up, if she would have thought to interview someone from the Mahua tribe at all. She wants to believe that she would have come here on her own, but she can't be sure. For most of the time she lived in the area, she and her family treated the reservation like a thruway—a place to pass on their way somewhere else.

Elinor knocks twice on the flimsy trailer door and jumps back as it opens toward her. A thin-lipped young woman stands in the threshold, looking deeply annoyed. Elinor checks her watch—it's 11:07.

"Shawnalee?"

"Yes, come in."

She starts to apologize as she enters the trailer, but a man shouts "Welcome!" at her before she can finish her sentence. His voice is booming and almost musical; it sounds like someone is banging on a drum inside her head.

"Welcome, welcome, welcome, miss!"

Randy Hudson is at least six foot five and solidly built, with a craggy face framed by salt-and-pepper hair that he wears in a low braid. He buzzes with goodwill and a kind of energy for people that Elinor doesn't have, now or ever. When he leans in to shake her hand, she straightens her arm, trying to keep him at a distance. She doesn't want him to notice her breath, her bloodshot eyes, or the greenish tint of her skin.

"I'm so sorry about this morning—"

"Don't worry, don't you worry about that. Shawnalee, did you offer our guest here some coffee?"

Shawnalee is still standing beside the door, her glum demeanor the complete opposite of his. She doesn't bother to ask Elinor if she wants any coffee. She just turns toward the kitchenette and begins filling a hot pot from the water cooler.

As Elinor settles into the folding chair that Randy offers, she remembers that Richard's notes mentioned the importance of using the correct titles for tribal leaders. She asks how Randy would like to be addressed during the interview, whether it's "Mr. Chairman" or "Chairman Hudson" or something else.

"Oh, no, no." He sits down across from her at his desk, surrounded by stacks of moving boxes and dented filing cabinets. "I don't stand on ceremony. I'm just Randy. Plain old Randy. To you and everybody else around here." He leans back in his chair, crossing a long leg over his knee. "I have to admit—when Mr. Hall said he was sending over a student, I expected someone younger. You know, someone straight out of school."

"Technically I am straight out of school. I went to college late."

"Well, good for you. What made you want to study writing?"

"I just always liked it," she says, offering an incomplete truth, but also a tidy, self-contained answer that invites no further questions. She opens her bag and fumbles around inside, searching for her recorders and notebook. "So . . ." She looks up, realizing that Randy has been watching her, probably because she's taking too long to get situated. "Do you mind?" She motions toward her recorder.

"Not at all. Not at all."

Randy has a curious habit of repeating words when he speaks. As she goes through Richard's preliminary questions, she notices it more and more. It's never enough for him to just agree or say yes. He often doubles and triples up, as if the quality of his feelings and the quantity of his assurances are somehow related. Randy is at his most repetitive when he tells her about the new office building and service center complex, partially funded by the royalties and taxes that the tribe collects from wells located on the reservation. Two hundred wells and counting, he beams. Up from ninety-five just the year before.

"When construction's finished, people who live on this side of the reservation will have one centralized location for everything, absolutely everything! Social services, veteran's services, a health station . . . Imagine the convenience! You'll be able to pay a fine in one building, get your kidney dialysis in another, and then pick up your food package before you leave."

The life that Randy just described—in debt to the tribe, in need of dialysis, dependent on a monthly box of government peanut butter and shelf-stable milk—seems like a sad one, no matter how new or modern the buildings that house these services are. But perhaps he's just a realist. Randy is two years into his third elected term in office, voted in by a landslide each time. He knows his people. He knows how some of them have to live.

A few minutes into the conversation, Shawnalee returns from the kitchenette. "Here," she says, depositing a Styrofoam cup on the desk.

Elinor thanks her and takes a sip of the inky coffee, which is clearly instant. She can feel the grit of undissolved crystals on her tongue. The taste is unpleasant but the caffeine momentarily revives her. "And how would you like me to address you, miss?"

Randy seems taken aback by the question. "Oh, this is Shawnalee Turner Whitebush. She's my assistant, my jack-of-all trades. Jill-of-all trades, actually. She won't say much while you're here. She just keeps me organized so I always know where I'm going."

Shawnalee flicks her eyes up at the ceiling and quickly looks away. Elinor wonders if he's accurately describing her duties or obliquely telling his young assistant to keep quiet during the interview. Whatever annoyance she just saw, it's gone before she knows it. Randy continues talking about the boom, how it's transforming the reservation one family at a time. Even in her addled state, it doesn't take long to understand that the chairman of the Mahua Nation is pro-oil. It also takes only a brief sweep of his person to see that he's probably profited from it in some complicated way. He's wearing a two-tone gold watch that she's almost certain is a Rolex and an enormous ring on his right pinky with a square-cut diamond in the center, as large as the diamonds she sees on newly engaged women after bonus season on Wall Street. Within arm's reach, Randy has three newer model iPhones in different-colored cases. She imagines one is for personal, the other for tribal business, and the other, she's not sure what.

"The old office," he continues, "wasn't much bigger than three of these trailers put together, and it had black mold everywhere. Black mold! The stuff that gets in your lungs. And that's just what we had to live with because there wasn't any money to fix it, to really fix it the way it needed to be fixed. So every six months or so, a couple of volunteers would open all the windows and clean the walls with bleach, just so it wouldn't take over the place, but it always came back. That's why we moved out here to this trailer during construction. Usually, somebody from Indian Affairs would be like, 'Hell, no. There's not any budget for that.' But because of all the oil money we're bringing in, we don't have to settle, which is how we always lived before, settling for whatever we got, settling for 'good enough' or 'better than nothing' because that's all we had."

Elinor is taking notes as fast as she can, her hand cramping as she scribbles. She doesn't have the wherewithal to summarize or abbreviate like she usually does. Her brain simply can't process more than it already is. Instead, she writes with a slavish fidelity, which she realizes must look odd to Randy, or perhaps oddly complimentary. When she finishes taking down his last sentence, she notices that he's staring at her notebook, smiling.

"You want a tour of the new office building?" he asks. And then, without waiting for an answer, he turns to an unsmiling Shawnalee and says, "Come on. Let's give her the grand tour."

27

The hard hat she's wearing is too big for her. She has to hold it up with two fingers so it doesn't slide down over her eyes. Despite this, it's not her hat that she's most preoccupied by. It's Randy's. He has a bright orange one with the words THE CHAIRMAN printed on the front and back in oversize, boldface letters. It's an odd choice for someone who claims not to stand on ceremony.

With or without the personalized hat, everyone on the construction site seems to know him already. He slaps backs and shakes hands as he passes, asking guys about their girlfriends and what they did last weekend and whether they finally bought the truck they've had their eye on. He reminds her of Richard working the crowd at a party, but even more effortless, which she didn't think was possible. All activity comes to a halt as he nears, which is a relief. The noise level on the site is punishing. Her ill-fitting hard hat only serves to amplify it. She continues pushing up on the edge every few seconds until Shawnalee sighs and grabs the hat from her head. With two quick tugs of the plastic strap inside, she adjusts the fit and offers it back to her. She doesn't say "you're welcome" when Elinor tries to thank her.

At the tallest of the six buildings, the three of them climb aboard a large temporary construction elevator, operated by a young man who introduces himself as Denton Lemarie. He and Randy talk amiably as the platform rises, seemingly unbothered by the rickety metallic noises coming from the elevator's hydraulics or the thin walls separating them from certain death below. Elinor stands in the corner, making herself as small as possible. She tries not to watch as they climb, higher and higher, but she can't help herself. Her rental car, parked in the lot below, shrinks to the size of a postage stamp; the road she drove along thins to the width of a twig.

At one point, she glances over at Shawnalee, who seems as uncomfortable as she is. Worry lines punctuate her mouth and dimple the space between her eyebrows. Elinor wonders how old she is—twenty-five? Maybe thirty, at most? Too young for lines that deep. When their eyes meet, Elinor offers her a weak smile. Shawnalee quickly looks away and Elinor wonders what's wrong with her, what happened during her short lifetime that made her so hard. She wishes she could get her alone for a few minutes, without Randy and his likable but outsize personality taking up all the available oxygen.

The elevator stops on the eighth floor, and Denton—whom Randy is already referring to amiably as "Dent"—slides open the accordion doors and lets them off.

"You be sure to give me a call, okay?" Randy tucks his business card into the young man's shirt pocket.

"I will, thanks. You all be careful up here—it's windy today."

Randy steps off the platform, crossing a three-inch gap between the elevator and the building. Elinor closes her eyes and takes a deep breath as she follows.

"Any guesses how much that boy is making an hour?" he asks when she catches up.

She shakes her head, nauseous again.

"Twenty-six dollars."

"That's good, right?"

"A couple years ago, it'd be unheard of. Completely unheard of for a Mahua boy, not even twenty years old yet, making that kind of money. But he's reliable, from what I hear. That's why I told him to call me. He could do better than construction, better than twenty-six bucks an hour. Can you believe that?" He shakes his head, chuckling. "Unemployment on the reservation used to be around forty percent before the boom. Now there's more jobs than people, so it's the workers who have the advantage for once, not the other way around."

Elinor trails after Randy and Shawnalee as they walk near the edge of the roof. There's no barrier to keep them from falling off, not even a thin stretch of hazard tape. She wishes they'd move closer to the center, safe from the gusting wind. Randy, however, seems too excited to register any sense of danger. He keeps pointing at things as they pass. A huge battery of oil tanks, a half-dozen rigs, construction sites, a road-widening project. Farther off in the distance is Avery, which Elinor hasn't seen from this perspective before. It's an ugly sprawl of development, tallest in the center with two extensions on each side that resemble arms. It's not quite a mid-rise city yet, but it will be soon, which is shocking—the possibility that what used to be a small town might be an actual city one day, that oil did all of this.

"For once," Randy says with an air of satisfaction, "for once, my people aren't being left behind."

There are details that complicate the story he's telling. Everything she's read suggests that the problems people complain about in Avery are exponentially worse here. Violent crime on the reservation is up; meth and heroin arrests are up; domestic violence incidents, sexual assaults, overdoses—every indicator is up, probably because every indicator on the North Fork was up, long before the boom even began. Elinor wonders if the oil field jobs are really worth all the trouble they bring and whether the Mahua can even get the highest-paying ones, or if they simply have more access to the jobs that white men used to consider "good." Despite reports of companies offering lower royalties and signing bonuses for leases on the reservation, she suspects that Randy is too much of a cheerleader for oil to give her a straight answer. Still, she knows she has to try.

"Are there any downsides to all this development? Like the crime, maybe?"

He stops walking and looks over his shoulder at her, smiling. "You know much about policing on reservations, miss?"

"No," she admits. "Probably not as much as I should."

"Well, we have about a million acres of land on the North Fork and not enough tribal police to cover them all, never have. And because this is sovereign land, our police and your police are different. Outsiders commit crimes here, but our police can't touch them. So let's say a Mahua girl gets raped on the reservation by a white man, which we know happens from time to time. Because he's white, the tribal courts don't have any authority and the Feds tend not to prioritize the cases involving us. So sure, there's more crime because there's more people. That's just simple math. But the complicated math—the geometry, the calculus, whatever it is that you folks study—the complicated math is that the systems around here were broken long before the boom started. They've been broken pretty much since the days of Columbus."

Elinor nods, hoping her recorder caught all that despite the wind. She pushes the hair out of her face and continues following Randy and Shawnalee, mentally replaying the words "our police and your police" and "whatever it is that you that folks study." She doesn't feel any whiter than he is; she never has. But it's obvious that Randy doesn't think about her in terms of how they're similar. Only how they're different. She can't fault him for this, not when she's guilty of doing the same thing. All those years she lived in Marlow, she was either teasing the Mahua girls like her white classmates or looking right past them as if they didn't exist.

At the far edge of the building, he stops and raises his arms out in front of him. "It's beautiful, isn't it?"

The land is desertlike, as if it's been cleared of anything green or living. What's left is a devastated landscape, dotted with amber flares that stretch all the way from Kittery to the horizon. Elinor doesn't see any beauty here, but she's not Randy. She can't judge what looks like opportunity to him. She turns around in a circle, stopping when she notices a sprawling building with a slate-gray roof—bigger than any other building in the area except the one they're standing on.

"That's our casino," Randy says. "You want to head over there for some lunch? They've got the best buffet in the area."

It's just past noon, according to Elinor's watch. She doesn't know if she can hold down solid food right now, but she's only halfway through Richard's list of questions. Given what it took to get here, she might as well ask them all.

"If you have time, sure."

"But you have all those contracts to sign," Shawnalee says. "And then that conference call at two."

Randy waves her off. "Doesn't take more than a few minutes to sign contracts. Besides, if we're giving our visitor here the full tour, we can't skip the casino."

They return to the ground level of the building, passing the same commotion they walked through earlier. A trio of men call Randy over, so he excuses himself and leaves Elinor and Shawnalee in a corner, watching someone wield a metal sander that shoots sparks through the air.

"So . . ." Elinor says, but her voice is drowned out by someone else using a table saw. She starts again, almost shouting now. "How long have you been working with Randy?"

"Going on five years," Shawnalee shouts back.

"He seems to rely on you a lot."

Shawnalee says nothing. It's unclear if she even heard.

Randy's comment about incidents of rape on the reservation reminds her that Leanne was last seen here. It's not a great leap to imagine that something like this probably happened to her too. She knows that her disappearance has no place in the article, but she can't help herself. She feels the need to ask.

"A couple years ago, there was a woman from Avery who went missing while she was out running. Some witnesses said they saw her here, on the reservation. Do you happen to remember that case?"

"Is this for the interview, or are you just making small talk?"

The man with the saw stops sanding, and suddenly Elinor can hear her thoughts again. However curt and unpleasant Shawnalee has been since her arrival, she's still surprised by her reaction to the question.

"I was just curious . . . Small talk, I guess."

Shawnalee's eyes flick toward at the ceiling, the same way they did earlier when she could barely manage to contain her irritation. "Listen," she says sharply, "when Randy comes back, I think you should tell him you changed your mind about lunch."

"Why?"

"Because we don't need to spend any more time with you than we already have."

Despite the rough start, Elinor thought the interview with Randy was going fine. Well, even. But now the hostility she's felt all morning from Shawnalee has finally broken out of its lower register. "I don't understand. I apologized for being late—"

"God, you must think we're so stupid."

"What? What are you even talking about?"

"Car trouble." Shawnalee laughs, but it's obvious that she's not laughing at the thought of something funny. "You know I've lived on this reservation my entire life, right?"

A workman passes, carrying a long metal beam that forces both of them to step back. Elinor doesn't know why she's asking.

"*And?*"

"And you don't seem to understand how many people around here drink themselves to death. But I do, so I can tell when someone's hungover, okay? You still have last night's liquor on your breath. And now you come stumbling in, two hours late, asking about what? The one white lady from Avery who went missing like two years ago? Do you even know how many Mahua women we've lost?"

Randy returns from his conversation with some newfound bounce in his step. "Alright." He claps his hands loudly, rubbing them together. "So who's hungry?" He's happy about something, so happy that he starts toward the exit without them, not noticing how slow Elinor and Shawnalee are to follow.

28

The River Bend is an older casino, originally built in the mid-nineties. Now the tribe is expanding the facilities. Adding a section for more one- and five-dollar slots. Adding another section for private card games. The 210-bed hotel is booked solid through Christmas, so they can't update any of the guest rooms yet, but they will, they will, Randy says, as if to remind himself of one more thing that needs to happen on his watch. He explains all of this as they walk through the casino's main floor, with its colorful lights and sounds coming from every direction. Bells, trills, music. The clatter of coins, both real and fake. Elinor tries to keep up and pay attention, but the only words she can really hear are Shawnalee's. *God, you must think we're so stupid.* She's still trying to figure out how to excuse herself from lunch, but she worries that she'll offend Randy, who doesn't seem like the type to take yes, then no for an answer.

The restaurant at the casino is called the Golden Fork. Long before they reach its double doors, signs tacked to stanchions advertise the $8.99 lunch buffet as the best deal in the Bakken. Although there's a line at the entrance, Randy sweeps right past it, winking at the pretty young hostess as he heads toward the only empty booth in the dining room, a horseshoe-shaped one that could seat a group at least twice their size. Elinor rubs her eyes. The carpets and seat cushions are all done up in swirling gold paisley, a pattern that's hard to look at for long. The smell of the food and the brightness of the overhead fluorescents make her want to crawl out on all fours, and just the thought of this shames her, amplifying the words that she's already hearing on a loop. *God, you must think we're so stupid.*

The truth, she decides, is probably better than any excuse.

"I'm so sorry, but I'm not feeling well. I think, maybe, I should go back to my hotel . . ."

"Well, sit down." Randy all but pushes her into the booth and slides in beside her. "Sit down if you're not feeling good. Shawnalee, go get her a Coke from that soda machine over there, will you? Actually, get her a ginger ale instead."

She doesn't want to see the expression on Shawnalee's face as she's once again dispatched for a beverage on her behalf. She stares at her hands, which are resting on the table, her fingers interlaced to prevent them from shaking. She's too old to be this hungover, too old to not remember large swaths of the night before. The last time she felt this bad, she woke up with a tattoo on her left forearm. Five inches tall by four inches wide, itchy and inflamed because she'd torn off the plastic wrap while she slept. Absolutely no memory of getting the work done. No memory of the pain, even. By that point, Elinor had been circling the drain of her modeling career for a while, booking those embarrassing jobs for the sewing pattern company that paid too well to turn down. At first, she assumed that someone could just airbrush the tattoo out in post-production, but it wasn't that simple. People looked at her differently because of it.

"You used to be exotic but approachable," her agent said.

"That was your thing," her manager agreed. "Now we don't know how to market you."

The tattoo effectively ended what she couldn't. The second biggest decision of her life, second only to leaving Marlow, and she didn't even really make it.

Randy cocks his head, giving Elinor a careful once-over. "If you don't mind me saying, miss, I thought you looked a little green back at the construction site. I just figured you were afraid of heights."

"I am. That probably didn't help."

"My fault then," he replies, so kindly that it almost hurts. "I should have asked if you wanted to go up to the top floor. I'm sorry about that."

"No. You're not the one who needs to apol—"

"Here." Shawnalee deposits a glass of ginger ale on the table. "If you two are having lunch, I'm going upstairs to the business office. I'll be back in half an hour to pick you up, and then we really have to go."

He doesn't appear to be listening. He's waving at two men sitting on the other side of the dining room. As Shawnalee leaves, Randy gets up from the booth.

"Excuse me for a minute, will you?" It sounds like he's asking a question, but he's gone before she has a chance to reply.

Elinor watches how the two of them make their way through the busy restaurant. While Randy says hello to everyone he passes, Shawnalee hugs her shoulder bag to her chest, trying not to get jostled as she moves past the diners gathered around the crowded buffet. Elinor takes a sip of ginger ale, which immediately goes down the wrong pipe. She coughs into her fist, mortified by the smell of alcohol still on her breath. It occurs to her that if Shawnalee knew she was hungover, then Randy probably did too. He must have. That's why he ordered her a coffee as soon as they shook hands. It may even be why he took her to the roof of the new building, to get some fresh air. Unlike his assistant, he just decided to be polite and play along, a thought that makes Elinor feel even worse than she already does. She leans back in the booth and takes another sip, slower this time.

A waitress comes by with a large stack of buffet plates. She's an older Native woman, dressed in a uniform the same color as the upholstery. Pinned to her lapel is a name tag that reads MARGO.

"How many of you are eating?" she asks.

"Not me, thanks. I think . . . I think only he is." She feels guilty for occupying such a large table by herself, so she points at Randy, hoping this will explain whose idea it was to sit here. She watches as the woman's eyes track across the room and her mouth sinks into a sneer.

"Well, there goes my tip," she mutters.

"What?"

The waitress slides a single plate onto the table. "Old Randy never tips. Most of the time, I don't even think he pays." She pauses and looks Elinor up and down. "You mind me asking who you are?"

Elinor doesn't understand in what context she's asking, so she simply says her name.

"No, I meant who are you to *him*. How do you know Randy?"

She wonders if the waitress is a former girlfriend or wife. There's a blade edge of something in her voice, but she's not sure what. "I'm interviewing him for an article I'm writing about the oil patch."

Margo chuckles, revealing a fat pink wad of gum parked in her cheek. "Another reporter. Christ. That man is nothing but out for himself, isn't he?"

"Excuse me?"

Margo looks over her shoulder again. Randy now appears to be holding court. A small crowd has gathered around him, everyone smiling, laughing, and slapping each other's backs as if they're all in on the joke.

"You must be like the third or fourth reporter he's trotted through here in the past month or so."

"I guess because he's an important local fig—"

"Something I always wonder about you people?" Margo asks.

"What's that?"

"You all know he's pretty much the biggest crook there is, right?" She pauses, waiting for a reaction, but she seems to understand that Elinor has no idea what she's talking about. "He's an elected official, but he owns a business that services oil fields on reservation land. That shouldn't be allowed. He's getting all these fat contracts from the same companies he's supposed to be keeping an eye on. He's basically dealing himself the best cards."

Elinor thinks about the three iPhones laid out on Randy's desk back at the office. One for personal, one for tribal business, and maybe one for this other business, which she's only hearing about now. *Amateur,* she imagines Richard muttering under his breath, the same way he used to whenever he thought her research wasn't up to par. *You don't even know all the things you don't know.*

"Did you and Randy have some sort of prior relationship?" she asks. "Is that why you're telling me this?"

"You mean like was I his old lady or something?" Margo can barely get the question out before she starts laughing. "Shit. You think I don't have enough problems without inviting someone like that into my bed? I'm third-generation North Fork. My family's been screwed over by people with money for at least a hundred years. We're used to it by now. The only thing that's different about Randy is that he's the first Indian to do it."

A man in a uniform walks past the booth. He gives the two of them a sideways glance, not quite smiling as he does it. Judging from the way Margo straightens up and lowers her voice, Elinor assumes he's her manager.

"Ask around if you don't believe me," she says when he's out of earshot. "But once you run out of people who need old Randy to make money—and there's a lot of them, I'm not gonna lie—but get past all those minor-league crooks and you'll see. He wants you to think everybody loves him, but if you still believe that by the time you leave here, then you weren't really asking the right questions."

Shawnalee returns to the table, breathing as if she ran all the way to the restaurant from wherever she came. It hasn't even been ten minutes yet.

"Margo," she says with a nod.

"Shawnalee." Margo nods back.

It's an odd greeting, both friendly and tense at the same time. It's obvious they know each other but prefer to keep their distance, although it doesn't seem like there's any real enmity between them. The two women simply exchange a word and a look, as if they both know what the score is.

"Where is he?"

Elinor turns her head for a split second and motions with her chin.

By the time she turns back, Margo has already moved on to the next table.

Shawnalee scans the dining room for Randy. When the two of them make eye contact, she raises her cell phone in the air and shakes it as if she wants him to look at his. As he returns to their table, he keeps his head bent low over his screen, his thumb scrolling down, down, down. Elinor moves toward the center of the booth, expecting the two of them to slide in on either side of her, but they remain standing, staring at their phones, which she can hear now. They're both vibrating with activity, as if they're getting the same messages.

"Is something wrong?"

"I'm sorry. We should . . . we need to get going. Something's come up," Randy says, still staring at his screen, appearing troubled for the first time since they met. "But feel free to stay as long as you like and enjoy your meal."

Shawnalee is already leaving, backing out of the restaurant one impatient step at a time. When Randy catches up to her, she turns and they both walk away as if they're racing toward something. Elinor wonders if anyone else just saw what she did, but the other diners seem happily unaware. This is the answer to Randy's question, the one she avoided earlier. Writing had always been her way of making sense of the world and all the things she didn't understand.

Elinor rummages through her wallet and puts a ten-dollar bill on the table. It's probably three or four times more than the cost of her soda, but it feels like the tip Margo deserves.

29

Randy's truck is heading west on Highway 12. Elinor struggles to follow; the thin red needle of her speedometer bounces dangerously close to ninety-five. She's no longer keeping a safe distance to avoid being spotted, as she was when they first left Kittery. At this point, she's just trying not to fall behind. If Randy or Shawnalee are aware that she's been trailing them for nearly ten minutes, her presence is probably the least of their concerns. Several miles away, there's a twisting black pillar of smoke rising in the air, a sign that something is wrong. Something is burning.

Along the shoulder of the road, parked cars begin to appear. At first, there's only a scattering of them, but the farther she drives, the more congested it gets. Dozens of people are standing outside their vehicles, taking videos with their phones or shielding their eyes from the sun as they stare off into the distance. Slowly, she starts to let up on the gas. The futility of what she's doing has been wearing on her for a while. Elinor has no idea how far Randy is going or what she intends do if she catches up, although he's actually not the person she wants to talk to again. It's Shawnalee. For miles, she's been thinking through how best to apologize for her lateness, her dishonesty, her general ignorance of what Mahua women have to endure. But her list of offenses is long and the gap between their vehicles too wide, so she eventually decides to pull over.

The smell of burning rubber hits her as soon as she gets out of the car. The fumes are so acrid, even from a distance, it's difficult to breathe. Her entire body resists it. Her eyes start to tear up and her throat constricts, pinhole small to defend against the air. She covers her nose and mouth with both hands, but only manages a few steps before she stumbles and has to lean against the bug-splattered grille for support.

"Jesus. What is that?" she asks a man walking past. She's so lightheaded, her question barely makes sense. She could be referring to the smoke or the smell or both.

"Rig blew up," the man says, not breaking his stride as he continues along the shoulder, aiming his phone at the fire.

Elinor realizes that what she's smelling isn't burning rubber but burning crude oil, and the wind is blowing the fumes right at her. She pushes herself away from the hood of the car, dusting off the crusty bug carcasses now stuck to her hands. She covers her nose and mouth again as she walks up the road toward a small crowd. Standing in the shade of a bread delivery truck, there's an elderly couple chatting with the driver. She's about to ask if they know how serious the fire is when she overhears the husband.

"I bet they just lost a couple million bucks right there," he says, scratching his sunburned neck.

His wife shakes her head. Around her shoulders, she's clutching a ratty old sweater, even though the midday heat is stifling. "Oh, you don't know."

"But you weren't even looking. I saw it blow up."

"I saw it too," the bread truck driver interjects. "It was one big fireball." He raises his hands to his chest, opening and closing them like a magician conjuring something out of thin air. "Kaboom!"

The wife ignores him. "We should get going now," she says to her husband. "We got a car full of groceries that I need to put away before everything spoils."

"But don't you want to see what happens?"

"You know what's going to happen," she snaps. "They'll put out the fire and that'll be that. Same as always. We don't need to watch them do it. Come on now, you want all that meat we just bought to go to waste?"

The couple head back to their car as three little boys streak past, the last of them shouting, "I'm gonna get you!" None of them appears to be having trouble breathing. In fact, they're carrying on as if they're at a playground, seemingly unsupervised by an adult. Elinor lowers her hand from her face and takes a shallow breath. It's still not easy, but it's not as hard as it was just minutes before, and the thought of this is alarming—how quickly the body can adapt to something so toxic.

Several emergency vehicles drive by with their lights on and sirens wailing. During the quiet pauses in between, Elinor overhears fragments of nearby conversations, surprised by their casual, occasionally indifferent tone.

"Well, that's what they get for being greedy."

"You know those companies barely train all those boys they keep hiring. It's no wonder—"

"Whose land is that? Good luck trying to squeeze a dollar of insurance money out of whoever owns that well."

"I wonder if it'll blow again? I want to get a video this time."

To her, the fire looks serious. But serious is apparently relative here, which shouldn't surprise her as much as it does. All the OSHA stats and public safety articles she read described these oil fields as some of the world's most dangerous places to work. Maybe that's why everyone gathered along the road seems unfazed by what they're seeing, why they talk about the fire like it's something that's happening to a company rather than to a community, to people. How different this is from her childhood when an extended cast of characters banded around her father, trying to help him transition to single parenthood after Nami left. Although their offers of casseroles and school pickups often came with the worst kind of pity—thinly veiled and highly critical of her mother—Elinor was still aware of a deep-seated desire to lend a hand to Ed, whose abandonment returned him to a state of being one of the community's own. She doesn't recognize anything resembling that neighborly sense of care or concern now, and she wonders how a change like this is measured. What kind of stat or metric registers this kind of loss?

A large metal chunk of the rig crashes to the ground and a murmur travels through the crowd, rolling toward her like a wave. The smoke continues to rise even higher and darker than it did before while the wind plays a curious trick of the eye. The fire and several nearby flares look like they're all tilting at the same angle. Elinor pats herself down, grabbing her phone out of her back pocket. She snaps a few pictures, rising on tiptoes to avoid the heads of the people in front of her, but every image she takes is blurry, either because the air is so hazy or she's high on fumes. Elinor decides to double back to her car. Her head is throbbing violently now, adding to the misery of an already miserable hangover. She doubts she can have a productive conversation in this state and feels too sick to even try.

The combination of rubberneckers, emergency vehicles, and road construction brings traffic to a near halt. Eventually, the police arrive to let more ambulances and fire trucks through. After ten minutes of inching along, making hardly any progress at all, Elinor's phone vibrates. She glances at the 212 area code from New York and almost chokes out a laugh. Of course this would be the moment when Richard finally contacts her, when she's hungover, trapped in bumper-to-bumper traffic, and there's an oil well burning down in the distance. She considers not picking up and just letting the call go to voice mail, but she no longer wants the anticipation of it hanging over her head.

"Hello," she says, not giving herself a chance to second-guess.

Richard doesn't respond. Elinor pulls the phone away from her ear and checks the screen, wondering if he hung up, but the call is still connected.

"Hello?" she repeats.

"Yes, hi. Hi. I'm sorry, I didn't expect anyone to answer." It's a woman's voice. Thin and distant, and there's a baby crying in the background. Elinor doesn't know anyone who has a baby. "Could you give me a second. . . ." There's a loud clunk, like the phone is being moved from one ear to another, making the baby's cries sound slightly more distant than they did before. "I swear she wasn't fussing a second ago. She just started when you picked up."

"I'm sorry. Who is this?"

"It's Kathryn. Kathryn Tasso, from school?"

The end of her sentence lifts into a question, as if it would ever be possible to forget her. Elinor is confused for a moment. She has a very clear memory of blocking Kathryn's number earlier this week. She must have switched to another line, dogged as she is. Elinor is tempted to hang up and block this one too. She'd braced herself to talk to Richard. Now her chest finally expands, filling with air.

"Yes, I remember you," Elinor says, so sharply that the now-whimpering baby is the only sound she hears for a while.

"Well . . . I'm so glad to finally connect. I've tried calling and emailing a couple of times, but I wasn't sure I had the right contact info. How are you? How have you been?"

The sound of Kathryn's voice—so pleasant now, so free of the condescension that always marked it before—infuriates Elinor. It should be harder than this for people to wipe the slate clean.

"I haven't returned your messages because I've been busy. Also, I have to say . . ." She considers her mother, how she never got to tell people off, not even when they deserved it. Such delicate little birds. Such thin, fragile necks. What could it possibly matter now? "I'm not really sure why you think you can just call me up for a favor like this." She remembers the way Kathryn used to whisper under her breath whenever she said anything in class, how she'd cut her off midsentence when she was struggling to make a point. Perhaps she wasn't always talking about her or talking down to her, but it felt like she was. To remind Kathryn of her transgressions would be to admit how much she's still affected by them, which Elinor is unwilling to do. But thinking about them again raises the specter of all her old insecurities. It was hard to go back to school at her age, to be surrounded by younger and better-educated classmates, to transition out of a career that always made people assume she was dumb. It was hard, and then Kathryn made it even harder.

"To be clear—we don't, we've never had a relationship like that. It seems crazy to me that you think we do." Elinor isn't sure where she's going with this. All she knows is that the momentum of her anger keeps pushing her forward. "And if you talk to any of your little friends . . ." She almost says "lemmings," which is how she used to think of the women Kathryn surrounded herself with—women who probably would have been kind to Elinor, if only Kathryn had led them there. "Make sure you tell them not to call me either."

The baby is crying again, louder than it was before. "Take her," she hears Kathryn say. "Just take her." Elinor imagines someone—a nanny, probably—whisking the baby out of the room because the crying soon fades away. "I think there's been some kind of misunderstand—"

"No. I understand you perfectly. I always have. Now that I'm writing for the *Standard*, suddenly you can't be nicer. Do you have any idea how sad that is? How you're the absolute last person in the world I'd ever want to help?"

Her questions hang in the air, suspended in years' worth of hard feelings, kicked up like a cloud of dust slowly settling to the ground. Behind her, a driver honks, telling her to close the gap that's formed between her car and the next. She lowers her window and holds up a defiant middle finger, emboldened by everything she just managed to get out. For once, she won't be left with any regrets about what she did and didn't say.

"I'm—I'm sorry," Kathryn stammers, and Elinor feels good for the first time today, hearing the tiny crack in her voice, knowing that she's the one who put it there.

"I wasn't . . . I'm so sorry. But . . ."

Her apology barely has a chance to land before the "but." Elinor bristles at the thought of Kathryn trying to make excuses for herself. "But what?" she snaps. "What?"

"I wasn't going to ask you for a favor. Not that one, at least. I didn't even know you were writing for the *Standard*."

"So why do you keep calling then?"

"I wanted to talk to you—about Richard."

30

There's a woman standing outside her window, yelling. Twice now, Elinor has waved her away, but the woman refuses to go.

"I dare you!" She slaps the glass with her open palms, leaving behind large, smeary prints. "I dare you to get out of that car."

The woman's eyes are bloodshot and buggy. She looks like she might be on drugs. Elinor shoos her off again, but this only seems to upset her more.

"We're suing him," Kathryn says. "Me, Lauren Post, and Natalie Diaz—the three of us are suing him for sexual harassment."

The woman's palms smack the window again. "Give me that middle finger one more time and I'll break it in half."

Elinor covers her phone and rolls the window down an inch. "Will you go away? I'm trying to have a conversation."

"What the fuck did you flip me off for? You're the one holding up traffic."

It's no use trying to explain that she hadn't fallen that far behind the next car. Maybe fifteen feet at the most, and what did it even matter? Traffic wasn't moving then and it isn't moving now. Honking never helps. A reasonable person might understand this, but the woman seems incapable of reason. Elinor wonders if she's high on meth, or maybe paint thinner or bath salts, something that's making her act erratic and aggressive. And then the hard, sharp point of what

Kathryn said finally pierces through. She puts the phone back to her ear.

"Elinor? Hello? Are you still there?"

"You're suing Richard?"

"Are you alright? I hear shouting."

"You're suing him?"

"Yes, and the university too, for not following up properly on the complaints we filed. For keeping him employed, basically."

"Bitch! You are *not* just gonna sit there and ignore me."

She covers the phone again, her grip so tight, it feels like she might snap the thin aluminum case in half.

"I'm not leaving till you say you're sorry." The woman leans over, barely inches away from the window, rapping on it with her knuckles as her breath fogs the glass. "Am I making it hard to hear?" She looks like she's enjoying herself now. Her mouth splits open into a grin and then she raps even faster. "Am I? Am I?"

Elinor throws her phone on the passenger seat and flings open her door, hitting the woman in the face. She stumbles backward, holding her forehead in both hands. Elinor gets out of the car and stands over her, the asphalt stretching her shadow out long. She's younger and fitter than the woman, taller by at least a foot, things that probably weren't as obvious to either of them until now.

"You—you hit me," she says, seemingly confused by the blow.

"Go away," Elinor tells her, not loudly or angrily, but in a tone steeped with threat. "I'm going to hurt you if you don't go away."

The woman blinks and rubs her head. She looks around, but no one is coming to help her. She rubs her head again and takes a slow step back, and then another and another. As she opens the door to her truck, she shouts, "Who the fuck do you think you are?" but her question sounds more impotent than enraged.

Kathryn is still on the line when Elinor returns to her car. "What's happening over there? Who was that shouting?"

"Tell me what you were going to say."

"But are you okay? Where are you right now?"

"Nowhere." Elinor turns her air conditioner on full blast, sweating from the few seconds she spent outside in the sun. "I'm nowhere. Please, just tell me why you called. Tell me everything."

One by one, Kathryn recounts how Richard pursued her and their classmates, dangled opportunities in front of them, and then graciously backed away when they declined his advances. But then the repercussions began, professional repercussions that they often couldn't trace back to him until much later. Lauren learned that she lost a major fellowship because Richard failed to submit a letter of recommendation for her. Natalie, one of the standout students in their graduating class, had been a finalist for several staff writer positions, always coming close to landing the job but not close enough. When she called a woman she'd interviewed with and asked for advice that might improve her chances in the future, the woman suggested removing Richard from her list of references but refused to explain why. She also swore that she'd deny it if Natalie ever told anyone about their conversation.

Of the three stories Elinor hears, Kathryn's disturbs her the most, not because of the consequences to her career, which she'd put on hold after graduation to have a baby, but because of the pattern of events. Richard seemed to take an interest in mentoring her from early on. He encouraged her to drop by his office, where they had long conversations about her career goals and what she'd have to do in order to achieve them. Eventually, they started meeting in coffee shops and bars, and then at his home, where they jumped from school- and work-related topics to personal ones. Why was she so driven? When was the last time she'd gone on a date? What kind of men was she interested in? Kathryn's voice began to falter when she alluded to past traumas in her life, traumas that he coaxed out of her with whiskey and weed and carefully worded affirmations about how hard it must be to be such a beautiful woman.

The longer Elinor listens, the more she recognizes the similarities between Kathryn's experiences and her own. Elinor once told Richard about a man she'd met at a bar and taken back to her apartment at the end of a long evening. The man seemed irritated when she sobered up during the walk home and changed her mind about inviting him in. Then he pleaded and cajoled and asked to use the bathroom, and she—not wanting to seem like a bitch—agreed to let him in. Despite saying no, despite trying to fight, the police said she didn't have a case against him and discouraged her from filing one. Too many witnesses had seen them together at the bar, making out as they left. Although her father had passed away years earlier, Elinor couldn't help but hear his voice, raging at her and asking what did she expect, taking a man she'd just met back to her apartment? *This is what you get.*

Richard, in contrast, said all the right things. He told her it wasn't her fault and she had nothing to be ashamed of, a reaction that almost surprised her. There was such an ordinariness to her story, an utter lack of originality. It sounded like every other account she'd ever heard, which made her feel so much worse, the fact that she knew about the possibility of such violence in the world but didn't see it coming until it was bearing down on her throat. Because she revered Richard and doubted herself, his reassurances were more comforting than her own. How stupid she was not to see it. The way he treated her and Kathryn—snake charming his way into their confidence— she realizes these weren't genuine, independently thought-out acts. They were methods, reused and recycled from one woman to the next, no different from the man at the Depot who tried to pick her up by making her feel insecure.

It sickens her to learn that even his first move was a ploy that he'd used on them both. After an elaborately expensive dinner that Richard referred to as a "meeting," he brought Kathryn home to his apartment. As she stood on his balcony, peering down at Gramercy Park below, he touched the small of her back. Instead of letting his hand wander, she told him to stop. And when he reached under her shirt, she quickly collected her things and left. Afterward, everything he promised—letters, introductions, offers to recommend her for assignments that he'd passed on—evaporated. But he was smart and strategic about meting out his punishment. Kathryn continued to earn

As in his classes, and his behavior toward her in public remained as complimentary as ever. Elinor even remembers feeling jealous of his admiration for Kathryn's shrewd instincts, unaware that a rift had ever taken place between them. It was only after he shut her out that Kathryn realized how careful he'd been. He never put anything in writing to her, to anyone, that could be used against him. It was the women's word against his.

"That's why we decided to reach out to you. We were wondering"— Kathryn hesitates—"hoping, really, that you might be able to help us with this. Maybe you have records of things that he sent you? Like text messages? Or emails? The two of you seemed, you know, friendly, for longer than any of us were. We thought maybe he lowered his guard after a while."

Despite the initial similarities, when their stories finally diverged, Elinor's jumped the track. Whereas Kathryn and the others had rejected Richard's advances, she'd opened herself up to them, accepting his romantic attentions willingly. At first, she did so because it was flattering that someone like him would take an interest in her. Then later, long after the patina of his affections had grown dull, when his eye would frequently wander and he was quick to anger or irritation or criticism, she stayed with him because she thought she was learning things about the business that she couldn't pick up elsewhere.

"Does he know?" she asks. "About the lawsuit? Does he know that you're doing this?"

"He was notified last month."

Elinor imagines a calendar, flipping the pages backward. "When last month?"

"I don't know the exact date. It was around mid-May though. Why?"

They served him with papers and then he passed off the assignment to her. That was the order of events. Of course it was. He didn't convince Lydia to give Elinor the article because he needed to have hip surgery, or because she grew up in North Dakota, or because she was right for the job. It was none of those things. He gave it to her because he wanted to keep her busy and beholden. Silent.

Elinor covers her eyes. The air conditioner has been on high for several minutes, turning her fingertips cold and blue. "I'm sorry," she says. "I can't help you. It wasn't—it wasn't like that with us."

Kathryn is quiet for a while, and then her tone takes on a familiar edge. "That's what I told the others. But they kept insisting I get in touch." She makes a noise, something that sounds like a cross between a sigh and a laugh. "I can't believe he's got you working on something for the *Standard*."

Elinor nods. She understands that there's nothing she can say in her defense. She's also preoccupied, connecting the dots scattered around her until she's able to see what they've been pointing to all along. Unlike Kathryn, Lauren, and Natalie, Richard never enticed her with professional inducements, before or during their time together. He never praised Elinor's work or complimented her in public like he did with the others. He never introduced her to his colleagues as one of his most talented and promising students. It was as if he knew no one would believe him.

"This is why we all hated you, by the way," Kathryn says.

"Because I chose to be with him?"

"Because women like you make it so much harder for the rest of us."

31

Elinor doesn't remember driving. One minute, she was sitting in traffic on the reservation. The next, she's standing outside her room at the hotel, staring at a blinking red light on her door. She inserts and removes her key card, inserts and removes it again. Three more red blinks and still nothing. She takes a deep breath and wipes the card on her shirt, polishing the magnetic stripe until it's free of dust and lint. Then she dips the card in with one smooth, deliberate motion, waiting for the door to unlock. When the light blinks red again, Elinor grabs the handle in her fists and shakes it, knowing this won't help matters at all, but it feels good to shake the fuck out of something just because she can.

Her neighbors are being noisier than usual. She hears coughing and deep voices and a snort of laughter right before their door flings open and a middle-aged man walks out, followed by two, three, four others, all dressed in similar uniforms of T-shirts, work boots, and jeans. She braces herself for a comment—something that will finally make her lose her mind at them in this narrow hallway—but the group simply nods or tips their baseball caps in greeting, seemingly startled to be living next door to a woman. Elinor glances at her watch. It's nearing the 4 p.m. shift change. If their room is empty now and she could just get into her own, maybe she'll finally be able to sleep. This is what her entire body wants to do, even though her mind understands the unlikeliness of it. The second she closes her eyes, her conversation with

Kathryn will simply play and replay on a loop, the words worse than any noise that her neighbors could ever make.

She slides down with her back against the door and sits cross-legged on the floor, too exhausted by the thought of sleep to return to the lobby. The sun is angling in through a nearby window, forming a warm square of light on the rough blue carpet. She runs her fingers back and forth across the square as she tries to figure out what to do—about her room key, about everything. Continuing with her work here as if nothing happened doesn't seem like an option. But neither does quitting. She takes out her phone and examines the speed dial list. Richard used to occupy the first position, followed by her sister, her building manager, the bodega around the corner from her apartment, and Damon. Removing him from this order after their breakup—which had been presented as mutual but was in fact his idea—had seemed like such a loss.

Elinor stares at the cracked screen, trying to understand what it is that she actually feels toward him before she dials. The sensation swells and pitches like anger, or maybe even outrage, but it can't be. What is her actual grievance against him, after all? Richard had an eye for women; she always knew that. He could be ill-tempered and unkind. She knew that too. But like he said on the phone—now she understands why he said it—he never made her do anything that she didn't want to do. And maybe that's the part that bothers her most, the part that makes her feel so hopelessly taken in. Her classmates saw what she didn't and ran, while Elinor stayed by his side for as long as he was willing to have her.

Even now, she's curious about Richard's reaction to the lawsuit in a way that feels like a betrayal. To whom, she's not sure, especially since she'd never been friendly with Kathryn and the others. She's not about to invent some notion of sisterly solidarity now. The longer she sits there, rubbing her hand across the carpet, the more obvious it is that her hesitation to call has nothing to do with Kathryn. It doesn't even have anything to do with Richard. She's simply ashamed of the questions she wants to ask. They're all wrong. Instead of demanding to know what he did to her classmates, her immediate concern is the article. Did he actually think she could write it? Or was he just trying to buy some goodwill? Elinor always tried to deny it whenever Maren called her selfish, but she wonders if that's not the very definition of her behavior in this moment. Shouldn't she be furious at Richard for what he did to other women even though he didn't do those things to her?

She imagines being hauled into a roomful of lawyers to explain that her relationship with him had been consensual, that he never offered her anything before they started seeing each other, or during the year they were together. He didn't need to. His attorney will ask what she used to do for a living, no doubt aware that her response will introduce a damaging question. If Richard was the type of man who could date socialites and successful businesswomen and even a former model, then why in the world would he sexually harass his students? She finds this deeply troubling, the idea of being a wild card kept in someone's pocket and played when Richard needs a win. *This is why we all hated you*, she thinks.

At the far end of the hall, she hears humming and the squeaky metal wheels of a rolling cart. Elinor jumps to her feet and walks toward the elevator where a cleaning woman is unspooling a large black bag out of a box. She lifts and lowers the bag like a parachute, letting it billow open with air, and then crouches next to the garbage can, which is stuffed full and surrounded by trash again. Elinor doesn't understand how so many pizza boxes and empty beer bottles can accumulate like this. But at least twice a day, maybe more, some poor woman has to get on her hands and knees to clean up the mess.

"Excuse me. Would you mind letting me into my room please? My key's not working."

The woman looks up, blowing a strand of hair out of her eyes. It's the same one Elinor saw the day she checked in, the one muttering about pigs.

"Which room?"

"I'm in three fifteen, at the end of the hall. On the left."

The woman follows the direction of Elinor's pointed finger, and then motions toward the elevator. "You go to front desk," she says in heavily accented English. "They help you."

"But couldn't you just—"

"They help with bags at front desk."

"No. I don't need any bags. I'm locked out." She waves her key card at her. "*Locked out?*" Elinor repeats, the words loud and slow and pronounced with too much pique. She feels like a hypocrite, doing the same thing that strangers sometimes do to her when they assume she doesn't understand. It's startling, how quickly she resorted to this. She, of all people, who knows how insulting it is. "I'm sorry," she says, jabbing the elevator button until the car finally arrives. "Never mind."

Elinor returns to the lobby, bracing herself for the run-in with Hannah that she was trying to avoid. She caught a glimpse of her behind the desk when she first walked in, and sure enough, Hannah's round pink face is the one waiting for her when she moves to the front of the line. There are too many things going on right now to spend what little energy she has crafting an apology. She doesn't know why she would. She was concerned that Hannah might be doing something harmful to her child. She's not about to apologize for that.

"Could you please reprogram this?" Elinor slides her card across the counter. "I think I demagnetized it. I'm in three fifteen."

"No, we've removed you from three fifteen."

She pauses, expecting more to follow, but Hannah just stands there, tapping her palm with one of the Thrifty's complimentary pens.

"Moved me where?"

"Removed, as in checked out. Not moved."

"But that's a mistake. I have a reservation through next Wednesday."

Instead of consulting her computer or running the key card through the machine, Hannah simply tosses it into a small pile on her desk. "You *were* reserved through Wednesday, but you violated the hotel's no smoking policy, so we've removed you from your room and charged you a two hundred and fifty dollar cleaning fee. Here . . ." She reaches under the counter and pulls out Elinor's bag. "Housekeeping packed your things for you. You should find everything inside, but it's your responsibility to double-check before leaving the property." Suddenly, she's looking past Elinor's left shoulder. "May I help the next customer, please?"

In the corner of her eye, Elinor sees the person behind her take a few steps forward. She places both hands on the counter and widens her stance, blocking his approach as she processes everything she just heard.

"You're kicking me out for smoking?"

"We're a nonsmoking property, ma'am. We're very strict about that. And the housekeeper said she did give you a warning."

Hannah is stone-faced as she speaks, but Elinor senses that she's enjoying this, using what little power she has to make things difficult. Does the cleaning woman putting a No Smoking sign next to her ashtray really count as a warning? Aren't there other rules being broken here, bigger ones that matter more? Elinor thinks through how best to respond, aware that asking these questions is unlikely to get her anywhere.

"I didn't realize I could be kicked out for something like this. Obviously, I won't do it again. And I'm happy to pay the cleaning fee—"

"We already charged you for that, so it's not like you have a choice."

"That's fine, but this isn't really about me smoking, is it?"

"Well, what else could it be about?" This time, Hannah's expression cracks a little, flickering with amusement.

"We had a misunderstanding last night. I'm really—"

"Ma'am, when you checked in, you initialed on your paperwork that you'd reviewed our guest agreement, which includes our rules and policies. The fact that we're a nonsmoking property—that's like the very first rule on the list. Would you like me to show you?"

"But no one actually reads all that fine print."

"Well, next time, you probably should. Because it says we have the right to remove any guest who causes a disturbance to—"

"A disturbance?" Elinor finally snaps, incensed by Hannah's repeated use of the word "we," as if anyone else was involved in this decision besides her. "I've been living next door to half a dozen guys who keep banging around at all hours of the night, and I'm the disturbance for having a couple of cigarettes?" She pauses, reminding herself not to argue the wrong point. She's not being kicked out for smoking. She's being kicked out because of what she said at the Depot. "Look. I'm sorry I misspoke yesterday. I wasn't trying to offend you or your boyfriend, or imply that you're bad parents or anything. I just wanted to—"

Hannah's jaw visibly tightens. Elinor regrets saying "bad parents" out loud, within earshot of her coworkers and customers. The change in Hannah's demeanor is immediate. She seems agitated and ready for their conversation to end, as if she was looking forward to the sport of it at first, but now the whole thing has gone on for much longer than she expected.

"Ma'am, I'm not going to keep repeating myself," she says curtly. "This is a nonsmoking property. That's all this has ever been about."

"Then I'd like to speak to the manager on duty."

"I *am* the manager on duty."

"The person you report to then."

"Come on, lady," groans the man behind her. "Don't you see all of us waiting back here?"

Elinor glances over her shoulder. The line for the front desk is now curled around a column, extending into the breakfast buffet area. The men standing in it aren't admiring or ogling her anymore. They're staring at her with dark expressions, their steel-toed boots tapping impatiently against the tile. Riskier than being wanted by these men is being in their way. Elinor turns back and stares at Hannah's bright blue eyes, framed by spidery black lashes.

"Do you mind, ma'am?" She blinks innocently. "I've got a lot of customers to take care of." Noticeably, Hannah is speaking louder now, probably to ensure that the men in line know who's to blame for the wait.

It's the blinking that sets Elinor off—the playfulness of it, as if this is all just a game and not a decision with real repercussions, at least for one of them.

"You know there's not another vacant room for at least a hundred miles. So where the hell do you expect me to go?"

Hannah shrugs. "I'm not sure, ma'am. But that's really not my problem. Maybe—maybe you should just go home."

32

In the parking lot of the Thrifty, Elinor sits in her car, smoking cigarettes and making calls. At first, she tries the big hotel chains up and down the length of Highway 12, hoping to stumble into a last-minute cancellation. Then she calls the lodge at the River Bend Casino, followed by the cluster of roadside motels with the bright blue swimming pools on the outskirts of town. She searches online for other housing options, finding bare bones websites for random RV parks and old Craigslist postings that people forgot to take down. She calls every number she finds despite knowing what she'll hear, if she can get through to a person at all. No vacancy. No vacancy. No vacancy. When she has to turn on the engine to charge her dying phone, Elinor reluctantly tries Peg, the travel booker at the *Standard*. The line rings and rings until it finally goes to voice mail. With the time difference in New York, she realizes that the office is probably closed for the evening, so she hangs up without leaving a message. It's better this way, she thinks. Given what Peg went through to find her a room at the Thrifty, Elinor doesn't know how to explain that she lost it, or what kinds of flags it might raise, and with whom.

Her only real choice, if she can call it that, is to stay with Maren. But the thought of this makes her uneasy. It's not because the farm is two hours away from Avery; two-hour drives are nothing in North Dakota. It's not even because Elinor feels embarrassed about how much she drank last night at the bar. It's the discomfort of being near

Maren's family given what she knows about Gary. She can't imagine talking to her nephews or sitting across from them at the dinner table without thinking about the children that she and her sister used to be. She worries that Maren will leave her boys as they were left.

When a tow truck appears, slowly making laps around the lot, she knows her time is almost up. Elinor dials her sister's number. She barely has a chance to brace herself for the conversation before Maren answers, as if she's been waiting for her call.

"Well, look who it is. What have you been up to, I wonder?"

"Working," Elinor says sharply, put off by her greeting, the way it sounded like she was smiling when she said it. Through the window of the Thrifty, she can still see Hannah behind the front desk, chatting pleasantly with customers. Elinor can't handle another smug woman smiling at her today.

"I was just kidding. You don't have to bite my head off."

Elinor thinks this is an exaggeration, but she's about to ask for a favor, so she decides not to argue the point. "What's that noise?" she asks, trying to identify the tap-tap-tapping in the background.

"I'm chopping onions for dinner. Your favorite," Maren says dryly. "Mrs. Sievert's cheeseburger casserole."

Mrs. Sievert was their next-door neighbor on the base, a former home economics teacher married to a likable airman from Des Moines. Everyone assumed she was barren, a cruel little rumor that made the rounds because Mrs. Sievert always stopped to coo at babies in strollers but never had any of her own. Twice a month, she'd arrange with Ed to come over and give Elinor and Maren a cooking lesson. She was well meaning enough, and even went to the trouble of sewing personalized aprons for them both, but Elinor was too small for hers. She had to tie a baseball-sized knot in the strap so it would hang properly. The knot sat right at the base of her neck, making it stiffen and ache. She hated wearing it. She also hated learning how to cook a stranger's family recipes, all of which relied heavily on cans of condensed soup and frozen hash browns and big, rubbery blocks of Velveeta. Although she didn't make mistakes on purpose, she eventually learned that making enough of them flustered Mrs. Sievert, so she began substituting sugar for salt, measuring out too many cups of flour, and leaving bits of shell in the mixing bowl after cracking the eggs. For her ineptitude, Elinor eventually found herself banished from the kitchen.

"You don't have any sense for cooking at all, do you?" Mrs. Sievert used to ask good-naturedly. "You and your dad are lucky to have your sister around or else you'd probably starve."

Compliments like this would make Maren visibly swell with pride. Her rounded posture improved; she stood what appeared to be several inches taller whenever she put on her apron. Mrs. Sievert seemed to enjoy watching Maren's progress, treating it as evidence of her skills as a teacher. She referred to Maren as her "star pupil," a fairly meaningless title since she had no other students. Still, it made Maren and their father beam whenever they heard it. *Don't you understand?* Elinor wanted to ask. *If you keep trying so hard, she'll keep coming over.* But someone in their household had to cook. By now, Maren has probably made Mrs. Sievert's cheeseburger casserole a hundred times over, and Elinor understands that her sister had to learn because she wouldn't.

"So what are you up to?" she asks.

"I already told you. I'm making dinner." There's a clunk of something in the background, and then a quick burst of water from the sink. "What did you do today?"

Elinor mentally runs through the list of things she wishes she could tell her. *I showed up late and hungover for a meeting. I learned that my ex is being sued for sexual harassment. And I was just kicked out of my hotel, so I'm hoping to stay with you.*

"I interviewed someone on the reservation."

"Oh, really? Who?"

"The chairman of the Mahua Nation."

"Randy Hudson? He's kind of a character, I've heard."

It's not clear how she means this. Elinor is about to ask when the tow truck loops toward her again, temporarily blinding her with its headlights even though it's too early to use them. She wonders if the driver is doing this on purpose, telling her it's time to go without actually telling her.

"I didn't really get a good sense of him. He had to cut the meeting short."

"I'll bet. You hear that one of his wells blew up?"

"His wells?"

"A well that his company services, I mean. I think that's the third or fourth accident they've had this year. They'll probably get shut down after this, or fined, at least."

Elinor remembers how the color drained from Randy's face as he scrolled through the messages on his phone, the way the dust swirled behind his truck in violent clouds as he sped toward the drill site. She assumed he was worried about injuries on the reservation, or maybe even deaths. She should have known it was about money. Everything in the Bakken seems to be about money.

"How did you find out about the explosion already?"

"Tom heard it on the radio."

In the background, a young boy's voice whines, "Mommmmm!" Maren covers her phone, muffling their conversation to the occasional word or phrase: "Stop . . . Not kidding . . . Your brother . . . Right now . . ." When she returns to the line, there's a distinct, firm click of a closing door. Elinor imagines her ducking into the pantry, probably surrounded by jars of colorful fruit, preserved the way Mrs. Sievert taught her.

"So, you must have had one hell of a hangover this morning." Again, it sounds like she's smiling.

Elinor doesn't know what the better response is, saying she did or she didn't. She can't bring herself to admit to either. "The aspirin and water helped. Thanks."

"For what?"

"For setting them out for me."

Maren is silent.

"What's the matter?"

"You don't remember who took you home last night?" She says this in the form of a question, but there's no mistaking the undertone of judgment.

Elinor scans what little remains of her memories. She had a cigarette with the bartender. She saw a fight in the alley. Then she ran into Hannah and her boyfriend. Afterward, everything turns to mud.

"It wasn't you?"

"No, it wasn't me," Maren says, more annoyed than incredulous now. "Dani was the one who took you."

At first, Elinor thinks she hears the name "Danny" and her heart begins to pound at the thought of being left alone in that state with a man. Although it only takes a few seconds to corral back the memory of who Dani is, it forces her to see Dani bent over the bathroom sink again, the image as disturbing now as it was then. Elinor's alarm quickly turns into anger. She shouldn't have gotten so drunk last night. Of course, she knows this. But still—how could her sister pawn her off on a stranger?

"So you just sent me back to my hotel with someone you barely know?"

"It's not like I met her for the first time last night, and the two of you really seemed to be hitting it off. I saw you exchanging numbers at one point. Besides, she said your hotel was on her way home."

There's nothing in Maren's voice to suggest that she understands what she's done, or why this is so upsetting, which is the thing that bothers Elinor most.

"You really couldn't cut your date night short with *Gary* to make sure I was okay?" The way she says his name—loudly, obnoxiously, emphasizing each stupid syllable—makes it clear what she thinks of him.

"No," Maren almost shouts. "No, I'm not doing that aga—" She catches herself, as if she realizes that her kids might overhear. Then she resumes in a whisper, her volume low but her tone vicious. "I'm sick of always being the one who has to take care of everybody, like I don't have any other purpose in life. So excuse me for deciding I'm done with all that, especially for you. It's not like you ever showed me the tiniest bit of gratitude anyways."

Suddenly they're at it again. Having the same old argument, cast in the same old roles. The selfish one. The sacrificed one. Back and forth they go. Still resentful about things they did to each other long before they understood the weight of a grudge. Maren's constant warnings that Elinor would turn into a slut if she wasn't careful, just like their mother. Elinor's decision not to return home for their father's funeral. The two of them, locked in this unwinnable battle over which parent was wrong, which parent was more wronged. The only difference is the mention of gratitude, which Maren has never said out loud before. Elinor can't believe she'd expect it. The thought that she does is ridiculous. It makes her want to act out, to be cruel.

"What exactly should I be grateful for? Not having a mother and getting stuck with you instead?"

"How is that my fault though? She was the one who ran out."

"Because she hated it here, and you were as miserable to her as everyone else."

"No, Elinor. You've been telling yourself that same old story all these years, but you never put any of the responsibility on her. She didn't want to be our mom. She definitely didn't want to be a wife. Some women just aren't like that. Don't you get it? She wanted to come to America and Dad was her ride. But she didn't love him any more than she loved us; otherwise, it would have been impossible for her to leave."

By the end of her sentence, Maren is almost yelling again, the sound of her voice creating an echo in the closet or pantry she's standing in. Elinor has to jerk the phone away from her ear as the tow truck stops in front of her car. The driver lowers his window and stares at her for a moment before making an exaggerated gesture of tapping on his watch. Previously, she found his oblique signals and attempts to communicate with her annoying. But he's exactly the parachute she needs right now.

"Someone's here," she says. "I have to go."

"What? Are you serious?"

"Yes. I'm sorry. I really have to go."

Maren sighs into the phone—a long, slow exhale, as if a valve just broke open and she's releasing all her fight. "Jesus Christ, El. I don't know why we even try anymore."

33

The tow truck driver isn't moved by her explanations. He simply stares at her, his head tilted and arms crossed, looking like someone who's heard it all before, probably from people worse off than she is.

"It's too bad you lost your room at the Thrifty, miss. But if you're not staying at the hotel, you can't keep sitting in their lot all night." He points at something just past her shoulder. "It says so right there on the sign."

Elinor is exhausted. She has been for a while. Every argument with Maren, no matter how familiar or repetitive, always leaves her feeling abraded, all tender skin and raw, exposed nerves. Afterward, it's hard to believe how close they were as little girls, falling asleep in the same bed and holding hands when they walked to and from school. Elinor doesn't recognize who those children are anymore. Her memories of them almost feel false, planted by someone who wants to look back and believe they were closer than they actually were.

On the spectrum of major and minor fights, the one they just had hovers somewhere in the middle. Recoverable, with time. In a month or two, Maren will probably call her up or send a text about something innocuous, and Elinor will eventually answer. Neither of them will mention their conversation today. To do so would risk wading into the quicksand of another argument. They'll add the unkind or insensitive things the other person said to their ongoing list of resentments, preserving them for later use. Elinor will probably never hear another word about Gary unless she asks, which she won't. How desperate she was to think that she could stay with Maren for the rest of this trip. In her panic about losing her housing, she ignored the fact that distance had always been the key to maintaining any semblance of peace between them.

"Hey." The tow truck driver waves at her. "You listening?"

"Yes, I heard you. Will you give me a minute?"

"I think I've given you plenty. Now, rules are rules, miss. It's time for you to go."

The way he keeps calling her "miss," combined with his invocation of rules, needles deep under her skin. Rules seem so arbitrary here. Just small demonstrations of power by people who have very little, used against people who have even less. She glances at Hannah through the window of the hotel and feels the same spike of anger all over again.

"Where the hell do you expect me to go then?"

The sharpness of her voice surprises her. It seems to surprise him too. She's been doing this more and more lately, letting her feelings toward one person spill over into her interactions with others. It wasn't the cleaning woman's fault for having a job to do. It's not his fault, either.

"I'm sorry," she says, briefly covering her face with both hands. "I'm just frustrated because I can't find a place to stay tonight."

The driver takes off his baseball cap and scratches his pink scalp, most of which is visible through thin gray wisps of hair. He looks off into the distance, but it's not clear whether he's thinking about possible suggestions or trying to keep his cool. She waits for him to say something until the silence stretches on for too long.

"So . . . do you have any ideas?"

He looks at her, exasperated, either with the premise of the question or her impatience for an answer. Normally, a reaction like this would prompt her to apologize and back away. Something about being a woman, a nonwhite woman, has made her sensitive to inconveniencing others, swift to assume that her presence isn't wanted. But the Bakken doesn't reward this kind of behavior. She thinks about the Mexican kid that Harry Bergum told her about, the one he never referred to by name. Nineteen years old, arrived in Avery without a plan or even a winter coat, Harry said. Somehow, he figured out how to survive here, probably because he had no other choice. Elinor has to be as dogged and determined as he was, as all these roughnecks are, coming to a place that beckons with opportunity but quickly spits out the unresourceful. If she can't summon the strength to do this, then maybe Hannah was right. She should just go home.

"The Motel 6, the Days Inn, the Sunnyside Lodge . . ." She begins reciting the list of places that she's already called, counting them off on the fingers of her left hand before moving on to the right.

"But those are all motels," the driver interrupts. "You're not going to find a room at a motel anywhere near here."

"That's why I'm trying to figure out if there are places I'm not thinking of. Word-of-mouth places like boardinghouses or—I don't know— campgrounds?" She calculates how many days she has left until her flight back to New York. Only five, which can't be right, but it actually is. It feels like she wasted the first half of her trip, doing all the things that Richard wanted her to do. His bidding, which was exactly what she'd hoped to avoid from the start. "Where would you tell a new roughneck to go if he didn't have any housing lined up?"

He scratches his head again. "I heard the Lutheran church lets guys stay overnight if they're really desperate. They say it's part of their Christian mission," he adds sourly. "It's the big brick church near the high school—the Good Shepherd."

"The Good Shepherd," she repeats, wondering why he's looking in the back of her car now, holding his hand over his eyes to shield them from the glare. "And you think—you think they'd rent me a room there?"

"Wait. It's just you?" he asks, pointing at the lone bag in her back seat.

"Just me what?"

"Just you in town. You're not here with someone? Like a boyfriend or a husband or something?"

She hesitates, not certain why he's asking. "No? I'm here alone."

"Oh. Then you probably wouldn't want to go to the church."

He seems to think this comment requires no further explanation, but Elinor doesn't follow. "I'm sorry. Why's that?"

"Because it's not a hotel, with actual rooms or doors that lock or anything. It's a bunch of guys on cots and sleeping bags in the basement, with everybody out in the open. It's like a . . ." He raises his eyes toward the dusky sky, which is a color somewhere between violet and blue. Pretty, if not for the cloud of gnats buzzing overhead.

The driver waves his hand in the air to scatter them. He frowns, still struggling with the word he can't remember. "What do you call those things they set up for people after a hurricane or a tornado?"

"You mean an emergency shelter?"

He snaps his fingers at her. "That's it. That's how they set up the church at night, like an emergency shelter. You wouldn't have any privacy at all."

She understands that he's telling her this because she's a woman, because despite an occupation that demands a certain amount of indifference to people's hardships, he's not entirely without a heart. He doesn't want to be responsible for sending her to a place where something bad could happen. The thought of this, however well intentioned, almost makes her want to laugh. I'm here, she thinks. I'm already goddamn here.

"But I've been calling around for hours and can't find a room anywhere, so it sounds like the church might be my best bet?"

He looks at her with a slow shake of his head, as if she doesn't understand what she's getting herself into. "I'm not sure the pastor would let a single woman bunk with all those men. Don't you got a friend or somebody you can stay with?"

She tries not to appear stung by the question. Elinor is terrible at friendship, not for a lack of desire but a lack of practice. In her twenties, everyone she knew was transient. The girls she lived or hung out with passed through each other's lives quickly, either because they quit modeling or moved up in the world to more expensive apartments and wealthier crowds. Later, in her thirties, Elinor often felt like she'd regressed, sitting in college classrooms, being stared at by kids who were as intimidated by her looks as she was by their intellects. This is probably why she continues to circle back to Maren despite all the grief their relationship causes. The list of people in her life is short and keeps getting shorter.

"I don't have anyone I can stay with," she says. "That's why I've been sitting here, trying to figure something out."

He takes a swig from an oversize travel mug. "Actually, now that I think about it, if you don't mind the drive, you'd probably be better off going to Emerald's—that big truck stop on your way out to the reservation? Not the first set of truck stops, the one that's like twenty miles past them, the brand-new one. They don't got a towing contract yet so people have been parking there overnight."

She drove by Emerald's earlier that day, registering little more than its bright green signage before speeding past. "They really let people sleep in their cars?" she asks, skeptical given all the bans on overnight parking in the area.

"For now. But people are pissed off about it because the whole place pretty much turns into a junkyard for RVs at night. It won't be long before someone steps in and breaks it up, whether it's the company or the county or whoever." He takes another swig from his mug, wiping his mouth on the back of his hand. "I can't guarantee you'll be able to find a space this late, but if you do, that'll be a whole lot safer than the church. At least you can stay in your car."

The irony that she'd be safer in a parking lot than a church seems lost on him. Elinor lets it pass and simply thanks him.

"Good luck to you, miss. And, hey . . ." Something in his voice changes, as if he's trying to choose his words carefully but sound casual when he says them. "When you get there, don't forget to lock your doors before you go to sleep, okay? Make sure you do that."

The corners of his mouth lift, but the effect is awkward, as if he's not used to smiling. Even so, the attempt changes his expression for the better, allowing Elinor to see the type of man he probably is when he's not on the job. A father with adult children of his own. Maybe even a grandfather. Someone who understands what it means to worry about another person but doesn't have any control over what happens to them in the world. She could have asked what he was afraid of, why he seemed so intent on steering her away from the church, or why he felt the need to remind her about locking the doors, but she already knows. It's the same reason she got so upset when she thought Maren had left her passed out with a man named Danny. All during the drive to Emerald's, she thinks about how strange this is—two people with seemingly little in common, possessed by the same unspoken fears and conclusions about what might happen to a woman like her, alone in the Bakken, alone anywhere really. That shouldn't be. The things they're afraid of should be impossible to imagine, not the first thing they assume.

34

It's a quarter past eight when she arrives at Emerald's. The parking lot is huge and well lit, with signs directing semis to one side and passenger cars to the other. It's both exactly what she hoped and nothing like she expected. The tow truck driver said it turned into a junkyard for RVs at night, which she assumed was an exaggeration. But as she drives up and down the long rows, searching for an empty space, she sees campers and pop-up trailers and mini RVs—all old and deteriorating. Not a newer model in sight. Men sit outside their vehicles on folding chairs, drinking beer or cooking on miniature grills. Several have gone out of their way to make themselves comfortable, to create some semblance of home. Coolers double as ottomans, iPads do the work of televisions, T-shirts as large as flags hang out to dry on makeshift clotheslines strung from awnings or antennae. She drives past a couple with an elaborate setup in front of their otherwise ramshackle trailer. They have an area rug—to keep the dirt at bay, she assumes—and a half moon of mismatched lawn chairs positioned around a small folding table. Tiki torches burning bright with citronella separate their space from the people parked on either side, who have similar setups. It's clear they've all been living here for a while. She imagines Gary trolling the aisles of Walmart in search of things to make his RV more inhabitable and finding her sister instead. She shakes her head, trying to rid herself of the thought of Maren visiting him in a place like this.

At the far end of the lot, Elinor loosens her grip on the steering wheel, relieved to find some empty spaces in the back row. Surrounding her are a couple of trucks; a minivan; a battered Ford Escort, its front end resting on cinder blocks instead of tires—all with out-of-town plates and hints of people sitting inside. A tinny sound of a radio, a glow of a phone screen. Some of the cars have aluminum foil sunshades, made for keeping parked cars cool. Instead, they're being used as curtains to block out the cars' interiors to passersby. Others have flattened pieces of cardboard or old bedsheets covering all the windows, hiding the occupants and their belongings. It's strange, knowing she's surrounded by so many people she can't see, but it doesn't feel as dangerous as she thought it would. She spots several women sitting around with their husbands or boyfriends, drinking beer and listening to music at a quiet, surprisingly respectful volume. A man walks past with a yapping Pomeranian, delicately holding a leash in one hand and a bag of dog shit in the other. He keeps pleading with it to hush and shush, as if he's aware that they're walking through the equivalent of strangers' bedrooms. The dog continues making more noise than its little body should be capable of, its short orange legs a blur of constant movement.

Having nothing but her bag and the clothes on her back, it doesn't take long for Elinor to settle in. As soon as she does, she dials Richard's cell, aware that she just has to do it, whether she's ready for the conversation or not. She'll never sleep again if she keeps avoiding it. The line doesn't ring before the outgoing message states that the mailbox is full—barraged, no doubt, by people like her, people who want and need to know things. She hangs up and tries the landline at his apartment, expecting a similar announcement until a woman answers breathlessly.

"Richard?"

Elinor hesitates. "No. I'm calling for Richard. Is he there?"

"Who's this?" the woman asks.

"Elinor. Elinor Hanson." She struggles with how best to describe herself—as a former student, a former girlfriend—so she doesn't describe herself at all. "Who's this?"

She hears the distinct metal strike of a lighter. Once, twice, before the flint finally catches and the woman exhales.

"It's Lydia."

"Oh. I didn't expect . . ."

At first, Elinor doesn't understand why Lydia is picking up Richard's phone, assuming that he's the one calling. Why would he call his own number? But then she realizes that they probably live together now. Lydia thought he was calling home.

"He's out, I'm guessing?"

"Yes. I don't know when he'll be back."

There's no point asking if she's aware of the things that Richard has been accused of. Although Elinor can't see her face this time, she hears the difference in her voice. It's morose and charmless, punctuated by the steady inhale and exhale of her cigarette, probably one of those thin brown 100s that only rich older women smoke. Lydia is fully aware.

"Are you alright?" Elinor asks.

"You've obviously heard."

"I have."

"News travels fast," she huffs. "It hasn't made the papers yet, but everyone seems to know already."

Something in the background squeaks. Elinor recognizes it as the door to Richard's balcony. The hinges always dried out no matter how frequently they were oiled. Suddenly she can hear the ambient noise of the city. Traffic and barking dogs, a lone siren in the distance. She has a guilty pang of nostalgia for Richard's apartment. She used to love the view from where Lydia is standing now, looking at Gramercy Park below in all its manicured glory. It used to seem strange to her, the thought of a city park that only certain residents had the keys to enter. It's a world away from where she is now.

"How's he doing these days?"

"Is that why you called?"

Lydia's tone suggests that Richard's mental and emotional state should be the least of her concerns. But Elinor can't help herself. She revered him for a year and dated him for another. When she writes now, it's often his voice that she hears in the back of her head, urging her to comb through something again, to go back to the drawing board and do it better. She almost never regrets listening to him, however harsh or critical she imagines his advice. "He's not handling this well, is he?"

"What do you think?"

Richard had always been a difficult person to accuse of bad behavior. She considered this quality the flip side of his charm. If Elinor mentioned that she saw him looking at another woman for too long, he'd defer and deflect until she began to question what she really saw. It made her feel crazy, like she couldn't trust her own eyes, combined with the added insult of having to apologize for starting a fight "over nothing." Sometimes, she wondered if his resistance to accepting responsibility was a function of his intellect. Richard was accustomed to always being right, or being able to lean on his rhetorical gifts to convince people that he was right. The more someone deserved an apology, the harder he fought not to give one, like it was some kind of sport that only he knew he was playing.

"How did you even find out about this anyway?" Lydia asks. "Aren't you still in North Dakota?"

"I am, but one of the women . . . she tracked me down out here and asked if I could help. I can't, obviously." She emphasizes the word "can't"—for her sake or Lydia's, she's not sure.

"Aggressive, aren't they? The witches won't be satisfied until they've ensured Macbeth's demise." She pauses for a moment. "Of course, that's what he deserves."

She's confused by the way Lydia refers to the women as "witches," while also suggesting that Richard should be punished. The ideas are oppositional. One seems like the thing she's supposed to say. The other seems like the thing she actually feels.

"Do you believe them?" Elinor asks.

"Don't you?"

The question has yet to be put to her as directly as this. She hasn't even asked it of herself. "Yes," she answers. And then once more, for good measure. "Yes."

It occurs to her that doubt never entered her mind after she spoke to Kathryn. Not only did she believe her classmates' claims, she believed wholeheartedly in Richard's capacity to do the things he was being accused of. She had seen, but not really noticed, variations of these behaviors all along. Favoring certain women, admiring them in ways he shouldn't, extending favors and gestures that in retrospect seemed inappropriately grand. Elinor's only resistance to Richard's guilt was how it forced her to see her own actions in a sharper light.

"I believe them too," Lydia says. "That's the problem. Because now I just feel like an idiot, dating someone—Christ, moving in with someone—who could do this. Me, of all people."

There's a small measure of solace in the fact that a woman like Lydia was as easily taken in as she was. It makes for an uncomfortable sorority. But absent from their conversation are the women whom Richard actually harmed. Kathryn, Lauren, and Natalie to start. And there were probably others—surely there had to be others—who chose not to get involved because they were afraid. They haven't spent a minute talking about what they went through. It's easier to make this about themselves.

"I think I was just excited by the idea of an accomplished man whose ego I didn't have to baby. It's hard finding one who's interested in dating an age-appropriate woman instead of some pretty little thing that looks good on the arm." Lydia pauses. "Sorry. I obviously wasn't talking about you. You write. You have a career." She laughs nervously, but then her voice catches. "You know, I asked him point-blank if you two had some sort of agreement about this Bakken article, and he said it wasn't like that with you. What did he mean by that?"

Elinor looks at her lap. It was one thing to have this conversation with Kathryn, someone whose respect she no longer cares to earn. But Lydia is different.

"He didn't . . . he never offered me things before we got together, as a way of getting us together. He didn't have to. Honestly, when he called about the article, I had no idea any of this was going on in the background. I just assumed—" And now it's Elinor's turn to laugh, embarrassed by how moved she was that he'd contacted her, entrusting her with something so personally and professionally meaningful. "I assumed he'd recommended me for this because I grew up here. Because he thought I could do it."

Lydia is silent for a while. "Well, fuck it," she says gruffly. "I think you can do it. And my name's the one on the masthead."

It should be a relief to hear this, but it's not. It seems like a knee-jerk reaction, not a full-throated or even genuine show of support. Still, it's better than Lydia killing the piece because she wants to cut ties to Richard and anything he was involved in. Elinor keeps hearing the same words over and over again. *Say thank you and good night. Say thank you and good night.* She still has an assignment to work on. That's more than she could have hoped for when Lydia picked up. The temptation is to end on this positive note, however hollow it might be. But she stays on the line, conscious of a nagging feeling she can't ignore, something she also learned from Richard—to trust her instincts when they were telling her that she'd taken a wrong turn.

"I don't want to write the article he pitched," she says abruptly. "That's not what this should be about."

"Alright?" Lydia says uncertainly. "What's the story, then?"

"I don't know yet, but it has to be about women—the ones who come to the Bakken looking for something. I want to write about the things that happen to them here. The violence and the misogyny. And race is part of this too. I'm just figuring out how."

Her inexperience is on full display now. No seasoned writer in her right mind would talk to an editor she barely knows like this. She's essentially spitballing, something that Lydia probably isn't used to because she seems thrown off guard.

"Alright," she repeats, elongating the word, sounding even more uncertain than she did before. "But you're not still thinking about that woman who went missing, are you?"

Thank you and good night. Thank you and good night.

"She might be a part of this. I'm not sure yet. All I'm asking is that you let me try. If it doesn't make sense to include her, I won't. And in the end, if I give you a story that's not worth telling, it's exactly like you said. Your name's on the masthead. You'll just kill it."

Lydia scrapes the flint of her lighter again as she starts a new cigarette. So much time passes. It seems like she's trying to smoke the whole thing before she decides.

"Okay," she finally says. "Go find yourself some women."

35

Elinor sits quietly for several minutes after the call ends, relieved but exhausted. She looks forward to waking up in the morning, free to figure out the story she actually wants to tell. But first—sleep. Hours and hours of sleep to make up for the hours she hasn't had. She locks her doors and crawls into the back seat, punching her bag with her fists until it forms a pillow. When she closes her eyes, she's so greedy for rest, she thinks it might come to her easily for once. But only a few seconds pass before she notices it. A nearby light post, as bright as a klieg light. Even with her eyes closed, she can sense its white glow through the blacks of her lids. She slides her bag to the other side of the seat and lies down again, but the effect is even worse in this direction. She tells herself not to think about it, which of course only makes her think about it more. In a fit of desperation, she digs a sweater out of her bag and drapes it over her face, but it's too hot to breathe so she yanks it away. Elinor returns to the front seat, brushing the staticky hair off her forehead as she surveys the cars parked nearby. Earlier, she noticed that all of them had their windshields covered. Most have their side and rear windows covered too. Now she understands why.

She walks over to the gas station to buy a windshield screen, bracing herself for comments from the peanut gallery she has to pass. She's relieved to find that most of the people sitting in front of their cars are couples, drinking or grilling their dinner, too distracted to register her presence. The stray aromas of food drift toward her from every direction. Hot dogs and cheap, fatty burgers, cans of baked beans with bacon. Her stomach rumbles, a reminder that she needs to eat soon. When she enters the gas station, there's a rack of windshield sunshades displayed next to the door, outrageously priced at $39.95. She suspects she's not the first person to wander in looking for one. Elinor quickly finds an inoffensive beach print with palm trees and sandcastles on it. What she can't find so easily is food, other than junk food. She serpentines through the narrow aisles, seeing only chips, candy, and cookies—things that will probably make her blood sugar go haywire.

"You don't have any sandwiches?" she asks the kid texting behind the register. "Something other than just snacks?"

"Sold out," he says, not bothering to lift his eyes from his phone. "Next fresh food truck comes at 3 a.m. Diner's still open though."

All Elinor wants to do is return to her car and sleep, so she grabs a bottle of water, two granola bars, and a fistful of beef jerky, individually wrapped in plastic. She declines the bag that the kid offers, a decision she regrets as soon as she leaves the store, the sunshade being larger and unwieldier than she expected. She drops the water bottle first, lunging for it before it rolls under someone's pickup, which causes her to drop one of the granola bars. Halfway across the lot, her hands wet with condensate from the bottle, she drops almost all the beef jerky.

"You need some help?"

Elinor looks up. There's a woman sitting in front of a VW van, an old one with a patchwork of mismatched and rusted replacement panels. The woman is younger than Elinor by at least a decade, a petite brunette who looks like she recently spent too much time in the sun. Although she's thin, the low-slung angle of her chair, combined with her posture, make her stomach rise up like a table. On it, she's balancing a can of beer.

"I'm okay, thanks." Elinor grabs the beef jerky pieces, which have fallen like pick-up sticks. She wonders what possessed her to buy so many.

"You're new," the woman says matter-of-factly.

Elinor doesn't know if she means new to the Bakken or new to the parking lot. Either way, she's not sure how she can tell.

The woman introduces herself as Lisa and motions toward the chair beside her. "You want to sit and take a break?"

Her car isn't that far away. But Elinor hasn't seen many women like this—young, alone, and seemingly receptive to having a conversation. If she's a roughneck or even a job seeker, she's worth stopping for. It's just an unfamiliar situation. Women are usually more standoffish to her, bordering on dismissive. Damon once attempted to console her about this by suggesting that her looks probably intimidated people who were insecure about their own. It was the same reason he didn't have many male friends, he reasoned. Although she knew he was trying to make her feel better, his logic always troubled her. Being attractive was supposed to be a good thing. It often seemed like the one true, good thing about her, given that people rarely commented on anything else. She didn't like the idea of her appearance being a wall that was hard to get past. Lisa, however, shows no signs of being insecure, much less intimidated. She picks up the sweatshirts piled in the chair beside her and pats the vinyl seat.

"Come hang out," she says.

Elinor sits down, resting the sunshade and snacks in her lap. On the ground, equidistant between them, is a miniature grill. Lisa gives the charcoal briquettes inside a sharp poke with the end of a stick, sending flecks of ash snowing through the air.

"How could you tell I was new? Did I look lost or something?"

Lisa motions toward the sunshade. "Everyone buys one of those when they first get here. Then they figure out that plain old cardboard works best." She turns and points at her van, which has a cracked headlight and a Montana license plate hanging on by a single screw. The windshield has been plastered from the inside with flattened boxes that read ABSOLUT VODKA and OLD GRAND-DAD BOURBON. "There's a liquor store down the road that'll sell you those for a dollar apiece, which is kind of a rip-off since they were probably just going to recycle them. But at least it's the cheapest rip-off in the area." Lisa catches Elinor looking at the open tall boy in her hand. "You want one?" she asks, but she's already reaching into her cooler, pulling out another.

"That's okay. I don't want to take your beer."

Lisa opens the can with a loud crack and holds it out to her. "Too late," she says, smiling. "Plus we have more in the van."

Elinor has no choice but to accept it now, not that she really minds. The can is ice-cold, a nice contrast to the muggy summer heat. She presses it against her forehead before taking her first sip, which goes down like water.

"So what part of Montana are you from?"

Lisa looks confused.

"The license plate—it says Montana. You're from there?"

"Ohhhhh. No, we're from Grand Forks. When we first got to town, we met this older guy who was just leaving. I guess he'd had it with this place, so he sold us his van for a couple hundred bucks."

Elinor is familiar with Grand Forks, where the state's other air force base is located. Suddenly she has so many questions. Is Lisa from a military family as well? Why did she decide to leave her hometown? Who's the "we"?

"We?"

"Me and my boyfriend. Hey, Travis!" she shouts at the van. "Travis! We got a visitor."

She waits, but nothing happens. "He's beat. He just finished his first week on the job over at a site in Ruxton. We're actually celebrating tonight." She points at the plastic bags on the ground next to her feet. Spilling out of one of them is a Styrofoam tray of steaks marked a dollar off. The other contains a fat round loaf of bread and cans of something she can't make out through the grocery store's logo. "Travis!"

Elinor is disappointed that Lisa isn't alone. She drinks her beer faster, aware that it would be rude to leave with an almost full can, but she doesn't want to intrude on a private celebration.

"Is that all you're having for supper?" Lisa asks, glancing at her beef jerky and granola bars. "You should stay and eat with us."

"Oh, no . . ." Elinor is alarmed by Lisa's friendliness, unaccustomed to it. "I ate already. These are for tomorrow. Besides, I'm really tired . . ."

The side door of the van opens and out stumbles a barefoot man with the worst farmer's tan she's ever seen. His chest is as white as a full moon, but his face and arms are the color of terra-cotta. Travis pulls on a T-shirt, nimbly stretching the collar away from the lit cigarette hanging out of his mouth.

"Steak's done already?" he asks, his voice a low mumble.

"I haven't started cooking yet. We have company."

"Company" is such a Midwestern word, a throwback to Elinor's childhood when the apartment always had to be spotless in case company dropped by unannounced, which rarely happened. Sometimes, Elinor's father would receive an invitation to visit his fellow officers' homes and bring his family along, as if they were the jet trail he dragged behind him. Whenever they were the company, Ed insisted they all wear their nicest clothes—matching outfits and tight patent leather shoes for Elinor and Maren, a pretty dress and good jewelry for Nami—even though they usually arrived to find everyone else in jeans or shorts. He also made Nami carry the gift for the hostess, hoping the gesture might help her ingratiate herself with the other wives.

"A good guest always has to bring something," he said. "They don't come empty-handed, like they're just begging to be fed."

Elinor puts her beef jerky and granola bars on the folding table with a quiet "help yourself" while Travis pulls out another chair. It feels silly offering these things to them when they're about to have dinner, so she pats herself down, wondering if she has anything else worth sharing.

"Cigarette?" she asks, extending her pack.

Travis waves her off, still finishing the last of his, but Lisa leans over and plucks one out.

"Don't mind if I do."

She lights her smoke and introduces Elinor to Travis, who seems neither bothered nor excited to have a stranger joining them for dinner.

He just listens while Lisa puffs away and tells Elinor their life stories, which she merges together as if they've always been intertwined. Elinor learns that they were both born and raised in Grand Forks to civilian parents, and they've been dating since the age of fourteen, except for a two-week period in high school when Travis decided to chase after a new foreign exchange student. "Some skank from Costa Rica," Lisa adds with a sly giggle, which fails to elicit any reaction from him. Three months ago, they came to the western part of the state because they were tired of jumping from one minimum-wage job to another. It seemed undignified—a word Lisa hits every beat of—totally *un-dig-ni-fied* for both of them to be approaching thirty and still earning minimum wage. Despite the warnings of the previous owner of their van, who couldn't get hired anywhere, all the rumors they'd heard about the Bakken's hot job market turned out to be true.

"Now that I think about it, that guy must have had something really bad on his record," Lisa says, pausing for Travis to chime in. "I mean, short of murdering somebody or being a kiddie diddler, anybody with half a brain can get hired in this town." She glances at the van with a grimace. "I just hope he didn't do any of that bad shit in there."

At a certain point, it becomes both noticeable and uncomfortable that Lisa is doing all the talking. Despite being interested in what she has to say, Elinor worries that Travis is unhappy about the presence of a third wheel, which is taking the focus off him and his special night.

"Congratulations on your new job," she says, raising her beer at him. "You just finished your first week, I heard."

He shrugs, plunking his can against hers without enthusiasm.

"He's *full-time* now," Lisa says proudly.

"Big deal," he mutters.

She pets him on the back like he's a dog or a child. "He was hoping to land something that came with housing, but that'll be the next job after this one. We haven't even been here that long, and he's already a full-time ginzel."

Oil workers have a vocabulary all their own for the myriad jobs in their industry. Some of the job titles sound made up. Roustabouts, chain hands, derrickmen, tool pushers. Elinor is vaguely familiar with the term *ginzel*, but she doesn't think it's a good word. It's slang, if she remembers correctly, the kind of name guys use when they're giving each other a hard time, though Lisa doesn't appear to know this.

"So what kind of work does that involve?" Elinor asks.

Travis shrugs again. "Dirty shit."

She waits for him to elaborate, but Lisa cuts in again. "He means the grunt work that the higher-up guys won't do." She pokes the coals, decides they're ready, and throws three steaks on the grill before Elinor can protest. "If you've never worked in an oil field before, you have to start at the bottom and pay your dues before companies will hire you for the really big money jobs. But it's still way more than he was making back home."

She nods, hoping that Travis might have something more to add, but he's just staring at the grill, absentmindedly pushing and pulling the tab on his beer can until it finally snaps off in his hand and he throws it—really hurls it—across the parking lot.

"And what about you?" Elinor turns to Lisa, trying to fill the increasingly awkward silence. "Are you working too?"

Right away, she can tell that she's touched a nerve because Lisa's face tightens and Travis leans into the conversation, resting his elbows on his knees.

"Well, go on," he says after a beat of silence. "You told her everything else about us. Why don't you tell her how you're dancing at a club now?"

The sound of his voice startles Elinor. She realizes he's not quiet or shy, or even tired. He's definitely not a mumbler. He's mad. He's been mad this entire time and now she's tapped into the very thing that probably made him mad in the first place.

"I just started dancing at this club on Route Ten," Lisa says, ignoring him. She scans Elinor up and down. "You could too, you know, if you're looking for work. I can introduce you to the manager. The money's *in-sane*."

Out of the corner of her eye, she sees Travis jump up from his chair.

In one swift motion, he kicks the grill, as hard as someone trying to kick a football over goalposts. Steaks and hot coals fly everywhere. The metal grate rolls away, spiraling in a bright silver blur until it finally clatters to the ground.

"What the fuck?" Lisa shouts. "That was our *dinner*, Travis."

But he's gone already, walking barefoot through the parking lot as onlookers peek their heads out of their vehicles to see what the commotion was all about.

"Choke on your dinner," Travis shouts back. "Fucking choke on it."

36

One summer, the agency sent a young Ukrainian model to fill a vacant room in the apartment. Nadeeja was thin, blond, and blue-eyed, a look that was universally in demand, and she also had a prominent beauty mark on her cheek that was very on trend that season. She'd barely unpacked her bags before landing an enviable succession of editorial shoots that went straight to her head, especially when she learned that her new roommates mostly did catalog work—steady, stable, decidedly unsexy catalog work for companies whose clothes they would never deign to wear in real life. Instead of trying to get to know Elinor and the others, Nadeeja treated the apartment like the way station they all knew it was. On her days off, she holed up in her room, watching TV with her hanger-on of a boyfriend, a quiet man who never bothered to introduce himself to any of the roommates. They took to calling him "Ivan" because he looked just like an Ivan should. Big, tall, and brooding, with a shock of white-blond hair that he wore in gelled spikes.

Elinor, whose room shared a wall with Nadeeja's, often heard them talking in their native tongue, punctuated with its long vowels and guttural consonants. Although she couldn't understand what they were saying, she could tell when one of their conversations was about to turn into a fight because Nadeeja would cry or plead, and then her voice became muffled, as if he was covering her mouth. Elinor was almost certain that Ivan was hurting her in some way that never left a mark or cost her any work, but she was afraid to ask. She assumed that no woman wanted to be on the receiving end of that question, and given how imperious Nadeeja was, Elinor expected her to react badly, possibly with anger, to being cast as a victim by someone she barely knew. It was almost a relief when Nadeeja abruptly moved out at the end of the summer, leaving only a Duane Reade receipt on the refrigerator as proof that she'd ever lived there. On the back of the receipt, she'd written her full name, a forwarding address for her mail, and nothing more.

Years later, when a booker at the agency casually mentioned that a former client named Nadeeja had jumped off a balcony in London, Elinor felt a strange, sharp pang of guilt that she knew she wasn't entitled to. She hadn't given her former roommate a second's thought since she'd moved out. And she hadn't intervened or offered her help when the younger woman desperately appeared to need it, even if she didn't appear to want it. The booker, upon hearing Elinor's suspicions about Ivan, tried to absolve her of any responsibility by suggesting that Nadeeja could have had a drug problem or money trouble or a serious bout of depression—things that happened with alarming frequency to people in their line of work. There was no reason to believe that Ivan was still in the picture or his abuse had anything to do with her decision to end her life. But that was exactly the problem. Elinor wasn't sure what effect, if any, her inaction had, and wondering without the possibility of an answer was actually worse than knowing what the answer was. She made a rare promise to herself that the next time she felt the question needed to be asked, she wouldn't avoid it again.

If not for the incident with Hannah at the Depot, Elinor probably would have blurted it out already. But now she's wary of making the same mistake twice, coupling good intentions with less-than-careful phrasing. Fortunately, Lisa has given her plenty of time to think. Ever since Travis took off, she's been talking nonstop, cycling through embarrassed apologies and petulant name-calling, sometimes all at once.

"I just thought it might do him some good to be around new people, you know? Like being sociable would maybe snap him out of the shitty mood he's been in all week." She swats at a mosquito buzzing too close to her face. "I'm sorry you had to see him act like that. Big fucking baby."

The two of them are walking through the parking lot in the blast radius of Travis's outburst, picking up the dust- and gravel-crusted steaks and stomping out the occasional live coal. Under Elinor's arm, she's carrying the miniature barbecue grill, which landed nearly twenty feet away from the van. It's empty now, but still warm to the touch, and there's a huge dent on the side where Travis kicked it. They have yet to find where the cover rolled off to.

"He just can't get it through that thick head of his—I actually *like* dancing. I always have. And I'm good at it too. I mean, I'm not Friday or Saturday night kind of good. Those girls are like fucking acrobats. But I'm way better than the Tuesday morning freak show." She kicks a black coal down the long row of cars, waving at a man listening to the radio in front of his camper. He responds with a friendly wave back and a "Hi, Tina" that she doesn't bother to correct.

"Look, I'm not trying to pry or anything . . ." Elinor's brain is swimming in cortisol, still shaken by the image of Travis punting the grill across the lot. She couldn't sleep now if she wanted to. She's too worried about what will happen to Lisa when he returns, which will probably be soon given that he left without shoes on. Elinor has always been deeply uncomfortable with male anger, the ways in which it can manifest. She doesn't understand how something can feel both predictable and unpredictable at the same time.

"Please don't take this the wrong way . . ." She hesitates again, but reminds herself that if she doesn't take advantage of the break in conversation, she might not get another one for a while. "But I need to ask. Does he lose his temper with you a lot?"

"Oh God, no," Lisa says, laughing almost. "Travis isn't a hitter, if that's what you're getting at. He just blows up at *things*. He'd punch a brick wall a million times before he'd ever lay a finger on me."

Her response, while relaxed and good-natured, isn't very reassuring. Elinor also wonders if it's the truth, or if it's simply what a woman in a bad situation might say to a stranger. She examines Lisa out of the corner of her eye, searching for bruises or scratches, but sees only a few dark moles and a wine-colored spot on her thigh that appears to be a birthmark. The absence of physical evidence doesn't necessarily mean anything though. If dumb, silent Ivan knew enough to hide his handiwork, then maybe Travis does too.

"I'm sorry I asked about your job," Elinor says. "I had no idea he'd react like that."

"It's not your fault Travis bugged out. All anyone wants to talk about around here is what people are doing for money. He should be used to it by now. By the way, I was dead serious about introducing you to my manager. He's always on the lookout for exotic girls—as dancers, not because he's got a fetish or anything."

Despite disliking the word "exotic" and all the baggage it carries, Elinor decides to ignore it in favor of something she should have mentioned earlier. She explains that she's actually a writer, working on an article about women in the Bakken for the *Standard*. It's the first time she's been able to say this out loud without feeling uncertain about it, wondering if someone was preparing to yank the rug out from under her feet. It feels good, but still surreal.

"I'm obviously not going to write about you," she continues. "Or Travis either. I don't write about people without their permission, just to be clear."

"I like writing," Lisa says, seemingly unbothered by this information, and slightly off topic. "And I don't mind being in your article if you want to include some dancers in it. Or hey—" She grabs Elinor's forearm, shaking it gently. "I work on Sunday and Monday nights. If you want to swing by the club and see what it's like, I could show you around."

Elinor had mentally disqualified Lisa as an interview subject as soon as she learned she was stripping. So many articles she'd read had already gone down this route, focusing on women who were making a small fortune in the Bakken by taking their clothes off for men. It was too easy. As far as she was concerned, writing about strippers was as lurid as writing a dead girl story. "I don't need any dancers for this particular piece," she says, being careful to use the same euphemism that Lisa does. "But I could use some help finding female roughnecks to talk to. Do you know any of those?"

"Oh, sure. There's a bunch of them around here in the lot. Travis is actually friendly with a couple of older ladies—*lesbians*," she whispers curiously, as if she's scandalized by the idea of two women in a relationship. "I don't think they work on weekends, so I bet he could introduce you tomorrow if you want."

She does want, but the mention of Travis reminds her that he could be anywhere right now. She turns around, walking backward for a few steps to make sure he's not behind them.

"You don't have to bother looking for him, if that's what you're doing. He's probably hanging out in his friends' RV. He'll have a couple of beers and then come home when he's calmed down." She says this so casually, as if Travis has blown up with enough regularity to establish a pattern, which also isn't reassuring.

"I hate to bring this up again, but are you sure—are you absolutely sure he's not going to come back and do something to you?"

Lisa shakes her head. Thankfully, she doesn't seem annoyed to be asked the question twice. "I swear, he's not like that. And I'm not like that either. I knew girls in school whose boyfriends used to slap them around and I always thought they were so sad. Some of them even married those assholes."

It's hard to tell what part of this argument Lisa believes, and what part is meant to make Elinor believe. She studies her expression, trying to find some evidence of a lie, but she neither knows what to look for nor sees anything that would give her cause to doubt. She has to let it go. "Well, I hope I didn't offend—"

"It's fine, it's fine." Lisa waves her off and then puts a hand on each hip as she surveys the distance they've walked from her van. The plastic bag of steaks that she peeled off the pavement dangles loosely from her wrist. "There's no way the cover could have rolled this far, is there?"

"I doubt it."

"Fucking Travis. I just bought that grill too."

They walk to the gas station, where Lisa deposits the bag in an overflowing dumpster that specifically forbids its use by anyone other than employees. Judging from the mountain of garbage and the casualness with which Lisa adds to it—flinging the bag high in the air so it falls on the pile with a splat—no one who lives in the parking lot pays any attention to the signs or to the pair of security cameras angled at the bank of dumpsters. The act of defending Travis appears to have calmed Lisa down because on the walk back to their cars, she changes the subject and begins giving Elinor an unsolicited orientation to life at Emerald's.

The rules are actually much stricter than she imagined. There's really only one rule that matters and multiple variations of it. *Be invisible.* This means using the dumpster at night when the manager isn't around, and not blasting music or getting caught stealing from the gas station. There are four pay showers for truckers and parking lot residents in the lounge area. The natural temptation, according to Lisa, is to buy a shower and have sex behind a closed door for a change instead of in a vehicle, but don't do it, she warns. The management wouldn't put up with that for a hot minute.

"We've got to be self-policing," she explains. "Emerald's has been threatening to call in a tow company for a while, which would suck for pretty much everyone living here, so we're all really careful about respecting the property and not causing any trouble." She bends over and fishes a rock out of her shoe, throwing it at an angle like she's skipping stones. "And if you leave during the day, don't forget to be back in the lot by ten every night; otherwise, you might not find a spot, and you definitely can't park on the grass."

"It seems like you know a lot about this place."

"I should. We've been here going on six weeks now. We staked out a spot as soon as we heard they weren't towing."

"And before Emerald's?"

"We were renting a patch of dirt in some farmer's field about ten miles north of here. That guy was a jerk though. He kept jacking up the price every week, saying he could always find someone else who needed a space if we couldn't pay. Actually, he and Travis almost got into it a few times."

Elinor lifts and lowers her eyebrows. Lisa must notice because she quickly follows up.

"Travis is a good guy. He just has this really strong sense of right and wrong, so he gets pissed at the thought of customers disrespecting me at the club, or if people try to push him around on the job or make him feel small."

Elinor wants to wave her hands at the parking lot, row after row of cars filled with people whose labor Avery needs, but whose presence the town neither welcomes nor wants. "But isn't this a bad place for him then? I mean, doesn't that kind of thing happen all the time around here?"

Lisa is silent for a moment. Then she tips her head back and releases a single, loud "ha!" straight into the air. "Jesus. I never thought of it like that."

37

At first, all she sees are the knuckles. White knuckles, knocking against her window and then pulling away. As she rubs her eyes, Travis slowly comes into focus. He's standing beside her car, peering in at her under a visored hand. He knocks again and says her name. Muffled through the glass, it sounds like he's calling her "Elenora," which he very well may be. She's more confused by his presence than afraid, especially when she removes the sunshade from her windshield and notices an older woman hovering behind him, smiling like she's embarrassed to be there. Elinor brings her seat to an upright position, accidentally jerking the lever and thrusting herself toward the dashboard. Her neck and back feel terrible. She turns on the engine and lowers the dusty window, trying to sit up straight. Small pockets of air crack and pop in her spine, bursting in places where they don't belong.

"Lisa said you needed help finding some ladies for that thing you're writing?"

Travis looks like a dog that just shat in the house. Tail curled between his legs, unable to make eye contact. He shoots his thumb back at the older woman. "This is Annie. She hauls dirty water for Kincannon."

Only a man eager to make up for his bad behavior would do this, she thinks, introducing two strangers—one of them fast asleep—at the crack of dawn. Elinor and Annie wave at each other, both hesitant and awkward. They make arrangements to meet in the diner after Elinor has a chance to tidy up, which amounts to little more than brushing her teeth and washing her face in Emerald's restroom. It's early and the facilities appear recently cleaned, with streak-free mirrors and dry countertops that smell like lemons and bleach. Remembering Lisa's advice from the night before, she wipes off the water she splashed on the tile, careful to be a good and respectful guest, a ghost.

Annie is sitting in a booth in the back corner of the diner, nodding off over a cup of coffee. Elinor slides into the seat across from her and orders two glasses of water from a passing waitress, feeling parched and certain that one won't be enough. As she removes her recording equipment and notebooks from her bag, she regrets not having more time to prepare for their conversation. She has no questions written out. Nothing remotely resembling a plan. She unpacks her bag a little slower until the strangeness of the silence prompts her to say the first thing that comes to mind.

"So how are you?" she asks.

Annie's expression softens a little. "Tired. Same as you, I bet." She points at the jukebox attached to the side of their table. "You mind? I could go for some music right now to wake me up."

Music might interfere with the quality of her audio recording, but this isn't the kind of request Elinor can say no to, not when she sees the quarters already in Annie's palm. She watches her deposit them one by one into the slot, giving the side of the machine a gentle tap so they fall in. The last time Elinor saw a jukebox like this, she was in her twenties, on the tail end of a long first date in a twenty-four-hour diner. The guy she was with made a big deal about taking turns, probably to show off his taste in music or evaluate hers. As soon as he picked out a song, he made her pick one, back and forth until they spent down every credit. Thankfully, Annie makes all the choices herself, punching in several four-digit codes that she seems to know by heart. The song that begins to play through the tinny speaker is something from the Motown era, one of those trios or quartets of Black women in matching dresses who made upbeat hits but were poorly paid.

"You like Motown?" Elinor asks.

"Love." Annie nods. "It reminds me of home."

"You're from Detroit?"

"Fargo, actually. But I grew up listening to this kind of music."

The fact that they're both from North Dakota gives them a few minutes of easy small talk. Elinor asks if the old movie theater in downtown Fargo is still in business. Annie asks if she ever ate at the Chuckwagon Buffet in Marlow before it closed down. She waits for the inevitable question about how her family ended up in the state, and is pleasantly surprised when she doesn't hear it.

"I don't think I've ever met a writer before," Annie says, glancing at the stack of notebooks on the table.

"I never met a truck driver before this trip to Avery."

"Get out." Annie seems shocked. "We're everywhere, though."

Elinor doesn't know what to tell her. She can't imagine many circumstances, except possibly a variation of the current one, in which she would ever cross paths with a truck driver. Despite her guardedness and discomfort whenever she meets someone new, this is one of the things she appreciates about writing, how it forces her out of her bubble.

The waitress returns and deposits two glasses of ice water on the table. Then she takes out her pad and holds her pen over a blank page, as if to say they can't occupy a corner booth for just a cup of coffee and some water. Elinor orders the most expensive item on the menu, a large breakfast platter called the All-American. She encourages Annie to order something too—the *Standard's* treat—but she declines, probably because a meal is more than she wants to commit to. The waitress sniffs as she collects their menus and moves on to the next table. It's hard not to interpret the sound as annoyance.

Annie leans forward after she leaves and lowers her voice to a whisper. "That's Stacey. She's always in a bad mood."

"Why's that?"

She shrugs. "Because of people like us, I guess."

"Us?"

"You know, the folks camped out in the lot."

What lengths Elinor would have gone to as a child, what lengths she actually did go to, to feel like she belonged to an "us." Now the group she's been swept into, albeit temporarily, is no more wanted in this community than she was, an irony that isn't lost on her.

"So how long have you been living at Emerald's?" Elinor asks.

"About four months. Pretty much right when this place opened to the public."

Physically, Elinor has never felt her age. But now every muscle in her body is sore and tight and miserable, a condition she attributes directly to sleeping in her car. It's hard to imagine doing this for more than a few nights.

"Yup. You heard that right," Annie confirms, rubbing the corners of both eyes with her knuckles. "Months."

She explains that her employer has a contract with a man camp that doesn't allow women. Instead of finding her another housing situation, Kincannon gives her a monthly stipend. It's not quite enough to rent a place of her own, but at fifty-five, she thinks she's too old to live with roommates. Sleeping in her truck allows her to pocket the extra money, so she claims not to mind it anymore. The faster she saves, the faster she can head back to Fargo, where her goal is to open a truck driving school for women. Annie is eager to talk about why a school like this is necessary, and for several long minutes, she goes on to describe what would make hers unique. The things Elinor jots down in her notebook—small classes where female students would feel free to talk and ask questions, a self-defense course to prepare them for life on the road, practicing with licensed female drivers during the permit period instead of men who might bully or harass them—seem like reactions to the difficulties that Annie experienced, rather than changes that will address why she experienced what she did. Even if it were Elinor's place to comment on this, she wouldn't. When Annie talks about her school, she seems happy in a way that few people she's met here are.

"One All-American, over easy, wheat toast," the waitress interrupts, depositing Elinor's breakfast on the table.

When she walks off, Elinor asks Annie if the two of them had some sort of falling out. The service has been so gruff from the start, she's certain the answer will be yes, but Annie just shakes her head.

"Me and her? We barely even know each other. She's like that with everybody who's parked in the lot. She treats us all like we're homeless or something."

Annie sounds more upset about being snubbed by their waitress than being hazed by the men she went to driving school with. The sudden spike of resentment is noticeable, and strange. The two women are probably about the same age, both working jobs that can't be easy on their bodies, both dealing with men in the oil patch every day. In an alternate version of reality, Elinor could imagine Annie and Stacey being friends, bound by what they have in common, rather than looking for ways to set themselves apart. She wonders how many of her own passing encounters have turned out like this, opportunities for connection wasted by some combination of judgment and defensiveness, insecurity and shame.

"I don't know where she gets off either, thinking she's so much better than us," Annie grumbles. "It's not like we're really homeless. I probably make at least five times what she does."

Elinor isn't sure what Annie's salary has to do with anything, except that it seems to make her feel superior.

"Some of the nicest, most decent people I've ever met are living out in that lot. He's a good example right there." She motions toward the window at Travis, who's smoking in front of the diner with a woman who isn't Lisa. "That kid helped me change a flat in the rain one night. He got totally soaked too, and we barely even knew each other back then. He just stopped because he saw all these people speeding by, not giving me an inch."

She's not sure how to reconcile this description of Travis with the version she saw last night. She can still see him leaning forward in his seat, glowering at the mention of his girlfriend stripping for other men, and then screaming at her to go choke on her dinner. Elinor must be frowning when she thinks about this because suddenly Annie is leaning forward, looking almost offended.

"What? You don't like Travis?"

"No, no," she says quickly. "I don't know him well enough to like or dislike him . . . I saw him lose his temper yesterday, that's all."

"Well, the kid's got a temper for sure. But show me a guy who doesn't, right?"

38

Travis's chosen form of apology appears to be providing Elinor with not just one woman to talk to, but a steady stream of them. After she finishes her conversation with Annie, he brings in a wire line operator named Lorraine, followed by a dispatcher who goes by Honey, and then another dispatcher who declines to give her name after she learns how large the *Standard*'s readership is.

"Batshit ex-husband," she explains apologetically.

Somehow, Travis always seems to know when the interviews are wrapping up. Just as she's saying her thank-yous and goodbyes, he reappears in the diner, trailed by another tentative-looking woman he rounded up from the lot. He slips in and out without saying more than a quiet word or two, usually an exchange of first names. And he doesn't ask if there are certain types of female oil workers that Elinor needs to talk to, or if she even wants to talk to more. He just rightly assumes that she does and continues leading them in. Elinor is both grateful and stunned. She hoped he might introduce her to the couple that Lisa mentioned, which he does at one point, but she never imagined he'd go this far out of his way to help.

The hours pass quickly in conversation. From her windowed corner booth, Elinor notices the volume of traffic pick up on the interstate and the sun rising to ever higher points in the sky. She goes from offering to buy the women breakfast to encouraging them to order lunch. No one ever takes advantage of her invitation to have a full meal, preferring instead to politely pick at muffins and coffee or french fries and Coke. Elinor continues ordering more food than she actually wants to eat—an extra side of bacon for her All-American Breakfast, a triple decker turkey club with fries, a garden salad, a slice of lemon meringue pie, a root beer float—sensitive to the fact that she's been monopolizing the same table for hours, but she has nowhere else to go.

Some of the women, she likes—usually the sharp-tongued and quick-witted ones who are easy conversationalists, eager to have a new person to chat with. Others are harder to warm to, not that warming is the point. Elinor can tell that a number of them are sitting down with her simply as a favor to Travis or Lisa, not out of a genuine desire to discuss their experiences or be part of an article. These are the ones she has to prod for substance, trying to get past their terse or vague answers. Donna describes her work as a tank welder as "hard," then "stressful," and finally "dangerous." The closest she comes to opening up is when she talks about her four-year-old son, who's staying with her parents in Wisconsin. She's quick to add that she Skypes with him every Sunday night, as if she feels accused of something that Elinor neither thought nor said.

The women she meets are oil field veterans and relative newcomers to the industry; old and young; married, single, or "it's complicated." The single ones, she notices, choose not to date. Many of them laugh at the thought of even trying to, citing some combination of time or energy.

"I'm too tired." Cherri chuckles. "Just too fucking tired."

Whenever she asks about the men they work with, the mood usually shifts. Elinor notices a fair amount of fidgeting and broken eye contact, a sudden caginess that usually wasn't there before. A few of the women feel so good about the money they're earning, they claim they can ignore the harassment they're often subjected to, while others can barely describe the conditions they work under without pausing to collect themselves. A handful look at Elinor, mystified when she asks about harassment, having never experienced it at all.

"If the other girls you're talking to are having trouble with that," a tool pusher named Andrea says, "they're inviting it in some way. They may not know it, but they are." Andrea has been nothing but pleasant during their time together. Still, Elinor hears Kathryn's voice, as crisp and clear as day. *This is why we all hated you.*

"Why do you think they're inviting it?"

Andrea's big green eyes widen, as if she can't imagine why she's being asked. "Well, because I certainly don't have problems like that."

Theories and rumors and opinions abound, sometimes conflicting with and canceling each other out. The boom won't last for much longer. The boom is here to stay. Women can earn as much as men in the Bakken. Men get paid more here for the exact same work, no different than it was back home. Avery feels safe. Avery feels like the Wild West. The housing market collapse was caused by Russia. The housing market collapse was caused by China. The housing market collapse was caused by the banks.

Noticeably, two common threads connect every woman she talks to. They all came to the Bakken to find opportunities that they couldn't find elsewhere. And they're all angry about things that feel out of their control. Sandy's eldest son refuses to go to rehab, even though she can finally afford to help him pay. Elena, who was born in Mexico, is often mistaken for Native American and complains about having to put up with white people who can't tell brown from red, "people too stupid to even know why they hate me." Joanne asks if she's off-the-record three times before discussing her boss, the manager of a water depot who makes at least one comment about blow jobs every time she works a shift.

Out of all the women she talks to, Rae and Dana, an interracial couple, have been in the Bakken the longest, going on two and a half years in July. Elinor expects their issues to be somewhat different from each other's, but they both steadfastly agree: they hate what passes for funny here. If their coworkers aren't cracking jokes about gays and lesbians, then they're joking about Blacks or Indians or Jews. Dana says the guys on her crew often thump her on the back and compliment her for being one of the few Black people they know with a sense of humor. But their jokes are vile, so vile that Dana often goes to bed thinking about them at night. She wonders out loud if she should say something to their boss, and then answers herself in the next breath. If she complains, her coworkers will start calling her "sensitive," which will only make things worse, so she simply laughs along with them, all the while raging inside. Elinor understands what this feels like; she's been doing it for most of her life. It's a weight, but not the kind she carries on her shoulders, which almost makes it sound noble. Instead, she drags hers around like a net, catching more and more refuse in its wake.

Shortly after lunchtime, the interviews end almost as abruptly as they began. When Elinor finishes talking to a woman named Rhonda, Travis walks over with his fists shoved into his pockets and tells her that he can't find anyone else. He seems embarrassed and apologetic—about last night or the number of volunteers, she's not sure. Either way, there's no need. She never expected to do so many interviews in one sitting.

"Thank you, Travis. This was the most productive day I've had si—"

He shakes his head. "You don't have to thank me. Lisa said you needed help and I didn't mind helping."

"But you spent all morning doing this. I don't know how—"

Travis waves her off, clearly uncomfortable with appreciation, much less praise. "Alright, well, I'm glad it went good for you. I gotta take off now. Good luck with"—he gestures toward her table—"whatever it is you're doing here."

As he turns to leave, he almost bumps into Stacey, who sidesteps him with an eye roll and a sigh. The part of Elinor that wonders if she misjudged Travis wishes he'd just stand still for a second and let her thank him properly, but he's gone already, as quickly as he left the night before. Stacey stops at her booth, examining the nearly untouched turkey sandwich that she delivered at least two interviews ago.

"Something wrong with it?" she asks.

"No, it's fine." Elinor tries to straighten up the mess she's made of her table. She stacks her notebooks in a pile and slides her belongings away from the carafe in Stacey's hand, the spout of which is tipping closer to her laptop than she'd like. "It's just hard to talk and eat at the same time."

Stacey nods. "You all done now?"

"I think so. You need the booth? I can clear out if you—"

"No, you're fine where you are. The rush is winding down anyway."

After the first few interviews, Stacey took a noticeable interest in Elinor's work, delivering plates of food slowly, often in multiple trips, and circling around to offer more coffee refills than necessary. Sometimes, when she had no other customers to tend to, she simply hovered nearby and listened in. They haven't had a chance to discuss what Elinor's been doing all morning, but she imagines that Stacey has put it together by now.

"Those girls really know how to complain, don't they?"

After so much eavesdropping, Elinor assumed that some sort of question was coming, but not this one. "What do you mean?"

"You think they'd be happy, making as much money as they are, living out in the lot for free. But every time I walked by, all I heard was them complaining about one thing or another."

A customer asks for ketchup. Stacey leaves without excusing herself, gives the man a bottle, and then delivers two plates of eggs waiting in the pass. When she returns to Elinor, she picks up their conversation as if she never left.

"It's like the Indians on the reservation. 'Oh, my water supply's getting polluted,'" she says in an exaggerated whine, grimacing in a particularly ugly way as she says it. "'Oh, there's too many outsiders coming on our land.' I just get sick to death of listening to people complain. If you don't like it here, then leave, I want to tell them. If your boss is chasing you around the desk, then get yourself another boss. Life is pretty simple if you choose not to make it hard."

It's clear that Stacey has thought about this before, that the line isn't coming to her spontaneously. More so than the substance though, it's the sentiment that gives Elinor pause. Stacey is angry too, but in a way that makes her incapable of empathy, only judgment. Elinor wonders if she's inching toward the very same edge, if she stepped over it already and didn't even notice. Before she gets a chance to follow up, the man who asked for ketchup says he needs hot sauce. Then a pair of men ask for menus. Despite her interest in the interviews, when Stacey returns, she declines to be interviewed herself.

"I don't care if you sit here and do your work. You, I don't mind. But I like to keep my private thoughts private."

This hardly seems true, but Elinor doesn't urge her to reconsider. She's overwhelmed by the volume of material she has to transcribe now. After Stacey moves on, she reviews her notes, paging through the women she spoke to in reverse order, going all the way back to Amy Mueller, arguably the angriest of them all, with two wells in her backyard that she didn't want, a dead husband, and also possibly a dead niece by marriage. Elinor takes advantage of the diner's Wi-Fi to see if she can finally track down Mrs. Mueller's nephew. Predictably, there's no public listing for Shane Foster in Avery. And there are too many Shane Fosters listed in the *I* states. Thirty-four of them in Indiana alone, plus hundreds more on Facebook and Twitter. She clicks around for a while, finding all the wrong Shanes, before returning to her scribble of notes. There was someone else that Mrs. Mueller suggested she talk to, another woman, but she can't make out the name slanting off the edge of the page. She puts on her headphones and finds the interview on her computer, scanning the recording backward and forward until she cues up the right section.

"You should go over there and talk to her, if you get a chance," Mrs. Mueller says, sounding as irascible as Elinor remembers. "Her name's Louise Eddy, E-d-d-y. She's got four EnerGia wells on her property. Four! You'd get a kick out of talking to her, I bet."

Elinor replays this part again, turning the volume up to drown out the diner's ambient noise. For the first time, she notices the mischievous lift in Mrs. Mueller's voice at the end of her sentence, as if she was smiling at the thought of bringing Elinor and Louise Eddy together.

39

By now, it feels like she's driven the same two highways over and over again, so the unfamiliar county road provides some much-needed visual respite from Avery's long commercial sprawl. Miles and miles of farmland stretch out before her, interrupted by the occasional three- or four-stoplight town before returning to farmland again. The quiet scenery is just what she needs after hours of back-to-back interviews. It's that time of the year when the fields are dense and saturated with color, reminding her that the old sayings and songs she learned as a child still hold remarkably true. The corn is nearing "knee-high by the fourth of July," and the wheat that has yet to be harvested does appear almost amber in the afternoon light.

Along this new expanse of road, signage welcomes Elinor to towns so small and unmemorable, she's not sure if she's ever passed through before. Most of them have been named after men. There's Dean, followed by Ryan, Victor, Elroy, Lucas, an outlier named Laverne, and finally, Heath, where Louise Eddy lives. It was surprising, how easy she was to track down. For someone in her seventies, she has an unusually large digital footprint. Although Mrs. Eddy's phone number is unlisted, her address came up in multiple court records because of the lawsuits she filed against EnerGia, starting in 2008. Two years ago, she was arrested for threatening oil workers on her property with an unloaded weapon, a charge that prosecutors dropped due to Mrs.

Eddy's age and declining health, as well as the influx of more serious cases in the area since the start of the boom. The year before that, she allegedly made a bomb threat to EnerGia's parent company in Texas, a charge that the court dismissed due to insufficient evidence.

Whatever hesitation Elinor feels about paying an unannounced, unsolicited visit to Heath is mitigated by Mrs. Eddy's past willingness to talk with seemingly anyone on the record. The list of articles her name appears in is even longer than the list of court records. Dozens of marginally reputable publications with smaller circulations than the *Standard* have quoted her about all the things that Mrs. Mueller mentioned in her interview: well water that tastes like kerosene, freshly washed hair snapping off by the fistful, showers and baths capable of making eyes sting and open wounds burn. Upon first read, Mrs. Eddy's quotes sounded cantankerous, sometimes even unhinged. But Elinor decides to make the trip anyway, aware that people have long been conditioned to confuse women's anger with instability.

After driving past the five or six businesses that make up Heath's town center, she keeps a lookout for Mrs. Eddy's farm. The GPS doesn't work here, so she glances at the directions in her notebook, worried she might miss the address and not notice, something that's actually very hard to do. Every time a property approaches, she can see it coming from miles away thanks to the presence of trees. There are hardly any on the horizon except for the telltale copses planted to shield people's houses from the wind. The Eddy farm announces itself with an arrangement of tall cypresses that look like closed beach umbrellas standing up in the sand. Four wells and several tanks hover in the distance, exactly as Mrs. Mueller described. Elinor turns onto the private road, her car jerking and rumbling over the loose gravel, making a terrible noise that signals her presence before she even arrives. She keeps her eyes glued to the road, crawling along at barely ten miles an hour to avoid the occasional pothole as big as a tire. It's not a particularly long driveway, but its state of near disrepair makes it feel endless. She's relieved to finally come to a stop in front of a modest two-story farmhouse, all white peeling paint and gray rotting wood.

Behind it are several outbuildings in similar condition, including a barn that appears to be leaning dangerously on its foundation.

Her brother-in-law was fond of saying that real farmers didn't have time to make things look pretty. According to Tom, if given the choice between painting a fence or fixing a broken post, fixing always won out. While she understands the value of function over appearance in a place that demands almost nonstop labor, she thinks the Eddy farm looks more abandoned than poorly maintained. There aren't any cars parked near the house or tractors out in the field. No sounds of people or machinery either. And there's a wild, soon-to-be overgrown quality to the place, with weeds crawling up the sides of buildings, spiraling around drainpipes and antennae and wires. Three of the five stairs leading up to the front porch are broken, worn straight through the middle of the treads. Elinor doesn't dare put her full weight on the ones that remain, so she hoists herself up with the help of the railing, getting a splinter wedged into her palm for the effort.

Elinor knocks on the door, but already, her hopes are less than what they were. Thick layers of dust coat every surface, untouched for some time. The only prints she sees on the floorboards besides her own are from a family of possums or raccoons or some other animal with paws that look like greedy little hands. She sucks out the splinter with her teeth and then gives the doorknob a tentative jiggle, not sure what she'd do if it were actually unlocked, which it isn't. Elinor knocks again, rattling the rickety metal screen, which has been patched and repatched with yellowing pieces of tape.

"Hello?" she shouts, shielding her eyes from the sun as she tries to look inside. All she can make out is a dark kaleidoscope of shapes in the leaded glass window.

The porch wraps around the house, so she follows it to the back and walks toward the barn, crossing paths with two skinny white cats. They study her for a second, their faces mean and angular with hunger, before they prowl off into the high grass.

"Hello?" she repeats, hearing only bugs, birds, and wind.

As she nears the barn, she gets a better view of the wells behind the property, their slow-moving heads all working in unison. It hardly seems fair that the wells are here, but Mrs. Eddy isn't. This used to be a home once. Someone's children, perhaps Mrs. Eddy's grandchildren, played on this land not that long ago. She can see the evidence of them everywhere. The tree house in the backyard, complete with its tire swing; the deflated beach ball in the yard; the sandbox that the feral cats are surely using as a litter box now. She wonders when Mrs. Eddy moved away and whether she attempted to sell the property or simply packed up what she could and left.

After peeking her head in the barn and finding it empty—the final sign she needed to confirm that no one lives or works here anymore—she gets in her car and heads back toward the main road, pausing at the end of the driveway. In her rearview mirror, she looks at the house one last time and notices a flag in the top floor window, possibly an attic window. It's an American flag, hanging upside down like the one at Mrs. Mueller's. Seeing it displayed this way once felt like a fluke, just the work of an addled, sleep-deprived old woman not paying attention to how she was doing things. Seeing the same display twice feels like it has more meaning than she understands. Even though she's never met Mrs. Eddy, she doesn't think she or Mrs. Mueller are the kind of people who would ever intentionally disrespect a flag. Midwestern-ers, farmers, people of an older generation—rightly or wrongly, she throws them all into a group that values its symbolism too much.

She's so startled by the sight of the flag in her rearview that she doesn't notice the dust cloud at first. It's coming from the driveway diagonally across the road, accompanied by a buzz that sounds like a swarm of insects growing louder and closer. An old man in a golf cart stops at the end of his driveway and climbs out as the dust settles. His movements are as slow as his stomach is big, spilling out over a tightly cinched belt. He's about to reach into his mailbox when he no-tices Elinor sitting in her car, so he lowers his sunglasses and waves. Apparently, her waving back is all the invitation he needs to hike up his pants and start walking toward her.

"You lost or something?" he shouts. He doesn't look left or right before crossing the road, as if he knows no one is coming.

His unhurried pace allows her to study him. He's wearing a short-sleeved undershirt that used to be white and jeans that have gone soft at the knees. Perched high on the bridge of his nose are amber-tinted sunglasses, the kind she used to see on late-night TV in the eighties when she wasn't supposed to be awake.

"No, not lost. I was looking for Mrs. Eddy. I assume she doesn't live here anymore?"

"What business do you have with Louise?"

It's an odd, off-putting way to respond to a question, but something about his tone gives her pause. He's not being unfriendly, not exactly. He sounds more concerned.

"I'm writing an article about the oil boom. A woman I interviewed, she suggested that I talk to Mrs. Eddy while I was out here."

The man smiles. "Oh, I don't really think you'd want to do that."

Elinor isn't sure what confuses her more. His smile or his suggestion. "Well, I came from Avery just to talk to her. You know what traffic is like over there these days." She makes out the slightest bob of his head in agreement. "How long ago did she move?"

"Around the holidays. Her kids had to put her in assisted living."

Was this the reason why Mrs. Mueller sounded so amused when she mentioned her? Because Elinor would drive all this way for nothing? It's hardly funny though. The more likely scenario is that Mrs. Mueller didn't know her friend had moved. She wanted the two of them to meet for some reason.

"Are you still in touch with Mrs. Eddy? Would you be able to pass on a message to her?"

"Sorry, no. I don't have her new contact information."

"Well, what about her family, then? Could you reach out to one of her kids?"

The man looks around. Not a single car has driven by since he crossed the road. Still, he surveys the area as if he fears being overheard.

"Louise and her family can be—unpleasant," he says, although it's obvious that "unpleasant" isn't really the word he wants to use. "I don't think you'd particularly enjoy talking to her."

"But she doesn't seem to mind the publicity. And I write for a magazine with a really large readership, much larger than any of the other publications she's spoken to."

The man frowns. "No. You're not hearing me, miss. I don't think you—*you*—would enjoy talking to her."

All those years her family lived on the base, being stared at and slighted by their neighbors, they still knew better than to talk badly about people with strangers. They could never be certain who was friendly with whom, or who enjoyed gossip and stirring up trouble. The man appears to be doing the same thing, holding back an opinion that he actually wants to share. Elinor wonders if the concern she heard in his voice earlier was for Mrs. Eddy or for her.

"Did you know her well?" she asks.

"As well as I wanted to." He catches himself at the tail end of his sentence. It looks like he wishes he hadn't said it. He crosses his arms over his chest, resting them on his stomach. Hidden in the wiry white hair on his forearms, she can make out a faded tattoo, probably decades old. It's an anchor with a banner. The words on the banner are illegible, but she's almost certain it's a US Navy tattoo. Judging from the man's age, she'd guess that he probably served in Vietnam.

"Tell me about the flag," she says.

"What?"

"You were navy, right?" She motions toward his arm. "My father was air force. The flag in Mrs. Eddy's window is hanging upside down. I think we both know it's not supposed to be like that."

The man shakes his head. "No. No, it's not." He turns and glances at his house, as if he's hoping his wife will shout his name to come take a call, eat his lunch, help her with the groceries. Anything to get out of this conversation. "Some people . . ." he begins hesitantly, "well, some people say that hanging the flag that way is a distress signal."

"Who was causing Mrs. Eddy distress? EnerGia? Or just the oil companies in general?"

"Them, I suppose," he says, kicking rock after rock into the grass. "But I think she was more distressed by people who look like you."

40

You'd get a kick out of talking to her, I bet.
You'd get a kick out of talking to her, I bet.
You'd get a kick out of talking to her, I bet.

The librarian is explaining something about the Wi-Fi in the build-ing, how it cuts in and out due to overuse. Elinor has been trying her best to listen, but all she can hear is Mrs. Mueller's voice, encouraging her to seek out a woman who once waved a shotgun at a work crew on her property. She assumed Mrs. Eddy had snapped because she was angry about the terms of her deal with EnerGia, which encroached upon her land and her living. But what if she was reacting to an entirely different sense of encroachment? What if the thing she couldn't tolerate was the color of the crew members' skin? Harry Bergum said there was a contingent of old-timers around Avery who felt that a certain "ele-ment" was taking over the area, a term she'd only heard white people use, usually in a whisper, to describe anyone who wasn't. Is it possible that Mrs. Mueller's reaction when she first met Elinor was more than just innocent, ignorant surprise about the mismatch between her Scan-dinavian name and her Asian face? Did she tell Elinor to seek out her friend because Mrs. Eddy was someone she'd enjoy talking to, or be-cause she was amused by the thought of setting up a confrontation?

The moment she keeps revisiting is the one in which Mrs. Mueller grabbed her arm and said she needed help. How desperate she was, and then she suddenly wasn't. The look in her eyes when she realized what she was doing and pushed her away—Elinor assumed it was regret for showing weakness in front of a stranger. But maybe the disgust she observed in her expression wasn't about that at all.

"If you have your own laptop and all you need is Wi-Fi access, your best bet is upstairs," the librarian says.

"I'm sorry—what?" Elinor was thinking about the reunion photo hanging above the Muellers' mantel, the one in which everyone was smiling and dressed up in patriotic red, white, and blue. Was Mrs. Mueller the outlier in this family, with her upside-down flag and her sense of distress about the world closing in? Or was she the norm? Is this what people were alluding to when they kept referring to her and her nephew as "quiet" or "strange"—all the words Elinor recalls being used to describe them, possibly as a replacement for the words that no one was willing to say. "What's my best bet again?"

"Your best bet for finding an empty seat is upstairs. The children's area doesn't get much traffic anymore."

"Kids don't come to the library in Avery?"

The librarian casts a quick glance around the room. "Well, we're serving a pretty different clientele these days."

The main floor is crowded with roughnecks. Nearly every chair is occupied by someone staring at his phone, and there's a line wrapped around several stanchions to get a twenty-minute time slot on one of three ancient-looking computers.

"Is it always this busy here?"

"If you're new in town and need free Internet access to look for a job, it's either us or the Job Bank. Other places, they'll usually make you buy something. And some businesses are just shutting off their public Wi-Fi altogether."

Elinor has several hours to kill before her police ride-along. After her visit to the Eddy farm, she decided to do research at the library, assuming the building would be mostly empty on a nice summer day, but the second floor is nearly as crowded as the first. The only free carrels she can find are near the children's area, where there's a man crashed out on a large beanbag shaped like a teddy bear.

The Wi-Fi is achingly slow, prone to stalling and taking up to a minute to load a single page of text. What Elinor eventually learns about upside-down flags confuses her more than it clarifies. The range of possible meanings is too wide and varied to know what's common. At its most innocuous, it was just like Mrs. Eddy's neighbor said. A distress call, used in cases of grave danger to life or property. But over the years, people began to widen their interpretations of what constituted danger and distress, co-opting the same symbol to signify very different things. Anarchists who disavowed the government's right to interfere in their affairs used it. Antiwar activists who claimed that the Bush administration had manufactured evidence about weapons of mass destruction used it. Tea Party members who wanted to protest the Obama administration's health care and trade policies used it. Elinor wonders if Mrs. Mueller and Mrs. Eddy hung their flags upside down because they believed their towns, and perhaps America at large, were being overrun by "nonwhite interests," a practice gaining in popularity among some white separatists. But this isn't the type of thing she can just wonder; she has to know.

She returns to her notes and recordings, looking for clues she can't define. She plays back her interviews, reads and rereads her transcripts, picks up on small details that she didn't notice before. The bitterness in Mrs. Mueller's voice when she described EnerGia's contracts as "sneaky little Jew agreements." The way Richard wrote "something going on with them" in the notes from his first phone interview with her. The undercurrent of worry when Harry Bergum said he didn't want to be part of a big-city hit job, followed by his comment that Mrs. Mueller and her husband got mixed up in something they didn't understand. She assumed he'd been talking about the oil. Now she isn't sure.

The details she has records of are unsettling, but no more so than the details she simply can't forget. The two old Daves using racial epithets in the Donut Hut every day, according to Tyler. Ned's resentment toward Harry's young Mexican employee. Mrs. Mueller's prodding insistence on knowing where Elinor's parents were from, followed by her rejection of the idea that her Korean mother was American. In between these interactions were too many others to count in which people looked over their shoulders in empty alleys, empty fields, worried that someone might overhear them talking about subjects they shouldn't.

The volume of what she sees differently disturbs her. But then there are the women. Not just the women she interviewed but the ones she didn't. If she ever crosses paths with Shawnalee Turner Whitebush again, she'll tell her she knows the number now. Twenty-eight Mahua women, teenagers, and girls have been reported missing in the state over the past two years, a figure that's both shockingly high and surely an undercount. For several hours, Elinor descends into a rabbit hole of names and faces and information. Rarely do the articles about missing or murdered Mahua women run longer than a paragraph or two. Some aren't even articles at all, just public Facebook posts written by family members or old police reports uploaded to the Internet with a photo and a request for assistance that probably never arrived. Now she understands why Shawnalee responded so furiously when she asked about Leanne Lowell, whose disappearance received more attention than all these other cases combined. Lydia gave Elinor an opportunity to write a story, nearly any story of her choosing, about women in the Bakken. And the one she keeps circling back to is the one that everyone has already been conditioned to care about.

Elinor turns around in her chair, distracted by a nearby noise. The man who was sleeping in the beanbag when she first arrived has moved on, his spot now occupied by another man who whistles when he snores. She wakes up her laptop with a tap of the keyboard, intending to block out the sound with some music. When her notes reappear on the screen, she sees two small icons in the upper right-hand corner of her Google doc. The red circle contains her initials, EH. The blue one, the one she's almost certain wasn't there earlier, says RH. Richard Hall. The two of them are logged into the same document. Slowly, she scrolls through the pages until she finds the blinking blue cursor labeled with his initials. Beneath it, she types:

What are you doing here?

She waits for a response. When one doesn't materialize, she wonders if the icon was always there and she just didn't notice. She's tired after all, operating on too little sleep. Maybe he left the document open on his computer and forgot about it, although that still doesn't explain why he accessed the file. She deletes her question slowly, letter by letter, unable to shake the feeling that he's watching her do it.

I created this folder.

She stares at his reply for almost as long as he stared at her question. These aren't the first words she expected them to exchange after recent events.

But this is my assignment now.

Then you should have downloaded my folder to your computer instead of leaving it on the cloud.

Elinor sits back in her seat, studying his responses, neither of which sound the least bit contrite.

That still doesn't explain why you're lurking around in my notes.

Is that what I do now? I "lurk"?

Without seeing Richard's face or hearing his voice, it's hard to tell what kind of mood he's in, whether it's dark and morose, or sarcastic and unrepentant. She imagines it's the latter, shaded with the former.

You're still not answering the question. Why are you looking at my notes?

I was curious to see how you were doing out there.

Why?

Because it's something to do.

The typing slows.

Because I'm trapped up here at the country house, about to lose my mind.

It's rare for Richard to acknowledge anything resembling a struggle. She's glad to hear him experiencing one now. His life has been gilded and golden for so long, with his exclusive park and expensive whiskeys and organic weed. Even his house in the Catskills, which he makes out to be some sort of prison, is one of the most beautiful places she's ever visited. He's probably in his study, sitting at his desk and looking out the window at the wooded green view down the hill.

Are you sorry for what you did to those women?

No pleasantries, then? We're just going to jump straight to this?

She cuts and copies her original question.

Do you know how many of my colleagues have dated their graduate students? Some of them even dated an undergrad or two.

There's a difference between dating and sexual harassment.

Should you really be explaining this to me? YOU?

So—clearly not sorry?

It doesn't matter if I am or not. I think we both know that. I'm going to be erased no matter what.

So, not sorry.

The man in the beanbag mutters something angrily in his sleep. Then he shivers and curls up into a ball.

I called last night and ended up talking to Lydia.

She mentioned.

Why did you ask her to reassign your article to me? What were you hoping for?

What do you mean? Hoping for?

Did you think if I owed you something, I wouldn't talk to Kathryn and the others? Because I couldn't actually help them with their case. You know that, right?

I told Liddy to give you the assignment because it was your story.

She thinks she must have misread the sentence, but when she reads it again, it still makes no sense.

How was it my story?

Richard doesn't respond for a while. She glances at his icon, confirming that he's still logged in.

Because you were the one who first told me about the boom. You're the reason I got interested in what was happening out there to begin with. It was your story, so I asked Liddy to give it back.

His answer should come as a relief to Elinor, but it doesn't. Why did she never think of the story as hers before? Why didn't she understand that he'd taken something from her until now? When they were dating, she used to read him excerpts of articles about the Bakken and imagine out loud how strange it must be for a town as historically white and segregated as Avery to diversify overnight. She didn't realize that he'd been listening all that time. How shameful that she often assumed he wasn't, and yet she still stayed.

Did you ever suspect Amy Mueller of being a racist?

No. Is she?

Maybe. Possible white separatist leanings.

Jesus, no. I didn't pick up on that at all.

Why would you? she wants to ask. And then, because she knows this is probably the last conversation they'll ever have, she simply writes back.

Why would you? You never had any reason to notice.

He doesn't reply for a long time—so long that she imagines several things he might be preparing to write in response. All cutting, all unkind. But when he finally begins to type, the words that appear on the screen are unexpected, almost startling in their grace.

Like I said—it's your story. You were always the one who needed to tell it.

She sits in silence with this, wishing it didn't feel good to be reaffirmed by this man, wishing she didn't still value his experience and advice. But despite Richard's many sins, the uncomfortable truth is that he taught her well.

So what do you do when a story doesn't feel right? Like you thought it should be one thing, but it's so much bigger than that one thing alone?

If you have to ask, El, then you already know.

41

Officer Peterson wants her to guess how many emails she sent to the police department about scheduling her ride-along. She opens the mail app on her phone to count, but he waves her off.

"No, just guess."

They're driving along Main Street in his squad car, a Dodge Charger that smells even newer than her rental. Elinor is in the passenger seat, hugging her bag to her chest. She sent a lot of emails. She wonders if she was assigned to Officer Peterson as some sort of punishment. It's been less than twenty minutes since they met at the station, and already, his energy is starting to grate.

"Oh, come on, guess."

"I don't know. Maybe four or five?"

"Nine!" he says with a laugh. "And that was before you got the town manager involved. He sent a bunch more."

She's not sure what his point is, except to suggest that she's been a pain in everyone's ass, including his. She hugs her bag tighter, trying to contain herself. All she wants to talk about are the upside-down flags. Is it common for people in the area to fly them this way? Do they mean what she thinks they mean? Her list of questions feels long and urgent, but something tells her to hold off, to get a better sense of who she's talking to before introducing a subject that might reflect badly on his town. A hit job, she thinks, unable to strike that phrase from her mind now.

"So how did you get picked to do this?" she asks. She scans the inspirational rubber bracelets on his wrist, the hair buzzed high and tight like her father's, the blond sideburns almost invisible against his skin.

"They always tag me for these public affairs jobs, probably because I was born here, so I know the area. Plus, I joined the department in 2002, so I can talk about how the work changed after the boom, assuming you're interested in that."

She is interested, but she's also distracted, struggling to make sense of so many competing things. She regrets not postponing the ride-along for another night, but there was no guarantee her contact would let her reschedule on such short notice. She looks out her window at the blur of passing storefronts, resisting the urge to rest her forehead on the glass. Among the thoughts she keeps circling back to is an assignment she wrote during her last semester of grad school—a profile piece about an elderly Chinese tattoo artist with a shop on the Bowery and a cultlike following that paid his steep prices without complaint. Mr. Liu was the person she'd sought out to replicate the tattoo on her left forearm, extending the pattern seamlessly from shoulder to wrist. Six months later, she returned to him to re-create the same sleeve on her right arm. Originally, Elinor had planned to highlight the similarities between Mr. Liu's struggles as an artist and an immigrant, but the essay soon spiraled out into something else. In an effort to explain how they first met, she found herself writing at length about her tattoos, which she eventually described as a misguided attempt to create her own armor, to disinvite people from looking at her after decades of believing she was worth more if they did. The professor she submitted it to said it was a poor example of a profile, which was supposed to focus on the subject, not the writer. But he couldn't deny that something about the piece opened up and broke free when she did.

"Hey, are you . . . you doing okay over there?" Officer Peterson is stopped at a red light. He's leaning forward in his seat, looking at her.

She turns to face him, not certain how long she drifted off. "Sorry. I'm just processing," she says, which is actually true.

He half smiles, half frowns at her. "If you don't mind me saying, after all those emails you sent, I kind of expected you to have more questions."

She nods, realizing this was the point he was trying to make all along.

"Isn't there anything you want to ask me about the town? Or about the Lowell case? You said you wanted to talk to someone who worked on that."

She doesn't remember sending nine emails, much less what she wrote in them. But she doesn't put it past herself to make this request at the height of her interest in Leanne's disappearance. Although her interests have shifted now, there's still some overlap that he might be able to address, but she finds herself resisting the urge to ask too directly. "What can you tell me about those roughnecks who were attacked after she went missing? The two who ended up in the hospital?"

"What do you want to know?"

"Anything, really." She waits a beat, hoping he'll share whatever comes to mind, but he doesn't. "Were the people who did that to them ever caught?"

He shakes his head. "Unfortunately, no. Both those cases are still open."

"Would the department be able to help me get in touch with them?"

"Possibly." Officer Peterson lowers his window as they pass a church. He waves and gives a thumbs-up to the man who's changing the letters on the sign out front. SLOW DOWN BECAUSE GOD IS WATCHING, the sign reads. "Hey! Good one, Arnie," he shouts.

Arnie waves back.

"It might take a while to find them, though," he continues. "I'd be willing to bet they aren't in the area anymore."

This seems like a bad bet to take him up on, given that the men had been attacked and beaten within an inch of their lives. "What makes you say that?"

"It's just what roughnecks do. They move around from one place to the next, following the money. Why would you even want to talk to those guys after two years anyway? Seems like you'd just be bringing back bad memories for them."

"Well, because the racial angle interests me." She watches him frown again, more confused than irritated now. "My understanding is that they were targeted because they were Black and Latino."

"Honestly, I think the papers made way too much of that. It was probably just a coincidence. The bigger issue was that they were two roughnecks in the wrong place at the wrong time, and that case kicked up a lot of bad feelings toward anyone who wasn't from here before the boom."

Her father had the same privilege that Officer Peterson is exercising now, assuming that race had nothing to do with the things that happened. Listening to her mother lose those arguments again and again doesn't particularly motivate her to debate this issue with a stranger. It also confirms something deep in her gut that says he's the wrong person to ask about the flags.

At the intersection ahead, two teenage boys are standing on the corner, shouting at passing cars. Shouting what, she can't make out, but they seem to think they're being hilarious. Officer Peterson pulls up next to them and lowers Elinor's window. He leans his elbow on the center console and stares at them, not saying a word, while the boys look up and around—at the sky, the streetlights, the signage on the storefronts—desperate to avoid eye contact. When the light turns green, he revs the engine and drives on. He doesn't notice, as Elinor does in her side-view mirror, that both boys are giving him the finger.

"That kind of public nuisance stuff was about as rowdy as things ever got when I first started. Back then, it was just me and eight other officers." He adjusts his rearview mirror, quickly taking stock of his reflection while he does it. "Now there's thirty-nine of us, which still isn't enough to handle the kind of action we see here, especially on weekends. If we don't get some money to hire and keep up with all these newcomers soon, this place is going to turn into the Wild West."

One of the women she interviewed at the diner used this term too.

Elinor surveys the length of Main Street, which doesn't look particularly wild. With the exception of the boys they just passed, the whole stretch is actually quiet for a change, without the heavy foot traffic or long lines she's used to seeing. The nine-to-five businesses are closed now, while most of the bars and clubs have yet to open. It's that transitional part of the early evening when the daytime people are heading home and the nighttime people are at home getting ready.

"I know what you're thinking," he says. "But it'll pick back up. It always does. You'll have plenty to write about."

She gets the sense that Officer Peterson is trying to convince her how necessary the police are in Avery, probably in the hopes of securing a line or two in her article about the need for more funding. She doesn't doubt this would be helpful. But the way he talks about the boom—like it's a switch that suddenly flipped on and changed everything—doesn't sit right with her.

"It sounds like you're saying there weren't any serious crimes in the area before all the newcomers."

"Serious." He hooks his fingers in the air, making quotes. "I guess it depends on how you define 'serious.' But it definitely wasn't as bad as it is now. Now we're dealing with assaults, rapes, drug trafficking. That Lowell woman going missing. Two murders in the past year alone. Things like this never used to happen here."

This is similar to what she said to Lydia, which is similar to what the town manager said to her. But repeating a falsehood over and over again doesn't make it true.

"Everything you just mentioned has been happening on the North Fork for years. The only reason we're talking about it now is because it's happening to a different group of people." She didn't mean to contradict him so directly, but hearing his act of erasure made her own offense so stark. She doesn't want to keep repeating her mistake or be an accomplice to someone else's. But now here she is, stuck in the awkward aftermath, a moment that can't possibly last forever but feels like it might. Slowly, she looks over at him to find that he's looking at her.

"Technically, that's correct," he says, his words careful, his enunciation crisp. "But the tribal police are responsible for what happens on the reservation. I was just talking about the Avery PD's jurisdiction."

Their conversation dries up for several blocks until the radio chirps mercifully and a dispatcher requests units to an address somewhere on Sixth Street.

"Alright. We're off," he says, turning on his lights and siren.

She reaches for the handle above the door and grabs hold as Officer Peterson does a wild U-turn. The move seems overly aggressive given how thin traffic is. It feels like he's being dramatic on purpose, either to put on a show for her or to make her shut up.

By the time they reach the call address—a quiet residential street lined with modest ranch-style houses—another unit is already on the scene. An officer is talking to a middle-aged man who apparently refused a Breathalyzer and roadside sobriety test. His SUV is parked on someone's lawn, the giant tires having torn up the nicely kept grass. A broken mailbox post lies a few feet away; the mailbox itself, a few feet farther. Another officer is talking to the homeowner, a woman with a baby perched on her hip and a toddler tugging on her leg. Several neighbors are watching the commotion from the safety of their front steps. Most of them are elderly. All of them are white.

When Officer Peterson gets out of the car, Elinor scans the houses on both sides of the street looking for upside-down flags, but sees none, just the amber glow of lights clicking on in living rooms and kitchens. She wishes it didn't have to be like this. A couple of people hang their flags upside down, and now here she is, looking for others. For the rest of her life, she'll always be looking for them, wondering what they might mean.

42

Officer Peterson wasn't exaggerating. After sundown, the volume of activity surges, as if the passage from day to night opened a gate somewhere. Elinor tries her best to make conversation, which she decides is marginally preferable to silence. When the radio crackles with police codes or nicknames in the cross chatter, she asks him to translate for her, which he seems happy to do. She learns that a 10–16 is a domestic disturbance, while a 10–55 is an intoxicated driver—not to be confused with a 10–56, which is an intoxicated pedestrian. A leaner is someone on heroin. A jumping bean is someone on meth. A wife beater is exactly what it sounds like.

Because he's on public affairs duty, patrolling without his usual partner, Officer Peterson's role at each site is limited. He can't help interview witnesses on the scene or put anyone in his squad car for a ride back to the station. His primary responsibility during the ride-along, perhaps his only responsibility, seems to be driving from one location to another so he can check in with his colleagues and tell Elinor what's going on. It's obvious now why the department was so resistant to doing this. He's a glorified tour guide. It's a terrible use of his time. Officer Peterson doesn't seem to mind, though. Whenever he responds to a call, he greets his fellow officers with fist bumps and throws a casual thumb back at Elinor, who has to remain in the car. Although she can't hear what they're saying, their gestures and glances aren't subtle. She knows when she's being discussed and dissected, which irritates her, the fact that Officer Peterson doesn't think she understands what they're doing.

From her passenger seat window, Elinor watches a parade of troubled people file past. The perpetrators, in particular, make her want to open them up like books. Ever since she first heard Lydia say "dead girl story," she's been annoyed by the casual cruelty of the term, but she wonders if the genre's allure is some kind of proximity to danger or suffering that most people don't have in their lives. Perhaps this is the same guilty prickle of fascination she feels as she watches two officers escort a handcuffed man out of what appears to be a nice, middle-class home. He's dressed in nothing but dingy gray underwear, so old and loose that it looks like he's wearing a baggy diaper. The man, who's red-faced and glassy-eyed, is obviously sky-high on something, maybe even drunk too. The officers—both of whom she could swear are trying not to laugh—have to hold his teetering body upright by the elbows. He's not walking to their car so much as being carried to it while he air pedals, his feet occasionally scraping the ground.

When Officer Peterson returns, he's holding both hands over his stomach like it hurts.

"What's going on?" she asks.

"The guy was passed out . . ." He wheezes with laughter, trying to catch his breath. "He was passed out . . . in the kitchen . . . with a . . . with a banana in each hand."

Aside from the minor sight gag, she doesn't understand what's so funny about this. Given the man's disheveled and disoriented state, it seems awful to laugh. "But why are they arresting him? Did he hurt someone?"

"No, no. It's not . . . it's not that." He waves his hands in the air, trying to pull himself together. "It's not the guy's house!" He blurts out the punch line as he folds over the steering wheel, honking the horn with his forehead. "I'm sorry. I'm sorry," he says, his shoulders continuing to shake. "It's not funny, I know."

Elinor watches him for a few seconds longer. He's still laughing too hard to notice that she isn't. "I guess you had to be there," she says.

The moments in which she observes Officer Peterson behaving badly alternate with occasional acts of kindness that could be genuine or could be performance. She honestly can't tell. At the Stop-N-Go, he spots a girl—maybe ten years old at the most—leaving the store with a bag of hot dog buns. He says hello and drives beside her slowly, talking to her through his open window about her favorite TV shows. Behind him, frustrated drivers divert down other streets or pass when it's legal to do so. A few are brave enough to honk, which barely earns them a glance in his rearview mirror. The girl is chatty and doesn't seem to understand that he's escorting her home, making sure she gets there safely—something Elinor hopes he'd do for any child, not just the ones who could be his own. When the girl reaches her front door, they wave at each other like old friends before she goes inside. Afterward, Elinor wonders if she's being unfair, assuming the worst about Officer Peterson because the one time she interacted with the police, they were condescending and rude, a secondary trauma to the one she'd already experienced. But her guilt never has a chance to expand beyond a pang or two before he turns around and does something upsetting again.

Shortly after seeing the girl home, he slows down at an intersection and examines two teenagers hanging out in front of a gas station.

"Some parents have no sense," he says.

"What do you mean?"

He motions toward the girls, both of whom are dressed in T-shirts and cutoff shorts. "Letting their kids stay out after dark, looking like that," he says, running his eyes up and down the length of their bare legs. "It's not that kind of town anymore."

Only three or four years separate the girl they just took home and the teenagers, but he responds to them so differently, like a pair of mosquito bumps passing for breasts is the dividing line between innocence and impurity. She's sick to death of the argument that what a woman wears dictates the behavior she deserves. It's hard to believe that people still think like this. She can never get over her dismay when she realizes how many people do.

"Please tell me you're not suggesting that what they're wearing is going to get them raped."

He jerks his head back, his expression both shocked and insulted. "Ea-sy. Easy now," he says, which is an infuriating response, the kind of thing someone would coo to a dog or a horse. "I'm not saying they're asking for it or anything. Give me some credit. But there's like twenty or thirty men in this town for every woman. If you think all of them care about the age of consent, then you're living in a fantasyland."

"Well, I guess those girls are lucky to have you around," she mutters, no longer caring whether he hears her or not.

Another long stretch of silence follows. Elinor has never been on a ride-along before, but she knows this one is going bad in a spectacular way. When Officer Peterson pulls into a Burger King and announces that he's taking a bathroom break, she gets out to stretch her legs, relieved to finally be free from the car.

The sky is dark and starless now, and the air is filled with crickets chirping from every direction. It's half past ten already, which hardly seems possible. Discomfort usually makes time crawl. Lisa said to be back in Emerald's lot by ten or there might not be an empty space for her. Elinor had forgotten, or perhaps chosen not to remember, being kicked out of the Thrifty. She had forgotten that a bed and a safe place to sleep were no longer guaranteed. How do people live like this? she wonders. How do they stay here without wanting to burn it all to the ground? She imagines Travis kicking the barbecue grill again, and she thinks she understands the impulse now. How else are people supposed to feel, living out of their cars, doing dirty shit for work, being pushed to the outskirts of a town that doesn't want to know they exist? And this is supposedly the best chance they have?

Elinor walks to the edge of the parking lot where there's a border of trees separating it from the lot next door. From the shadow of one of the larger trees, she smokes while watching a group of skateboarders attempt painful-looking tricks on the Burger King's bike rack. None of them are very good. Only one manages to ride the entire the length of the rail before he falls off and his board clatters across the asphalt. His friends hoot and jeer at him just as Officer Peterson walks out, drinking something out of a jumbo-sized cup. He does a confused double take, looking at them and her and back again, probably wondering if they were laughing at him. There's a split second when it seems like he's about to tell the kids to get lost, but he continues walking toward her, his eyes following the lit cigarette in her hand. She wouldn't have guessed he was a smoker, not with his clean-cut appearance and athletic build, but it's obvious now that he is. She recognizes the fiendish expression that only nicotine and certain hard drugs can inspire. She barely has a chance to offer her pack and lighter to him before he's inhaling a cigarette like it's the last one he'll ever have.

"I didn't know you smoked," he says. "Man, I would have stopped like an hour ago if I did. You mind?" He points at the tree she's leaning against, gesturing as if he wants to trade places with her. "We're not really supposed to do this in uniform—looks unprofessional—so I have to be discreet about it."

She lets him take her place under the tree's leafy cover. Just past his shoulder, a woman pulls into the parking lot with her headlights off. Elinor watches as she teeters past the skateboarders, her hands held out to the sides for balance. One of the boys follows her into the Burger King, laughing and mimicking her drunken gait.

"So, listen. I'm not sure what happened, but it feels like we got off to a rough start tonight and never really recovered."

She nods.

"Could we please start over?" He laughs and scratches his head. The rubber bracelets—yellow, pink, and red—slide down his wrist and fall back again. "I'm a decent guy, I swear. I think I just got nervous about putting my foot in my mouth that one time and then I kept doing it."

Elinor doesn't know which time he's referring to as his first. And she's wary of people who insist upon their decency, as if it's something to be claimed instead of demonstrated. She probably looks as unconvinced as she feels because suddenly his tone turns cajoling, like he's trying to sell her a car.

"Listen. I'll make you a deal. What else can I tell you about the

Lowell case? You said you were interested in that before, but we've barely talked about it. Ask me whatever you want if that helps buy back a little goodwill."

She wants to know what kind of person Shane Foster was, whether he hung his flag upside down like his aunt, and if so, was he doing that before his wife went missing or was it a reaction to the grief of losing her? But she doesn't feel comfortable asking Officer Peterson any of these questions, so she settles for an inferior one. "Does Leanne still have any family around?"

He shakes his head. "Her parents live in Montana, from what I understand. Her husband's the one who grew up here, but he moved to Idaho after all this happened."

An *I* state, she thinks. "He was never a suspect in her disappearance? The husband?"

"*Shane?*"

The cool professional distance lapses, and the sudden switch to a first name startles her, although it shouldn't. She of all people should know how few degrees of separation there can be in a small town. Officer Peterson and Shane Foster, both of whom are in their thirties she'd guess, probably went to school at about the same time, played in the same sports leagues, maybe even crossed over in age enough to go to the same keg parties in the woods, the ones that Elinor always went to but Maren never did.

"I just asked because I thought the husband was usually the first person you looked at in cases like this."

"He was off hunting with three or four other guys when she went missing, so we were able to rule him out pretty fast."

By now, she understands that reading about the case will only get her so far. There are things it would simply never occur to her to ask. "Okay then. Tell me something I don't know," she says. "A rumor or detail I couldn't possibly know from just following the news."

He nods, blowing smoke through his nostrils. Then he takes the pack out of her hands without asking and removes another cigarette that he tucks behind his ear. "Something you don't know," he repeats. "On or off the record?"

The fact that he's asking dictates her answer. "Off."

"Okay ... So here's one ... About four months before she went missing, Leanne cashed out an insurance policy her parents bought when she was a kid. It wasn't worth much, only a couple grand or so. But she never told her husband about the money, and she didn't deposit it or make any big purchases with it either. So for a while there, one of the theories was that she hadn't been abducted or murdered. She just decided to take off and that insurance policy was her bankroll." He lights his backup cigarette off his first, puffing the ember to life with several long drags. "There's no proof that's what happened, though. She could have loaned that money to a friend or—who knows—maybe had a drug problem no one was willing to talk about. Sometimes that happens around here. Anyway, that was a theory we kicked around for a while."

"That's it?" she asks. "She could have skipped town, but she probably didn't?"

Officer Peterson waves his hands at her. "Alright, alright. Here's another one, sort of along the same lines. The reward money her husband put up. Fifty grand. A lot of people didn't understand how someone like Shane Foster could get his hands on that much. I mean, if you grew up around here and knew him or his family, you'd understand there was just no way. When his parents were still alive, they were always getting their cars and farm equipment repo'd, and Shane was actually worse off than they were because he didn't even own a house to take a second mortgage on. So for him to come up with that kind of money for a reward? I don't know. There was something not right about it."

The way he looked in all those videos she watched—not angry or sad or worried. It still sticks with her for reasons she can't fully comprehend. "But a lot of locals started making good money after the boom—"

"No, but see? That's just it. Shane didn't want anything to do with the oil companies. Didn't like the element they were bringing in, he said. He was still working on landscaping crews when his wife went missing, so if he'd put up five grand? Okay, that probably wouldn't have made anyone blink. Maybe he could have gone as high as ten. But fifty? It seemed like he purposely picked an impossible number because he knew she'd taken off and wasn't coming back, and offering a big reward like that at least made him feel like a man." He puts his cigarette out in the grass, kicking the still-smoking butt onto the asphalt. "So how's that? You wanted rumors? Those are some of the rumors we chased around that first year. But nothing came of them. And to be fair, Shane always seemed like a nice enough guy from what I could tell. A little strange, maybe. Quiet. Not much of a people person, if you know what I mean."

43

Dani jumps to her feet and greets her with a sweaty hug, which she didn't expect.

"My wing woman!" she shouts, releasing Elinor with a hard clap to the back. "I'm glad you texted. I wasn't sure I'd ever hear from you again."

Dani, her brother, and Aaron have been drinking at the Depot since it was light out. Elinor would have assumed this even if Fat Mike hadn't said so. They're all red-faced and bleary-eyed. Teetering columns of empty glasses are scattered across their table. Elinor wishes she'd known that Dani wasn't alone before arranging to meet. As soon as she walked in and saw the three of them sitting next to the dance floor, she had a vague memory of being gently lifted into Dani's car by Fat Mike and Aaron a few nights earlier. She orders a round of doubles for the table from a passing waitress. It's part apology, part token of gratitude to all of them for getting her back to the Thrifty unscathed.

The Depot is more crowded than it was on Thursday. Before sitting down, Elinor exchanges a brief wave with Michelle, who looks like she's struggling to keep up with the onslaught of orders. Despite the long lines for drinks, most of the roughnecks appear to be in good spirits thanks to the presence of two large bachelorette parties—one dressed in pink JENNA'S SQUAD T-shirts, and the other wearing Tiffany blue sashes that read BECKY'S BRIDE TRIBE. There's also a group of about two dozen guys dressed in matching white polos. At first,

Elinor assumes they're from a bachelor party, but they seem too stiff in their pressed khaki trousers, relaxed-fit jeans, and tucked-in shirts. They look like a bunch of dads trying to loosen up by ordering shots for themselves and any bachelorette who happens to wander into their corner.

"I think it's some sort of company event," Dani says, staring off in the same direction.

The circumstances are less than ideal for a conversation. Elinor had hoped to get Dani alone, or at the very least, sober, which was probably an unrealistic expectation for a Saturday night. She considers trying again tomorrow, in a place that isn't thumping with dance music, but she's desperate to talk with someone who knows the town well and can help her make sense of the things she's seen and heard. She also has nowhere else to go at this hour. It's long past midnight, and she's too tired to risk the drive out to Emerald's only to find the lot full.

A fair-skinned redhead walks past their table, leaving a cloying trail of perfume in her wake. Fat Mike's and Aaron's eyes follow her across the room as they speculate about real tits and curtains that match the drapes, things she doesn't want to hear from two guys who have otherwise been pretty decent to her. She angles her back away from them, pulling her phone out and opening her recent photos.

"I need you to take a look at something and tell me what you see, okay?"

"Is it a dick pic?" Dani shouts.

Elinor hands her the phone and watches as her smile begins to flatline.

"Where'd you take this?" she asks, enlarging the photo of Mrs. Eddy's flag with her fingertips.

"A town north of here called Heath. Have you ever seen a flag hanging like this before?"

"Well, yeah." Dani reaches for her drink, which is almost empty. "Some of the houses on my route have them like that in their windows."

They talked about her job on Thursday night, she's certain of it.

But the pounding music and purple strobe lights are making it hard to think. Elinor envisions swimming pools and fires, something involving a hose.

"I service septic tanks," Dani reminds her.

"I've seen a couple like that too," Aaron cuts in.

Elinor didn't realize he'd been listening, but the redhead whom he and Fat Mike were ogling is on the dance floor now, sandwiched between two other men.

"So what does it mean?"

"People who hang their flags that way, they think they're under siege." Aaron takes the phone from Dani and looks closely at the photo. "Yup." He nods, handing the phone back. "My cousin's got his like that."

"No shit?" Dani says. "Nick's into this now?"

The "this" is what Elinor needs to understand, what she can't afford to get wrong. She's not out to ruin anyone's life or reputation, after all. She understands the importance of being careful. It's hard, if not impossible, to counter accusations like racism or sexism or anti-Semitism in the negative. How does one go about proving that they're *not* something? How do they account for what they haven't said or done or thought? Rarely do records like that exist.

"Who exactly does your cousin think he's under siege by?" she asks.

Aaron shrugs. He takes off his baseball cap and runs his fingers through his hair before putting the cap back on. "Nick's not a bad guy. He just liked Avery the way it was before all these people started coming. You know, when we had the town to ourselves."

She pauses at his use of the word "we." Suddenly, even a simple pronoun feels like a jagged piece of metal—harmless when it's resting in an open hand but also a potential weapon, depending on how it's being held, who it's being held by. "*Which* kinds of people, Aaron?"

He looks at Dani and Fat Mike and then back at her again. The fact that none of them will answer, not even Dani, is a type of answer. "I don't think he'd feel that way about *you*," he says carefully, perhaps realizing that he's waded chest deep into something he shouldn't have put a toe into. "You, I bet he'd like."

"Why? Because I'm a woman?"

"Well, that. And you're good-looking," he adds.

This isn't the compliment he thinks it is. Elinor doesn't want to be easier to accept or tolerate compared to other people of color because she's female, or half Asian, or part white. All this does is buy into the idea that some people have the right to do the accepting and tolerating and comparing, while others are simply there to be judged.

"Let me make sure I'm hearing you correctly. People who hang their flags upside down around here, people like your cousin—they think Avery's under siege by certain types of people of color who they don't want in their community? Did I get that right?"

Aaron glances at Elinor's hands, which are empty. No pad, no pencil. "You're not gonna say it was me who—"

"No, no. This is on background. I just need to be a hundred percent certain about this. It's important."

Behind them, there's a roar of laughter and shouting. The guys in white polo shirts all down shots of something in unison and then cheer. It appears that the tequila or whiskey they've been drinking since she arrived is having its intended effect. Elinor sees several untucked shirts now, along with bachelorettes playfully perched on laps. Some of them have even transferred their BRIDE TRIBE sashes or feather boas and tiaras to the men they're sitting on.

Aaron finishes off the last of his drink, glancing at his watch as he sets the glass down. "Yeah, you've got that right."

Fat Mike, who's not much of a talker, must be a friend of Aaron's cousin because he finally speaks up after sitting most of the conversation out. "Nick's harmless, just so you know. It's not like he's wearing a white sheet and rounding up Black guys with a shotgun so he can run them out of town."

No one says anything for a while. They're probably as chilled as Elinor is by the mention of a white sheet, which there's no mistaking the symbolism of. She thinks through how she wants to respond, aware that she needs these people badly, but they don't need her. And they're not likely to appreciate her pointing out that racism can sometimes be ugly and overt like this, but more often than not, it's the drop of poison in the well that people don't notice because they've been drinking the same water for too long.

Dani tips her head back and sighs dramatically. "Oh my godddd," she shouts at the ceiling. "I had such a good buzz going before this. Can we please talk about something else?"

"Just one more question," Elinor says. "Shane Foster—the guy who was married to that missing runner—is there any chance you knew him or knew whether he flew an upside-down flag when he lived here?"

All three of them quickly shake their heads. Elinor studies their expressions, not certain if the swiftness of their response is the result of just wanting to move on or actually not knowing. She's grateful for the arrival of the waitress, who appears with the drinks she ordered nearly half an hour ago. If not for the fresh round, she suspects that Aaron would have made a move to leave. The drinks were supposed to be doubles, but they look even more generous than that, which was probably Michelle's doing. She raises her glass to them, trying to restore some of the good energy she killed with her inconvenient questions. It's not an apology for what she's done so much as what she's about to do next.

"Okay, last question," she says, and they all groan loudly and drink. "I promise, this is really it. And then I'll grab another round for us, okay? I'll even go to the bar this time so it won't take as long." She scans their faces for a response. Dani still appears in be in reasonably good humor about her presence. Her brother, less so. And Aaron, not at all. Despite this, she gets nothing in the way of pushback on her offer, either because they wouldn't mind another round or they're relieved at the thought of being rid of her for a while.

"I heard a rumor that Leanne Lowell left town on her own, that she wasn't kidnapped at all . . ." She trails off, hoping one of them might jump in, but they just sit there with confused expressions, waiting for her to continue. "That's why I was asking about how people hang their flags around here. I started wondering—what if her husband got fed up with how Avery was changing and decided to make a statement? What if he was that kind of person?" she adds delicately, avoiding eye contact with Aaron. "Other people in his family were. But maybe Leanne didn't want any part of that, so she just took off instead?"

As Elinor spins this alternate version of events, filled with more what-ifs and maybes than any responsible story should ever include, she remembers asking for Shane's contact information, which Mrs. Mueller refused to provide. She's not sure if Mrs. Mueller said "He'll never talk to you," meaning "you as a writer," or "He'll never talk to someone like you," which could have meant something else.

"It's humiliating to be a man whose wife leaves him," she continues, thinking of her father, who never remarried, never dated, never got over his sense of betrayal and loss. "So maybe he just went along with the idea that his wife went missing instead of acknowledging what really happened. Is that . . . is that something you've ever heard people talking about, or maybe thought about on your own?"

The three of them look at her like she's drunk and they have to take her back to the hotel again. After a while, Dani just shrugs.

"It's a nice thought," she says, frowning almost. "But you know that's not how these stories usually end, right?"

44

The crowd on the dance floor is like a wall now. Elinor slowly pushes through the bodies and makes her way to the side of the bar that Michelle is working on. She even manages to get two seats like she did before, offered up by a pair of guys who try to make conversation before giving up and moving on. Dani squeezes in beside her, having insisted on coming with, probably to re-create the conditions that worked so well for her on Thursday night. Elinor decides to take a break from asking about Shane and Leanne while they wait to order their drinks. She's aware that she's been testing the limits of everyone's patience since she arrived, so it's a surprise when Dani returns to the subject unprompted.

"I wasn't trying to be a jerk when I said it was a nice idea," she says. "You know, about that lady not being dead."

"You think she's dead?"

"Well . . . yeah. Don't you?"

She isn't sure what to think or hope. But the casualness with which they're discussing a human life gives her pause. How worn out they are by the same old story, told and retold so many times.

Michelle glances at her from behind the bar. She's grim faced; her expression says she'd quit right now if she could. She's holding a bottle of Cuervo upside down, moving it quickly over at least two dozen shot glasses arranged in tight rows. She doesn't measure. She barely even looks. She just pours, swapping one bottle for another when the first runs dry. A barback appears from a side room hefting a steaming tray filled with nothing but freshly washed shot glasses. Elinor imagines the number of customers shooting hard liquor tonight has everything to do with Michelle's bad mood.

"I mean, what are the chances?" Dani continues. "Someone goes missing like that, she has to be dead, right?"

No, Elinor thinks. Not necessarily. Not always. Sometimes, women really do just leave. A few years earlier, she found her mother on Facebook, of all places. By then, Nami had changed her first name to Naomi, something Elinor discovered simply by searching for "Nami Hanson" and scrolling so far down the list of results that alternate spellings began to appear. The second she saw the thumbprint-sized picture, she recognized the face staring back at her as if it was her own.

Nami's profile page was just a shell, the kind started by someone who hadn't been fully committed to the task. There was no mention of where she lived, or whether she'd remarried or had more children. Her list of friends was private. She hadn't included any information about her jobs, past or current, much less taken the time to share her favorite hobbies or books. The only content was an album with six uncaptioned photos, all taken at national parks in the western US— Glacier Lake, Bryce Canyon, Moab, Joshua Tree, Yosemite, the Grand Canyon. The photos were always of Nami alone, but she didn't appear lonely. Far from it, in fact. Irrational as it was, the longer Elinor looked at them, the more she began to think of the smiling images as private messages from her mother, a sign that she was alive and well and in the world.

Maren wasn't even curious or interested when Elinor brought up the account, as if she'd already discovered it on her own. She seemed more upset that Elinor was thinking about trying to reconnect. Given her reaction, Elinor didn't mention how she'd scoured the rest of the Internet for evidence of Nami, looking for a phone number or address as she'd done countless times before. Having her correct name didn't help as much as she thought it would. There were simply too many

Naomi Hansons, none of whom appeared to be their mother. For months, Elinor considered just sending her a message on Facebook, but she talked herself out of it every time, convinced that Nami had given her a small glimpse of her life, and it was happy and free.

Dani drums her fingers against the bar, either impatient with the wait for drinks or Elinor's slowness to respond. "I think that whole conversation about Aaron's cousin just put me in a weird mood. I mean, Nicky's not my favorite person, but we pretty much grew up together, so it sucks to hear where his head is at now. . . . Anyway, I'm sorry. I'm not sure why I had to be such a dick about some lady not being murdered."

It seems like Dani is apologizing for things she's not really guilty of. But for the moment, Elinor has a more immediate concern.

"Hey," she shouts over the music at the guy standing behind her. "Could you stop pressing up on me like that?" She's relieved to see how spooked he is by her request, how quickly he takes a step back from her stool. The club is so crowded now, she decides to give him the benefit of the doubt that he wasn't leaning against her on purpose. She turns to Dani again. "You don't have to apologize. It sounds crazy when I say all of this out loud, I realize. I've probably just been thinking about it too much."

"Why?"

She shrugs. "Because it's interesting, right?"

Dani blinks sleepily. Despite insisting that she lost her buzz, she still seems a little drunk. "How's that again?"

"It's nice to imagine that she got a chance to start over." As soon as Elinor hears herself saying this out loud, she knows why it's interesting to her.

"Hey, don't I know you?" someone shouts, tapping her roughly on the shoulder.

She rolls her eyes, not turning to face him while Dani tries to suppress a grin. Elinor isn't sure what bothers her more, the uninvited touching or "Don't I know you," which had always been her least favorite line when she was modeling. She wasn't famous or successful enough to actually be recognized by anyone. It was such an obvious lie, designed to play into some perception of shallowness or vanity that men assumed she had, that she actually did have for a while.

"I'm sssserious," he continues to shout. "I've seen you before."

The man sounds completely wasted. He taps her shoulder again. She assumes he's going to keep doing this unless she tells him to go. Elinor swivels her stool around to see a white polo shirt just inches from her face, the armpits damp with sweat. She's eye level with the breast pocket, which has a black circle on it and a letter *H* drawn inside. Haines, she thinks. Haines Hydraulics. She looks up, landing on a bright red face that flickers with recognition at the same time hers does.

"Seeeee?" he slurs, his breath thick with Jack and Cokes like it was on the plane. "I knew it was you."

Elinor stands up, pressing her back against the brass rail of the bar as she reaches out and grabs Dani's forearm. Even when she's no longer seated, the man towers over her by several inches, so close that she can smell his aftershave and sweat. She looks around, pinned in on all sides by the crowd. She squeezes Dani harder.

"What's wrong?" she asks, trying to loosen Elinor's grip. "Hey—*hey*, that kinda hurts."

"Are you just going to stand there and ignore me like you did on the plane?" The man sways from side to side as he speaks. "You remember that? You remember how I was trying to make conversation and you were such a cunt to me?"

"Watch it," Dani warns.

The man glances down at her, and suddenly his expression darkens. "Was I talking to you?" He sways toward Elinor this time, trying to lean on her stool for balance but he misjudges the distance and brushes the side of her arm. She jerks back so violently that her elbow knocks over a melting glass of ice on the bar. As water drips down her back and onto the floor, his mood takes another wild swing and he starts to laugh.

"Oops! Youuuu're cut off! Bartender! No more for this one over here!"

She can feel him breathing on her again. Again, she thinks. Again. Despite her best efforts to convince herself otherwise, she knows this sensation, knows it was real. Panic wraps around her throat and tightens like a fist. She turns and stares wide-eyed at Dani, digging her nails deep into her skin.

"What?" Dani shouts.

"Is there a problem over here?" Michelle asks.

Elinor looks at her with the same paralyzed expression. Please, she thinks. Please. But what she's pleading for, she's not even sure.

The man shakes his head at the three of them and points at Elinor, tracing the air around her face with his finger. "Ssstuck-up, that's what you are. Don't talk to me, she says. No talking. Sstuck-up." Something about this exchange is giving him such pleasure. He smiles at her—big, smug, righteous—and then begins to walk back to his coworkers in the corner. The crowd, probably sensing that he's about to be sick, lets him shove and stumble past without complaint.

"What happened?" Michelle asks. Then she looks at Dani, whose arm Elinor is still clutching. "What the hell just happened?"

Dani slides off her stool and slowly pries Elinor's grip loose, finger by finger. When her arm is free, she reaches out and tips Elinor's face toward hers. "That guy do something to you on the plane?" It's a question, but she doesn't ask it like a question. Elinor wouldn't be able to answer anyway. Her entire body is shaking, overwhelmed by a surge of rage and terror that's about to arrest her heart.

"Maybe you should take—" Michelle starts.

"Yeah. Okay, come on," Dani says, leading her away. "It's too crowded over here."

As they return to their table, Fat Mike and Aaron glance at their empty, drinkless hands. At first, they look disappointed, but then they do a double take at Elinor. Both of them quickly stand up, searching her face for an explanation before moving on to Dani's. Suddenly the three of them are huddled together, and then Michelle appears with two bouncers in tow and all six of them are huddled together. They talk and glance over their shoulders at Elinor, then talk and glance some more. Before she understands what's happening, the four men elbow their way into the corner and soon the pushing and shoving and yelling begin.

"What did I do?" someone shouts.

The polo shirts aren't roughnecks. They're not tough, even when they're drunk. Most of them scatter at the first sign of trouble, abandoning their bachelorettes and each other. A few of the younger ones try to step in for a while, patting the air with their hands and urging everyone to stay calm. But none of them are willing to throw down in the end, not even when the bouncers, Aaron, and Fat Mike pick up their coworker, each of them holding him up by a limb.

"What the fuck did I do?" the man from the plane keeps shouting.

The four of them walk toward the exit, carrying him off like a pig they're about to slaughter. The man tries to kick his way free, all the while cursing and demanding to be put down. Fat Mike stops as they pass Elinor, forcing the others to stop alongside him, as if they're awaiting further instruction. She knows she could put an end to this if she wanted to. She just has to tell them to let him go. But one look at him brings all the rage she's been carrying up to the surface, memory after memory of being touched, leered at, diminished, demeaned, assaulted, humiliated, ridiculed, and shamed. She hasn't known what to do with this anger except reflect it back at the world that gave it to her.

Elinor leans down toward the man, who appears more confused than frightened at first. It's only when she's hovering directly above him that his watery red eyes seem to focus and he actually sees her.

"I know what you did to me," she says.

He remains still for a few seconds. A thin line of sweat trickles down his cheek. Then he bucks and wrests an arm free, taking a wild swing at the air that catches one of the bouncers on the shoulder. It's not the bouncer, or his partner, or even Fat Mike who puts him back in his place. It's Aaron. Skinny, scrawny Aaron who seemed so annoyed with her not that long ago. Someone taught him to fight, or maybe he was forced to learn, because suddenly a light turns on inside him and he's beating the man like it's the last thing he'll ever do.

45

In the fourth grade, everyone in Elinor's social studies class had to do a poster presentation about one of the US presidents. Before the teacher had even finished explaining the project, Elinor shot her hand in the air—something she rarely did at school—and asked if she could choose Teddy Roosevelt. Twice that summer, her family had visited places where his presence loomed large—first at the national park named in his honor and later at Mount Rushmore. She returned home to Marlow fascinated by the idea of him, how he'd been so many different things during his lifetime. A cattle rancher, a war hero, an explorer, a lawman, a naval officer, a governor, a president.

Elinor put more work into that poster than any other assignment she'd ever done for school. Using the photos and souvenirs she'd collected on her trip, she filled every available inch with details about Roosevelt's life and career. On one side, she pasted several images that she'd cut out of a brochure about his rise to the presidency. On the other, she enlisted Maren's help drawing a faux scroll on which she wrote the highlights of his accomplishments in office—the Panama Canal, the conservation of national parkland, trustbusting, the Square Deal. Around the edges, she carefully glued all the pine needles, rocks, and flakes of gold- and rust-colored earth that she'd secreted away from the national park in her pockets, despite her father telling her not to.

The teacher praised Elinor's uncharacteristic dedication to this project. Her only criticism was how the middle of the poster—the largest section by far, decorated with a construction-paper frame and multicolored confetti—could have been put to better use. Instead of featuring an oversized photograph of Elinor's family, the one taken under the four presidents at Mount Rushmore, she said it should have focused more on Roosevelt. Normally, criticism of any kind would have wounded Elinor. It was the reason why she rarely spoke up in class to begin with. But she didn't particularly care what her teacher thought about the photo. Her family looked like a family in it. Showing it off to her classmates had been her only motivation.

Decades later, Elinor enrolled in a class on nineteenth- and twentieth-century US history to fulfill a degree requirement. Thirty-eight was an embarrassing age to be what was essentially a college junior. It was also an embarrassing age to learn that she'd internalized a memory of Roosevelt that was little more than a child's rendering of him, whitewashed to the point of myth. There was no denying that he'd been and done all the things she remembered. Even the hyper-masculine, tall tale–like stories about chasing boat thieves downriver and getting into a bar brawl to defend his honor were true. But there was a darker side to him that she'd never read about in any museum or book. She didn't, for example, know that one of the things that had led him west from New York to the Badlands was a profound sense of grief for his mother and wife, both of whom had curiously died on the same day, the former of typhoid and the latter due to complications from childbirth. She also didn't know that he'd left his infant daughter in his sister's care for several years, unable to be a parent to the child arguably responsible for his wife's death. And to her great shame, she didn't know that despite Roosevelt's love for the western territories that would eventually become part of the United States, his attitudes toward the indigenous people to whom these lands belonged could only be described in modern-day terms as genocidal.

The sun is slowly rising over the national park now, casting thin splinters of light across the dark horizon. Soon, caravans filled with tourists will take over the scenic inner loops to admire the park's views and take photos of deer and bison ambling across the road. At the visitor's center just off the interstate, Elinor sits in her car and waits, thinking through the events of the past few hours.

After the Depot closed, she stayed behind with Dani and Michelle, unnerved by how quiet and empty it was, this place that she'd come to associate with noise. Michelle lined up three shot glasses on the bar and poured, not bothering to ask if anyone wanted a drink or what they'd like to have. Elinor appreciated how neither she nor Dani pressed her for details about the man or what he'd done to her on the plane. Instead, the three of them simply raised their glasses to one another, each privately toasting something that they chose not to say out loud. Although Elinor was still in a state of shock, she recognized something unexpectedly tender about this moment, a sense of connection that she rarely felt with people. Dani had defended her. Michelle had come to her aid. Even Aaron and Fat Mike had tried to help her in their own misguided way. Noticeably, the two of them didn't return after carrying the man outside, leaving Elinor to wonder what they'd done to him. The idea of causing the man pain didn't give her any particular sense of satisfaction. She knew enough not to confuse vengeance with power or justice, or even principle. She also knew that an uncomfortable reckoning lay in store for her, allowing men to use violence on her behalf as a remedy for the violence that another man had inflicted.

Before parting ways, Michelle offered her a place to crash for the night, which Elinor gratefully declined. She wanted to take a drive.

"Are you serious? You want to drive now?"

Dani shook her head. "It's three in the morning. Where would you even go?"

"I'm not sure," she said, even though she was. Since the day she first arrived, she knew that she'd eventually return to this place.

Maybe they understood her need to get some air and be out in the open, or maybe they saw the look on her face and realized she wasn't going to stay. Whatever the reason, they didn't try to dissuade her.

The visitor's center off Exit 32 overlooks the Painted Canyon, a huge

expanse at the park's southeastern edge. Such an alien landscape—
Roosevelt said so himself in his writings—formed by layers of sedi-
ment and ash. As the sun continues to rise, the canyon comes to life
with morning color. Inch by inch, shades of rust, gold, pink, brown,
and green begin to illuminate and ignite. Elinor tracks the sun's
movement, reminding herself on occasion to breathe. When it finally
breaks from the horizon, blaze orange against the cloudless sky, it's
all fire and awe. The most perfect sight she has ever seen. The most
perfect sight Roosevelt ever saw. How strange that this place she loves
most in her home state is named after him, a man who did so much
good for people and yet believed in the supremacy of white Europe-
ans above all others. It's hard to reconcile how these truths can even
occupy the same plane. That's probably why this land means so much
to her. It's a reminder of how complicated this country is, how great
beauty and terrible ugliness have coexisted here from the start.

Elinor's eyes flutter closed as the sun shines brightly on her face.
Somewhere in that weightless stage between exhaustion and sleep,
she begins to tells herself a story. It comes to her in fragments—small,
splintered ones that eventually come together to form a whole. The
story is about a woman who lived in a beautiful place but never felt
like she belonged there. Once upon a time, this woman was loved—by
a man, by a family. And maybe she loved them too until she no longer
could, because that love came at the expense of things that made her
who she was. When a door to another world cracked open, she seized
her moment and charged through, not thinking about what her absence would do to the people she left behind. Maybe this woman re-
gretted what she'd done later. Maybe she didn't. But by then, it hardly
mattered. What was passed was past. There was no fixing all that
she'd broken, even if she wanted to. Wherever this woman landed,
she had to start over, because isn't that what you do when the story
you've written isn't what you hoped for or planned? You start over.
That's what Nami did. That's what Elinor did. And if she allows herself
to abandon her senses and imagine a different ending, maybe that's
what Leanne Lowell did too.

This is the answer to her question, the one she asked Richard before they parted ways for good. All this time, Nami and Leanne have been leading her to a different story, one that she wasn't able to see at first. It's not about the women who arrive in this hard and unforgiving place, looking for something better. It's about the ones who were always here and chose to stay.

Elinor isn't certain if she's dreaming or planning now, or whether there's even a difference, but she sees the road ahead so clearly. It winds through golden grasslands and small, sleepy towns, past tired farms and fields filled with pumpjacks nodding at the earth. It takes her through the vast reservation she never saw clearly as a child and deposits her in front of the trailer with the stripe around its middle. When she knocks on the door, Shawnalee will open it as she did before, pausing at the sight of her.

Maybe, she hopes, this is where things will begin again.

Acknowledgments

In February 2020, my agent, Jen Gates, arranged a phone call between me and Anna deVries of St. Martin's Press. I remember very little about that conversation except the thing that mattered most—the excitement of knowing with each passing minute that Anna was the right person to edit *O Beautiful*. It's hard to believe that the two of us still haven't met in person because of the pandemic, and yet her imprint on this novel has been profound. If you're an aspiring writer, I hope you'll one day be able to work with an editor who sees you on the page as clearly as she saw me—someone who knows what you're trying to achieve and supports that vision with grace, good judgment, and encouragement. My sincere thanks to Anna, Alex Brown, Jennifer Fernandez, Brant Janeway, Beatrice Jason, Young Jin Lim, Martha Schwartz, Rima Weinberg, Dori Weintraub, and all of their colleagues at St. Martin's for bringing this book into the world with such care and professionalism during a period of time when the world often felt so uncertain.

To my husband, Joel: I always tell you that I can't do this work without you, and you—being the person you are—always tell me that I can. Let's continue disagreeing about this for the rest of our lives. In the meantime, thank you for being the first to read these pages, for reading them over and over again whenever I asked, and for telling me to keep going when I wanted to walk away and write something easier. You are the very best person I will ever love. To both of our families—siblings, in-laws, pride-of-my-heart nephews—a book like this requires spending a lot of time in darkness, so I'm grateful to all of you for being such a bright and constant source of light. And to my parents, Moo Yong and Young Ja Yun, without whose intrepidness this book would not exist: Mom and Dad, thank you for being so brave when you decided to come to America all those years ago. Your fierce determination to give your children a better life never fails to humble, astonish, and inspire me.

To my Baltimore writing group, Molly Englund and Jeannie Vanasco: thank you for reading the early pages of this book long before they were ready for your eyes. Our conversations as women writers living through a truly dystopic time in American history influenced me in countless ways over the years, and your friendship has helped Baltimore feel like home. I also want to thank my online writing group—Hannah Bae, Jessie Chaffee, Krys Lee, and Julia Phillips—for making Tuesday nights during the pandemic something to look forward to and for reminding me that the next story is always waiting to be told. Big thanks to Boomer Pinches, friend and reader extraordinaire, who provided such helpful and timely feedback on this manuscript, and to Elizabeth Evitts Dickinson and Jia Tolentino, who were so gracious in helping me understand how their writing world differs from my own.

To my wonderful colleagues in the English department at the George Washington University: not all pre-tenure faculty receive the time or space to actually do the work that earns them tenure. How lucky I am—not only that you chose to hire me but that you also provided the conditions that have allowed me to create and thrive. Much gratitude to all of you, as well as to the university at large and the Columbian College of Arts & Sciences for awarding me substantial grants and resources during my pre-tenure years. This book is truly the product of my time at GW and the investments this entire community has made in me. A very special thanks to my students, past and present. Whenever I see your kindness and empathy in class and on the page, I think the future is going to be alright; one day, it's going to be in your good and capable hands.

To the following organizations, thank you for honoring me with generous grants to fund the research and writing of this book: the Maryland State Arts Council, the Greater Baltimore Cultural Alliance, the Robert W. Deutsch Foundation, and the Massachusetts Cultural Council. Our communities are truly better places to live and work because of your recognition that art matters. I am also indebted to the Ucross Foundation, MacDowell, the Virginia Center for the Creative Arts, and the National Humanities Center for the invaluable gifts of time and space in which to write, and for introducing me to such wonderful cohorts of fellow artists. Also, special thanks to Melissa Girard, Jason Massey, and dearly departed Cutty the Cat, not only for the gift of your friendship, but for twice lending me your home so I could quietly revise.

Finally, let me return full circle to my agent, with whom these acknowledgments began. In December 2017, Jen and I met to discuss an earlier version of *O Beautiful*, which had arrived at an unexpected crossroads. Jen, thank you for listening with such an open mind that day and for encouraging me to write the story that only I could tell. I am grateful to you and your dedicated colleagues at Aevitas Creative Management for always being there when I need you most.

To all the people mentioned here and anyone I may have inadvertently left out, I look forward to hugging you, or at least seeing you, in real life one of these days. Until then, heartfelt thanks for helping me bring this book into the light.